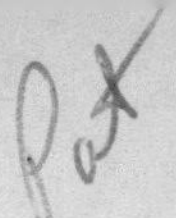

"With *Dark Angel*, Cassandra Collins paints a brilliant and mesmerizing portrait of love more powerful than death."
—Deb Stover, author of *A Moment in Time*

TOUCHED BY AN ANGEL

He took several steps toward her, his eyes never leaving her face. Standing close enough to touch her, he reached past her and planted his hands firmly against the counter. She was caught in the circle of his arms. The smell of sandalwood coiled through the air. His leather jacket crinkled slightly as he leaned forward. A sultry smile creased his face, turning her insides to mush. She imagined how it would feel to stroke his clean-edged jaw and let her finger linger at the cleft in his chin.

"You are so special, Scarlett." His voice was husky, needy. Then he touched her on the neck, his fingers warming more than her skin.

"I'm sorry you were hurt," he mumbled hoarsely.

He caressed the bandage's perimeter. Where his fingertips touched her skin she felt a slight stinging sensation, yet it didn't hurt her. Then he pressed his hand over the bandage and closed his eyes. And when he opened them again, they shone with a crystal purity that astounded her.

"You are my destiny." His fingers trailed along her jawbone to underneath her chin. He tilted her face so that she was forced to meet his gaze. "I don't know why I'm here, only that being drawn to you, being with you, is inevitable. Maybe you're a test for me."

"A test?" she whispered softly. The nearness of him charged the air, the way it feels before a storm breaks. "How could someone like me test a renegade like you?"

Dark Angel

Cassandra Collins

LOVE SPELL  NEW YORK CITY

A LOVE SPELL BOOK®

November 2000

Published by

Dorchester Publishing Co., Inc.
276 Fifth Avenue
New York, NY 10001

ISBN 0-505-52414-7

Printed in the United States of America.

To my angel

Dark Angel

Chapter One

Scarlett flicked her wrist and checked the time on her watch. Twenty to nine. Almost closing time.

She rubbed her neck and peered out the darkened plate-glass window. Incessant rain smeared its surface, transfiguring passing cars into giant fish that glided through a murky underworld. The street's solitary lamppost wavered like an elongated strand of gray-green seaweed. Los Angeles in March. Enough rain to slow the city's frantic pace. But never enough to cleanse the city's sins.

Lightning crackled, followed by a pop of light that glazed the street blue. In that split-second light show, raindrops sparkled around the outline of . . . a man.

Adrenaline surged through Scarlett's tired body, jolting her awake. She strained to see the man's form, but her eyes were momentarily blinded. The lightning's flare had obliterated the street scene into one splotch of fluorescent periwinkle.

She pressed the heels of her hands to her eyes. Of course there was no man standing outside. The lightning was playing tricks with her. Men don't materialize out of rain droplets, even here in Tinseltown.

Lowering her hands, she again fixed her gaze on the plate-glass window. Beyond her reflection, the streetlamp's pyramid of muted light drew her attention. Gusts of wind rippled and swirled the glistening downpour like breath against velvet. She felt lulled by the waterworks' display until a string of drops solidified into a silver line that again outlined a man's silhouette.

Scarlett managed a craggy gasp before her mouth went stone dry. The silhouette seemed to lean forward as though it wanted a better look. At her?

Move, she commanded herself. Get to the phone. Dial 911. But she couldn't have been more grounded to the spot than if she'd stepped in a vat of glue. Even if she did make it to the phone, what would she say? "There's a Day-Glo imprint of a man staring at me"? They'd chalk her up to another crank call, just like the gazillion others L.A. police undoubtedly get every night.

She followed the shimmering line that contoured what looked to be a man of about six feet—maybe less. Lean. Dressed in some kind of bulky garb. A jacket maybe? This had to be a neighbor's prank. Roger, Doris's son, lived in a third-story apartment a block over—maybe he was playing a trick with a flashlight and a cookie cutter.

The thought made her smile. That kind of cookie

cutter could make gingerbread men a hot seller.

She squinted at the silver-lined figure. It contained no substance. When she looked into what should be a face or a chest, she saw only the slanted rain and through it, the faint dark thread of Gabrielle Street. How did Roger do that?

It moved.

The air seeped from her lungs in a low and frightened moan. She looked down at her dirty tennis shoes and fixated on the shoelace's loopy bow. "Don't be a baby. It's nothing but a trick of light and rain."

Trick. Light and rain. The words echoed in her mind as she slowly inched her gaze upward. She couldn't stay here next to the grill all night. What would tomorrow morning's customers think if they found her bleary-eyed, dressed in the same clothes, and muttering things about cookie cutters?

She gasped.

He stood under the streetlamp and returned her gaze. Not just an outline of a man. No, this was the real thing, a man in the flesh. His shoulders hunched in a leather jacket, he seemed oblivious to the swirling deluge. Instead, his attention seemed riveted to something inside her business.

To her.

His forthright look sent tremors of anxiety through her body; yet, for the life of her, she felt compelled to stare back. Those dark eyes, nearly hidden beneath loose strands of glistening wet hair, mesmerized her.

The pounding of her heart competed with a sudden crash of thunder.

Despite the heat inside the room, she now felt the

outside cold against her face, the taste of chilling raindrops as they slid down her cheeks and onto her lips. A trace of sandalwood teased her nose before a lethal mix of emotions rocked her gut: love, desire, abandonment. Painful, brutal abandonment. Emotions so raw, they tore at her insides, unearthing her own anguish when her mother died.

Her head sank until her chin rested on her collarbone. She felt drained, as though she had relived a year's worth of grief in the last few moments. Minutes passed before she chanced another look.

No one stood underneath the streetlamp.

She flicked her gaze to either side of the streetlight. Not a blessed soul. A car cruised by and sloshed through a puddle.

He never existed. The thought was matter-of-fact, as though she were explaining something tiresome to a child. *You're tired. So tired that you're imagining bogeymen.*

Dipping her hands into a plastic bucket, Scarlett scooped out a dishrag and squeezed it, the excess drops mimicking the rain as they spilled back into the sudsy water. The cool water was reassuring. Real.

"Am I becoming one of those spinsters who resort to illogical fantasies, Mom?" When she was alone, she still spoke to her mother. They had always helped each other see the humor in a situation, no matter how seemingly hopeless or crazy things seemed. "Or are you sending studly angels to watch over me?" Scarlett chuckled at the thought as she rubbed a stubborn smear of mustard off the counter. "It'd be just like you to send me James Dean to ease my loneliness."

Loneliness. Since her mom's death a year ago, each day had been a lesson in coping with loneliness.

She gave her head a little shake to dislodge the memories and glanced again at her wristwatch. Only fifteen more minutes until closing. It'd feel good to go home and kick off her shoes, wrap herself in her old chenille robe, and sip a glass of wine while watching an old movie on TV. She smiled to herself. Preferably something with James Dean.

The raspy creak of hinges interrupted her thoughts. Someone had opened the front door. For a thrill-rushing instant, she prayed it was the mystery man from under the streetlamp. She straightened, stretched her back slightly, and managed her best smile.

Which faltered immediately.

The man in the open doorway was a swollen parody of the man she had just seen. Instead of a lean animal slouched in a leather jacket à la James Dean, this stranger was stuffed into a black jacket and jeans combo—a Johnny Cash–for-fatso's look. His ruddy face and bloated stomach indicated a glutton who drank and ate too much. A blast of cold air stunned the room before he shoved the door shut behind him. Then he shook his head in one jerk, like a dog, spraying rainy droplets into the air.

"Evening," Scarlett said, hoping she sounded more pleasant than she felt. She was accustomed to weirdos and street people in this section of Venice.

He grunted a response as his small dark eyes scoured the single room.

"Today's special is a chili burger. Two ninety-nine. With fries, three-sixty." Another habit she had learned from her mom—always tell 'em the special of the day. Scarlett tossed the rag back into the bucket where it landed with a small splash, then doused her hands under the tap. "Rain letting up?"

He grunted again. "No night for man or beast." His voice scratched the air like a Brillo pad.

From across the room, a faint whiff of body odor grated her senses. She wondered which he was—man or beast. Wiping her hands on a nearby towel, she decided to restart this conversation. "So, what can I get you?"

A mocking smile quivered at the edge of his lips as he reached behind him. She heard the slow, grating slide of the dead bolt. "You can get me your signature, Miss Ray."

The fine hairs on her arms stood on end. She continued wiping her hands, more slowly now. The towel's fabric felt coarser, heavier than she remembered. A distant police siren screamed to life.

Careful to modulate her voice so that her own inner alarm didn't ring through, she said slowly, "I don't under—"

"Yeah you do." He unzipped his jacket and pulled out a sheaf of rolled-up papers. Eyeing the wet countertop, he hesitated. "Over here, doll." He motioned with his head toward a drier section of the L-shaped counter, crossed the room, and plopped onto one of the stools. It creaked under his weight. Carefully, he laid the papers out before him so she could read. "Mr. Chandler thinks you playin' hardball."

He pulled open his jacket and extracted a pen from his shirt pocket. Her gaze dropped down his pudgy midriff, recognizing something she'd only seen in the movies. A holster. Fear crested inside her, threatening to crash her inner world.

A gun.

She fisted her hands in an attempt to quell their shaking. The grease in the fryer popped and her gut convulsed.

Cold fingers slid over her scalp, down her neck, squeezed the breath from her throat. He was one of Chandler's thugs. Kenneth Chandler, the big-moneyed investor who wanted to own this block. Now she knew how badly he wanted it. "I told Mr. Chandler 'no.' " Her voice sounded thin, anxious.

His lower lip dropped to display an uneven row of small yellow teeth. He cocked his head and squinted at her. "No time for games, doll. Ain't leavin' without your signature."

Her cheek twitched. She couldn't control it.

With a quick glance at the paper, she recognized Chandler's scrawling signature—the same signature she'd seen when Chandler's lawyer showed her this same document two weeks earlier. They thought she'd sell Ray's Hamburgers—the business her mother loved and bequeathed to her—for a measly thousand bucks? She wouldn't sell it for fifty, a hundred times that.

He gave the pen another push. "This is his last offer. You get my drift, doll, or do I gotta spell it out?"

"If I refuse?"

A smile that looked more like a grimace creased his face. "Your ma's dead. No family. State'll auction the property . . ." In one slow motion, never taking his eyes off her, he slipped his hand down to the holster and played his fingers across the worn leather.

A second cold wave of fear rose within her. It was true, she had no heirs. So that's how Chandler had wrested control of the other businesses on this block—he'd either extorted a sale or bought them, dirt cheap, at state auction. The man got what he wanted, one way or another.

A soft crackle interrupted her thoughts. In her peripheral vision she spied the fryer's wooden handle, its wire metal basket submerged in burning hot grease. If she was quick . . .

In one swift moment, she pivoted, grabbed the handle, and swung.

Time shifted to a lower gear. In slow motion, she saw the mesh basket arc through the air, grease streaming behind it like thin amber ribbons fluttering in a breeze. Stinging drops fell on her forearm, her neck. She winced, tightened her grip on the handle, and pushed the basket toward the man's face. His mouth dropped open. A gold tooth sparked light. He raised one fleshy arm to block the impact. His other hand reached inside his coat. The metal basket made contact, the sound of sizzling flesh like one long prolonged hiss. He yelled, the sound rolling through time like thunder.

He raised the gun, its barrel dead level with her eyes. She held up her other hand and spread her fingers wide. The basket fell from her grip. It clanged and rattled against the counter.

A bright flash.

The sound of the world cracking open.

She never felt the hard impact of the floor—it was

as though hands gently lowered her onto pillows. Above her the man's face loomed, contorted with rage and hatred. A stream of blood coursed from his lower lip down his stubbly chin. Flecks of red shot into the air as he screamed obscenities and waved the gun in large, spastic motions. The stench of lead and smoke engulfed her.

Something clouded her vision. Warm. Sticky. She couldn't breathe. She opened her lips, but lacked the strength to take a breath. The taste of iron flooded her mouth.

I'm going to die.

Surprisingly, the thought didn't scare her. If anything, she felt a little awed. Her eyelids felt so heavy. She closed them and felt herself drift off. . . .

Music. Tinkling music like a thousand distant wind chimes. Darkness. Ahead, a pinpoint of light twinkled, like an evening star in an empty sky. On her left she heard the murmuring of voices and soft sobs. She started to turn her head and look, but intuition—or was it a voice?—warned not to stray from the light.

As she approached, the light turned into a glowing, burning ball of the purest white. It radiated an energy that felt like . . . love. An endless stream of love. A joy sprang loose from within her and she realized she had kept that feeling tightly bottled throughout her lifetime.

Her lifetime. No sooner did she think this than images appeared before her, as though she were watching a movie. One by one, the pictures materialized and faded. Her father. Her mother. Pain cascaded through her, trailed by the comforting thought—her own?—that all things pass. She concentrated again on the light, which now took the shape of a door. Somehow she knew there was nothing more important than to enter that doorway, to pass the threshold.

A form blocked the doorway. Rays of white and gold streamed around it. A man? The edges of his silhouette sharpened against the dazzling backdrop of light, yet she couldn't decipher his features. The image reminded her of something, but the memory vanished as the swirling scent of sandalwood surrounded her.

"It's not your time." His voice vibrated in her head, and she realized he spoke to her telepathically. "You must go back."

"She's back," announced a male voice.

Scarlett blinked open her eyes. Faces floated above her. Beyond them, a large light glowed. She focused on it and tried to remember why it looked familiar. Bulbous. White. It hurt to stare straight into it. She closed her eyes, the light's impression burning yellow against her darkened lids. Foggily, she recalled it was the ceiling light at Ray's.

Ray's Hamburgers? The second shock wave hit. What was she doing lying on the floor of her business?

Fluttering open her eyelids, she avoided looking directly at the light and shifted her gaze to the left. Crouched next to her was a man with curly brown hair—the light burnished the ends of his frizzy curls, giving him a halo effect.

He smiled, but it didn't diminish the anxiety etched in his face. "You're going to be okay. We're taking you to the hospital." He spoke carefully, as though his words tiptoed through a minefield.

"Hospital?" Scarlett frowned at the muffled sound of her voice. She glanced down and saw a clear plastic cup over her mouth.

"Oxygen," the man answered. He pulled what looked to be a strap around her elbow and yanked it tight. Scarlett started to bend her head to get a better look, but her body refused to move. She tried to lift her arm, but it didn't budge.

He must have seen the wild fear in her eyes, because he spoke in soothing tones as he lightly patted her shoulder. "You're strapped onto a stretcher that holds your body immobile. We don't know if the bullet damaged your spinal cord, so until you have X-rays taken, we can't chance any movement."

Bullet? Spinal cord? Sheer, unadulterated panic galloped through her. "What bullet?" she mumbled into the oxygen mask. Her heart thumped so hard in her chest she would not have been surprised to hear its echo bounce off the walls.

But the man was busy talking to a woman dressed identically like him in a blue uniform with "A-1 Ambulance" stitched in thick white letters on the front pocket. Scarlett's eyes darted over the woman's short blond hair up to the bottle she gripped in the air. Clear liquid dripped down a dangling plastic tube straight into Scarlett's arm.

The blonde glanced over. "How do you feel?"

A sharp pain in Scarlett's neck throbbed to life. A scant memory of falling floated through her mind. "Awful. What happened?" She closed her eyes, but the memory refused to surface.

In the darkness of her thoughts, stars exploded as

another sharp pain detonated in her neck. The pain shot through her with the force of a hammer's blow, discharging hot spasms through her chest. She groaned and attempted eye contact with the man again, but his angular, tanned face blurred and sharpened as though someone were focusing a film. With excruciating effort, she tried to speak, but an unfamiliar gravelly male voice overrode her efforts.

"Detective Ramsey, LAPD. What happened?"

"Don't know, but she's one lucky girl," answered the paramedic with curly brown hair. "Someone saw her lying on the floor and dialed nine-one-one. . . . She'd lost a lot of blood by the time we got here."

Blood. Suddenly she remembered the man in the black jacket, blood dribbling down his chin. Her swinging the fryer basket. The hot stings of flying grease. Staring straight into a gun barrel. The flash.

She groaned at the avalanche of memories. "He tried to—"

"Save your strength," the paramedic intoned. "The police will take their report at the hospital, when you're stronger." He nodded curtly to the woman. In one efficient movement, they eased the stretcher out of the cramped kitchen space.

As they pushed her through the front door, Scarlett was astonished to see people milling about on the sidewalk. There stood Doris—her mother's best friend—her round brown face glistening with tears. Standing next to her was her oldest son, Roger, his arm cradling his mother's sagging form. He caught Scarlett's eye and gave her the thumb's up sign. She scanned the crowd filled with people from the neighborhood, people she'd known since she was a kid, and smiled weakly. She made eye contact, hoping they remembered her strength when her mother had died suddenly—that same strength would see her through this as well. Didn't they know that?

Just then she caught elderly Mrs. Johnson praying, her lips silently moving over her tightly clasped hands. The image struck some raw intuition. *Did I almost die?*

Right before the paramedics slid her into the back of the waiting ambulance, Scarlett saw the man.

He stood in the middle of the crowd, doused in a pool of light. Just the way he'd looked standing under the streetlamp. Longish brown hair framed his angular features. He raked a few loose strands from his brow, unveiling rich brown eyes that riveted her with their intensity. A ripple of déjà vu passed through her.

I've known him before tonight.

Yet, at the same time, she was certain she had never seen him before in her life.

He stepped forward, his eyes never leaving her face. She no longer heard the sounds of the crowd and was only vaguely aware of the paramedics' maneuvers behind her. The man approached with confidence, as though he had every right to be at her side. When he was a few feet from her, she smelled a hauntingly familiar trace of sandalwood. Something within her responded, and she inexplicably knew that he was part of her not only now, but forever.

He quickened his pace and reached toward her. The doors of the ambulance shut just as he mouthed her name.

* * *

"I'm Detective Ramsey. I'd like to ask a few questions about what happened in your restaurant—if you're feeling up to it."

Scarlett turned her head and felt the pillow's coolness against her cheek. A small mountain of a man stood next to her hospital bed. Restaurant? He referred to her hamburger-slinging business as a *restaurant*? Either he knew her secret dream—to own a restaurant—or he was being painfully tactful.

"I can come back another time," he prompted.

"No. Now's okay."

Her gaze traveled down his starched black uniform to the rectangular gold name tag with "A. Ramsey" etched in neat block letters. Farther down, the holster and the gun met her at eye level. A sickening surge of fear rose within her as she remembered facing another gun. She glanced back up into his gray eyes and thought she caught a look of worry pierce his reserve. No doubt he already knew the whole story.

No way was she going to be pitied. "Thought detectives dressed in street clothes," she said airily, remembering Dana Andrews in a '40s detective thriller.

"Department shindig," answered Ramsey.

She detected a drollness in his voice. Probably hates to get dressed up, she mused. She adjusted the covers around her dusty pink chenille robe while silently thanking Doris for dropping it by the hospital. Being wrapped up in her favorite old robe gave Scarlett a small but much needed comfort. "Do you smoke, Detective Ramsey?"

From where she sat, his bulbous nose almost blocked

the surprised look in his eyes. "What's that got to do with the price of tomatoes?" he retorted.

She smiled. "Thought I'd bum a cigarette."

"They let you smoke in your hospital room?"

"Don't know."

"You've been here over twenty-four hours—or haven't you craved a cigarette before now?"

"Craved, yes. Smoked, no."

He did a double take, as though debating whether to continue this line of questioning.

"Quit smoking a year ago," she explained with a slight shrug.

"But you're willing to start again now?" He flashed her a bemused grin.

"Willing, but not able." She tightened the robe's sash around her waist. "I promised Mom I'd stop, and I did. Can't go back on my word. Even though the thought of sneaking just one cigarette keeps me going sometimes."

"Good. Hate to think I'd driven someone to smoke. Plus, you don't want to let your mother down."

She felt her eyes moisten, and looked away. "No, I don't."

In the seconds that followed, Scarlett avoided the detective's eyes. Outside the open door, the soft squeak of nurses' shoes faded in and out. Down the hall, the elevator bell dinged once, followed by babbling voices as passengers exited.

Ramsey finally broke their silence. "Doctor says you're lucky."

She looked up and found him gazing at the bandage on her neck. "Yeah, it missed the major stuff and only severed a minor vessel." She nervously twisted the edge of the sheet between her fingers, not wanting to add that she had been clinically dead when they found her. According to her physician, the paramedics detected no pulse when they first arrived. All she remembered was waking up and seeing the ceiling light. Strangely enough, that image had been haunting her ever since, reminding her of another light. But the harder she tried to remember, the hazier the memory grew—like a dream that, upon awakening, flees your consciousness.

A soft scraping brought her attention back to the present. The detective was pushing a chair across the linoleum floor to the side of her bed. He sat down heavily and flipped open a notebook. "Shall we begin?"

She spent the next fifteen minutes describing what happened that night. What the guy looked like. What the gun looked like. What he said. What she said.

"*Exactly* like I told you guys earlier," she added, hearing the exasperation in her voice and not caring. It exhausted her to repeat everything—couldn't the police get it right the first time?

He barely glanced up from his notes. "Earlier?"

"This afternoon when you guys—the police—called. I told them exactly the same story."

His eyes bore into hers. "What time?"

"Two. Three." She frowned at the consternation on the detective's face. "Something the matter?"

He tapped his pen against the clipboard. "You gave them a description of the man who shot you?" The cold calm in his voice prickled her skin.

"Yeah." Her voice broke and she cleared her throat.

"Is there a problem? I mean, it was the police who called. Right?"

His broad face broke into the toothiest grin she'd ever seen. "I just remembered. Captain Emerson said he'd called you earlier today for a preliminary interview. Slipped my mind."

She swore the glint in his eyes didn't match the warmth of his smile. But nothing matched anything anymore. Her life today certainly didn't match her expectations from a year ago. Give it up, Scarlett. Don't make a mountain out of a phone call.

"When're you lugging Kenneth Chandler to jail?" she asked while the detective closed his book. "Extortion. Attempted murder. This man's straight out of an old James Cagney movie. He deserves to spend the rest of his life pacing a small cell."

Detective Ramsey's eyebrows lifted slightly. "We'll be investigating your claims."

Investigating?

"That's all? You mean Chandler's free to—" Swallowing hard, she fought the rising hysteria in her voice. The last thing she'd expected was for the man who had threatened and nearly killed her to be merely investigated.

Detective Ramsey stood and tucked the notebook under his arm. "According to Dr. Bowman, you'll be out of here in a few days."

She heard the kindness in his voice, but it didn't assuage her fears. Kenneth Chandler wanted her property and was willing to kill her for it.

"LAPD Pacific Division—Venice police—will patrol your business when you reopen."

She leveled back a stare. "Patrol my home too?"

"Absolutely."

"Until Chandler's off the streets?"

"You have my word." He punctuated his intent with a nod, his gaze unwavering.

Relief washed through her, relieving the pent-up fear that had lodged in her gut. With the police between her and Chandler, she was safe. Her armor loosened and she closed her eyes. "Thank you," she whispered.

After Detective Ramsey left, she realized how exhausting it had been to rehash the particulars from that horrific night. She picked at her dinner, then turned off the reading light and snuggled under the warm covers. She missed her soft bed—this hospital mattress felt as though she were sleeping on an ironing board. And she missed her old tomcat, Rhett. He'd started hanging around soon after her dad deserted them—now with Mom gone, he was the only family Scarlett had left.

Outside the door, she heard the brisk footsteps of nurses and their hushed conversations. Down the hall, someone's TV emitted canned laughter. The wheels of a cart creaked past her door. The jumble of foreign sounds reinforced her homesickness.

She closed her eyes and hugged her arms around herself. A mist enveloped her thoughts as she succumbed to the comfort of sleep.

She was back on Gabrielle Street, yet it wasn't the same. The street glowed and undulated like a river of molten gold, its radiance lighting the faces of the people around her. Scarlett leaned back and drank in the heavens, feeling the light infuse her, fill her with a profound joy. Then, as though she were watching a fast-speed film, dark clouds swirled and mushroomed until they blotted the sky. Black, sticky shadows crept in, clinging to lampposts, sidewalks, even to people. Their dank smell like rotting garbage.

Glass shattered. Someone grabbed her and yanked her into the running crowd, which slowed to a stop at the edge of an inferno. The fire crackled menacingly as it devoured the structure in front of them.

Ray's Hamburgers. The fire was destroying her business.

Her face burned with the flames' heat as a cold dread filled her. Yet her feet refused to move, forcing her to stay and witness the devastation. Within the roaring flames a man materialized. An invisible breeze whipped his longish dark hair about his face. Unaffected by the roaring blaze and voluminous smoke, he simply stared at Scarlett, as though nothing else mattered.

Panic jolted her. Someone had to help him. She looked around, but the others had disappeared. It was up to her.

Heat, smoke, and roaring winds threatened to overwhelm her as she dragged one foot, then the other, toward the blaze. Realizing the odds were against her, she staggered back and cried, "Get out! I can't save you!" Ash filled her mouth as she struggled to yell again, but strangled on her words.

He remained unfazed and continued standing in the fire. Transfixed, she stared back into his dark eyes. Strangely, they held no fear. They reached out to her with an intensity, an urgent need. *He wants me to understand something.*

Then it hit her. He was the man who had stood in the crowd the night she was carried to the ambulance.

A surge of exhilaration rushed through her like a great wind.

Something binds us together. More powerful than either of us, it binds us for eternity.

She awoke with a start and gazed into the shadows. Gradually, she recognized the hospital room. The basin. The chair in the corner. She tossed back the top cover to cool her heated body. To her surprise, her hospital gown was drenched with sweat. She was fumbling with the buttons on her handrail, searching for the nurse's call button, when the door opened.

Light from the hallway flooded the room.

"Nurse?" She didn't want to say she'd had a bad dream and needed a friendly voice. How childish. "I . . . I can't sleep."

No response. Scarlett blinked at the startling white light that swirled in incandescent clouds. The faintest scent of sandalwood drifted past her, teasing her memory. She wanted to look, but the light's intensity forced her to shut her eyes. On her face she felt the warmth from the light's brilliance. It reminded her of her dream and how the fire's heat scorched her skin.

Impossible.

She had to still be dreaming. Not wanting to witness the hellish blaze again, she squeezed her eyes shut tighter, willing herself to wake up.

"Open your eyes." A man's deep voice reverberated through the room.

She cautiously obeyed.

From the center of the light a form took shape. It

moved toward her and she again detected a faint trace of sandalwood. A man. Closer now, his features sharpened. Clean shaven. Unruly hair that matched the deep bronze of his eyes. He wore jeans, snakeskin boots, and a whiskey-colored bomber jacket that had seen better days.

His dark gaze ignited her memory. The man from outside her business. The man in the crowd who'd mouthed her name. How did he know her? Why was he here? Terror curdled her insides. Was this one of Chandler's men to finish the job the other thug hadn't?

His deep brown eyes held hers in a steady gaze. "Don't be afraid."

She had the strange sensation that he had just read her thoughts. Attempting to smile, she failed miserably. "Look," she began hoarsely. "If Chandler wants my business this badly, he can have it. If you have the papers with you, I'll sign now."

He took a step toward the bed and she instinctively shrank against the handrail behind her. She grimaced as the hard edge made contact with her lower back.

A flicker of pain crossed his face. *He knows what I'm feeling.* She gave her head a slight shake. Crazy thoughts. She wasn't thinking clearly.

He held his hand up in a calming gesture. "I won't hurt you." His voice echoed as though from far away. "You are my destiny."

Then he did the strangest thing of all. He smiled. A slow, easy smile that curled one side of his mouth upward. That sensual grin, and the way he slouched in his leather jacket, made her think of the Dean bad boy in *Rebel Without a Cause*.

Dumbfounded, she found herself smiling back. Like they shared some secret.

Then he began to change.

First the edges of his clothes and his hair grew transparent. Then the rest of him faded, like a picture left in the sun too long. Within moments, she couldn't tell if she saw him at all . . . except it seemed, for the briefest of moments, that his smile lingered.

The next thing she knew, she was staring into total darkness.

Chapter Two

Night descended on Los Angeles with more fanfare than a movie premiere. Voluminous clouds paraded into dusk, their edges tinged with shades of persimmon and rose. Down at Santa Monica Beach, Scarlett knew people were standing stock-still, watching the last drop of golden sun dissolve into the ocean. Some would applaud, like they did every sunset. In L.A., everything was a show.

"So what'll it be, Enrique?"

The elderly gentleman's white handlebar mustache jiggled when he spoke. "Usual."

"Extra onions?"

His faded hazel eyes, nearly hidden beneath sagging lids, twinkled. "And slap on some peppers too."

"You've got a gut of steel, Enrique," she teased as

she reached beneath the counter for a jar of marinated jalapeños.

She slapped a hamburger patty on the grill and watched a drop of grease skitter a crazy path across the hot metal. The sizzling sounds triggered the memory of swinging the fryer basket at the man who almost killed her. Gingerly, she touched the thick bandage on her neck.

"Hurt?"

She smiled, realizing Enrique watched her. "A little sore." She heard the forced cheer in her voice. But damn, the last thing she wanted was to encourage pity, so she always tried to make light when her customers asked about her wound. Or the man who caused it.

An involuntary shiver ran through her.

Enrique muttered something in Spanish. She glanced over her shoulder and saw him wagging his head, mumbling to himself.

"Enrique," she said with mock annoyance. "I'll have none of that around here. If you want to feel sorry for me, feel sorry for all the onions I gotta peel before the night is through. That's enough to bring tears to anybody's eyes."

"*Si,* Little One. You're safe. That's all that matters."

She pressed the spatula against the hamburger. Was she safe? The police, true to Detective Ramsey's word, had been patrolling her business and home since her release from the hospital a little over a week ago. Fat chance that thug might get within spitting distance of her with cop cars continually cruising by. Plus, she was certain the locals had a silent agreement to be "back-ups" to the police patrols. Like Enrique tonight. He used to visit Ray's Hamburgers once or twice a week. Now he warmed a counter stool almost every night. The locals—her friends and neighbors for the last seventeen years—were "taking care of their own."

Yet fear still clung to her like a second shadow. She thought of the butcher knife under the counter. And the sharp paring knife she'd hidden in a niche above the front door. She was "taking care of her own" too. Strange what destiny brings.

She flipped the patty over with a fresh smack and watched a flurry of steam rush upward. Destiny. *What did that man in my dream say? "You are my destiny." Strange dream. Must have been the medication they'd given me in the hospital. Although that still doesn't explain why I saw him in the crowd.*

She pressed the spatula on the hamburger, which sputtered and fumed against the grill. I was obviously in shock, she mused. Or delirious. So my mind fabricated him in that crowd. Some mind. I hover on the brink of death and invent some young stud coming to my rescue.

She picked up the salt shaker and shook it over the cooking meat. He had that James Dean stance. And attitude. A bad boy up to no good. She remembered the slouch of his shoulders and how the jacket's worn leather molded itself to his physique. The bottom of the jacket fit snugly against his lean waist, probably hiding one of those muscle-ridged stomachs that flinches slightly under a woman's touch. And those jeans. They didn't leave a whole lot to the imagination.

She set the shaker down with a little too much force.

"*Estás bien?* You okay?" asked Enrique.

She closed her eyes, wondering if the heat in her cheeks was from the grill's warmth or her naughty thoughts. Glancing over her shoulder, she saw Enrique looking at her with a quizzical expression.

"You feelin' okay?" he repeated. His mustache drooped as his jowls slackened with concern.

"You all worry too much about me. I'm fine. Shaker slipped." *Or my mind.*

Later, she glanced out the window at the dusky shadows. Instinctively, she flipped her wrist to check the time. "Six?" she asked in astonishment. Glancing up at Enrique, she held up her hand, displaying the wristwatch. "I just got new batteries for this 'cause it stopped working!" She shook her wrist and glared at it. "Just what I need. A temperamental wristwatch."

"Take it back. Get a refund," Enrique offered.

"I'd have to call that jerk ex-boyfriend and ask for the sales receipt. He'd probably view it as an overture and start asking me out again."

Enrique's eyes twinkled. "Wasn't he the one that wore those ripped tee shirts?"

"Night 'n day."

"I always wanted to slip that kid some *dinero*—tell 'im to buy some decent clothes."

Scarlett rolled her eyes. "Think it was fun to be seen with him in public? Anyway, he wasn't poor, he was advertising his business. Custom-ripped tee shirts by Rafael. He'd sell hundreds every weekend down at Venice Beach. Mainly high school kids who wanted custom-ripped tee shirts to match their personally ripped jeans."

After a moment's pause, Enrique asked, "Rafael? I thought his name was Bob."

She snorted a laugh. "This is L.A., remember? The land of dreams and stardust? Bob thought 'custom-ripped tee shirts by Bob' sounded like some hick with a steak knife getting creative. But Rafael—well, that, Bob decided, conjured images of some dark-skinned Marlboro man passionately ripping at tee shirts with his dazzlingly white teeth."

The line of Enrique's lips tightened, as though he was trying to suppress a smile. "I take it you weren't—how do they say?—sweet on him."

She exaggerated a sigh as she set the correct time on her watch. "Unfortunately, he had the body of Tarzan and the brains of Godzilla. When Bob—Rafael—walked, I'm sure all he thought was, 'Left. Right. Left. Right.' "

Enrique chortled. "Then why'd you accept the watch?"

Scarlett raised her eyes and grinned sheepishly. "To keep the time?" She flashed Enrique what she thought was a wide-eyed appeal for approval. Either she didn't have the knack to mimic ingenues, or Enrique wasn't in the approval-giving mood. Instead, he crossed his massive arms over his chest and shook his head slowly.

"Okay." She dropped the effect and leaned against the counter, lowering her voice. "Here's the scoop. I hadn't had a date in so long, I feared I'd end up in a nunnery. Then one day I meet this guy whose shoulders block out the sun and whose big white-toothed smiled makes me think it's snowing in Southern California." She tapped the face of the watch once, letting her forefinger rest there for a moment. "Guess that's my lesson—never accept gifts in a relationship that doesn't work. Chances are the gifts won't work either."

An hour later, at nine, she'd cleaned the grill, washed the dishes, turned off all the appliances, and insisted Enrique leave. He stubbornly refused until she reminded him that the police were patrolling twenty-four hours a day and no harm could possibly come to her with cop cars wearing a groove down Gabrielle Street. Finally, he bought a piece of pie to "drop off at Doris's" and left. Now it was time to go home and soak her tired feet. Before locking the door behind her, she gave the place one last look.

In the shadows she felt, more than saw, all the knick-knacks that adorned the walls. The quirky collectibles she and her mom had found over the years: the *Wizard of Oz* plates, the stuffed bear named Charlie with the bright orange tummy, the antique radio that sat on a special shelf behind the cash register.

"Goodnight, Charlie," she whispered before shutting the door. For years, this had been her and her mother's closing ritual. Sometimes Alice would tilt her head and say, "Listen. Charlie's snickering because . . ." And tell some fanciful story of what had happened to Charlie that day.

"Maybe overactive imaginations run in the family," mused Scarlett as she turned the key in the lock. Something had to explain that man in the bomber jacket.

Outside, the hot and smoggy March evening weighed on her like a sticky blanket. Heat waves could descend with a vengeance in early spring and fall. . . . Maybe L.A. didn't have a winter like other parts of the country, but it did have an unforgiving summer that taunted other seasons like a neighborhood bully.

As usual, cars lined both sides of the street, bumper to bumper, thanks to the congestion of apartments that crowded the periphery of this business block. L.A. never had enough parking space. Scarlett turned her body slightly, stepped off the sidewalk, and scooted sideways between a canary-yellow Pinto and a blue Honda. Crossing the street, her footsteps brushed the silence. A distant barking made her glance at the hazy night sky. What could bother a dog on a peaceful night like this? Was the moon hanging too low?

The piercing squeal of tires shattered the quiet.

To the right, a car rushed toward her, its headlights searing the darkness with laserlike intensity. Blinded by their fierce gleam, her thoughts tumbled in confusion—she was halfway across the street. Could she make it to the far sidewalk? Or should she run back? Which way meant safety?

She jerked her head toward the engine's heightened roar. The car's back tires disgorged clouds of burning rubber as the car careened toward her. She screamed as her feet made the decision her mind couldn't—she spun and ran back toward the canary-yellow Pinto. Faster, faster.

Her feet hit the pavement clumsily. Her body lurched forward in jerky movements. Her toe caught on something and she stumbled. *Don't fall. Run!* She tripped, caught her balance, and kept going.

Her mouth fell open as she gasped for breath. Over her shoulder, she saw the car swerve toward her. Its bright beams stung her eyes. Momentarily blinded, she slammed full-length into the side of a parked car. In its passenger window she saw the slash of headlights looming behind her—the bright feral eyes of a beast intent on its prey. A sob ripped from her throat and she scrambled along the side of the car, her fingernails scratching its cold metal surface.

Too late. I'm dead. She hastily glanced back, her galloping breaths riding a building scream.

In that instant, a man's form took shape in front of the headlights. Scarlett's breathing halted, the scream lodged mid-throat. His shadow darkened, his outline cutting a sharp-edged silhouette into the harsh light.

God, someone else is going to get killed!

Time seemed to stop as he floated toward her. Massive arms seized her. After a dizzying upward motion, she suddenly realized they were suspended far above the chaos.

Suspended?

She peeked over his shoulder. Below, Gabrielle Street was a dark line bordered by lights and box-top buildings. Impossible. Yet there was the dot of a yellow car she'd squeezed past only moments ago. Next to it, the car with murderous intent looked like a bullet hole in the middle of the street. Even from this distance, she heard its engine chugging. It reminded her of the labored panting of a beast after a chase.

"Don't be afraid."

She jerked her head in the direction of the voice, trying to see her rescuer's face, but the night's shadows cloaked his features. Exhilaration threaded through her, as though some current of feeling ran between her and this superhuman creature.

Either I'm dreaming, or Superman broke up with Lois Lane.

She heard a chuckle. Low and rumbling, like distant thunder. A fluttering of joy passed through her. Yes, this had to be a dream. And she was starring in it with the Man of Steel.

She tilted back and enjoyed the infinite panorama of stars above. Giddiness filled her head. For the briefest of moments, she felt within the sky, surrounded by cooling breezes that stroked her like hundreds of comforting hands.

The next moment, she lay crouched on the sidewalk, her face pressed against the still-warm pavement that reeked of dirt and grease.

A surge of fear overrode any remaining twinges of rapture. She was back in the nightmare. This was the reality, not whatever had just happened.

Fearfully, she chanced a glance to the side and found a space between two parked cars that offered a view of the street. Although she couldn't see her attacker's car, she heard its engine's rumbling growl. The same sound she'd heard while hanging from the heavens.

Hanging from the heavens? *I must have been so terrified, I had one of those "out of body" experiences.*

Her thoughts halted as a gravelly voice—seemingly from the car—barked something about the "wrong one," followed by a muffled response.

The wrong what? A sickening revulsion shuddered down her backbone. Instead of her, they had hit the man who stepped into the street. She stifled the urge to cry out, to beg someone to call the police. Her chest heaved in silent spasms. She flinched as her body fought the instinct to run, to escape to safety. But any movement might draw their attention. Cautiously, she listened as the tires rolled forward, grinding something in the road. The motor gunned once before the car sped off.

Only then did her body respond fully to the trauma. Her hands shook so badly that she had to fist them against the concrete to lever herself into a sitting position. A waft of exhaust lingered, a reminder of the car's venomous intent.

She had to check the man lying in the road. Shakily, she started to stand when another scent curled through the air.

Sandalwood.

She spun around and gasped.

The streetlamp's luminescent glow cascaded down on him, silvering strands of his dark unkempt hair. Shadows masked his eyes and darkened the hollows of his cheeks. A sliver of light highlighted the line of his lean jaw. He didn't move, but remained motionless within the pyramid of illumination, observing her.

She shivered with cold recognition. The man who had appeared in the rain the night she was shot. The same man who had stood in the crowd and visited her hospital room.

Or was this another out-of-body experience? She pressed the cracked concrete beneath her hands. Smelled the putrid remnants of exhaust. Felt the horror that mushroomed within her. She was definitely here in this stark ugly reality.

A chilling shiver skittered across her shoulders and down her back. Why did he stand there watching her?

What did he want? She tasted her own fear, sour in the back of her throat, as she remembered: There were two voices in the car. Had he been left behind to finish the job?

She felt nakedly vulnerable hunched on the sidewalk with no means to protect herself. "Please—" but her voice gave out as she choked back a sob. He loomed closer and she instinctively slumped back, ducking her head.

Nothing happened.

Shuddering an intake of breath, she cautiously looked up. The light from the streetlamp played with the edges of his hair, infusing the air around his head with a golden glow. Slowly, he opened his arms, palms up. Light swam down the caramel-colored leather jacket and, for a moment, Scarlett swore something sparked at the tips of his fingers.

"I'd never harm you, Scarlett."

Strangely enough, she felt his voice. Like waves of energy that rolled through the atmosphere and resonated with her soul. Touching her so deeply, so intimately, that she imagined her soul exposed to him. Instantaneously, the roiling fear within her evaporated, replaced by a soothing comfort that warmed her insides.

The man in the road. She had to help him.

"Someone's been hit." She gestured toward the parked Pinto. "He's in the street, behind that car. We have to help him—"

"That was me."

She found herself shaking her head in disbelief as she stared at the man before her. He adjusted his leather jacket slightly with a shift of his shoulders, his eyes never leaving her face.

This is crazy. Impossible. She had seen the car bearing down, roaring toward its victim. He had stepped out when the car was—what—maybe twenty feet away? Hardly time to escape from the vehicle's path, yet somehow he had managed to not only push her out of harm's way—but also save himself?

"How?" She breathed the question more than spoke it. Nothing was real anymore. Yet she still felt the sweltering heat on her face, heard the distant barking dog. Everything else was as it had been before the car appeared . . . or was it? "How did you do it?"

"It's not easy to explain." The rich tones of his voice rippled through the air. "I knew you were in danger, so I . . . stepped in. They thought they hit someone, but—as you can see . . ." He opened his arms wider to prove he was intact. ". . . that is not so."

Scarlett's eyes traced how the light pooled in the leather's worn crevices. From within the shadows of his half-opened jacket, a flicker of brilliance caught her attention—some kind of pendant that dangled at the end of a chain from around his neck. She looked back up into his face and found him staring intently at her, impassioned concern in his eyes. No, obviously, he hadn't been hit by a car. Yet . . .

She flicked her gaze toward the street. "I heard someone in that car say they'd hit the wrong one. I'm certain of that," she persisted.

His eyes narrowed. "Yes, that's what they think happened."

She waited, thinking he'd finish his explanation, but

he said nothing more. What did he do? Throw something in the road? How did he have the time to save her and foil their murder attempt within a matter of seconds?

And what about that celestial Ferris wheel ride where she looked back down on Gabrielle Street?

I'm losing my mind.

"Don't worry, Scarlett."

His words rumbled through the dusky night air. It took her a moment to realize he'd responded to her thoughts, which made the fine hairs on her arms stand on end. A breeze stirred the air, carrying with it the unmistakable scent of sandalwood. She rocked back on her knees and absently grazed her hands across the cooled skin on her arms. I'm not dreaming, yet this man appears in my life when I'm near death . . . or maybe not near, but . . .

She met his gaze warily. "Am I dead?" She wasn't sure that was a better alternative than being off her rocker. Or maybe this is what being loony tunes felt like.

A slow smile curled his lips. "Scarlett, you're asking me what you are?" He threw his head back and laughed deeply. Looking back down at her, he raked his fingers through his mane of hair as he shook his head. "You don't know how rich that question is." But the mirth in his eyes clouded over and he looked away.

A sudden mist passed between them, blurring his shape. The air thickened and cold fog dampened her face, weighted her eyelashes. She blinked, straining to see him through the murky veil that now separated them. The swirling gray teased her mind's eye, creating shapes that mimicked his stance or the turn of his head before vaporizing into nothingness. Then the fog parted, briefly, and she spied the clear outline of the lamppost.

He had vanished.

Jake stood underneath the streetlight, watching her as she continued to stare at him, her green eyes serious. *Should I return to the human dimension?* he wondered. He fingered the crucifix around his neck and gave her another assessing look. To return required more strength and willpower than he had—these recent journeys from purgatory to Earth's plane had exhausted his precious inner resources, what he once called his soul.

Yet Scarlett had been planted squarely in his path. There was no way to avoid her, or hide from what propelled them toward some united fate. He knew that too well. Too painfully well. *Fight the memories,* he commanded himself. *It's over. You're being tested again.*

Through the gray veil of his world, he circled her, critically eyeing her small body half-crouched on the concrete. The few feet between them crackled with energy. *Yes, you're my destiny. This is how it felt before when I was drawn to aid two other people, before you, on Earth. But this time, I feel more.*

As though in response to his thought, a heightened urgency sprang loose within him—its ferocity almost more than his being could contain. So fierce, he shook with its power. Since when did he experience such a human reaction on this side of the curtain?

It had never been like this before.

He willed himself to control these new sensations as he moved behind her and continued to observe this human, this woman, who undermined his existence—a transmutation of what he once called life. She remained staring straight ahead at the spot under the streetlamp. Perfectly still, like a porcelain figurine. Her short, red curly hair bobbed down her neck in copper coils that glistened with stray moonlight. Her slender arms, stretched out before her, propped her up as she strained to see where he had gone.

With quaking fingers, he rubbed the raised pattern on the crucifix, the metal chilling to his touch. A wispy cloud of ash floated over her head and veered wildly in a zigzag pattern to miss hitting Jake. Evil sifted through this realm in patches of smoke—remnants, Jake had long ago decided, from the belching fires of Lucifer himself. That they recoiled and avoided Jake gave him hope that his presence repelled evil. Which meant, or so he desperately wanted to believe, that he was trapped in purgatory for a higher purpose. God's purpose. An angel made earthbound until some unknown goal was met, some mission accomplished.

He clutched the crucifix in his palm, feeling its sharp points dig into his hand. *Or maybe I'm God's joke. Part human, part supernatural, doomed to roam the earth in this parallel dimension for eternity.*

"Where are you?" pleaded Scarlett. Gradually she rose, her silk blouse rippling with the movement.

He felt her emotions: confusion, fear. Their power rocked through him with a force he had never intuited before from a "destiny." He couldn't leave her like this, frightened and alone. But he couldn't return to Earth's plane. Not right now. Instead, he concentrated on his own thoughts and willed a message to her: *Remember your strengths—they will see you through this difficult time.*

The fog began to spin, whipping her hair and clothes in its growing frenzy. Scarlett gasped and hugged herself, her eyes locked on the swirling gray wall that surrounded her. Then, with a deafening whoosh, it caved in on itself with lightning speed, funneled into a pinhole of space. She was left staring, dumbfounded, down the empty street mottled with splashes of moonlight. In the distance the dog continued to bark. Muggy heat instead of chilling fog now caressed her skin. Had anything really happened in the last few minutes? To her senses, all was the same.

Yet in her head, she heard his voice as clearly as if he stood next to her. "Remember your strengths—they will see you through this difficult time."

The next afternoon Scarlett closed Ray's before the lunch rush and drove straight to the lawyer's office on La Brea, just south of Santa Monica Boulevard. She'd chosen this lawyer because his smallish ad in the yellow pages promised thirty minutes of free legal advice. The ad's size and cramped style, she decided, meant he wasn't one of those mega L.A. lawyers—megabucks, mega-ego. And the thirty minutes of free advice must mean he has a compassionate soul unlike in all the lawyer jokes she'd heard.

After doing a lousy parallel parking job, she peeled herself off the car seat, wishing—as she did every summer—that she'd thought ahead and saved enough to buy an air conditioner for her car. After plunking a quarter for thirty minutes into the meter, she lifted her hair and willed a breeze to cool the back of her neck. Dropping her hand, she glanced at her wristwatch, which was still stuck at six o'clock. "Why do I bother to keep wearing it?" she muttered under her breath.

No matter. Right before getting out of the car she'd heard the announcer on the radio say it was exactly twelve fifty-five in the third day of a record-breaking L.A. scorcher. A drip of sweat inched down the small of her back into the waistband of her skirt as Scarlett eyed the door before her. Stenciled across its shiny beige surface were the words *Venice Bar Association*. Actually, *Venice Ba Association*, the "r" plucked by some mischievous kid, no doubt. Or a disgruntled client who didn't get his thirty minutes' worth?

If it wasn't so hot, she would have laughed at her little joke.

A rotund receptionist looked up, her dull eyes reflecting nothing. When she didn't offer any greeting, Scarlett barged ahead. "I have an appointment to see Mr. Sartorelli."

In the corner a fan creaked as it slowly pivoted in a 180-degree arc. It sat on the top of a chipped metal filing cabinet—the only uncluttered surface in the room, Scarlett noted wryly as she looked around. Magazines obscured the coffee table. The receptionist's desk was a burial ground for paper, coffee cups, Scotch-tape dispensers, and a hodgepodge of other objects.

With one fleshy hand, the receptionist shoved several

papers aside and stared at a monthly calendar taped onto the desk's surface. "Name?" she croaked, not bothering to lift her eyes.

"Scarlett Ray." The fan pushed a gust of air over the receptionist's head. Not one lacquered hair budged.

"You're on time," the receptionist finally stated, her pudgy finger pressed on a spot in the calendar. "Lemme get Mr. Sartorelli." In one bulky movement, she shoved herself away from the desk and yanked down her wrinkled skirt. Scarlett swore the floor shook as the massive woman lumbered down the hallway.

Within moments, a thin, wiry man dressed in a gray suit walked briskly down the hall, his hand extended to Scarlett.

"Ms. Ray, please come back to my office. I was expecting you."

His office was a tidy wood-paneled box that allowed for one bookcase, a desk, and two chairs. *Guess clients come in ones or twos,* Scarlett mused as she quickly glanced around the room. A third would have to stand pressed against one of the walls or sit sideways on his desk. Her eyes drifted over the highly polished desktop covered with a few neatly placed items: a pen and pencil holder, a clock, a yellow note pad, a silver-framed picture of a woman with mousy hair and a frozen smile. His wife?

The room felt refreshingly cooler and Scarlett breathed with relief as she settled into her chair. No wonder Shamu the Receptionist was so uptight—it must be godawful hot out there relying on one rickety fan to pump stale air while Mr. Sartorelli luxuriated in a refrigerated Shangri-la.

"Did my receptionist offer you anything to drink?"

Are you kidding? "No, I'm fine. Thank you."

He leaned back in his cushioned chair, steepled his fingers, and cast upon her what Scarlett construed to be a benevolent gaze. "Tell me your problem."

She cleared her throat. "Before we begin, your ad states that you provide thirty minutes of free legal advice, correct?"

He nodded. "Correct."

Scarlett scooted forward to the edge of her seat. "Two and a half weeks ago, Kenneth Chandler sent a . . . gentleman into my business, Ray's Hamburgers . . ."

She explained about the man shooting at her after she refused to sign the purchase agreement with Chandler Enterprises, about the car that nearly ran her down, how other property owners on that same block had lost their businesses through mysterious circumstances—with Kenneth Chandler ultimately replacing them as the legal owner. All the while, Mr. Sartorelli jotted down notes on his pad.

Finished, Scarlett exhaled heavily. "Can you help me?"

He gave the notes a last cursory glance before meeting her eyes. "Yes. If what you say is true."

She bit off her protest and flicked an imaginary piece of lint off her skirt. *If.* Is that what she was up against? Proving what had happened to her was real? She didn't need any reminders that even she doubted what was real anymore.

He continued, his voice smooth like a salesman's. "From what you say, however, Chandler Enterprises is absolutely guilty of illegal activity and we can litigate this as a civil action in court."

She felt lulled with the promise of relief. Safety. There was a way out of this madness.

"My rate is two hundred dollars an hour plus a five-thousand-dollar retainer."

The room chilled to an uncomfortable degree. After a lengthy pause she found her voice. "You've got to be kidding."

He set his pencil down and stared at her, unblinking. "Hardly, Ms. Ray." The icy tone of his voice now matched the room's dropped temperature. "I'm a lawyer, not a philanthropist."

"You said you offered free counsel—"

"For thirty minutes. Flicking his wrist, he glanced at the time. "Which, by the way, is up. If you wish to continue this discussion, Ms. Ray, I'll have to send you a bill."

She stood and glared at him. "You advertise free legal advice to attract people like me who are desperate for help, yet have no extraordinary resources of money. What do other people do? Hawk their life savings or sell their few treasured possessions because you'll fix all their problems in a time-consuming, expensive legal battle?" He lowered his eyes and she knew she had hit the crux of his scam. "Don't answer that question. . . . It's not worth two hundred dollars."

As she stomped through the stuffy waiting room, Scarlett thought she caught a "told you so" smirk on the receptionist's face.

Outside, Scarlett welcomed the heated air and familiar hum of L.A. traffic. So she met a dead end searching for legal restitution. The detective was continuing his investigation of Chandler Enterprises, and the cops were faithfully patrolling Ray's Hamburgers and her home around the clock. She wasn't exactly alone in this. But alone enough to be a target for another of Chandler's murder attempts. And so alone that her mind was playing tricks, imagining some strange man who materialized and vaporized with gusts of fog.

A man who stirred her so deeply she wanted to see him again—figment of her imagination or not.

Chapter Three

As she vigorously chopped the onion, Scarlett sniffed back the tears that filled her eyes. With business slacking off, it would be a while before she could get the Cuisinart fixed and escape this miserable kitchen duty. And the Cuisinart definitely took precedence over getting her watch fixed. Thinking of money, or lack thereof, refueled her anger about her afternoon visit to the "Venice Ba Association."

"I should have scrawled a 'd' after 'Ba' and ripped off 'ociation'," she muttered. Whack. She neatly sliced a whole onion in two. "At least then he'd be advertising himself truthfully. Lawyer. Humph."

The creep had the gall to ask for two hundred dollars an hour plus a five thousand-dollar retainer. Did he think people who sought free legal advice had the means to shell out that kind of money? What did his clients do—sell their homes for the honor of his services? No wonder that lawyer died such an ignoble death in *Jurassic Park*. Whack. Three cheers for Hollywood.

"I won't sell our home, Mom, just to line a lawyer's pockets." Whack.

She stopped and looked at the vegetable slaughter before her. "Should I go for a compromise?" Could she really say it? Lowering her voice, she whispered huskily, "Hold onto our house, and sell Ray's?"

She slouched against the work counter and etched an imaginary design into the chopping block with the knife. "Lose Ray's?" The knife slowed to a stop as her thoughts congealed.

Ray's is my past, my legacy. My future. I can't give it up.

Can't.

She shoved the shreds of onion aside, plopped another fat yellow onion on the cutting board, and whacked hard at it.

The front door creaked open and she wiped her wet cheek against her sleeve before shooting a glance toward the entrance. A couple of teenage boys strolled in. Doris's son Roger chatted amiably with one of his teenage buddies. Behind them sauntered Enrique, a Dodgers baseball cap perched jauntily on his head. He started to wave hello, then stopped.

"Problema?" he demanded, his eyes darting around the room.

She sniffed. "Onions." Sweet Enrique, ready to defend her from evil at a moment's notice.

The wrinkles around his small hazel eyes deepened as he squinted at her face, at the chopping board, then back. He nodded. "Onions, eh?" His voice revealed relief. "Okay if they make you cry, I guess. As long as it's not one of—" He pressed his lips together, frowned thoughtfully, then waved the air as though erasing the thought. "Don't mind us, Little One. We'll warm these stools until dinner time. Keep you company."

Little One. That's what her mother called her. Even as she grew into adulthood, her mother had still called her "Little One." Some of the regulars, like Enrique, continued to do so.

She refrained from battling another onion and instead neatly sliced the next one. The old hinges on the front door squeaked again as the door opened.

A whiff of vanilla blended with the onion vapors. Only one person in the world used a supermarket's spice aisle as a perfume counter. "Afternoon, Judyl," Scarlett called out.

A stool creaked behind Scarlett. "Greetings. Hullo Enrike."

Enrique's mumbled response didn't disguise his disfavor.

Another wave of vanilla. "Scarlett, did you know Cleopatra used onions to protect her bathing quarters?"

Judyl was about to launch into one of her infamous vegetable stories. Best to cut her off at the pass.

"What'd she do? Make her guards eat raw onions? That'd keep anybody away." She continued over Judyl's protest. "Nah, these are regular ol' smear-'em-over-the-hamburger-patty-type onions. The only thing they protect is the taste of the juicy meat."

Meat stories were a strong amulet to vegetable lores. Judyl made a sound somewhere between a groan and utter disgust. Enrique chuckled. The boys were in their own world, yapping and laughing about something interesting only to teenagers.

"Scarlett, someday please put a vegetarian entree on your menu so the rest of the world can eat here." Sometimes Judyl sounded like Maggie Smith in *The Prime of Miss Jean Brodie.* At times like this Scarlett wondered what Judyl had done in the real world before she started living out of her car and growing bean sprouts. "The body's a temple," continued Judyl. "Peoplekind were not meant to eat cows."

Peoplekind. Judyl's odd vocabulary matched her name—Judyl LowMoon. She claimed that one night twenty years ago, the heavens zapped her brain with the name "LowMoon" while she stood stark naked in the middle of Central Park. Scarlett never asked about the naked part—it was enough to accept that the name LowMoon was a message from God.

Enrique guffawed. "Then why d'you come into Ray's if you don't like people eating meat?"

A brief, uncomfortable silence followed. Scarlett knew Enrique didn't approve of Judyl's lifestyle. It didn't help that she mispronounced his name every time she saw him. Enrique came from the school of old-fashioned chivalry mixed with a healthy dose of common sense. Judyl's fierce independence he could probably accept. It irritated him that she refused to pay money for an apartment ("landlords are medieval warlords in disguise"), and disturbed him that she grew trays of sprouts in the backseat of her car ("grown with love for the betterment of peoplekind's bodies and spirits"). But it enraged him that she had a son named Sun who also lived her freaky lifestyle.

"Because Ray's is like a second home. And I wanted to ask Scarlett if Sun could stay here after school lets out today."

Enrique grumbled something unintelligible.

Scarlett put down the knife and turned around. Today Judyl looked like something out of *Aladdin.* She had wrapped her head in a blue-and-gold-threaded scarf—probably one of her treasures she had ransacked from a Beverly Hills trash can.

With great effort, Scarlett lowered her gaze from the makeshift turban to Judyl's eyes. "I know Mom let kids use Ray's as an after-school hangout, but I'm just too busy to be babysitting and working at the same time."

Judyl's round blue eyes pleaded. The thin gold wire that pierced her nose vibrated slightly as she spoke. "Please, Scarlett. I have to deliver some sprouts to Glendale and Pasadena by three-thirty. I'll be back by five. I don't ask you often, only when there's an emergency."

"He's old enough to take care of himself," Enrique chimed in. "A young man needs to learn . . ." Enrique shook his head, obviously searching for the right word. His forefinger suddenly shot up in the air. "Discipline! Yes, discipline for himself."

"Self-discipline," corrected Scarlett.

Enrique nodded emphatically. "Self-discipline. *Sí.* And he needs a real home to go to after school. Not an automobile that grows . . . green things."

Judyl ignored the insult. "He's fifteen. Old enough to take care of himself, I know. But in this part of town, there's too many temptations. Even for a self-disciplined young man." Judyl's eyes misted over and her chin trembled dramatically.

Thanks, Mom, thought Scarlett. *Not only did you bequeath me this hamburger joint, you also bequeathed me your sterling reputation to live up to. If I don't help out the way you did, I'll look like a coldhearted bum.* "Okay," she conceded grudgingly.

"Cool. You have your mother's heart."

Judyl pressed her palm into the air in some type of greeting that Scarlett had never figured out. She nodded and twitched a smile in return, and watched as Judyl traipsed out of Ray's. Her mother's heart? Scarlett could never achieve that. Because her mother had loved and cared for this community in a way Scarlett had never really understood.

"*Sí,* you have your mama's heart," added Enrique.

"No, I don't. She was a saint to this neighborhood, always ready with a helping hand. Free food. Free babysitting services. I'm her selfish, capitalistic daughter. All I want to do is make a living." She avoided Enrique's eyes and turned back to the grill.

If the locals like Enrique didn't make it a point to eat at Ray's Hamburgers, she wondered if she'd have any income at all. Since the shooting, business had drastically dropped off. Thanks to the bad press, no doubt. She couldn't blame people for steering clear—would she frequent a joint where the owner had been shot point-blank? Most people probably thought it was gang related, considering it happened in this part of town. Which undoubtedly pleased Kenneth Chandler, because her shrinking income strengthened his chances to move in on her business. Like a shark sniffing blood.

I won't sell, she reminded herself. *Someday this'll be behind me and I'll be the proud proprietor of a restaurant that serves quiche, not hamburgers.* She chuckled to herself, imagining how it would feel to break forty eggs instead of chopping forty onions.

The onion fumes launched a second assault, making her nervous stomach do an extra flip-flop. She needed a break. Scarlett wiped the knife clean, covered the onions with a clean dish towel, and poured herself a tall glass of cool water. Smiling a greeting at the boys, who were now seated on two stools next to Enrique, she sauntered past the grill to the cash register. Leaning against the counter's edge, she stared out the plate-glass window at the street.

Outside cruised an occasional car, sunlight sparkling along its chrome and windshield. The street seemed so normal with its slow-moving traffic and meandering pedestrians. Hardly the same street where a hit-and-run driver had tried to take her life.

Or the street where the man in the leather jacket disappeared in a swirl of fog.

She had tried not to think of him, to deny that something that spooky had occurred. Yet his image kept returning, haunting her. How he slouched underneath that streetlight, watching her with those impassioned dark eyes. How he answered her thoughts, how light sparked at the tips of his fingers. *It's a trick of my mind, that's all. Supernatural beings don't hang outside Ray's Hamburgers, for God's sake. Get a grip on yourself, girl.*

Gingerly, she touched the bandage on her neck. Obviously, she had been through a lot of stress. And stress made people do and see odd things. Like men who materialized out of the heavens. *Wonder if his name's LowMoon,* thought Scarlett with an inward chuckle. *Nah, I'm not as far gone as Judyl. Yet. I'm simply recovering from a stressful episode. That's it, plain and simple.* She smiled to herself, pleased with her tidy, logical explanation.

After another sip of water, she decided it was time to resume her chopping chores. But when she started to turn away, something flared in her peripheral vision. She swerved her gaze to the window as an icy chill glazed her insides.

The plate-glass window was a solid wall of flames. Her eyes stung with the savage rippling of oranges and yellows. Heat singed the air, teased her skin. Her jaw dropped open, yet she had no air in her lungs with which to yell. She was frozen in this spot, as though Fear stood behind her, his fingers digging into her shoulders, forcing her to witness the conflagration.

The fire leaped and danced silently. She released her held breath and frowned. She saw the fire, but she didn't hear it. Nothing crackled, sputtered, or roared. No, the impressive inferno was devoid of any sound. It flickered in absolute silence.

Was a movie studio filming on the street, creating some special effect? She inhaled slowly. No smell of smoke either. Only the vision of the fire and the feel of its heat.

As suddenly as the blaze appeared, it shrank and disappeared. A force—like a soundless gale of wind—blasted through the room. As it passed through her, she felt negativity at its most loathsome. Dark. Fearful. Insidious. Then it was gone, taking with it the gouging fingers from her shoulders.

The windows were again glass, but now they sparkled with glistening pinpoints of the clearest, purest light. The patchwork of tiny stars condensed into a solid mass of captured luminescence, so vibrant it made her wince. With a gasp of surprise, she realized they had formed a man's shape. His silhouette wavered, an image floating in midair like a mirage. The shimmering took on different colors. The colors of clothes: blue jeans, caramel-toned jacket. The color of black hair. Clutching her cold glass, she stumbled back a step.

It was him.

She jerked her head back toward the counter. Enrique was twisting one end of his mustache, chattering with one of the boys. No one seemed to be the least bit aware that the front glass window had projected excerpts from *The Towering Inferno,* followed by *It Came from Outer Space*. She stopped herself from yelling for them to look. If they didn't see it, did it really exist?

Cautiously, she looked back. The window was now plain clear glass, through which she saw a late-model Pontiac cruise slowly down the street, its radio blasting the pulsating beat of a rap song. Just a window. No aliens pieced together from twinkling lights.

Everything was back to normal.

She grasped both hands around her glass of water, reassured by its slick, cool touch. Shakily, she lifted it to her mouth. No sooner had the soothing liquid touched her lips than she realized somebody was standing on the other side of the cash register, directly to her right.

Shifting her gaze over the rim of the glass, she saw a tall, lean form fiddling with the antique radio that sat on a shelf above the register. His long arm blocked his face. One of the boys? He'd have had to cross right in front of her to get to the radio and she would have seen him.

He lowered his arm and her insides caved in. "You," she whispered hoarsely.

"Doesn't seem to work," he said nonchalantly. His resonant voice stirred the air like an autumn breeze. She even felt the currents of air lapping against her bare arms. Just like before when he spoke.

She squeezed her eyes shut and downed the water in one gulp. The chilled fluid coursed a refreshing path down to her stomach. Without opening her eyes, she went to set her glass down on the counter, misjudged the distance, and instead slammed it against the Formica countertop with a loud crack.

Enrique and the boys stopped their chatter. "You okay?" called Enrique.

Scarlett turned in a half-circle and blinked open her eyes. At the far end of the counter sat Enrique. Even at this distance, she saw his sunken eyes glisten with concern. On either side of him sat the two boys, their faces scrunched with confusion.

"Behind me." Her voice was little more than a rasp, so she dipped her head in the general direction. She licked her lips and willed herself to speak in clear, calm tones. "There's a man in jeans and a leather jacket standing next to the cash register."

All three of them raised their eyebrows in unison.

"Don't look at me!" Her voice had taken on a guttural tone. "Look at him." She jabbed her thumb slightly, indicating behind her.

Enrique leaned his body slightly to the right to see where she indicated. The two boys exchanged a look, then followed Enrique's lead. Scarlett thought they looked like flowers wilting the way they each drooped to the side. The glazed expressions on their faces told her nothing.

"Well?" she whispered.

One of the boys looked at his buddy and mumbled something in rapid Spanish. Enrique straightened and shrugged. "*Nada*. Nothing, Little One."

"That's impossible!" she said indignantly. "He was fiddling with my radio and now he's—" Their dumbfounded looks stopped her from continuing. They have no idea what I'm sputtering about. Which means I imagined him again.

She turned around and nearly screamed. There he stood, resting his elbows on top of the cash register. He grinned, one side of his lips curling mischievously.

As she stammered for words, he raised one hand to silence her. "They don't see me. Only you do."

"B-b-but why?"

"They don't hear me, either. But they do hear you. Everything you say to me. You might want to take that into consideration." He scratched his chin and winked.

How dare he mock her! She started to speak, but changed her mind. Even if she really saw and heard this man, the others saw nothing. Zilch. Empty air.

Okay. That proves it—he's a hallucination. A result of my stressful trauma. I'll ignore him.

She bit the inside of her lip. *I mean, I'll ignore my hallucination.*

Tossing back her hair with a flip of her hand, she began fussing with the salt shakers and napkin holders that dotted the edge of the countertop.

"Want to go home, Little One? We'll escort you to your car," suggested Enrique from the end of the counter.

Scarlett grabbed a box of salt underneath the counter and filled a random shaker. "No! No, I'm fine." She winced at her voice's new high octave. *God, I sound like Minnie Mouse.* She tried surreptitiously to clear her throat as she poured the salt. Her gaze traveled everywhere except back to the cash register.

"You forgot to take the top off," Enrique said quietly, wagging a finger at the salt shaker.

She flicked her eyes down and saw a waterfall of salt spraying off the shaker's silver lid. She yelped and quickly righted the box of salt. White granules were everywhere—on the counter, the napkin holders, the floor. It looked like a miniature sand storm had blown through this area of Ray's Hamburgers.

In a flash, Enrique was at her side, his callused hand gently cupping her elbow as he steered her from behind the counter. "You say 'fine,' but Enrique thinks different. Go sit and let an old man baby you, eh?" Enrique shooed her away and grabbed the broom from its niche behind the refrigerator. When she still hadn't moved, he pretended to sweep her away, which forced a feeble smile to her lips.

With quick steps, she passed the boys. One of them snickered, but was quickly hushed by Enrique. She walked to the front of the counter, the section closest to the door and farthest from the boys, and sat on one of the well-worn red vinyl stools with her back to the counter. Sighing heavily, she feathered her fingers through her curly hair and debated whether to look over at the cash register again. If he was still there, what next? Did she have the strength to face her alter-ego, or whatever her mind was fabricating?

Absently, she fingered the bandage on her neck. Should she make an appointment with a shrink? The local mental health clinic advertised services on a sliding scale. Sliding scale for sliding minds . . .

"You don't need a shrink, Scarlett. You only need to believe."

Like distant thunder, his voice rolled through the room. A current of electricity raced through her as she tried to assemble her jumbled thoughts. This was madness. She leaned back against the counter, terrified to look up. She fought to inhale a breath, but her lungs refused to expand.

"Look at me, Scarlett."

He sounded closer. So close, she swore she felt his warm breath against her cheek.

She managed a stilted breath. Her insides burned with a liquid heat, as though she'd just taken a long swig of liquor. Scotch, if she wasn't mistaken by the lingering taste on her lips. Scotch? It had been years since she'd touched hard liquor.

"Sorry," he said with a chuckle. "Should have asked if you wanted a swig of spirits."

She lifted her head slightly and watched as he sank a flask back into his jacket pocket. She noted how his crucifix sparked a feeble light and how the leather jacket crinkled softly as he moved.

Her insides weren't hot just from the effects of whiskey, she admitted grudgingly to herself.

He stood in front of the window, his eyes boring into her with their heat. An unseen light streaked paths of platinum through his onyx locks. He lifted his arms. Streams of light shot from his fingers, piercing the air with blades of radiance.

Her mouth went bone-dry. All thoughts fled her mind. It seemed a small eternity that he stood in front of her like that with his arms open, seeming to beckon her. Or appeal to her. Sandalwood traced the air, intoxicating her senses. And in the distance, did she hear the faint tinkling of chimes?

I can't succumb to this . . . this . . . craziness. She gulped a mouthful of cool air, willing herself to gain control of her mind.

No sooner did she think these thoughts, than the streams of light from his fingertips dissipated. Now she saw him clearly, without any dazzling electric show. He stood in front of the window, as real as any man.

Behind him, through the glass, she saw moving cars and ambling pedestrians. A chubby little boy patted the window and gurgled before his mother pulled him away. Had he seen the man?

A sharp pain announced that she was clutching her hands together with the ferocity of a desperate prayer. She unraveled her fingers, her eyes never leaving the man before her. He wore the same attire as when he had appeared in her hospital room, the night she'd decided he'd simply been a dream. Jeans. Snakeskin boots. Whiskey-colored bomber jacket. She halted her inventory and met his eyes with a steady gaze. He returned her look, his dark eyes serious. *Who are you?*

He smiled, a slow easy smile—the kind shared between intimates. "Jake," he answered.

She clutched her hand to her chest as the realization hit her—she hadn't said anything, only thought the question. What was he doing? Reading her mind?

"Yes."

Her mouth dropped open. Not only was she imagining this rogue in a leather jacket who seemed to step directly out of the sun and disappear in waves of fog, she now had him reading her thoughts. Wasn't that redundant? Why imagine someone who reads your own thoughts? She frowned as the question looped over and over in her mind. . . .

"You're not imagining, Scarlett."

His voice, warm and beckoning, stilled her questions. She sank against the counter. Its hard edge dug into her back, but she didn't care. If nothing else, it reminded her that this moment, and the next, were indeed reality.

He shrugged away from the window and took a step toward her. His gaze drifted over her hair, her face, resting finally on her eyes. He seemed hesitant to speak and shook his head slightly. Once. The movement released a strand of dark hair that curled lazily across his forehead.

"Scarlett, there are so many things I could tell you. . . ."

How'd he know my name? But her astonishment turned into self-mockery. Huffing an exasperated sigh, she crossed her arms and glared at the apparition. *Of course he knows my name. I made him up!* Absent-mindedly, she flicked her wrist and tapped the glass face on the wristwatch. Maybe Enrique was right. She should go home, rest.

"When did your watch stop working?"

She looked up and caught him frowning at her.

He didn't wait for her reply. "It stopped the night you were shot. After you nearly entered the light."

"After I . . . ?" Pieces of a memory floated together in her mind, forming a vague recollection. There had been darkness and a light shaped like a door, and at the doorway, a dazzling brilliance filled with love and a man's voice.

This man's voice?

No. Straight-jacket talk. This rebel without a cause didn't stand in some golden doorway telling her to go back.

The fragile image shrank back to the dark edges of her mind.

"Have you told anybody else about you near-death experience?"

No, I haven't. Which meant . . . dare she realize the truth? *You know what happened to me that night?*

He crossed his arms and nodded.

A lump formed in her throat. This was no repercussion of an overwrought mind. He was there, as real as anything in the room.

The seriousness in his dark eyes softened; tenderness softened the creases of worry in his forehead. "This isn't easy, for either of us. You and I share a special bond, Scarlett. A destiny. Why? I don't know."

Was there a hint of sarcasm to his words?

He adjusted his stance and she thought, for one thrilling moment, that he was going to approach her.

She peeked behind her at Enrique sweeping the floor. Humming a quirky tune, he looked up and smiled pleasantly before looking back down at his work. She flicked her gaze over to the two boys. They were laughing and punching each other playfully. From where they sat, they could easily see anything unusual at the front window, yet they obviously didn't.

Slowly, she looked back. Jake stood several feet in front of her, his head tilted as he seemingly assessed her thoughts. "Remember, they don't see me. Only you do."

She felt drawn to his dark, compelling eyes. Strangely enough, she felt connected to him, yet there were no words to express exactly what this meant. It was simply a deep knowing. He smiled and a wave of peace flooded her insides, bringing with it a sense of euphoria that threatened to spill over from herself to all things. No fear. No worries. Just a vibrant sense of peace that soothed her soul.

And even stranger, she knew he understood how she felt. His invisible radar detected her every thought, her every emotion.

His gaze locked with hers for a long moment, his dark eyes cooling into fathomless black. The stony defiance that hardened his features also diminished the incredible peace she'd experienced only moments before. What brought on this brewing storm when moments before they'd shared a bond, a "destiny"?

He stalked several steps back, eyeing the radio again. "Haven't seen one of those in . . . years. Why don't you ever play it?"

She followed his glance to the antique radio. "It's an antique. Never did work." Words. Enrique would insist she go home if he heard her talking to herself. A quick check caught Enrique telling a joke to the boys. He obviously hadn't heard her.

"Another gift that doesn't work?" Jake arched one eyebrow and flashed her a teasing grin.

The cold front had vanished as suddenly as it had blown in. Scarlett felt a rising heat fill her cheeks as Jake's dark eyes glittered with his in-joke. *My mom and I brought it. A gift to each other.*

He looked at her with such compassion she thought she'd cry if she didn't concentrate on something silly and nonsensical. She glanced at the radio and carefully formed her thoughts. *Mom wanted it because she said her family had one just like it when she was a little girl. We pooled together all the change we had in our purses and bought it on the spot.* The irony of purposefully buying a broken gift hit her as she cut a look at her wristwatch. Unlike Bob—Rafael—the broken gift she and her mom shared wasn't indicative of a nonworking relationship. Her mom had been her best friend.

His long fingers caressed the glossy wood that encased the radio. His forefinger circled one of the white knobs. "This is the volume knob. Did you know that?"

She shook her head slightly.

He tapped the next knob and flashed a wide grin over

his shoulder. "And this is the station selector. We had one like it, too. Back when . . ." His searching fingers stopped and, for a long moment, he stared at the radio. "But that was another life," he muttered.

He leaned against the counter next to her and crossed his arms. A distant flame sparked to life in the depths of his eyes.

"Later, when you think of me, try not to be afraid. Or tell yourself you're suffering from . . . exhaustion, or whatever. Ah, Scarlett, you are so—"

He took several steps toward her, his eyes never leaving her face. Standing close enough to touch her, he reached past her and planted his hands firmly against the counter. She was caught in the circle of his arms. The smell of sandalwood coiled through the air. His leather jacket crinkled slightly as he leaned forward. A sultry smile creased his face, turning her insides to mush. She imagined how it would feel to stroke his clean-edged jaw and let her finger linger at the cleft in his chin.

"You are so special, Scarlett." His voice was husky, needy. Then he touched her on the neck, his fingers warming more than her skin.

"I'm sorry you were hurt," he mumbled hoarsely.

He caressed the bandage's perimeter. Where his fingertips touched her skin she felt a slight stinging sensation, yet it didn't hurt her. Then he pressed his hand over the bandage and closed his eyes.

She looked up at his face, mesmerized by his intense concentration. This close, she saw how his thick black lashes cast small spiked shadows under his eyes. And how, when he opened his eyes again, they shone with a crystal purity that astounded her.

"You are my destiny." His fingers trailed along her jaw bone to underneath her chin. He tilted her face so that she was forced to meet his gaze. "You're a mystery for me too, do you know that? I don't know why I'm here, only that being drawn to you, being with you, is inevitable. Maybe you're a test for me."

"A test?" she whispered softly. The nearness of him charged the air, the way it felt before a storm broke. *Why would someone like me test a renegade like you?*

She thought she detected the faintest shadow cross over his eyes. A stab of anguish pierced her heart more cleanly than any sword. She gasped, but the moment passed as quickly as it came. Following close behind it was the odd understanding that what she felt wasn't her pain, but *his*.

He cocked his head and narrowed his eyes. "Why would God have you experience my pain? That never happened with . . . the others." Abruptly, he dropped his hand and pulled away.

He didn't take steps. It was more that he glided back several feet, then stopped again in front of the window. Golden rays of sunlight pierced the window and coiled about him in long gilded threads.

In a flash of resplendence, he disappeared.

Behind her, Scarlett heard Enrique sweeping the floor while teasing one of the boys about a girl. Traffic droned down the street. The fryer bubbled. Everything was back to normal. Scarlett continued to stare at the window, uncertain if the encounter had really happened or not.

But that night, when she changed the bandage on her neck, the wound had completely healed.

Chapter Four

Waterloo Street bloated midblock to accommodate a palm tree growing smack in the middle of the road. Four houses west of the palm tree sat 2120 Waterloo, the house Scarlett had shared with her mother for sixteen years. After her mother's death, it had been hellish to go home alone. The memories taunted her, disrupted her sleep. But now, a year later, Scarlett found comfort in the pieces of their shared life.

Fumbling in her purse for the key, Scarlett scanned the front door. Even now, at nine-thirty at night, she clearly saw the shreds of faded beige paint like dried-up pancake makeup on a spinster's face. At the bottom of her purse, she touched the key's serrated edge. As her fingers curled around the familiar cold metal, she pivoted slightly and surveyed the moon-splashed shadows of her front yard. She knew the clumps of gray and black were thriving weeds and dried-out juniper bushes. Undoubtedly an excruciating humiliation to her neighbors, who spent every spare moment hedging and weeding their lush rectangles of lawn.

She twisted the key once to the right while giving a swift kick to the door's bottom left corner. It popped open with a sucking sound.

Dipping her fingers into the darkness, she flicked the light switch next to the door, which brought the room to life. Rhett lifted his head from where he lay on top of the refrigerator and mewed a raspy greeting.

"Evening, your majesty," Scarlett mumbled as she tossed her purse on the kitchen table and made a bee-line for the bedroom. There, she plunked down on the bed and slowly removed both of her scuffed white shoes, moaning as she wiggled her toes in delicious freedom. Rubbing her feet, she stared at the pictures scattered over the top of the walnut bureau. A pigtailed Scarlett in her brownie uniform. A more mature eleven-year-old Scarlett whose smile revealed braces, and her mom hamming it up in front of Ray's Hamburgers on its grand-opening day.

Scarlett touched the cool pewter frame that encased her favorite picture. A cherubic four-year-old Scarlett in her mother's arms—her father conspicuously absent. "You sure had it tough, raising a kid and building a business all alone . . ." She stroked the slick glass over her mother's young, beaming face. "Amazing how you still managed to slip an extra ten or twenty bucks to some needy mom or kid. Face it, Mom, you were a social worker at heart. Problem is, people think like mother, like daughter. Can you believe I babysat Judyl's son the other day? Okay, so he's fifteen and doesn't need a babysitter—but I did make him a chili burger, and poured that kid enough Cokes to give him hyperglycemia. I'm not as nurturing as you, but I gave it my best shot. How you doubled as a kiddie-drop-off-center and a hamburger joint, I'll never know."

Scarlett's smile dropped and she sighed heavily. "Hamburger joint. You would not believe the problems I'm having—and we thought making ends meet was sometimes tough. I gotta figure out how to save Ray's."

A scratchy mew beckoned from the other room.

"Coming, your majesty," Scarlett responded, knowing Rhett had no intention of climbing down from his sacred spot to properly greet his mistress. But approaching seventeen years of age, he had earned the right to sovereign rule.

An hour later, Scarlett sat slumped in her favorite spot, an overstuffed wing chair placed strategically in front of the TV. Dinner had been a bowl of cottage cheese and fruit. Now she sipped a glass of chilled white wine and watched a Loretta Young movie classic. This was her evening ritual: dinner with Rhett, movies with the stars of yesteryear.

Loretta played the young, neglected wife of David Niven. Cary Grant played an angel. I wouldn't mind an angel like that coming into my life, thought Scarlett as she swirled some of the cool wine in her mouth. It tasted faintly of apples and lemons and she swallowed the liquid slowly, savoring it.

Cary Grant sat in a restaurant with Loretta Young, looking at her with those slightly hooded, vulnerable eyes that melted women's hearts. Scarlett stared back, mesmerized. The velvet cadence of Cary's voice soothed her. She closed her eyes, letting his voice wash over her. Inside, a well of peace bubbled to life and Scarlett swore this was the best she'd felt since . . .

Since seeing Jake two days ago in Ray's Hamburgers.

She blinked her eyes open wide and concentrated fiercely on the movie. She wouldn't think about him. Did "hims" disappear in threads of golden light? It was the aftereffects of her trauma, that was all. A hallucination.

She concentrated on Cary Grant, who blurred to a blob of gray. Loretta Young remained intact as she tilted her head coquettishly and beamed at the fuzzy contours of Cary.

Scarlett rubbed her eyes. Could twenty-eight be old enough for bifocals? Blinking, she resumed watching. Loretta no longer spoke to a hazy Cary Grant. Instead, she conversed with . . .

Jake!

Scarlett squeezed her eyes shut. Impossible. No way did she just see Jake sitting next to Loretta Young. Ridiculous. The only thing on TV was an old black-and-white movie.

Opening her eyes a bare millimeter, she squinted at the movie. Through the dark fringe of her eyelashes, she spied Loretta batting her eyes at Cary, his back turned to the camera. Was he wearing a bomber jacket in the story? And was the food so potent in the restaurant that Cary's hair had grown a good three inches since she'd last looked?

Scarlett strained to listen to the conversation. Surely

she'd hear Cary's lilting "Judy, Judy, Judy" inflection. It didn't matter if Cary had changed his clothes, grown his hair. His voice was the one true test. Leaning forward, Scarlett eyeballed the TV, her ears finely tuned for the next line from Cary's lips. Loretta giggled something unintelligible and waited for Cary-in-the-bomber-jacket to respond.

Instead, Jake looked over his shoulder—right at Scarlett—and winked.

She jumped to her feet and shrieked.

The wineglass toppled from her hands and landed with several soft thuds on the threadbare carpet. Rhett scurried into the kitchen, his claws scrabbling a rat-a-tat pattern against the linoleum.

Panting shallow breaths, she stared at the TV. Jake blurred and became Cary again.

"There's a logical explanation for this," she began. Her voice sounded thin and wobbly, yet she continued to speak to the empty room. If nothing else, hearing herself offered a small reality check that yes, indeed, she was in the here and now, and not just now and then.

"You're tired. You've had . . ." she looked down at the empty wineglass. "Half a glass of wine. Obviously the combination of alcohol and fried brains makes one see leather-clad studs with supernatural prowess trade places with Cary Grant in a movie made years—okay, decades—before you were born." She rolled her tongue in her mouth. "Yeah. Right."

She flicked another look at the screen. Cary, trim and dapper in a dinner jacket, flashed Loretta one of those killer smiles. Scarlett glanced quickly away, then jerked her head back. Still Cary. Still Loretta. Still the black-and-white classic without any loose figments of her imagination also costarring.

On her way to the kitchen, she tapped the TV, its heated plastic surface another reassurance that this was indeed reality—but just for good measure she avoided looking at the screen. "Judyl's the one who gets brain-zapped by mysterious forces, not you," she mumbled.

Passing Rhett, she noticed the cat weaving a lazy figure-eight pattern, back and forth, the way he did when he rubbed against someone's legs. His loud purring mimicked fingers thrumming an old washboard. Since when did Rhett get off on rubbing air?

"Getting old," Scarlett muttered as she ripped off several sheets of paper towels. Not only was she losing her mind, so was her cat. Some shrink somewhere must have a name for this. Human-Feline Schizoid Transference? Or maybe Loose Marbles Hairball Syndrome?

On her way back to the living room, she stopped for a moment and eyed the old cat as he brushed back and forth, his bent tail curling indolent circles in the air. "Maybe we're both going senile, ol' boy. I can see it now. The headline of *The Enquirer* will read: 'Crazed woman tries to crawl into TV set—claims Cary Grant needs a new bomber jacket. Her cat brushes imaginary feet for hours.' "

A deep, throaty chuckle sent a hundred fears scurrying across her skin.

Her fingers went limp. The paper towel dropped soundlessly to her feet. Rhett continued weaving back and forth, oblivious.

The faintest imprint of a man teased the air. Then,

to Scarlett's astonishment, it filled with color. Living, breathing color. First the long legs solidified in navy blue jeans. The chest expanded into a whiskey-hued bomber jacket, zippered only halfway. Then the bronzed neck, the lean jaw, the unruly tendrils of hair. And those eyes. They shaded gray to indigo as he fully materialized.

She gulped and held her breath, her gaze dropping down to his feet and back up to his face. He looked real, all right. Just like he looked sitting next to Loretta Young. Only now he was out of the TV and standing next to her kitchen table. Maybe that wine had fermented too long. . . .

He winked and grinned. "It was only a few sips, Scarlett. Just enough to relax you, I'd say."

She felt her eyebrows raise as her mouth dropped open. Stealthily, she moved her right hand over and touched her left arm. Warm. This was no dream. She watched as he bent over and scratched the top of Rhett's head, who continued to rub against his legs while purring loudly. Clearing her throat, a difficult task with a mouth as dry as cotton, she tried to ask why. Why her? Why now? But all that came out was a raspy sound, like a fingernail scratching silk.

Jake straightened and paused, watching her reaction. "On the other hand, cheap wine'll do it every time." One side of his mouth curled up, giving his smile a rakish edge.

She found her voice, barely. "I think I have to lie down now." The last thing she remembered was her legs crumpling and Rhett's incessant purring.

When she opened her eyes again, she was lying on

the couch, a pillow propped under her head. David Niven was now on the TV, speaking sternly to a stiff-lipped Loretta. Rhett cuddled against Scarlett's feet, his gold-speckled eyes watching her intently.

"You look worried, ol' boy," she said in a half-croak.

Then it struck her. What am I doing lying on the couch?

A hodgepodge of scenes flashed in her mind. With a jolt, she remembered what had happened. Jake appearing like a Etch-a-Sketch drawing in her kitchen. Laughing and making some droll comment about cheap wine. Then her knees had buckled.

Great. Another visitation by the rock-n-roll alien.

"He's only a figment of my sex-starved imagination," she commented feebly to Rhett, who twitched his ears in response. "I haven't had a date since Neanderthal Bob. That, and the recent film-noir attempts on my life, have made me . . . mentally unstable. That's it. I collapsed because my mind overloaded and blew a fuse."

But that still doesn't explain how I ended up on the couch.

Pushing herself onto one elbow, she scrutinized the room. No East-of-Eden types lurked in the shadows. On TV, David Niven waved a menacing finger at Cary Grant. She leaned forward.

Rhett butted his furry head against the soles of her feet. Scarlett stroked him behind the ear with her big toe. Everything was normal. Just her and Rhett and Cary and David. A typical evening at home.

She fell back onto the pillow, exhausted. "I've got

to get a life," she said to Rhett. "One where strange men don't point guns at me. Where strange cars don't try to run me down. And where strange—images—don't materialize . . ."

Jake stood over her, a washcloth in his hand. "You're better, I see. Like a cool cloth? I thought it'd feel good on your forehead."

She opened her mouth to speak, but all that came out was a hoarse squeak.

"You tumbled into quite a heap back there. Didn't mean to scare you like that."

He gently placed the cold cloth on her forehead. Her eyelids, her mouth, her hands, quivered with fear. Even if she imagined him, she sure as heck was not imagining the cloth. She could feel it on her forehead. Cool, wet.

As though in response to her anxiousness, soft breezes washed over her, carrying with them a soothing comfort. She became aware that she no longer shook. Even more surprisingly, she felt calm.

"Why?" She finally asked without opening her eyes. She knew Jake stood next to her. She sensed his presence. And, oddly enough, felt his concern. It reminded her of being a little girl and having her mother take care of her. Scarlett felt safe. Safer than she had in weeks.

A giddiness bubbled within her thoughts. She shook her head slightly, trying to remember what she had wanted to ask. But it didn't matter. Whatever had bothered her no longer mattered.

"I won't leave you until you're feeling better."

Barely opening her eyes, she peeked out from underneath the cloth at Jake as he leaned over and adjusted the compress. Sandalwood laced the air. When he pulled away, his fingers brushed against her cheek, leaving a heated imprint that made her skin tingle.

She lifted her hand to her neck and remembered how his touch had also healed her.

Bolder now, she lifted the towel off her eyes and observed his face, which hovered above her own. She scoured his roughened cheek, the dark indentation above his upper lip. A thin white scar laced the edge of his eyebrow.

She looked up into his eyes, which were no longer black, but silver. Like mirrors. Reflected in them, she saw the man who shot her. A cold wall of fear rose within her, yet she couldn't tear her gaze away. In those shiny pools, she watched the horrific replay of the night she got shot.

The squat dark man raised the gun, its barrel meeting her eyes point-blank.

She ducked and grabbed at Jake's jacket, burying her face in the pungent leather. She started to speak, but a sob broke the words.

Jake's strong arms embraced her, held her close. "You saw my thoughts. I'm sorry."

Thoughts? She felt a tear trickle down the side of her cheek. Tasted its salty wetness as it rolled past her lips.

Madness.

This was madness!

And Chandler's ploy. It all made sense now. She didn't need to sign an agreement. Chandler didn't even need to kill her. No, he planned to simply drive her to the brink of madness and give her a push. If she was deemed mentally incompetent, her life was up for grabs.

Pain coursed through her fingers from their rigid grip on the jacket. *I've let one of Chandler's men get this close—*

With all the strength she could muster, she shoved hard, pushing Jake to the end of the couch.

"Get out of here!" Her voice rang through the room, unfamiliar and shrill. Rhett streaked by, bumping against a table in his frantic flight.

Jake stood, holding his hands up as though to calm her.

"Out! Out!" In a flurry of movement, she half-fell, half-clambered off the couch. Her foot hit something and she glanced down at the empty wineglass. In a rush, she grabbed its stem and smashed the cylinder top against the coffee table. It shattered with a loud crack. Particles of reflected light sprayed the room.

The rim was now spiked with broken glass, which she jabbed menacingly at Jake.

"I said out." She ground the threat through tight lips. "And tell that bastard Chandler he'll never get his filthy hands on my business." Pointing her weapon at Jake, she slowly stepped to the left, toward the phone couched on the bookshelf. "Never."

Jake's splayed hands pushed against the air, as though to press back her anger. "This isn't what you think . . ."

"What I think?" Now next to the bookshelf, she fumbled for the receiver, her eyes never leaving Jake's.

"Don't—" But instead of finishing his thought, he

expelled a weighty sigh and dropped his hands. Even if she lunged at him, she would fall right through him into the wall. That jagged glass could do some serious harm . . . to her.

He rolled his eyes toward the ceiling. "You plunk me into this situation—and for what? To watch her hurt herself? What if I don't get her to the hospital in time? Kinda like what happened to the last 'destiny,' only this time, God, if I lose my charge . . ." Jake widened his arms in a helpless gesture. "I'll give up. Just open the gates of Hell and release me. I don't want Heaven if it means losing an innocent life again."

He lowered his gaze. Scarlett stood open-mouthed, holding the broken wineglass limply at an angle. "I don't know who's crazier, you or me."

"Odds are in my favor," he answered. "Know a good bookie?"

Scarlett jumped as several loud thumps sounded on the front door. She glanced at Jake, then to the door.

"It's okay. Answer it," he said.

She started to ask why she should take his word about what was okay considering he did many un-okay things like materialize like Casper the Ghost, when a booming voice yelled, "Miss Ray. Police. Are you all right?"

"Police," she mouthed with great exaggeration to Jake, after which she scurried to the door and briskly undid both latches and the doorknob lock. As she opened the door, a swirl of cool night air scented with jasmine swirled into the room. In the feeble yellow glow from her porch light, she saw a tall, slim figure topped by the familiar triangular shape of a policeman's cap.

"We were patrolling past when we heard yelling . . ." In the dim lighting, she caught his eyes shift to her hand. His voice lowered—so low she had to strain to hear his question. "Are you all right?" His words were heavy with another meaning: Are you in danger?

The broken glass! Of course, that's why he was staring at her hand and talking like a theatrical aside. He probably thought she was fighting off some intruder. God, how to explain the broken wineglass in her hand.

"Oh, you mean this?" She tried to act casual as she lifted the glass for his inspection. "I accidentally sat on this wineglass and it broke. That's probably when you heard me yell."

His gaze flicked to her lower torso and he winced before looking back into her eyes. "Sat on it? I hope you're not hurt."

"Did more damage to the glass, I'm afraid." She waved it coquettishly and emitted a high-pitched giggle.

Behind her she heard Jake chuckle. "Oh, stop it," she said, glancing over her right shoulder at him.

Jake pressed a finger to his lips, warning her.

She tossed a look back at the policeman. "Oh, I forgot." She bit her lower lip. "Damn." The expletive popped out before she'd had a chance to think what to say. "Damn," she repeated, nodding quickly. "That's the cat's name."

The policeman waited a beat before responding. "Damn. Funny name."

"Yeah, damn funny name." She twitched a half-smile, hoping it passed for charming.

"You said to 'stop it.' "

"Oh, right. I said that, uh, to—"

"Damn?"

"Right. Damn." She dipped her head again to the right. "He was . . . clawing the couch."

As though on cue, Rhett peeked around the kitchen corner, to Scarlett's left, his scruffy head lobbing between Jake, Scarlett, and the policeman.

"He's over there. . . ." The policeman ducked his head slightly to Scarlett's left.

She barely glanced over, aware that a hot flush was inching up her neck. "Well, I'll be," she croaked. "He certainly gets around."

"Uh-huh." The policeman lowered his gaze to the broken glass, then back to her face. "Better throw the broken glass away, Miss Ray. And maybe you'd better take it easy with the wine."

"And easy with me," chimed in Jake from behind her.

She held her tongue lest she looked like a genuine fruitcake to this police officer. "Will do." She cocked her head and squinted at him. "Aren't you . . ."

"George Bradshaw, ma'am."

"George, yes, that's right. You came into Ray's Hamburgers a few nights ago and had some coffee, right?" She found herself staring at his eyebrows, which slanted up toward his forehead like the top of the letter "A." It gave him a perpetually sad look, not unlike a basset hound.

"Yes, ma'am."

"Well, thanks for patrolling my business and home. Let me fix you up with a free hamburger next time, okay?"

"Never offered *me* a free burger," Jake quipped behind her.

She flicked a look over her shoulder. "You don't eat—" She caught herself and smiled sweetly at the officer. "You don't eat enough from the looks of you." *God, now I sound like a den mother.*

After they exchanged good-byes, she closed the door and glared at Jake before heading for the kitchen to toss the broken glass into the trash.

"You blamed poor ol' Rhett," Jake teased with a nod to the cat when Scarlett walked back into the room.

"What was I gonna say? That an invisible man behind me is cracking jokes?" Scarlett glanced over at the cat, then back. "And how'd you know his name was Rhett?"

"It's still Rhett? Thought you'd rechristened him something more . . . memorable."

"I had to cover my slip."

"Good thing your curses are short. Imagine if you'd said, 'sonof—' "

"That's enough. Besides, you didn't answer my question. How'd you know his name is Rhett?"

"Scarlett. Rhett. What else?"

"I suppose you also know my mother's name. I mean, what her name was." Her voice trailed off.

"Alice," he answered softly. He paused, clearly gauging her reaction. His eyes held hers for what seemed a small eternity.

"Alice." She drew a strained breath. "Yes, her name

was Alice." She twisted her hands together. How did he know these pieces of her life? It's not that it felt bad, but the whole thing was . . . unnerving.

Even more unnerving was that she had protected Jake, in a sense. She had not admitted to the officer that an apparition—or whatever Jake was—stood behind her. And had appeared unannounced several times in her business and now, in her home, claiming he was her destiny.

Was she succumbing to evil forces? She shivered, warding off a chill that tickled her spine. After all, there were documented cases of exorcisms and evil spirits—could she be a victim of such dark powers?

But when I passed out, she reminded herself, *he could have killed me. Instead he took care of me.*

He didn't want to listen to Scarlett's thoughts, but it would be like not hearing the patter of rain on glass or the swish of the wind through leaves. He heard her questioning herself, falling back on the worry that maybe she was losing her mind. Heard the repetitive questions about how he got in, and should she still call 911. And if he really was a figment of her imagination, what would the cops do when they again arrived at her home and listened to her babble about spirits and ghosts? Did they let crazy women go free? Or did they drag them into jail for observation?

He shook his head sadly. "Scarlett, it saddens me that my presence makes you question your sanity. Believe me, I wouldn't be here if I had a choice." Clasping the cross around his neck, he decided it best to delve into the inner knowledge he carried about Scarlett. Maybe it would convince her that his mission was for her sake. That's what he hoped, anyway. He, too, had to believe.

"Your mother always stuck a ten-dollar bill into the toe of your right shoe when you went on a date."

She stood stalk-still, and seemed to contemplate his statement. "Nobody knew that," she finally whispered.

"You found Rhett the same month your dad deserted you for good. You were eleven, gangly and shy. You pretended Rhett was an angel in disguise who had come into the world to take care of you and your mom—"

"Stop." The single word was barely audible. Scarlett's green eyes, now sunken in her ashen face, pleaded with Jake. "Please stop."

His heart swelled with her pain. Before he realized it, he had crossed the room and sheltered her in his arms. Holding her tightly, he smelled a faint rose perfume, felt the frailty of her body as she sank against him. He rubbed his chin against the silky softness of her hair, murmuring words of comfort.

She clung to him, the deep resonance of his voice soothing her more than his words. Nestled against him, she released her fear and succumbed to his offered strength. She needed his strength. A gentle stirring within her signaled that she wasn't immune to his charms, despite the confusing circumstances. His arms tightened around her, as though in answer. Too tired to question, she sank deeper into his embrace, grateful for his warming refuge.

"Scarlett." He said the word like a prayer. "Don't be afraid of me. I promise, I would never hurt you."

Her lips brushed against the jacket's soft leather as

she spoke. "Why did I see the man who shot me?"

"I didn't mean for you to."

She swallowed back half-formed questions. After a long moment she asked, "Why are you here?"

"To guide you."

"Who sent you?"

"The one who also tests me."

She heard the pain in his voice. They were in this together, although what that meant eluded her. She just knew that she had to trust that he'd never bring her harm. Willingly, anyway.

She ran her fingers over the leather, its texture buttery under her fingertips. She inhaled deeply and luxuriated in the traces of sandalwood that always scented the air when Jake was near. Pulling back, she looked into his face, unafraid to confront what she'd find there.

Although the rigid lines of his face exuded toughness, his eyes brimmed with a tenderness that made her heart ache. The sense of peace returned, with something more. She also experienced the undeniable undercurrent that occurs between a man and a woman.

"It's all so confusing," she whispered. "I touch you and feel you're human. Yet . . ." She shook her head slowly. "Yet you appear and disappear . . . like a ghost." A chill prickled her skin as she reflected on his psychic insights. "That's it? You're a ghost?"

The protective weight of his hand on her arm was her answer. No ghost could touch like that.

"I must talk to you about Chandler." His hand slipped down to hers, the touch of his fingers like liquid fire. Gripping her hand in a tight clasp, he led her to the couch, where he indicated he wanted her to sit. She complied.

He paced a few steps, then turned and faced her. "Later, it might frighten you to remember what I said. If that happens, also remember that I, like you, have been thrown into these circumstances. My concern, my wish, is only for your happiness." He stopped and crossed his arms over his chest. Only when his eyebrows slanted in a question did she realize he was waiting for an answer.

"Yes, I'll do that if I'm afraid."

He nodded, pulling his thumb along his jaw as he scanned the rug, deep in thought. "I lived before. On Earth, as you do now." He waited a moment, as though testing if she could handle this information. "I was a young man in the 1950s. I worked for a man who stole from innocent people—that's how he earned his living. I learned to steal as well. I took no responsibility for what I did. I hurt people. Betrayed them. I think that's why I'm a prisoner in this purgatory."

A schism of pain flared within her. She caught her breath as the hurt subsided. It was from him, she realized. Just like before, she felt his torment.

He dropped his head slightly, but not before she caught his nod. Then he looked back at her, his face tightened with resolve. "I'd take the stolen money back to my employer and he'd give me a cut. Except he, my employer, decided I had double-crossed him and murdered me one night in my sleep. My employer was Chandler."

Her head spun. For a fleeting moment, she felt as

though she were falling from a great height, plunging into a bottomless abyss.

"Don't give in to the fear, Scarlett." His warning sounded from far away. "Chandler uses fear as a weapon. He is evil. I'll be with you, to help you, in all the ways I know. Please believe that I'll do anything within my power to save you from Chandler."

She wanted to cry at the profound sadness in Jake's dark eyes. Studying his profile, she became aware of a glow that emanated from wherever his skin was exposed. It was a living light that poured off his hands, his face, his hair. She glanced around the room and became aware of an order of things, yet precisely what this meant escaped her. From outside, she heard the singing of trees and the low, deep roar of stones and rocks. Rhett passed by on his way into the kitchen, etched with a thin golden line from the tip of his nose to the end of his tail. The radiant line wavered and danced with the cat's movements. Holding up her hand, she saw the same ethereal light shimmer around her hands and up her arms.

When she looked back up, the light had grown around Jake so that he stood in the center of a dazzling luminescent ball.

Yet his eyes still bore a great sadness.

Gradually, he faded into the radiance. For a moment, the golden brilliance remained. It took the shape of a door, triggering again that same vague memory. A door that emitted streaming golden rays? Had she been here before? In the distance, a thousand wind chimes tinkled. Hushed voices murmured. Then, with lightning speed, the effulgence shrank into a pinpoint of dazzling white before disappearing altogether.

Chapter Five

Late-morning L.A. sunshine. It never ceased to amaze Scarlett how the rays of light managed to sneak through the smog. Layers of brown hovered over Tinsel Town like a bad reputation. She looked away from the dirty sky and started to unlock the door to Ray's when a lumpy shadow darkened the sidewalk at her feet.

Someone stood behind her.

She swerved around, the key gripped strategically between her fingers in what she vaguely remembered doubled as a lethal instrument. As her body pivoted, her thoughts raced back to that self-defense class she had taken ten years ago. How did that key thing work anyway?

Fully facing the source of the shadow, she yelped in surprise, then fumbled and dropped the key.

"I thought the same when I saw my face in the mirror this morning," quipped Enrique. Tightening his hold on a brown-papered package, he smiled sheepishly and bent over to retrieve the fallen object.

Scarlett took a deep breath of smog-filtered air and clutched at her heart. I've got to get a grip. Next thing I know, I'll be defending myself against Rhett with the kitty scooper.

Enrique handed the key back to her. "Would it help next time if I say, 'Boo'?"

She swallowed a half-hearted laugh. " 'Hello' will suffice. Sorry I jumped."

"Jumped? More like some kinda karate lunge. I expected you to kick-box this ham out of my arms." Enrique's white mustache jiggled as he laughed at his own joke. "And you hold that key like a little—" He squinted and Scarlett knew he was searching for the word. Then he nodded with satisfaction. "Like a sword. Enrique ready to use the ham as a shield if need be." He playfully held the package up in front of him.

Taking a shaky breath, Scarlett welcomed the returning warmth to her insides that only moments before had rocked with cold terror. "I don't know which is the bigger ham—you or what you're carrying!"

In the hazy light, Scarlett noticed for the first time the deep grooves that ran the length of the old man's forehead. Tired? she thought. Or worried. God, she'd probably scared him half to death.

He juggled the ham from one arm to another. "Told Doris I'd bring her a gift."

The change of subject took her by surprise. "What?"

"This!" He patted the packed bundle with two sound swats.

"A ham? At eleven in the morning? I've heard of steak and eggs, but coffee and a hunk of ham?"

Hurt ceased his face and she immediately regretted her unthinking comment. "A ham," she smiled, hoping her new tact didn't reek of sticky-sweetness. "Much better than a power tool. Really. It's . . . romantic."

She remembered how the other night he had taken a piece of pie to Doris. So that's it. He has a crush on her—she should have guessed. Sweet-faced Doris had singlehandedly raised five kids after her husband's fatal heart attack sixteen years ago. Ray's Hamburgers had only opened the year before, and Scarlett's mom took Doris shopping bags full of food, sometimes daily, until she got back on her feet. After that, she and her mom were best friends—yet, in all those years of closeness, Scarlett had never seen Doris with a boyfriend.

"Yes, very romantic," Scarlett added softly. It was about time Doris had herself a gentleman caller. Unexpected tears tickled the corners of Scarlett's eyes, which she quickly blinked back.

The lines in Enrique's forehead relaxed. "Romantic? A little. Plus Doris has four overgrown boys who don't always bring home the . . . bacon." He chuckled at his play on words.

Just as she pushed open the door to Ray's, Scarlett noted how the string looped at the top of the package. "And it even has a bow. Nice touch."

"You know Max? The butcher? Old friend. He let me pick out the biggest, freshest ham—and being an old Merchant Marine, I tie it up with one of my fanciest knots. Enrique maybe not a man of wealth. But I am a man of—how you say?—style."

The way he drew out the last word with self-satisfaction made Scarlett smile. "Wish you were a few years younger, Enrique. I'd love to be courted by a man with your style."

His shoulders shook as he laughed. "Few years? You flatter an old man. Ah, if only I were born thirty years later, I'd court the lovely rojo-haired Scarlett."

"And I'd be the lucky owner of a ham!" She patted Enrique on the shoulder and gave him a big wink before entering Ray's.

Throughout the rest of the day, while she chopped onions, took orders, and turned hamburgers, her thoughts returned to her morning conversation with Enrique and the way he'd rolled the word "style" off his tongue. And every time she thought of it, she would reflect on how she had never known a man with style.

Except for Jake.

Which triggered another set of memories.

Every single time Jake entered her thoughts, something fluttered to life inside her and she was transported above the mundane acts of slicing tomatoes or spreading relish. Her actions became automatic, like a robot's, while her imagination caressed every detail of Jake's visit the night before.

She ruminated on how nice it felt to be in his arms for that too-brief moment. How his strength enveloped her, sheltered her. They could have been on an island in this crazy world, all to themselves and needing no one. It was more real than anything she had ever experienced before.

She retraced every nuance of Jake's visit over and over recalling the tannic scent of his leather jacket, the heat of his breath against her cheek, the rich vibration of his voice as he mouthed small comforts into her ear.

It had been real, all right—until he'd faded into a ball of golden light.

The last memory jarred Scarlett back to the here-and-now, prompting her to take a giant step away from her daydreams. How many women, after all, starred in a real-life version of *The Ghost and Mrs. Muir*?

The thought sobered her more than if she'd dunked her face in a bucket of ice water.

At nine that night, Scarlett didn't know what exhausted her the most: a full day of chopping, serving, and cleaning—or the ten hours of mental aerobics as her thoughts bounced from Jake-the-man to Jake-the-phantom.

At closing time, she stood next to the front door and flicked off the light. Glancing over her shoulder, she whispered her nightly farewell to the teddy bear. "Goodnight, Charlie." With the lights off, Charlie looked like a small lump of shadow on his shelf.

Was that a sound?

Her eyes darted across the single room. The darkness cloaked a variety of black to gray shapes, any of which could shift into a malevolent shape if she let her imagination take the upper hand.

I'm being childish. Nothing unusual is in this room.

She looked past the counter at the well of black she knew was the fryer. And beyond that to the large gray box against the back wall that she knew was the refrigerator. Was there music playing? Her gaze darted to the antique radio, which sat silently on its shelf over the cash register. Her ears had deceived her. Yet, there seemed to be an ominous hush that shattered the room's tranquillity.

An iciness bit at the nape of her neck and she shivered.

The knife. She remembered the paring knife she had tucked above the door frame. Cautiously, she reached up and gingerly touched the narrow wooden ledge. Finally, her fingers tapped the blade's cold metal, then down to the familiar wooden handle. She gripped the knife and left.

Outside, a faint wisp of orange clouded the evening sky. After locking up, she peeked back through the window into the restaurant's dim interior. But this time, she saw only the familiar darkened shapes of the counter, the stools, the shelves. Nothing eerie or out of the norm.

"I'm losing it," she muttered to herself. "Getting spooked over nothing. Like I don't have enough high drama in my life." She slipped the knife into her purse.

Turning, she inhaled deeply and caught a passing breeze from the ocean. A pang of jealously shot through her as she contemplated those lucky souls who had spent the day doing nothing more strenuous than sipping a cool drink and watching the surf tumble at their naked feet.

"Watch out, lady!"

She jerked her head toward the yell, but in the street's growing dusk, she saw nothing. From the muddled blue of early evening burst a kid with blond spiky hair, his wiry body crouched low on a skateboard, his unbuttoned shirt flying away from his skinny chest.

She jumped back with a shriek and dropped her purse, the contents scattering across the sidewalk. The boy angled his body and swept through the debris. In the moment that he passed her, she caught a mischievous leer on his freckled, sunburned face.

"Rad!" he screeched, obviously a reference to his success at maneuvering through the impromptu collision course.

Scarlett leaned against the wall and listened to the thundering beat of her frightened heart. "Rad?" She questioned the now-empty sidewalk. "Teenage terrorists yell 'Rad' these days?" In the distance, she heard the metal wheels barreling new paths over other sidewalks. And other pedestrians, no doubt.

She glanced down at the pieces of her life strewn across the concrete. Lipstick tubes, a mirror, her coin purse, chewed pens and pencils that had scribbled more hamburger orders than she liked to remember. Chaos was fast becoming a way of life.

Looking up, she spied a police car ease from an alley onto Gabrielle Street. It cruised by and slowed to a stop in front of her. In the gray light, she could barely make out two figures sitting in the car.

She was still leaning against the brick storefront, trying to catch her breath after the near-collision with the rampaging skateboarder. From the police car's passenger side, a face emerged, featureless in the twilight's deepening hues. The dark triangle on his head must be a cop's hat, she decided. Or a thatch of uncommonly thick hair.

"Anything wrong?"

She recognized the deep male voice. Gordon. George. Something like that. One of the officers who regularly patrolled her home and business. In fact, if she wasn't mistaken, the same policeman who had visited her home only last night.

"Fine." Her voice was a shell of its former self, thin and wispy. She cleared her throat and tried again. "Just had a little scare."

The passenger door opened and Gordon/George's tall form stepped out into the street. His slow, wide strides reminded her of some comic-cowboy sidekick, and she started to giggle.

He's going to think I'm out to lunch, she told herself.

Out to lunch? What am I doing relating my life in terms of food? How low can I go? Next I'll be comparing people to hamburgers. He's plain. She's rare with mustard only.

The silly thoughts instigated a second rash of giggles that grew in volume until she feared she'd lose control altogether.

My God, I'm hysterical. Get a grip. She straightened and aimlessly fluffed her hair "Gordon," she began, her voice riding a wave of suppressed hysteria.

"George."

She pressed her lips together, but a snort of laughter escaped anyway. Where in the heck had she gotten the name Gordon? She forced some levity into her voice.

"George," she said in a lower octave. "There's nothing to be worried about. A teenage boy nearly ran me over, that's all."

George lumbered onto the sidewalk. Closer now, she recognized the long face and peculiar bent of his eyebrows that gave him a perpetually sad look. Behind him, the police car idled, its slow chugging the only sound in the still nighttime air.

"Teenager?" asked George. "What did the car look like?"

Be serious, she reprimanded herself as another surge of hysterics threatened to explode. "He didn't drive a car. He drove a . . . skateboard."

"You nearly got run over by a skateboard?"

"They rule the sidewalks in Venice, believe me. Lucky he wasn't a Rollerblader—I've heard it takes forever to get those wheel marks out of your clothing."

She thought he would at least chuckle, but the sad look on his face didn't change. "You're okay now?"

"Just suffering a mild attack of survivor syndrome."

"Yeah." Sad George squinted at her, as though accessing something.

In the long pause that followed, she realized how true her words had been. She was a survivor. After all, she had lived through a murder attempt. The chilling thought erased her giddiness and left her feeling darkly somber.

"Let me help you." George bent over and started picking up the spilled items from her purse.

She joined him, wishing it were as easy to pick up the pieces of her own life. Don't like someone sticking a gun in your face? Just pluck him off the face of the Earth and toss him into a bag, she thought as she lobbed a dented lipstick tube into her purse.

"This yours?"

She looked up at George's face. His eyebrows

looked like a teepee the way they leaned toward each other. In his hands he held her knife.

She held out her hand to take it. "It's my paring knife."

"You carry it in your purse?" The teepee grew steeper.

"Sometimes I take my work home with me." She laughed softly at her witticism. George responded with stony silence.

He handed the knife to her. "Broken glass, knives. It's okay, Ms. Ray. I've known other women who survived traumas. Some go to extremes to protect themselves."

"I'd hardly call a paring knife going to extremes."

"If you ever want a referral . . . for psychological help . . . you can call our trauma unit. Ask for Mrs. Donald-Jones, she's a social worker who—"

She dropped her knife back into her purse. "I hardly think a kitchen utensil indicates I need a shrink."

She stood, stiffly, but avoided making further eye contact. A cool breeze wove around them, and she gritted her teeth to stop herself from shuddering.

"We'll leave now, unless you need anything else," George said.

"No. I'm fine."

"We'll check your home later during our patrols."

"I know. Thank you."

"Goodnight, Ms. Ray."

Only when the slapping of his footsteps disappeared did she chance a peek at his exiting form. His tall, lanky frame folded back into the police car, and she thought she heard a muffled exchange between George and the other police officer. Probably telling his partner that she was ready for a rubber room.

She sauntered down the sidewalk to her car. Now the moon cloaked the street in a pearly glow, slivers of light reflecting off chrome bumpers and windshields. Strains of rock music, laughter, and clinking glasses wafted through the air from some party in progress a few blocks over. There'd been a time, not so many years ago, when she'd scamper to a "happening" rather than fill her shift at Ray's. How many times had she let her mother down like that, leaving her to work extra hours because somebody had called to tell Scarlett a "hot party" was grooving somewhere in L.A.? The memory twisted at her gut as she thought of the burden it had put on her mother. Yet, a few months before her death, Alice had confided, "I didn't want you to miss out on your youth, with all its fun and parties—life's hard enough without a dad."

Reaching her car, Scarlett paused and looked at the moon, suspended like a single pearl against an endless backdrop of black velvet. "Miss you, Mom."

Something cold touched her neck. She straightened her body in one spastic jerk just before a force shoved her against the side of her car.

Her face pressed against the car's roof, the metal slick and warm under her cheek. The door handle dug into her rib cage, sending hot rivers of pain through her abdomen. Obviously her attacker was a man if she didn't mistake the lump that strained against her hip.

The knife. But it was in her purse, which was wedged somewhere between her thigh and the car door.

His breath soured the air as he whispered into her ear. "Don't scream or I'll kill you."

A crazy thought zipped through her mind. *That's what they say in the movies.* "I won't," she answered haltingly.

"You've been a royal pain, Ms. Ray, ya know that?"

The way he hissed "Ms. Ray" crystallized his face in her mind. The dark, squat man who'd shot her. He'd tried to kill her before, and he'd do it again. She focused on her breathing and willed herself to keep her wits about her.

Pain wrenched through her arm as he twisted her hand tightly against her back, effectively pinning her immobile against the automobile. "I have a message from Mr. Chandler. He wants the agreement signed within five days. Not one minute later. Five days. You understand?"

She started to nod her assent, but her head, jammed against the car's roof, could barely move. Scents of the day's lingering heat and dirt filled her nostrils.

"I said, do you understand?" He pressed against her, the force of his weight nearly pushing all the air from her lungs.

"Yes. Yes." Grit stung her lips. The taste of dust filled her mouth.

She felt his facial stubble grate against her neck. His tongue wet a path along the edge of her ear. She closed her eyes and swallowed a shudder of disgust.

The heat of his breath burned against her ear. "Mr. Chandler's givin' you a break, doll. If you don't take him up on this deal, you can say bye-bye to your life. Don't scream for help or you know what'll happen."

A chuckle, throaty and sinister, stiffened the fine hairs down her arms.

With a jerk, he released her hand. Clicking steps scraped across the asphalt behind her as she pushed herself slowly away from the car. Dropping her gaze, Scarlett searched the passenger window's reflection for a sign of the fleeing man. But all she saw was a lamp-post's splash of light, like a star caught in a dark pool.

She turned her head slightly over her shoulder and searched the grayness behind her for a sign of his retreat. Only trees' shadows were splattered against the side of the building. No man. Not even the lingering whisper of his footsteps remained.

The milling police in their black uniforms and gold-laminated name tags reminded Scarlett of buzzing bees. Cops scurried in, out, and around the police station—some escorted prisoners, others wove convoluted paths through the room, still others meandered, clapping their police buddies on the back while exchanging greetings. It appeared to be a veritable hive of activity from where Scarlett hunkered down on the slatted wooden bench next to the station's front entrance.

She'd driven straight to the local precinct after the devastating encounter with Chandler's henchman. Her hands had been wet with fear; more than once her fingers had slipped on the steering wheel as she drove up Bundy like a maniac. As soon as she recognized the police headquarters, she'd parked and run up the concrete steps into the station.

The night sergeant had dutifully taken notes while she breathlessly related the thug's vile threats. The sergeant's face had been a mask of nonemotion while he clicked away on his computer—until something on the screen made his eyebrows rise questioningly. His stubby fingers rested on the keys and his eyes darted across the screen as he read with intense interest.

"Have a seat on the bench," he said abruptly. "I gotta make a phone call."

Now she sat on the bench, her back shrugged against the hard wall behind her. She could still hear the whispered threats, like an incessant drone in her ear. Five days. Five days. All these years of hard work to build the business, and Chandler thought she'd throw it away in five days? Surely the police would put a stop to this madness now.

A policeman led a handcuffed man into the station. As they passed, she looked into the prisoner's face and gasped.

Jake.

His dark eyes fastened on hers, his mouth was downturned with the most immense sorrow she had ever seen on a human's features. The policeman nudged him with a gruff comment as Jake halted in front of her. A curl of dark hair hung over his forehead. His eyes entranced her. Held her. No words, no thoughts, were necessary. She knew that he knew what had happened, and now he was here to help her, to comfort her, to guide her. The moment opened outside of time, and all she had to do was step through and be with Jake. . . .

She stood. "Jake," she whispered.

Then his features rearranged, like in a kaleidoscope. The dark, unruly hair shortened into a crew cut. The dark, sorrowful eyes shrank into gray pebbles. The body enlarged into a thick-waisted, barrel-chested man wearing not jeans and a leather jacket, but wrinkled beige pants and an oversized tee shirt that hung loosely over a protruding paunch. Again, the policeman poked him, and demanded he move on. The man smiled at Scarlett, exposing a wide gap between his two front teeth. "Ain't no Jake, ma'am," he mumbled. "Wish I were."

She expelled her pent-up breath and sank back down onto the bench. God, had she grown so desperate that she saw this movie-star ghost in other people? But she didn't question her state of mind any further. Instead, an inner ache grew until she actively missed Jake with more ferocity than she had ever felt for another living being except her mother. A living being?

Even if you're not living. Even if you're only a wisp of my fractured life, I need you, she thought, half wishing he'd materialize right there and then to prove to her that these feelings, at least, were real. Could she will him into being? Was that the secret?

She closed her eyes and sought him with her mind. Jake. Please, come to me.

Holding her breath, she imagined the angular planes of his face, the onyx sheen of his unruly hair, the faraway light that smoldered in the depths of his eyes.

Those eyes. Hooded with a fringe of dark lashes. Unwavering, compassionate. An answering warmth flickered to life inside her. She saw him clearly, as if he were with her. . . .

She dared to open her eyes. There, walking toward her, strode a familiar form.

Detective Ramsey.

He bore through the hubbub of people without altering his path one inch. One scrawny bookish-looking fellow literally jumped out of the detective's way. And never once did Detective Ramsey say "excuse me"—he simply steamrolled a path to Scarlett like some kind of human machine intent on his destination.

Quickly she glanced about the room. No Jake. But there was barely time to feel her disappointment because Detective Ramsey loomed before her like a small building.

"Got the news," he barked and sat down. The bench groaned slightly. Detective Ramsey pulled out a notebook from an inner pocket of his windbreaker. "Chandler again?" No "hello" or "how do you feel?"

She shifted and folded her arms. "Yes. No. I mean, it was one of his . . . men."

Dropping her gaze to his opened notebook, she watched as he scrawled some sentences. The indecipherable writing lurched along in overgrown, coarse strokes like too many weeds in a neatly fenced flower bed.

The pen stopped and he shot her a glance over his broad shoulder. "Want some coffee?"

His gruff overture surprised her. It had been hours since she'd eaten, she'd realized. As though seconding her thought, her stomach growled in response.

"Coffee, hell. You need dinner." He shoved the notebook back into his pocket. "Let's get some meat sticking to those bones, then we'll talk."

After salad and lasagna at a small Italian restaurant on Santa Monica Boulevard, she solemnly recounted the harassment and threat by Chandler's man. Detective Ramsey nodded and wrote slowly. Before asking a question he would squiggle a series of concentric circles in the page's margin and purse his lips together.

At the end of the question-and-answer period, Ramsey huffed a mighty sigh. After a beat, he crossed his thick arms and met her gaze. "Got a problem."

She waited until the waitress removed their plates before answering. "What kind of problem?"

"You."

She folded her hands in her lap and twisted her fingers together. *I'm a problem? What does that make Chandler? A small war?* But instead of giving in to her defensiveness, she responded with as much politeness as she could muster, "Okay, shoot." She closed her eyes and chided herself. *Sheesh, you sound like you're acting in a bad Western. "Okay shoot?" When have you ever used that phrase?*

"You've been talking to . . . someone . . . that doesn't exist."

She opened her eyes. *Tell me about it.* "You mean, at Ray's? That's easy to explain." Her stomach flip-flopped. Her mind raced with different possibilities of how the LAPD knew Jake was in her life. She took a sip of water to buy some time while she debated how to answer.

"I've been under stress," she said, setting the glass back on the table.

She offered a meek smile as her thoughts returned to the afternoon when Jake had appeared at work and she'd insisted Enrique, Doris's son, and his buddy saw Jake too. She remembered how the boys had laughed behind her back, obviously making jokes about her imagining ghostly men. That had to be it—one of the boys. The one who knew her best. Doris's son, Roger. I can't believe Roger would tell the police I was talking to imaginary beings. What did he have to gain by doing that?

"Stress?" Ramsey queried. "Seems our patrol heard you yelling in your home. Loud enough to hear it from their unit in the street. When you opened the door, you held a broken wineglass."

The waitress again approached the table. They both sat in silence while she slid a bill toward Ramsey. He tossed her a credit card and Scarlett listened to the swish of the waitress's too-tight rayon skirt as she walked away. When the swishing stopped, Scarlett again spoke.

"Ever since that night when Chandler's thug pulled that gun on me, I've been emotionally edgy. Rightly so too."

"Were you emotionally edgy the night you got shot?"

It took her a moment to realize what Detective Ramsey had just asked. And another moment to understand his implication. She clenched her teeth and forced back down the sudden fury that rocked her insides. "You think I made up that man who shot me? That I lied? You think I shot myself and nearly died as a stunt?"

His eyes never wavered from hers. "No. I don't think you lied. But I gotta lay it on the table. There are those in the LAPD who think you don't know a marshmallow from a cloud."

"You mean . . ." She frowned, analyzing what in the

heck Ramsey was getting at. "That I don't know what's imaginary from what's real?"

"Yeah, that's another way of sayin' it."

She ran a finger on the outside of her frosty water glass. Several drops of moisture congealed, then trickled down the side like silent rain.

"There's another problem," Ramsey added.

She didn't take her eyes off the tiny streams of water. They made her think of the first night she had ever seen Jake through the rain-streaked window of Ray's. Their eyes had locked that night, as though they belonged together. But what had it gotten her? Now people thought she belonged in a padded cell.

When she didn't answer, Ramsey continued. "Chandler's best pals with the mayor. Seems Chandler called his buddy and threatened to sue the city for harassment if the investigation continues."

She made herself draw a deep breath before looking back into the detective's eyes. "Let me guess. The police don't want to pursue charges filed by a mental case against a . . . prominent citizen."

"In a nutshell." He reached over and gave her fingers a reassuring squeeze. She looked at his large, square hand with its simple gold band secured snugly on the ring finger. She knew, without question, that Detective Ramsey was a decent man with basic values who probably lived the American Dream—picket fence, loving spouse, good kids. The kind of life she would probably never have. Not at this rate.

He patted her hand. "Odds are against you, but I'm on your side."

She blinked back unexpected tears and looked away.

His gesture of kindness only reinforced what her life lacked. Family. Security. And except for Enrique and Doris, friends. Being a business owner meant no time for socializing, which meant she had no peers to turn to for support or just a friendly ear. Except for Jake—her "imaginary" friend.

Pulling her hand away, she swiped at a tear, fighting the urge to crumble into a blithering pile of self-pity.

A rhythmic swishing distracted her. Long red fingernails pushed the credit receipt toward Detective Ramsey. "Pick it up when you're ready. No rush," she said in a nasal accent that was definitely not Santa Monica.

As Detective Ramsey filled out the form, Scarlett eyed the waitress sashay away. If she could fit into one of those rayon-bondage skirts, and still breathe, maybe she could do the waitressing thing. No thugs. No death threats. Just regular hours and tips.

Detective Ramsey's voice intruded on her hopes for a simpler life. ". . . take you back to your car and follow you home. A separate unit will remain stationed outside your house tonight." He folded the receipt and slipped it into his trouser pocket.

Forget the rayon. They were back to reality. "You think I'm no longer safe in my own home?"

He scratched his chin. "You'll have twenty-four-hour police surveillance."

"You didn't answer my question."

"I think . . ." Ramsey paused and twisted his mouth as he thought. "I think Chandler's putting the squeeze on you. We want to ensure your safety, just in case."

"Just in case?"

"All I'm saying is, the police will remain with you for the next five days. A unit will be parked outside your home, outside your work, wherever you happen to be."

The lasagna and salad weighed heavily in her stomach. Everything felt wrong, upside down. Her insides, churned with nervousness then indignation, and finally a cold, raw anger.

She straightened her shoulders and bore a look at the detective. "I'm not going to live like a prisoner in my own home. Chandler has taunted me, threatened me, tried to kill me. I'm sick and tired of running from his slimy gofers, shrinking from my own shadow. You guys can park anywhere you want, just get that ba—" She bit off the expletive before it passed her lips. "Just get him off my butt and into jail."

She thought she caught a slight smirk cross Ramsey's face. "That's my girl. Let's bury the bastard."

Chapter Six

Scarlett held the door of her house open for Detective Ramsey. He eased his bulk past her and stepped heavily onto the front porch. His glance flicked over her shoulder, back into the living room. "That rusty lock on the back door—"

"I'll replace it."

"Sears down on Santa Monica has locks. Cheap. Try there."

"So you've told me." *Three times.*

"Almost spring. Air reeks of it." The porch light splashed yellow splotches on his broad forehead and massive jowls, making his face look like a full moon against the backdrop of night.

"Jasmine, I think. Hey, thanks again for dinner. And for battening down the hatches." The last she said in reference to the thorough once-over Detective Ramsey had given her little house. Not that she minded, really. It was nice to have a cop check that no bogeymen were hiding in a closet or behind the shower curtain.

"Battening down the hatches?" He squinted at her. "Sounds like somethin' from a 'B' movie."

Actually, it was a line she'd heard Tyrone Power yell in a '40s film classic. Clad in a ripped silk shirt from a recent to-the-death swordfight, Tyrone had swung one-handed from a rope, and—to the cheers of his shipmates—victoriously yelled, "Batten down the hatches, men! We're headed for the New World!"

"Are you okay?" Detective Ramsey's gruff voice interrupted the film reel in Scarlett's head.

"Fine. Fine," she murmured.

"You look a little glassy-eyed."

"Just thinking . . . about things."

"That creep, eh?"

She squared her shoulders and took a deep breath. A warm breeze pushed another scent of jasmine toward her. In the distance, she heard the rhythmic thrumming of crickets. This same peaceful night had also disgorged a man who threatened to take her life. Maybe he was still out there in the shadows, watching her. . . .

A sudden chill trespassed the evening's warm breezes. Scarlett shivered and rubbed the prickled flesh of her arm.

No. She backpedaled from her fear and took a deep breath. I won't let Chandler intimidate me.

"Five days," she said defiantly. "I have five days to come up with a plan to get that—" She raised her eyebrows at Ramsey to indicate the adjective they were both thinking, "Chandler off my back."

In the muted glow of her yellow porch light, she caught a smirk cross his face. Then his features rearranged back into his customary scowl. "Starting tonight, you get twenty-four-hour police surveillance. In case that creep wants to accelerate his threat."

A passing patrol car distracted them. One of the policemen—or women?—waved a greeting at Ramsey from the passenger side. He raised his hand in an answering acknowledgment.

"Tim's away at college. We have that spare room—"

"No." She meant to say it firmly, but it came out harsh. On the way home, Ramsey had offered his son Tim's room to Scarlett—claimed his wife Marge was still suffering from empty-nest syndrome and would love Scarlett's company.

"I appreciate your offering again," she said softly, "but I can't run my business efficiently if I'm commuting to and from Pasadena every day. Plus I'm still paying bill catch-up after losing business during my hospital stay. If I can't make ends meet, I won't need Chandler to wrest my business away from me. The bill collectors will."

Ramsey's mouth tightened, as though stopping himself from arguing the issue. "Okay, get inside—time for your beauty rest. You got my card."

She nodded. Earlier, he'd slapped one of his business cards on the kitchen counter with stern instructions to call if she needed anything. She'd had his number already from when he'd given it to her after the shooting. But she knew he was making a point: call at the smallest hint of trouble. "Yeah, I got your number." She laughed inwardly at her double meaning. He didn't fool her for a minute. On the outside he looked like a massive, balding lion. But inside he was a pussycat.

Before she shut the door, she watched Ramsey's tractor-sized body lumber down her front walk. For the first time, she noticed the stoop to his shoulders and wondered how much of the world's worries he carried.

After she changed into her pink chenille robe and fuzzy slippers, she sauntered into the kitchen to feed Rhett. The old cat had minded his manners and stayed on top of the refrigerator while the detective had investigated the broom closet next to the stove and checked that the kitchen windows were bolted. In fact the old cat had ignored the burly detective's antics—years of being "cat of the house" had given him the right to snub any of Scarlett's visitors.

Scarlett shoved a can of cat food under the can opener, which automatically whirred to life. "So how come you nuzzled Jake's legs last night?" she questioned Rhett over the metallic grinding. "Not like you at all, Mr. Rhett, cozying up to a total stranger."

"Because animals like me," answered a deep, familiar voice.

Scarlett froze. The whirring stopped abruptly.

Jake. He's here.

She felt him embrace her from behind. His hands roamed down the length of her arms. Through the chenille of her bathrobe, she sensed his strength and warmth. But when his fingers inched over her bare hands, it took all her willpower not to moan as the heat of his skin burned against hers. He stroked her wrists, then invaded the sheltering curl of her fingers to the sanctity of her closed palms.

"Jake." She murmured his name and swiveled around.

But he didn't stand in front of her as she'd expected. Instead, he sat ten feet away at the kitchen table with Rhett curled in his lap.

Had she imagined he stood behind her? That his arms encircled her? Detective Ramsey's words loomed in her mind, "There are those in the LAPD who think you don't know a marshmallow from a cloud."

Or a man's touch from thin air.

She leaned against the counter and scrutinized Jake. *I see you. That's real.*

As his long fingers wove through Rhett's fur, Jake slowly looked up. His eyes met hers straight-on. The dark orbs absorbed her, entranced her. She felt hopelessly lost in those eyes.

"I thought you were behind me," she admitted.

She looked like a child. Totally responsive to emotions below the surface, without reservation. Underneath a tousle of red curls, her complexion was clear and fresh and scrubbed. He'd never seen her like that before. Vulnerable, innocent. Had he ever sensed her heart so clearly before this moment?

"I was," he answered.

A thrilling shy smile came over her.

His heart beat faster.

In the heavy silence between them, he felt her answering desire. Warm, like sunshine, it heated his skin and ignited his imagination. It took every ounce of his strength not to walk across the room, pick her up in his arms, and carry her to her bedroom.

He closed his eyes and freed his imagination. He saw

her naked, bathed in moonlight that streamed in silver threads from the window. Her body, long and lean, reflected the mocn's glow like a pearlescent landscape. The curve of her shoulder reminded him of a gently rolling hill; the indentations of her rib cage, ripples on a lake; the fringe of dark curls, rain-moistened grass.

How he yearned to touch her. Taste her.

His eyes snapped open.

Stop it. You're not a man, you're a . . . a creature of purgatory. Making love is for humans, not you.

He clenched his fist against the cold kitchen table. Rhett jerked his furry head toward Jake and rasped a plaintive mew.

Jake flicked his gaze to the cat's diamond-shaped eyes. *I'm not even caught between a rock and a hard place. I'm caught between a rock and no place. Between two worlds. And the Big Man*—he glanced skyward, then back to the cat—*won't give me the key. At least you know where you belong.*

Rhett mewed again, this time louder, and jumped from the table. He landed with a soft thump on the linoleum floor and scrambled into the living room.

When Jake looked back at Scarlett, her face was an open question mark.

"You and Rhett were . . . talking?"

He laughed dryly, without mirth. "I've always been able to communicate with animals—I mean, ever since I entered this plane of existence. It's not how you and I communicate. You know, with words."

He'd never tried to describe this to anyone and now he watched Scarlett scrunch her face as she strained to understand. Her thoughts raced at him, crackling with energy.

He talks to animals? Like that character Rex Harrison played in that Disney movie? He saw her mouth twist as though she fought the urge to laugh. *That or St. Francis is sitting at my kitchen table.*

He knew she was preoccupied and had forgotten that he heard her thoughts as clearly as if she spoke them.

But no sooner did he think this, than she tugged at the lapels of her bathrobe and glared at him. *If he can read animals' thoughts . . . is he reading mine right now? Does he hear every single thought—or only thoughts I will him to hear? Jeez, I might as well parade around naked if my every thought is public property around this guy.*

He had to interrupt before she worked herself into a tizzy. "Scarlett, I—"

But a thought of hers stopped him. *Jake, if you can hear me, why do you appear at my work, my home?*

His fingers flexed as he debated how to address this. "Scarlett, you—"

A second thought zeroed in with the force of a heat-seeking missile. *Why didn't you appear when Chandler's gunman accosted me tonight?*

Her clear green eyes sparked anger and hurt. She crossed her arms defiantly and waited for a response.

He might as well jump into theory first. "You and I have a link—a destiny—which enables me to enter this plane and be with you," he began. *How can I explain this to you when I don't understand it myself?* "I don't know why I'm here, Scarlett. I wish I did. I know you're in trouble with a man who's also part of my past. I'm compelled to be with you—I call it our 'destiny.' Because of that destiny, I can will myself to your plane. But not arbitrarily."

Her haughty attitude had dwindled into a befuddled look. Was it worthwhile to continue this discussion? He shrugged apologetically, mostly to himself. If he was in this deep, might as well numb her with the complete truth. . . .

"I sometimes sense there's an "opening," like a tunnel, from my world to yours—" He shaped a cylinder with his hands, but her look only grew more perplexed. He dropped the mime act and continued. "And I travel through it to be with you. But there are times, like earlier tonight, when I—this is the only way I know how to describe it—I 'see' you far away in what looks to be a movie. I'll watch your story unfold, but I have no way to get to you."

His eyes darkened, as though a light had dimmed. "When that happens, as it did tonight, I am powerless to get back to you."

She turned pensive and seemed to phrase her response with great effort. "You saw what happened tonight?" She unfolded her arms, grasped the edge of the kitchen counter, and turned away. The kitchen light cast an aura around her profile, giving her the look of a life-sized cameo.

"Yes."

After a beat, she flicked her head back. Her lips quivered as she fumbled for words. "So that's it? You appear when all's well, claiming to want to help me—to be my 'destiny'—but when my life is on the line, you're sitting in some cosmic movie theater—?" He glanced down her stiffened arm and noticed her knuckles were white from squeezing the counter edge.

"Tell me, how does my story end?" she demanded.

His gut caved in. He preferred burning in Hell than causing her this anguish. Maybe this was nothing but a game of roulette. With God loading the gun.

"Please believe me, the last thing I want to do is cause you more pain."

She flicked open a cabinet over the stove and yanked a cigarette from one of her secret hideaways. Emergency stashes. Each room had at least one—just in case she needed an emergency puff. And this insane situation—discovering she starred in movies that played in never-never land—definitely qualified as an emergency. She plunked the cigarette between her lips and closed her eyes.

No can do. I promised Mom.

Slowly, she withdrew the pacifier and rolled it between her quaking fingers. Then she snapped it in two and tossed it into the trash container under the sink.

Heaving a sigh of resignation, she turned back to Jake, ready to announce that his gig was up.

But the change in his features melted her heart. Dark eyes brimming with despair. Gaunt cheeks outlined in shadow. The line of his mouth curved downward in a grim arc.

Her eyes moistened with compassion. And it hit her. They were both lost. Like two shipwrecked souls.

"Don't cry," he said soothingly. "I didn't mean to upset you. I only wanted you to understand."

He was apologizing to her when his wounds were

so starkly apparent? *Switch gears, Scarlett. Give the guy—or whatever he is—a break.*

She cleared her throat and affected a lightness to her voice. "So what did Rhett tell you?"

His brows arched in confusion. "We're talking about Rhett now?"

"Yeah. It's called changing the subject." She tossed her head and flashed Jake a dare-you look. *Still reading my thoughts? We're talking about the cat now.*

It took a moment for his face to relax. He fought a grin and stretched out his long legs. "Says you don't feed him enough, for one thing. I'm surprised at you, Red."

"Red?"

"Sometimes it fits you. After all, Bogie nicknamed Bacall 'Slim' . . ."

"And you've nicknamed me 'Red.' " Secretly, she liked the Bogie-Bacall comparison. But as soon as the thought flittered through her mind, she cut it off.

Grabbing a can of cat food, she finished opening it. On cue, Rhett trotted into the kitchen with a nonchalant air, as though nothing out of the ordinary had occurred in the last few minutes. After scooping the cat's dinner into a bowl on the floor, Scarlett joined Jake at the kitchen table.

Seemingly preoccupied with adjusting the sash on her robe, she muttered, "I have a hard time believing Rhett had anything else to complain about. His life is pretty good." She shot Jake a questioning look.

"Complain? No. But he is a tattletale."

"My Rhett? A gossip?"

"Told me you snore." Jake fought the impulse to grin

at the burst of surprise on Scarlett's face. She flushed until the color of her cheeks nearly matched her red curls.

"No!"

"He said it, not me."

Her eyebrow shot up. "I do not snore."

"Rhett says it wakes him up sometimes. In fact, he's surprised the neighbor's dog doesn't start howling." He couldn't resist the tease. This easy banter was unearthing a long-forgotten treasure: simple human companionship.

Her face flushed again, this time a vibrant shade of pink that reminded him of rose petals. Soft, pink rose petals. He breathed in deeply, half expecting to inhale their sweet, heady fragrance.

She thumped the table with her fist and narrowed her eyes teasingly. "The neighbors don't have a dog. Jake whatever-your-last-name-is, you tried to pull a fast one on me." She cocked her head to the side and her lips twitched in a half-smile. "Speaking of which, what is your last name?"

"Was," he corrected. "Miscusi."

"Miscusi," she repeated softly.

He hadn't thought about his name in a long time. There was no purpose remembering who he was, or how he once lived. But now, listening to how she said his name in that sweet feathery voice of hers—he felt real. Alive. As though he mattered in this world of humans and concrete objects, injustices and love.

Love? Something rumbled within him. Like molten lava pressuring the Earth's crust, its effects threatened to be cataclysmic. If he gave into these feelings, his world might be destroyed. *Fight it*, he commanded himself.

He opened his eyes, and found her green orbs fixed on him. Vibrant, sparkling emerald. Like sunlight on an endless sea. A knot tightened in his chest. He willed himself to stop right there. Hold back, Jake. Draw the line before you cross into something that can never exist.

For a prolonged moment their eyes held. Time seemed to stop as they shared the silence.

Her thoughts fluttered through the air and beat against his soul like the fragile wings of a butterfly. I don't care what you are, who you are. I only know it feels right.

She wanted him—a lost spirit—despite everything? How could she want him when he had nothing to offer?

He reached over and touched her hand. The velvet smoothness of her skin inflamed his senses. Long-forgotten feelings surged and roiled within him. Take her, one part of him demanded. Be of flesh. Another, harsher, voice reprimanded the first. You are not Man. It can never be.

He groaned and jerked his hand away. "Scarlett," he said hoarsely, "You and I can never—"

"Don't say that." Her fingers tightened around his.

"I can't give you the things you want from life . . ." He let the rest of his thoughts trail off. Damn, it hurt. More than he thought possible. For the first time, he ached for the simple pleasures of a man: a woman who greets him with open arms, quiet conversation into the night, the sound of children's laughter.

"You had two other 'destinies.' Who were they?

Other women, like me?" she whispered urgently.

I should stop this now. Leave. Return to my world. But the feel of her hand, the tender look in her eyes riveted him.

He haltingly began. "The first was a man who lived alone. The second was a homeless woman. I don't know why either was my destiny. I couldn't spare them pain. Or death." He unlocked his fingers from hers and slowly withdrew. *I swore I'd never let myself be drawn to another "destiny" again, and then God—or so I hope—brought us together. But this time I not only fear my failure to help you, I also ache to live a life with you.*

There. He'd thought it. The words he'd been fighting since the first moment he'd laid eyes on Scarlett. Impossible, crazy desires. There was no way in his fractured existence that such a simple dream could ever be.

He stood and shoved the chair away from the table. "I can't play this game, Scarlett. I can't go on like this." He stood rigidly before her, his hands fisted at his sides.

"Jake, what's wrong?"

He started to fade. The ends of his dark locks grew translucent, and the edge of his jacket began to blend with the air.

"No!" Her cry surprised her. She caught his look of astonishment as she faltered forward a few steps, closer to his vanishing form.

To her amazement and disbelief, he didn't fade in a swirl of golden light or fog. Instead, sorrow darkened his eyes as he mouthed her name. One of his hands stretched toward her, his fingers curled into an invitation. She didn't think twice before slipping her hand into his.

His entire being flickered as though pulsing with energy when they touched. In one instant, he was solid in his caramel jacket and blue jeans. The next, she saw directly through him, as though peering through a filmy gauze.

"Stay," she pleaded. She squeezed his hand, its warmth her only ally in this supernatural display. "I need you."

And then he was gone. She stood alone, staring into her living room at the empty couch, the floor lamp, the magazine-strewn coffee table. Rhett sauntered past, his furry tail weaving a lazy greeting to the air.

Scarlett looked down at her outstretched hand.

She still felt Jake's warm grasp.

From where Scarlett stood next to the grill, she saw how Doris's pudgy breasts nearly touched the counter's edge. Sitting on a neighboring stool, Judyl's angular body—dressed in what looked to be an assortment of tablecloths cinched at the waist—looked like a Jeff to Doris's Mutt.

"We have to help our own," explained Doris, her round face puckered with earnestness. "Home Meals gives us that opportunity. When a family suffers some setback—like when Old Man Harper died and left his widow penniless—Home Meals brought hot dinners to her apartment every night. Home Meals even has a van that tours neighborhoods like ours and when they see someone living on the streets—"

"Or in her car—" interjected Judyl, eating a leaf of lettuce with her fingers.

Doris nodded. "They'll drop off a lunch or dinner."

"You can request vegetarian," added Judyl through chews.

Scarlett fought the urge to smirk at Judyl's ingenious means of supporting herself while living the life of an over-the-hill flower child. Scarlett grabbed several empty plates from the previous hour's lunch rush. "I hardly have the time to drive a van around Santa Monica delivering meals." *My evenings are filled with life threats.*

A surge of anxiety shook her hands and she almost dropped the plates. *Don't think about that creep right now.* Taking a deep breath, Scarlett tossed the plates into the dirty-dish tray. They clattered onto a growing pile of plates, cups, and glasses.

Doris fastened soft, brown eyes on Scarlett. "What's going on?"

Willing herself to look calm, Scarlett blithely answered, "Just cleaning up. Why?"

"You seem jittery, child. Anything you want to tell?"

Judyl sat taller on her stool, her head cocked attentively. "Peoplekind are here to help one another."

Scarlett resisted the urge to flash Judyl a stop-it-with-the-peoplekind-quotes look. "A little tired, that's all." She decided to steer the conversation back to Home Meals. "I think I'm gonna pass on the Home Meals thing. After standing behind a grill and cooking several hundred burgers a day, I think I'd go a little wacko spending my off hours driving a van and delivering meals. My life would become one big food order, you know?"

Doris gulped a sip of her Coke. "No, I have something else in mind. Something less time consuming, but every bit as important."

Scarlett unscrewed the lid of a salt shaker and eyed her two friends suspiciously. "The van has a flat, and you want me to fix it?"

"You can do that?" chirped Judyl. "If I get a flat, I'll remember to call you."

Scarlett leveled an I-can't-believe-you-said-that look at her. "You live in your car, but you don't know how to fix it? Maybe you should take one of those automotive repair classes in case your home breaks down."

Judyl flashed her a slightly hurt and befuddled look. "I know it's on its last tires, but if I get a few extra dollars, I'd rather put food in my son's stomach than learn how to do a lube job."

A moment of awkward silence followed while Scarlett filled a salt shaker and fought a backlash of guilt. "Sorry about the home-breaking-down comment," she mumbled to Judyl. "What do you have in mind?" she asked Doris.

"We desperately need your help at the Home Meals fund-raiser tonight." Doris's words gushed out in one breath.

"Whoa." Scarlett set down the shaker. "Fund-raiser? This conversation is starting to sound like three Beverly Hills' matrons planning a benefit." She fought the urge to laugh. They were a far cry from the manicured types whose pictures plastered the society page with captions about raising enough money to build a hospital wing. Doris had singlehandedly raised five kids alone, Judyl lived in her car and sold bean sprouts for a living, and Scarlett ran a hamburger joint. "I've never been to a fund-raiser, much less know how to help at one."

Doris waved a dismissing hand at Scarlett. "I've been a volunteer at Home Meals for two years now—believe me, it consists of hardworking souls like you and me. Our problem is, three of our volunteers called in sick—and another can't find a babysitter. That means only two of us—Judyl and I—are serving drinks and appetizers to over a hundred people. We need your help."

Scarlett's mind reeled. Two people serving a hundred? If she had more than twelve people in Ray's, chaos was imminent. She glanced from Doris's pleading eyes to Judyl's imploring ones.

Maybe she was being overly selfish. How many times had she seen her mom slip a five-dollar bill into a young mother's hand, or drop off a bag filled with hamburgers to some family that was having troubles making ends meet?

"Oh, all right."

"You're as good as your mother, God bless her soul." Doris crossed herself quickly. "She loved our little community, just as you do."

Scarlett placed her hands on her hips and stared down her two old friends. "Doris, you've always worn rose-colored glasses when it comes to me. Mom was the saint and I was her little devil." A sudden well of sadness rose within her. Scarlett quickly turned around, grabbed a metal spatula, and began cleaning lunch's dried and greasy remains off the grill.

"Got no rose-colored shades on now, child," said Doris from behind her. "I see you better than you see yourself 'cause I see your heart."

Scraping the grill, Scarlett snuffled back a lump of emotion in her throat. Doris, for some wacky reason, had always thought Scarlett was worth salvaging.

Over the rhythmic grating, she asked, "Where do I go? What time?"

"Hayre and Doyle art gallery," answered Doris.

"You know the place?" questioned Judyl in that Miss Jean Brodie lilt. "It's the pink building with the neon tomato in the window."

Scarlett tossed the spatula into a pan of water, where it landed with a soft splash. "I've seen it. Never knew they sold anything—the stuff's so weird. Neon vegetables. Who in their right mind would buy something like—" she stopped upon seeing the insulted look in Judyl's vegetarian face.

"God bless you, Little One," cooed Doris. "You are so special. So caring. I don't know what we would have done without you and your mama."

The earnestness in the older woman's voice resurrected the lump in Scarlett's throat. She cleared it before speaking. "Don't count on me next time. I can do it this once, but after all, I'm struggling to run a business by myself, and . . ."

But the two women were already halfway out the door, blowing kisses and waving affectionate goodbyes.

* * *

Scarlett rushed home after closing Ray's an hour early. She tossed some dry kibbles into Rhett's food bowl while apologizing profusely for not remembering to buy his favorite canned ocean-fish food. Then she jumped into the shower for a frantic scrub—no way was she going to smell like hamburger meat at her first fund-raising event. Five minutes later she stood forlornly in front of her closet as she inspected her minimal wardrobe for something appropriate to wear.

"Black skirt and the pink sweater? Too hot. Black skirt and the white blouse with the Peter Pan collar? Nah, too virginesque. Black skirt and . . ." Whatever she picked, it had to go with her one decent black skirt.

Her gaze dragged over the last two blouses: an awful lime green rayon number with black spots that looked like watermelon seeds gone berserk. "Judyl," she muttered, "would pay good bean sprouts for this snazzy number."

"Hmmmm. You may be the winner," Scarlett mused as she eyed a short-sleeved teal crepe blouse with faux pearl buttons. It had only been worn a few times, the last being on a date from hell with Neanderthal Bob. "This outing will give you a chance to redeem yourself," Scarlett told the blouse as she pulled it from the closet. "Last time I wore you, Bob-the-Terrible stuck me with the tab. Make me feel pretty tonight, and we'll call it even."

As she put on the blouse, she wondered if she'd ever do anything normal with Jake, like go on a date. The thought brought on a rash of giggles. Doing something normal with a being that evaporated before her very eyes?

She pulled the blouse closed over her chest and scoured the room. "Are you watching me, Jake? Do you see me in that movie theater up there?"

From where Rhett lay curled on the bed, he perked up his ears and stared intently at his mistress.

"I'm not talking to you, Mr. Rhett, I'm talking to the visitor we had last night. Remember him? The James Dean look-alike who disappeared in the middle of the kitchen?" I sound crazy. Am I becoming one of those lonely spinster types who talks to imaginary friends?

Scarlett didn't want to seriously contemplate her current mental state. Instead, she quickly finished dressing and left the house.

The gallery was nestled on a side street in Venice, off the main drag. Suzanne Doyle, the gallery's owner, had organized the fund-raiser. From what Scarlett understood, it was cocktails and a silent auction, with all proceeds going directly to Home Meals.

Minutes after handing her car keys to a valet, Scarlett found herself jostled in the midst of the press of people at Hayre and Doyle. Over the tops of heads, she saw that the gallery walls were liberally decorated with paintings of food. Mainly still-lifes. And several provocative pictures that showed naked women draped in varying positions over bowls of fruit. Or she thought they were draped. Scarlett dared little more than a glance—she didn't want to know exactly what was going on amongst the papaya, strawberries, and fleshy bodies.

She made a beeline for Judyl, who was wearing a blue-and-gold towel on her head.

"Judyl?"

Judyl turned around. She carried a tray filled with stuffed cherry tomatoes. "Scarlett. Wonderful, you're here. There are more trays in the back. Grab one and circulate."

"Cows must feel this way," Scarlett muttered under her breath as she pushed an opening between two groups of chattering people toward the rear wall of the gallery. "Flanks slapping against each other, everybody mooing." Her mumbled words were absorbed by the crowd's din as she forged a trail to her destination.

In a clearing between bodies, Scarlett spied Doris busying herself over a long table laden with trays, bottles, and bowls of food. With one last squeeze between a man's broad torso and a matron's even broader behind, Scarlett broke loose of the crowd and half-staggered, half-walked over to Doris.

"Is this what fund-raisers are like? Cattle calls?" Scarlett pushed a stray curl out of her eye and leaned against the table to catch her breath.

Doris broke into a grin. "You're early."

"I closed Ray's at eight." Scarlett surveyed the crowd nervously. "Do I have to carry a tray through those people? Somebody's gonna end up with cherry tomatoes crushed into their designer outfit."

Doris chuckled softly. "You'll be fine. Judyl's been doing this for over an hour and there's been no disasters."

"Yeah, but people make room for a six-foot woman with a towel on her head."

Doris held a tray out to Scarlett and winked mischievously. "Want me to get you a towel?"

"Very funny." Scarlett took the tray, but didn't move. Instead she lowered her gaze at the crowd before turning back to Doris to plead her case. "Can't I stay back here with you? Do I have to be a Tray Girl? What if I trip?" Scarlett made a face. "That could be ugly. I'd probably never get the tomato stains out of my skin."

Doris chuckled. "Your skin would match your hair, that's all. Now don't come back until all those baby tomatoes are gone."

Within half an hour, Scarlett felt like an old hand at carrying trays. Like Moses and the Red Sea, the crowd parted wherever she went. Manicured fingers delicately lifted one or two appetizers at a time. Some even murmured "thank you" in the midst of their conversation. It was quite cultured despite the density of bodies.

An hour later, she was carrying a loaded tray into the crowd when a tall man with silvered hair turned and helped himself to one of her stuffed tomatoes. His angular face was striking for its chiseled planes, reminding Scarlett of the face in a German Expressionist painting she had once seen. Their eyes met, briefly, and she suppressed a shudder. Something about the look in his muddy-gray eyes reminded her of a predator. Sly. Cunning.

"Kenneth?" A thin woman swathed in a black crepe dress gently touched his shoulder with her bony, red-tipped hand. "I don't believe you've met Mr. Kinsler." She motioned to a man standing near them, the movement causing her bracelet of diamonds to spark small explosions of white light.

The men shook hands. As Scarlett edged by, she

heard the man introduced as Mr. Kinsler say, "Mr. Chandler, it's a pleasure to . . ."

The room's hubbub diminished, as though an invisible pillow had suffocated all sound. Scarlett turned, slowly, and eyed the man referred to as Mr. Chandler.

Kenneth Chandler.

Her stomach spasmed uncontrollably. Her fingers clutched the tray's slick, cold surface and, for a split second, she thought she'd be sick.

Kenneth Chandler.

Waves of fear washed across the surface of her mind, yet underneath flowed undercurrents of rage and grief.

The man who wanted to kill her.

She watched his head nod agreeably in conversation as his hand emphasized some point. Next to him the older woman in the black dress dipped her coiffed head in agreement, her eyes observing and adoring his every word and movement. It all seemed so refined, so civilized. He seemed so human.

No one knew that underneath his well-groomed facade beat the heart of a monster.

Chapter Seven

Frantic impulses shot through Scarlett's mind. Scream. Run. She wanted to yell at the top of her lungs, "This man is a monster! He'll destroy you—just as he's doing to me!"

All she could do was stand, rooted to the spot. Fear dug its claws into her, forbidding escape.

Pain throbbed in her fingers, but she couldn't lessen her death grip on the metal tray's edge. It was the only tangible contact she felt with the world. Cold. Hard.

Real.

Nausea threatened to overwhelm her. *Hold on,* she commanded herself. *It is no coincidence that Chandler's here. Don't let him know you're afraid of him. That's what he wants.*

In the eerie silence, she latched on to one of her old tricks for calming herself: counting. She ticked off the passing seconds. One. You're not alone. Two. There are people all around. Three. He wouldn't dare hurt you.

Not here, anyway.

Gradually, the cloying fear released its hold and she inhaled a jagged breath. Reaching ten, she released it. A mishmash of sounds flooded back into her consciousness. Tinkling glasses. Melodious laughter. Conversations whose voices, tempos, and rhythms intertwined into one multilayered hum.

The older woman parted her glossy red lips and laughed at something Kenneth said. Her mirth sounded false, practiced. She blinked her mascara-thickened eyelashes at the man introduced as Mr. Kinsler and murmured in a whiskey-thickened voice, "That's why I love him."

Him?

Scarlett glanced at Chandler. The woman had placed a possessive hand on his sleeve, yet he seemed oblivious to her endearment. On her hand a large diamond ring twinkled with tiny shards of yellow, white, and pink.

Must be his wife. Scarlett watched as Mrs. Chandler squeezed her husband's arm—a signal for a response, thought Scarlett. Yet he said nothing. Maybe he always ignored her.

"Darling, we don't want any more of those . . ." She waved her jeweled hand in dismissal at the proffered tray.

Scarlett nodded. Or tried to. Her head bobbed in a jerky motion, yet her feet still refused to move. It was as though she were glued to the spot. Warnings bubbled up from some dark recess in Scarlett's mind. *He's a killer, Scarlett. He destroys innocent people. Get away.* Not her own internal voice, but another. A familiar, deep, husky voice . . .

A stray scent of sandalwood caught her attention.

Scarlett jerked her head around. The crowd on her right was a clash of colors and body types. No bomber jackets and jeans. She looked back at Chandler's group. The scent of sandalwood was unmistakable now. Closer.

Someone passed behind the woman and Scarlett spied a ripple of leather. It stopped, and a body leaned forward. The jacket's lapels fell open, and a pendant, dangling at the end of a corded silver chain, sparkled. Under the harsh fluorescent lights, she recognized the crucifix she'd seen before under the streetlight.

A tremor shuddered through her.

Her gaze moved quickly up the chain, jumped to the line of his jaw, and shot straight to a pair of darkly troubled eyes.

Jake.

He stood hunched behind Mrs. Chandler, watching Scarlett with an animal intensity. A lock of hair fell across his forehead. Without taking his gaze off Scarlett, he swept the stray hair aside. Red-rimmed eyes and sunken cheeks told her he hadn't slept in days. Impossible. Ghosts—or whatever he was—don't sleep, do they?

"Scarlett, you're in too deep," he said in a low, gravelly voice. "He's a killer. Stay away."

Killer. Stay away. The same words she'd heard in her head. Jake's voice. Yet she hadn't seen him when she'd heard those words before. Had he transmitted his thoughts from elsewhere? Or been here all along?

He was here now. That was all that mattered.

A surge of gratitude passed through her.

Jake offered a half smile, as though too exhausted to give the real thing. He straightened, shrugged his shoulders into his jacket, but didn't move from his spot behind Mrs. Chandler.

Last night when the thug threatened her, Scarlett had felt abandoned by Jake. Since then, at odd moments, she realized she was nursing an inner hurt that Jake's appearances were at his convenience only and had nothing to do with her. His timetable, his needs, not hers.

Yet he was here now. For her?

Jake's dark eyes seemed to pale. "Scarlett, it's true. Something about my needs—" He pumped the air with opened hands, as though words weren't enough to express what he meant. "Later, we'll talk about that. Right now I'm here to tell you to get away. You're in over your head."

I can't. I need to tell Chandler to stop.

Even with the hubbub that surrounded them, Scarlett was keenly aware of an uncomfortable, tense silence between her and Jake. He ducked his head, then raised it again to flash her an annoyed look. "I swear to God, you're the most hardheaded . . ." He rolled his eyes upward. "Sorry. If that counts for anything." Then back to Scarlett. "Go home. Watch one of your movies. Get your mind on something else. I'll handle Chandler."

She felt like flinging the tray to the floor. He'd handle Chandler? He couldn't even see Jake. Or hear him. How much help was that?

"You might be around, but you're no help," she blurted out before catching herself.

"I beg your pardon," trilled a familiar voice. Judyl's turbaned head dipped in front of Scarlett. "I've passed around twenty trays of edibles compared to your ten." She lifted her nearly empty tray up a notch. "Make that nearly twenty-one."

It took Scarlett a moment to realize how Judyl had mistaken Scarlett's outburst. "Oh, I didn't mean—"

Judyl raised her chin. Given her height, all Scarlett could see was the underside of her jaw and the humongous towel that sat atop her head like clouds on Olympus. "Just because you're Scarlett Ray of Ray's Hamburgers, don't think you have the corner on food-serving techniques." Before Judyl left, she flashed Scarlett a parting look of dramatic hurt.

Scarlett winced and started to look back at Jake, when she caught a sideways glance from Kenneth Chandler. The glint in his eyes told her he recognized her—yet how could he? They had never met.

Judyl's retort rang in her mind. *Just because you're Scarlett Ray of Ray's Hamburgers* . . . So now Chandler knew it was Scarlett standing behind him. Now what would he do?

Nothing. He turned away with a slight shift of his shoulders and concentrated fully on Mr. Kinsler who babbled on about business and manufacturing.

She looked to Jake for support. The effects of her stinging remark could still be seen on his face, and, for the second time in the last few moments, she regretted her angry words. Biting her lip, she leveled a look at him. *I'm sorry.*

His hardened expression lost some of its edge.

She flicked her eyes at Chandler, then back to Jake. *He knows it's me.*

"All the more reason for you to leave," he countered.

She groaned inwardly. Jake didn't understand how desperate she felt. He'll never leave me alone if he thinks I'm weak. I must stand up for myself.

Jake's jaw bulged with a ferocity of feeling that stunned Scarlett. Ripples of anger charged the air and lapped against her like rough waves. "No!" he intoned. "Chandler always has bodyguards nearby. If he signals that you're hassling him, you'll be swept out of this room and shoved into the back seat of a car before Doris or Judyl even knows you're gone." He was gesturing wildly now, his voice bellowing over the other conversations. "Why are you willing to risk your life like that? For God's sake, get away. Don't open the door to his evil."

Not one person turned to see the flailing madman in the bomber jacket.

No one except Scarlett.

A look crossed Jake's face, as noticeable as a cloud passing in front of the sun. Another emotion crackled around her, skittering across her skin like sparks of electricity. The prickling sensation grew until she felt uncomfortably heated, as though she stood in front of a raging fire in eighty-degree weather. Different, much different, than anything she'd ever before felt from Jake's emotions.

Jake had shifted his eyes slightly to her left. Turning

her head, Scarlett followed the line of his gaze.

And found Chandler staring her down.

He regarded her with the interest of a hawk spying a field mouse. Chandler knew exactly who she was. But here in public, he'd act the opposite.

She would call his bluff.

"So we finally meet," Scarlett said. She didn't recognize her own voice. Cool. Monotone. Like a young, with-it Lauren Bacall. As though she were in control of this situation.

His wife tossed her a perturbed look. The man named Mr. Kinsler continued his discourse with Chandler, "So, Kenneth, we at Paradyne are interested in merging our manufacturing facilities with . . ."

Kenneth turned back to the conversation. With a flick of his wrist, he seemed to alert his wife that her assistance was required.

"No," responded his wife icily, lowering her eyes to indicate the food tray. "Thank you." She enunciated each word as though Scarlett didn't understand English. The woman's pencil-thin eyebrows curled up her wrinkled forehead.

I'm talking to him, not you, Cruella. Relishing her newly appointed role of thorn-in-the-side, Scarlett pressed her luck further. Literally.

She poked the tray into Chandler's back.

He flinched and cast a perturbed glance over his shoulder.

"What the—?"

"Mr. Chandler," began Scarlett.

The woman reached toward her with pointed red fingernails. "Don't be a pest," she hissed. Alongside Mrs. Chandler's hand, Scarlett saw Jake's reaching toward her.

Scarlett stifled a gasp. In his urgency to reach her, Jake had moved forward—and stepped right into the same place the woman stood.

His form bled into hers. Swatches of black crepe blended into triangles of brown leather. Because of his height, his head rested on top of hers, giving the surrealistic impression of a two-headed monster. His crucifix dangled down the center of her face, seemingly resting on her lips.

Her bony white hand still reached toward Scarlett. Through it reached Jake's large tanned fingers.

Scarlett expelled a gust of air and dropped her gaze. The phantom image left her feeling disoriented and momentarily confused. Had Jake merged with that woman? Did their hearts beat in tandem?

Could good merge with evil?

When she looked back up, only the woman stood there. Yet, if Scarlett wasn't mistaken, a faint glimmer of light sparked in her eyes. She tilted her head, like a curious bird, and fixed the most befuddled gaze on Scarlett. The faintest imprint of a cross shadowed her lips.

Scarlett looked away, anxious to assemble her scattered thoughts. *Jake, save me. But what is my life if I can't stand up for myself, my community?*

The thought was like an aftershock. It surprised her to realize how closely tied she was to this corner of L.A. The people, the neighborhood, all intertwined with her own spirit. For the second time in the past few days, she heard her mother's voice in her own words. It gave her strength.

Although her mother never had the chutzpah to do what Scarlett was going to do now.

"Mr. Chandler," announced Scarlett in a loud voice. Several people nearby made a hushing sound, as though they might miss an impromptu Hollywood show.

Chandler straightened his broad shoulders and turned around slowly.

Jake's voice filled her head. As though spoken from deep within a cave, his words vibrated with a faint echo.

"Scarlett. Be careful."

Chandler's sludge-gray eyes no longer looked at her with the remote interest of a predator. Now they examined her carefully, like a coldhearted scientist analyzing a bug under a microscope. "Is there a problem here?"

The groups of chattering people around them grew silent. Without looking around, Scarlett knew they were watching. To be entertained? Only L.A. smacked of such nonstop voyeurism. Everything was a movie.

"You're my problem, Mr. Chandler. And I believe you know why."

Against the crowd's grayish backdrop, Chandler's face lost color, dimension. The only thing left were his eyes, which narrowed until they were two glittering slits suspended before her. For a moment, she felt mesmerized by their light—a yellowish orange that glowed like fire.

You're scared, that's all. Don't back down now.

"You can't tell me I have five days to sign, Mr. Chandler. That's extortion." Her urgency gained momentum. She gulped a mouthful of air and continued. "It doesn't matter if you give me five days, five years, five lifetimes. I'll never sign away my legacy just so you can satisfy your greed."

She gasped as heat crackled through the air between her and Chandler. Its searing intensity was almost unbearable. Frightening. Around his eyes formed another face. Goatlike. Malevolent.

At that split second, Scarlett swore she was looking into the face of Satan himself.

She cried out, turned, and stumbled through the crowd.

"I believe you've mistaken me for someone else," she heard behind her. Chandler's voice. Teasing and cruel. The victor.

On top of Chandler's parting words, she heard Jake's voice. "Run, Scarlett. Escape."

Something pushed her forward toward the front door. Her hands were so slick with sweat that the tray slipped from her fingers and clattered in a teetering spin as she passed through the exit. Behind her she heard someone yell, but nothing could stop her now.

Without looking behind her, she bolted for her car and safety.

Scarlett drove home in record time. Squealing around corners, rushing red lights, she raced home in her desperation to be safe.

Safe.

As if that were possible now. She should have

thought of that before confronting Kenneth Chandler. In public, to boot. How many people witnessed her insult the man to his face? According to Detective Ramsey, Chandler had already complained to the police department that she was spreading falsehoods about his character. Wasn't there some legal term Ramsey used? Defamation of character? Hadn't Chandler threatened the city of Los Angeles with a suit if the police didn't squelch Scarlett Ray's illegal behavior?

"Smart move," she said out loud. "Why didn't I just take out an ad in the *Los Angeles Times*? 'Kenneth Chandler is an extortionist thug who threatens and murders innocent people. Signed, Scarlett Ray.' "

On her right, a police car pulled into view. She nursed the brakes, slowing momentarily. When she saw his taillights in her rearview mirror, she gunned the motor and shot ahead.

Turning a corner, her car's headlights illuminated the front of a corner business. Jail Bondsman. Tacky signs advertised twenty-four-hour business. Iron bars covered the door and windows.

A sinking depression lingered in her mind long after she'd driven past. "Smart move, Scarlett. You can't keep your mouth shut, can you? Even after Ramsey warned you that Chandler—that scum bag—has legal recourse to your complaints. You're in for it now. Big time."

She thumped the steering wheel in anger. "Legal recourse? What's wrong with the system when a scumball like Chandler can threaten your life, then complain that it didn't really happen and fire legal threats back?"

A stop sign loomed before her. She jammed her foot

on the brake and skidded to a screeching stop. A wino, huddled on a bus bench, jerked awake and blinked at her car.

"Sorry," she mumbled under her breath. She gently eased her foot on the gas and inched through the intersection.

Finally she reached home. Why hadn't she thought to leave the porch light on before she left? The small house looked like a gray block fringed with ragged inky shapes. Of course, they were the bushes and hedges she never trimmed—but sitting here in the dark, they looked like encroaching creatures, threatened to devour her small home.

"Stop imagining things," she said under her breath. "It's just your house. The same house you've been coming home to for fifteen years. Don't let that scumwad Chandler unnerve you like this." She laughed. "When did I fall in love with the word 'scum'?"

Her head fell back against the headrest and she let the laughter roll out, uninhibited. "Scumwad? Scumbag? And what was that other name I gave Chandler?" She squinted at her murky reflection in the windshield. Looking back at her was an oval splotch topped with red. "Oh yeah!" She started laughing again, harder. "Scumball." She held her sides as another cascade of laughter erupted.

A minute later, she had her laughing fit under reasonable control. Wiping away her tears, she sighed audibly. "I haven't had a good laugh in days." She shook her head in mild bewilderment. "Scum." She glanced in the rearview mirror and rubbed at a streak of mascara under her eye. "Guess I can thank Chandler for building my vocabulary."

She chortled softly and peered up and down the street. "Better get out of the car before your nightly patrol drives by and sees you sitting here all by yourself, laughing. That's all you need is another nutso report filed at the station."

Once inside her house, and after making sure to lock the front door behind her, she made straight for the bedroom and peeled off her clothes. Wrapped in her soft chenille robe, she poured herself a glass of chilled wine and plunked in front of the TV. She tried to watch her favorite station with its nonstop classic movies, but it was difficult to concentrate. Images of Chandler's face swirled in her mind.

She took a sip of wine and swirled the chilled liquid in her mouth. Those eyes. Yellow slits that seeped a fiery light? She swallowed the wine, vaguely aware of its acidic aftertaste.

"I couldn't have seen that," she announced to the room. "Must have been an image from an old movie. Kim Novak in that witch movie." She reflected on a close-up where Kim's eyes had sparked light when Kim-the-witch had cast a spell on the unwary Jack Lemon. "That must be it. Too many nights alone, watching movies. A crisis hits, and my mind plays reruns."

But an uneasiness prickled her skin. Jake was no figment of her mind doubling as a revival theater. Or so she believed at that very moment. If Jake was real, then what had she seen tonight in Chandler's face?

She realized she was gripping the armrests of the

chair. Her breaths came in uneven shudders. Was that a twig snapping outside the kitchen window? She glanced over, aware of the thunderous pounding of her heart.

Did the curtain move slightly?

Crazy. The window was shut, locked.

She swiveled her head and checked out the room. She had locked the front door. Checked the window over her bed. She was safe.

Or was she?

Rhett, flattened across the back of the couch like a furry manta ray, raised his head and met Scarlett's eyes. In silence, their gazes locked.

"Are you afraid too?" whispered Scarlett. "Did you hear something outside the window?"

Ridiculous, thought Scarlett. *I'm letting that scumbag Chandler scare me again.* A slight smile crooked the corners of her mouth. "Scumbag," she repeated under her breath, but the word didn't invoke the lightness it had before.

Rhett lowered his head and snorted lightly before succumbing back to his interrupted sleep.

Rhett wasn't worried. She just imagined that sound.

She took another sip of wine. Besides, the police were patrolling her house with regularity. What was Chandler going to do—harass her in her own home? Even if she did make a fool of herself—accusing him publicly of threatening her—the last thing he was going to do was stand in her bushes, peeking through the window.

The thought of Chandler in all his finery standing in

her Juniper bush outside the window made her smile. "Peeping Toms don't usually wear custom Italian suits," she kidded herself. "They usually go for more leisure attire. Sweats. Ladies' undergarments."

Her silly rationale calmed her somewhat. It was late. Time for bed. She flicked her wrist and checked the time.

"Six o'clock?" She groaned. Of course, the watch was broken. Unstrapping it, she made a mental note to get it fixed. When she had the extra bucks. After all this craziness was behind her.

Minutes later, she crawled into bed. Exhaustion suffused her body, making her arms and legs heavy. Sleep, blissful sleep. Tomorrow she would worry about Chandler. First thing in the morning, she'd call Detective Ramsey. Confess what she had done. Explain that her big mouth got the better of her. No, it was more dramatic than that. She'd tell him she went into an altered state and channeled Bette Davis. That she started spouting lines from that great scene in *All About Eve* where Bette tells everyone to tighten their seat belts because it's going to be a bumpy ride.

Scarlett chuckled to herself. "Maybe Ramsey will get a kick out of that. He'll be charmed enough to forget I made an idiot of myself. Then he'll help me figure out a game plan."

She yawned and stretched slightly. Outside, wind whistled through the night air. Leaves rustled. Branches tapped against each other.

Tapped?

Scarlett's mind shook off the cloak of sleep. Adrenaline shot through her body.

Another tap. If she wasn't mistaken, it was coming from the window directly over her bed.

Anxiety chilled her. The small hairs on her arms stood on end. She felt more awake than if she'd drank ten cups of coffee.

Had her ears deceived her? Not daring to move a muscle, Scarlett remained hunched under the covers, listening to every creak, every thump. The night suddenly seemed filled with an orchestra of sounds.

The chatter of leaves.

The thump of Rhett's feet as he landed on the carpet.

The shredding sound of Rhett scratching on the living room carpet.

Tap tap tap.

At her window. The same sharp, invading sound. On the window. Directly over her head. Cool, slick sweat coated her instantly. She swallowed hard, but the lump in her throat felt like a boulder.

Tap tap.

She shifted her eyes upward at the beige louver blinds. The thin slats were nearly closed, but not all the way. If someone was staring at her through those slightly opened slats, they'd see her form in the bed, slightly illuminated from the pale night-light near the door.

Damn damn damn. Why hadn't she thought about those blinds? Thought about the night-light. Anyone standing outside, in the dark, could see her. She might as well stand in front of a spotlight and yell, "Here I am."

She choked back a cry of fear. *Should I run? To where? The front door? They'd beat me there. Dash for the phone, dial 911? What if they have a gun? I'd be shot before I reach the bedroom door.*

A second surge of adrenaline coursed through her body. Thoughts bombarded through her mind. *Do something! Scare him! Run!*

She eyed the lamp next to her bed. In a spasm of movement, she grabbed it and slammed it against the louver blinds. A sharp crack. Jangling, crashing blinds. A scream. Not her own.

A woman's scream? Scarlett, lamp still in hand, was half out of bed, ready to flee.

A *woman's* scream?

Scarlett froze, perplexed.

"Scarlett?"

A woman's voice, calling her.

Scarlett stared at the now-bent blinds, which still vibrated from the recent attack. "Scarlett?" the woman repeated. Yes, definitely a woman. A woman who knew her name? Outside the window?

"Who—who is it?"

"Judyl. What's going on in there?"

Scarlett scurried awkwardly across the mattress on her knees and yanked the blinds back. Holding the lamp up to the window, the first thing she saw was the illuminated spider-shaped crack across the window. Through it, she spied Judyl's gaunt face, white and wide-eyed. The blue-and-gold towel was at a tilt. Undoubtedly from ducking her head when the lamp smashed against the glass.

"What in the hell?" Scarlett couldn't even begin to think where to start. "You're asking *me* what's going on *in here?*"

Judyl patted the turban back into place, her eyes following the splayed cracks in the glass. "You nearly broke your window."

Scarlett stuttered, brandishing the lamp in her hand like a wild woman. "I could have broken your face! What are you doing outside my window in the middle of the night?"

"It's not the middle. It's still early."

The logic escaped Scarlett. "Is this your idea of a house visit?" For a wacky moment, she wondered if Judyl was selling bean sprouts window to window. "You sneak up on people while they're sleeping and tap on their windows? I could have you arrested!"

"For what?" The plaintive tone of Judyl's voice didn't escape Scarlett.

"For intent to prematurely age a friend. Or at least to give a good scare. Haven't you ever heard of a doorbell?"

Judyl's blue eyes shimmered with emotion. "You left the fund-raiser so suddenly. Then I heard you'd mind melded with that three-piece."

Judyl's vocabulary was liberally sprinkled with everything from new age euphemisms to Star Trek jargon. Scarlett squinted at her friend. "I don't know what you're talking about, Judyl. But it's ridiculous for you to be standing out there. Meet me at the front door."

Judyl smiled and left.

Scarlett grabbed her robe and tossed it on while heading for the front door.

"What cracked the window?" asked Judyl as she crossed into the living room.

Scarlett shut and locked the door behind her. "A lamp."

Judyl stood in the center of the living room looking like some kind of draped monolith. "You hit the window with a lamp? Why?"

Scarlett shoved her hands into her pockets, mainly so Judyl wouldn't see her fists of anger. "I thought someone was trying to scare me," she said slowly, as though speaking to a four-year-old.

"By tapping?" Judyl looked incredulous. She folded her lanky frame into the armchair and continued to stare at Scarlett as though she'd lost her mind.

"No one's ever tapped at my bedroom window before."

Judyl shrugged. "People tap on my windows all the time."

"That's because you live in your car."

"It's my place of business too. Don't have regular business hours like you. People have to tap to get my attention."

The conversation had already taken a sharp right. Rather than pursue Judyl's bean sprouts business, Scarlett closed her eyes and tried to calculate how much a new bedroom window might cost. Definitely over a hundred bucks. It would have to come after getting the Cuisinart fixed. And before getting the watch fixed. With everything that needed repairing, she'd have a working watch sometime next year.

When she opened her eyes, Judyl was petting Rhett. "So why are you here, Judyl?" Scarlett tried to keep the irritation in her voice to a minimum.

"I was worried about you. What was with the mind meld?"

"The . . . confrontation?"

"You and that three-piece, I heard, were aggravating each other's karma."

"Chandler," muttered Scarlett under her breath. "Long story." She thought for a moment. "What happened after I left?"

Judyl hoisted Rhett onto her lap and continued petting the old tomcat. Rhett looked displeased with the smothering attention. "Don't know when you left exactly. I was heading into the crowd with another tray of those cherry-tomato things when I overheard some woman saying 'Calm down, darling. Scarlett Ray is a hotheaded girl, that's all.' I tried to be nonchalant as I looked over . . ."

Yeah. Who would look twice at a giant with a bath towel on her head, thought Scarlett.

". . . and this waspish women in a black dress—yech, I could feel the icky karma—was clutching this older gentleman's arm and talking to him. Like, she was holding him back, you know? And I looked around and didn't see you. I got worried. Told Doris I needed to check on you and drove straight over."

"He hadn't left, then?"

"No. Should he have?" A light bulb went on. Judyl's eyes twinkled with understanding. "That man would have followed you? Why?"

Scarlett didn't answer. Couldn't answer. She didn't want to anticipate anything Chandler might do. It was bad enough she had confronted him. Now it seemed silly and stupid. But at the time, she'd felt compelled to draw a line and let Chandler know that she wasn't going to lie down and take it.

She suddenly felt exhausted. "Judyl, I've got to go to bed. It's been a long night."

"Are you still afraid?" asked Judyl.

Scarlett met her gaze, and almost cried at Judyl's look of concern. "No. Police patrol my house at night. It's okay."

"Police?" Rhett jumped from Judyl's lap.

"Another long story. I'm too tired and it's too late to go into it."

"You have the police patrolling your home? What kind of trouble are you in?"

Scarlett rubbed her eyes and yawned. "I've got to open Ray's early tomorrow. Let's call it a night. I'll tell you the story later, when I'm rested." She had no intention of telling Judyl anything. Not until all this madness was well behind her. The last thing she needed was Judyl, the town eccentric, retelling and elaborating on Chandler's reign of terror. According to Ramsey, word from some of her customers had already reached the police's ears. Scarlett talking to nonexistent people. Scarlett carrying a paring knife for protection. Scarlett's buddy, who sells bean sprouts out of the back seat of her home/car, telling the world that Chandler was after Ray's Hamburgers.

No. That would only make Scarlett's problems look more ridiculous.

"Okay. Later, then." Judyl got up and straightened her shoulders. "But don't forget, you have Judyl LowMoon if you need a friend."

Scarlett watched Judyl's lanky form exit down the

walk way and blend into the darkness. "Friend?" Scarlett whispered to the night air. "Are you a friend to me too, Jake?"

The last thought filled her with remorse. A deep, tangible remorse. For the first time she realized how much she wanted Jake to be real.

Chapter Eight

Scarlett shut the door, pushed in the knob, and gave it a sharp twist. The lock clicked. She continued to grip the cold brass doorknob as a chilling realization shot through her.

Judyl said she'd driven out to Scarlett's home to check on her. But Judyl had never known where Scarlett lived.

Which meant Judyl had followed her home. And then what? Sat outside, waiting for Scarlett to go to bed? It didn't make sense.

She heard Judyl's old Buick chug to life. Scarlett glanced out her kitchen window. Through the dark, scraggly branches of the juniper bush, she spied the Buick's broken taillight as the Detroit monstrosity clattered down Waterloo Street. Long after the engine's low-throttled droning had blended into the night,

Scarlett remained next to the front door, frozen.

How could that old car have kept up with her Honda as it swerved and careened down Main, up Washington, and onto Centinela? Judyl's car was about as ambulatory as a street person's laden shopping cart. How many times had the locals wondered how Judyl saw through the piles, wads, and crates of clutter and out the windshield? Not to mention the stacks of bean sprouts that blocked the back window, for God's sake. When Judyl drove down Gabrielle Street, it looked like a flea market on wheels.

And tonight, she'd raced that engine-driven catastrophe seventy miles an hour to keep up with Scarlett? Driving recklessly in that car meant risking Judyl's business. Her home. Everything she owned. Plus, how many times had Judyl complained that the old car was "on its last tires"?

"She said she left the fundraiser after seeing me so upset . . ." Scarlett muttered to the empty room. But the words rang false. Did Judyl have another reason to trail Scarlett—a darker reason that had to do with Chandler? Judyl was the first to complain that she was nearly destitute . . . what if he'd paid Judyl to . . . to what? Frighten her? That didn't make sense either.

She met Rhett's wide-eyed stare. His ears, perked at attention, flicked back and forth like radar. "I wish you wouldn't do that—there's nothing in the room except you and me." Her gaze darted around the room. Besides her cat with the Flying Nun ears, nothing seemed out of the ordinary. Unless one took into consideration that this was a movie set for some ghost guy who sat perched in some other-world movie theater, watching her.

"Jake? You there?"

No response.

"Here I go again, calling out to some invisible James Dean. And I wonder why the cops think I'm crazy?"

"Need a cigarette," she announced matter-of-factly before striding to the kitchen cabinet that held one of her secret stashes. Her hands shook as she tapped the box of cigarettes lightly until several magical nicotine sticks protruded. But even as she clenched the spongy filter between her teeth, she couldn't bring herself to light the damned thing.

She gazed upward. "Mom, itsh just one cigarette." Speaking with the vice between her lips gave her words a distinct slurred quality. She pulled it from her mouth, and pointed it like a baton at the ceiling. "One puff. What's one puff? I've had a hell of a night. I deserve some . . . compensation after all I've been through. Some comfort. All I want is a mouthful of warm tobacco smoke." She frowned, then quickly added, "I promise to exhale immediately."

A raspy mew was her only answer.

She looked down at Rhett, who watched her with big green-and-gold-speckled eyes. Scarlett rolled the cylinder between her fingers, relishing the slight crunch of packed tobacco, raised it to her nose and inhaled deeply, savoring its toasty scent.

Then she snapped it in two and tossed it into the trash under the sink.

"You win, Mom. Good-bye crutch. Hello reality."

Suddenly drained of energy, she ambled into the living room and slumped into her favorite armchair. In the quiet, she again reflected on Judyl's vehicular kamikaze mission. Sure, Judyl had risked everything driving that bean sprout factory as if it were a race car. She'd undoubtedly had to clean "house" before she could walk up to Scarlett's porch. And after risking life and home, why give up if there's no answer at the front door? Tapping on Scarlett's bedroom window wasn't exactly normal behavior, but since when did Judyl follow polite society's rules? To her, the world was at a tilt, and she alone stood grounded.

Scarlett found herself laughing softly. She sounded like some wizened old hag. Bitching about a friend who was worried about her. Judyl probably overheard when Scarlett repeated Chandler's threat on her life. Even if it didn't make sense to her—or anyone else within shouting distance—Scarlett knew she cared about her predicament.

Scarlett picked up the remote and pressed the power button. "I can't believe I'd condemn someone for simply caring about me." She shook her head in self-disgust and watched as Rhonda Fleming and Ronald Reagan filled the TV screen. Ronnie was peering into Rhonda's eyes with a strained expression, as though he were searching those baby-blue depths for something he had dropped.

"You were never a good actor, Ronnie." Scarlett punched the power button. The screen blipped to black.

Tired from the day's stresses, she decided to try—again—to get some shuteye. After crossing to her bedroom, and before getting under the covers, she stopped in front of the dresser to gaze at the picture of her mother as a young woman holding her as a baby.

"The one time in my life I need you more than ever, and you're gone." She bit her lip. A hot tear of self-pity teased the corner of her eye. In Scarlett's mind, she almost heard the soft lilt of her mother's voice. "It's gonna be okay, sweetheart. Chin up."

She wiped at her eye and stared at the photograph. Even as a young mother of twenty-one, Alice had been far wiser than Scarlett's twenty-eight years. "Don't know how you did it, Mom. I would have crumbled if I were left with a young child to raise alone on zilch income. But not you. No, you built a business, enabling us to survive." She shook her head in amazement. "If you were here, you'd figure a way out of this Chandler mess. You had a knack for surviving tough situations."

After pulling off her robe, she tossed it on the hook behind the door. "Had a knack for people too. Picked them with a sixth sense." A thought hit her. "We didn't have a family, so you created one, didn't you? You brought people from the community—Doris, Enrique—into our circle." Scarlett tossed a look over her shoulder at the photograph and half-whispered, "Sorry for the things I thought about Judyl. She was being family, wasn't she, following me home like that." A warm flush of shame filled her cheeks.

After checking the cracked window over her bed one more time and reassuring herself it would hold—until next winter's rains, anyway—she snuggled under the bed covers.

For a split second, her ears searched the silence for any ominous tapping. But all she heard was the familiar hum of the refrigerator and an occasional passing car on the street. Sleep beckoned and her eyelids grew heavy. Before drifting off, she was vaguely aware of Rhett perched on her nightstand, his eyes glistening with hidden light as he observed her.

In her dream, she wandered on a beach during an overcast day. The endless sea reflected the sky's tarnished color. The pewter edge of the ocean's horizon—devoid of waves or boats—blended into the panorama of gray above, making it seem as though the world around her was a lifeless cocoon.

When she looked at the ground, she saw no chunks of earth. Only more gray, as though she walked on the surface of some sort of mirror that gave her a view of the sky's underbelly.

A swishing sound distracted her. Something brushed past her face, its texture cold and velvety. She jerked her head up.

Bats.

They flew in wild zigzagging patterns through the air. Some zoomed toward her, darted close, then veered away. As one whizzed near, she caught no distinguishing characteristics. No eyes. No mouth. It spun around and darted back. Then, for several moments it hovered near, its dark form wavering on an invisible current of air.

A superstitious terror gripped her insides as she stared at the undulating smudge. It started to fly in dizzying circles and she had the crazy sensation that it fed on her fear.

More inky swatches rushed past. Whenever one of them flew near, it gave off a faint high-pitched scream. She wrapped her arms around her body, hugging herself, but even her own warmth couldn't diminish the iciness in her gut.

She tipped her head back. Surely she wasn't alone with these surreal shadows. She searched the heavens for the sun, a cloud. But there was nothing. Only an eternity of dull silver hues.

One of the black bat-shadows swerved toward her and she screamed. The sound of her terror reverberated through the gray as though bouncing off the sides of a tunnel.

"Scarlett."

Had she heard her name?

Impossible.

She staggered forward several steps and listened intently. In the distance, did she detect a moaning wind?

"Scarlett."

There. Again. *A man's voice.*

She began running, yet even as she did it seemed ridiculous. Where did one run to if there was no beginning and no end?

"Scarlett."

Louder. Clearer. She ran blindly toward the voice. "I'm coming," she yelled, instinctively knowing that nothing mattered but her determination—her will—to reach this man.

No response.

"I'm coming," she yelled again, her voice breaking. He must know she was on her way. Some sixth sense told her that the mere sound of her voice gave him hope.

She thought, at first, that he was one of the black bats. A small dark speck floated in the distance, yet it never flew closer. It remained static, shimmering on the horizon like a miniature dark oasis.

That's when she felt the connection.

Currents of air stroked her face like thousands of needy fingertips. Pulling her forward, toward him. The breeze carried a message. It was an invisible message that took shape within her mind, became a voice within her thoughts. "Help me, Scarlett."

His speech was garbled with emotion, yet she heard the familiar rich timbre.

Jake.

Jake needed her, was calling to her.

She picked up her feet and pressed on, yet the fog seemed to thicken, slowing her progress. She lifted one foot, then the other, but it was like marching through thick syrup.

"Help me, Scarlett. I need you."

The gray air swirled with dust. She coughed as she breathed. Waves of heat beat against her. Her lungs burned. The chilling cocoon had metamorphosed into a broiling dungeon, as though someone had turned up the world's thermostat.

Ash. Heat. A crazy thought dashed through her mind. Was she running at the base of a volcano?

She tipped her head and viewed the ominous slate-hued sky. No orange or red glows. No towering black fortress of a mountain.

"Scarlett, hurry!"

She stumbled, then regained her balance and continued to run in slow motion, straining against the dense fog. Sweat coated her face and dripped down her neck.

She swiped at her brow to keep the trickling perspiration from clouding her eyes.

A writhing black shape loomed twenty or so feet in front of her.

"Jake! I'm coming!"

He turned his head, but from this distance she couldn't make out his features. The air felt like jelly now. Swampy, gelatinous. Just to lift a leg required tremendous concentration and effort. It was like running out of the ocean, away from the surging tide's pull.

Something held her back. It didn't want her to reach Jake.

She cried out and pressed her weight against whatever was snatching at pieces of her clothing, her hair, her arms. Tears burned her eyes and she cried out again. An anguished, desperate sound.

She felt trapped in a cross-current. Behind her the force tugged and ripped at her. Yet Jake's energy compelled her forward.

She spun and toppled. The next thing Scarlett knew, she was on her knees.

Dazed, she felt the ground with her hands. Cool. Like slick, hardened water.

"Scarlett." Jake's voice.

She looked up and gasped. He lay before her, dressed in his jeans and bomber jacket as always. Except the black batlike creatures pinned him down at his feet and sides. Jake's fingers stretched toward her. His brown eyes pleaded.

"What can I do?" she croaked. It terrified her to see those binding shadows. Yet if she got closer, what might happen to her? Would they fly at her, grasp her hands and legs, and imprison her as they had Jake?

"I need you," he repeated. His fingers stretched out again, beckoning her to take hold. The stark look of utter need in his eyes tore at her, yet she couldn't raise her hand to him.

"I can't." She shrank back, feeling like a helpless little girl. The same little girl whose father had left without an explanation. Painful memories assaulted her. A feeling of abandonment gripped her. Gazing at Jake, she felt her heart ache, just as it had when her father had turned his back on her so long ago. Except this time she could do something about it. Jake was begging for her help, whereas her father had walked away without even looking back.

More pieces of black shadow descended upon Jake. His torso, legs, and shoulders were now completely covered with what looked like hundreds of the inky shadows. His movement was constricted, but he still managed to reach toward her with stiffened fingers.

She jerked her head up and saw more of the batlike creatures flying toward them. They looked like hundreds of birds in the distance, intent upon their single prey. The sky darkened with their approaching armies.

Jake.

They would kill him!

Save him. Only you can save him.

The thought didn't seem to be her own, yet she knew it to be true.

Jake struggled against the descending shadows, the cords of his neck taut. Except for his head, no part of his body was free to move. His facial muscles strained and he grimaced. A groan not unlike an animal's escaped his lips. He turned his head toward her. For a second, she thought she saw a brief flicker of hope within the brown depths of his eyes, but the light quickly extinguished, leaving his eyes glassy and lifeless.

"No!" she shrieked, and lunged toward him. Falling on the mass of writhing black shadows was like descending on top of a mound of cold ash. They sank under her weight, cushioning her landing, yet none flew away. She spied the tips of Jake's fingers in the mass of black shapes. She touched them, delved her fingers down, and grabbed his whole hand.

Some of the batlike animals squealed, their eerie high-pitched chorus sending rivers of chills over Scarlett's skin.

She tightened her hold on Jake.

"Hold on," she commanded.

He felt warm. And strong. Through his touch, she felt a tingling. Like electricity. It traveled through her like liquid fire.

Several more bats screeched and flew off of Jake.

The tactile sensation that swelled through her body became a charged river. A rush of emotions rocked her insides.

Fear.

Panic.

Relief.

Love.

More bats rose into the air, flapping their triangular wings with rapid, seemingly desperate movements before shooting into oblivion.

The stream of emotions ebbed until only one was left.

Love. Its joyous sensations reverberated through every molecule within her.

A few shadow creatures remained on Jake. They peeled themselves off his legs and chest and fluttered pathetically before drifting away.

Jake's hold relaxed. "Your love," he said weakly.

She met his gaze. "My—?" A movement on his chest distracted her. A black piece remained over his heart. Scarlett swiped at it, hard. When her hand made contact, the shadow disintegrated into a puff of smoke.

It was over, yet Scarlett continued to grip Jake's hand. They had weathered a horror that defied words, but they had made it through.

With effort, Jake raised himself onto one elbow. He shook his head, as though waking from a long sleep. "If you hadn't come, I'd be . . ." His lips compressed into a thin line of anguish and he looked down.

"I don't understand . . ." she began.

Jake looked up and stared intently into her eyes. "I called you." He motioned for her to help him stand. When he was on his feet, he faced her fully and rested his hands on her shoulders. "You came to my world because I called you."

"I was dreaming . . ."

"I know. I saw."

Had he watched her on that movie projector? She looked around, half expecting to see a huge screen in the sky. But there was nothing. Not even a speck of black. Just the endless gray. She met his gaze again.

"In my sleep you have the ability to command me to come?"

"I can't command, Scarlett. I asked. Because you were in an . . . altered state . . . it was easier to communicate with you."

She drew in a deep breath, yet her voice came out whispery with emotion. "They would have killed you, those black bats."

He nodded. "I believe so."

"Was I the only one—?"

He finished her question. "Yes, you were the only one who could help me." He shrugged slightly, as though warding off the chill of what had almost transpired. "I don't understand it fully." He smirked with a derision that caught her by surprise. "He—or whatever rules this world—doesn't tip his hand. My entire existence here has been trying to fathom what I'm supposed to do. But one thing I do understand are those black butterflies. I've seen them in your world, Earth, but no human sees them. They gravitate toward evil, not good." He squeezed her shoulders hard, obviously unaware that his grip hurt her. "They've never attacked me before."

He lessened his hold and dropped his hands to hers. Weaving her fingers with his own, his eyes absorbed her with a look of pain and need. "My time—this life—is nearing its end."

"No." She pulled him toward her, as though their combined will could demand anything from the forces that be. She rested her head on his chest, reassured by the dull thudding of his heart. So real. So human. "No," she whispered. "I can't lose you."

She sank into the soft leather of his jacket and closed her eyes. She felt his chin rest on her head. His fingers pressed into her back.

His chest rose and fell as he sighed heavily. "My sweet Scarlett. When I was called to my third destiny, I had the stupidity to think I was to save you from evil. But you saved me."

He pulled away from her and looked deeply into her eyes. "You saved me just now. Why, I don't know. No other destiny has ever entered my dimension. You and I are more, Scarlett, although why God lets us stumble through this—" He bit off the rest of the sentence and shook his head. "I can't dwell on that. Not now, when the very act of your being here with me signals goodness. And love. Your love."

"I didn't do anything."

He cradled her face with his hands. "Your love dispelled the darkness."

"But I was afraid." She felt her chin quiver. The backlash of her terror was only now surfacing. "How could I save you with my love when I was overwhelmed with fear?"

His fingers stroked her temples, then wove into her hair. "Maybe you felt afraid, but you reached beyond that. You offered me your love."

"I—I only offered you my hand."

He smiled. "But you felt what happened?"

She nodded.

"That was love. Yours. Mine. You're a strong and caring being, Scarlett. Honest to God, why He put you with a loser like me—"

"Shh," she said, then put her arms tightly around his

waist. Together they stood, in the endless quiet, holding each other. She couldn't believe what he'd just said. His words hit her hard. It was the one thing she blamed herself for on Earth—not helping others as her mother always had.

"You're more worthy of love than you realize," said Jake.

That hurt. She literally felt the pang of his words against her heart. Worthy of love. She'd never felt that. Not since her dad had deserted them.

"Just because I saved you, that doesn't necessarily mean I'm worthy," she mumbled.

"Giving love insures its return. Twofold." He pulled back and looked into her eyes. The corners of his lips curled into a crooked smile. "Not that I knew that or even practiced it when I lived on Earth. But I know it now. Trust me on that one. What was in that Beatles song? 'The love you take is equal to the love you make'? They were a little off with the equation, but it says the same thing."

She frowned. "Beatles? I thought you died in the '50s."

"Destiny Number Two. 1967."

"Oh."

In the distance Scarlett swore she heard the sound of waves lapping against the shore. The sound was reassuring. "Why did they attack you?" she finally asked.

He sighed in resignation and looked up at the sky, his eyes filled with sadness. "Guess my soul is up for grabs." He looked back down at her. "Maybe my time is up and I never learned what I was supposed to. Guess the devil almost won."

Her insides dropped with a sickening sensation. "Why didn't you come to me? To Earth? Couldn't you have zapped yourself into the safety of my world, at least temporarily?"

"Scarlett, I—" But he stopped himself. His face grew more haggard. She felt his muscles quiver under her fingers where she lightly touched him around the waist.

"Tell me."

He stopped again and closed his eyes for a moment. "I can't get to you as easily as I did before. Let me try to explain this." His eyebrows knitted together. "When I want to get to you, I can't. But if you need me, it's still possible to get through to your dimension. To Earth."

"But you called me from my world. I'm here. The connection is strong. . . ." She was mentally grappling with the facts, trying to piece together some explanation.

"I called you, yes. But you've called me before, and . . ." He turned his head away. When he looked back, she started at the grim line of his mouth and the sunken depths of his eyes. "Something is holding me back when I want to go to you." His voice had lowered to a gravelly whisper.

A siren screamed in the distance and she jumped. Its shrill sound filled the air, surrounding them, but Jake acted as though nothing unusual was happening.

"Don't you hear that?" she asked. "The bell—"

She awoke with a jolt.

Blinking her heavy eyelids, she stared at the ceiling over her bed, trying to comprehend where she was.

Ring-g-g-g. Ring-g-g-g.

The phone's loud call pierced the silence.

Ring-g-g-g.

She rubbed her eyes and stared down at the clock next to her bed, trying to decipher the green digitized lines. Eight. Zero. Five. Five minutes after eight? Who in their right mind called her this early?

She lunged out of bed and staggered into the kitchen, catching the phone before it clanged again.

"Hello?" she answered breathlessly.

"Ms. Ray?"

"Uh, yes."

"Jerry Flynn. I'm the legal counsel for Kenneth Chandler, who is in my office with me right now. We have you on our speakerphone."

Speakerphone?

"You met Mr. Chandler at a fund-raiser last night."

"Yes," she answered slowly. *Legal counsel? Lawyer.*

"And you made certain derogatory remarks to him in front of people, namely Mrs. Chandler and Mr. Kinsler."

She felt like she was starring in a bad episode of *Dragnet.* Did she have to agree to everything this lawyer said? If this conversation was being taped, could it be used against her?

"Ms. Ray, I asked you a question."

She cleared her throat, mainly to buy time. Finally, she countered, "It sounded more like a statement."

A beat of silence. "Did you speak to Mr. Chandler last evening?"

"I believe I asked him if he wanted a stuffed tomato."

She heard a hefty exhale and some mumbling. Then the lawyer's voice again. "You also accused him of threatening your life."

Now it was her turn to be silent.

"Ms. Ray, did you or did you not accuse Kenneth Chandler of threatening your life?"

"What did you say your name was?"

"Jerry Flynn."

"Well then, good-bye, Mr. Flynn." It took three attempts to hang up the phone. Her hands shook so badly, the receiver kept clattering off the hook. She finally succeeded, then turned and eyeballed Rhett, who offered a raspy mew. "Yeah, you're right Mr. Rhett. We're in deep kitty poop now."

As she headed back to the bedroom, pieces of the conversation slammed through her mind. "We have you on our speakerphone." "Did you accuse Kenneth Chandler of threatening your life?"

"Scumbag Chandler not only threatened *my* life, he's now trying to take legal action against me for confronting him about it." Feeling overwhelmed, she fell onto the bed. Grabbing a handful of covers, she tucked them under her chin and glanced around the room. Past the pictures of her mother. Over the small bookshelf crammed with mementos they had collected. Past the framed black-and-white studio portraits of Jean Harlow and Myrna Loy that Scarlett had bargained for at a flea market. Small treasures that gave her life meaning.

"Am I going to lose everything I have?" she asked the room. *What do I have if I lose everything?* The amazing ability to cook twenty burgers in fifteen minutes flat? Yep, that outstanding talent would land her a spectacular job as a short-order cook in some Sunset Strip dive.

Despite all that had happened, she had never felt defeated—until this moment. Now the feeling washed over her, numbing her. "Guess I'd better kiss my dream of owning a restaurant good-bye."

Dream.

She squinted, trying to grasp the significance of something that seemed just beyond her reach. Dream?

She gulped a breath of air and clutched the covers more tightly.

Jake.

She'd dreamt of Jake. He had been bound by shadowy creatures, calling for her.

Now the images rushed back to her consciousness. The gray void. The black specks like bats—what had Jake called them? Black butterflies. They'd attacked Jake. Nearly killed him.

She sat up in bed. "Jake?" She listened, but all she heard was the next-door neighbor's lawn mower sputter to life. "Jake, can you hear me?"

She searched her mind for some shred of evidence—had she heard his voice in her sleep? Had he really called to her, and had she broken through this world into his?

"I entered purgatory and saved Jake." The sound of her words reassured her that what had happened must have been real.

She lay back down and followed the line of a zigzagging crack that creased her ceiling. "Right, Scarlett. You're cracked too, thinking you entered *The Twilight Zone* and rendezvoused with James Dean. I bet Chandler's lawyer would love to get his hands on that tidy confession. Then, if he couldn't nail you for criminal intent, he could fall back on insanity."

Yet, the dream seemed so real. Had she, in fact, breached some physical law and entered Jake's dimension? Can people do that in dreams?

The neighbor's mower hummed in the background as she contemplated this thought. Had Jake ever described his world? No. But often when he visited her he seemed unhappy. Morosely unhappy. Sometimes even angry. Maybe, for some reason she couldn't fathom, she had been given the keys to his world.

But for what purpose?

Maybe I saved him because we're meant to be together.

"Like Moon Doggie and Gidget," she said sarcastically. "Grow up, Scarlett. How can you spend your life with someone who at best is—is some alien dressed in blue jeans? At worse, some figment of your imagination."

"Don't joke too quickly, Scarlett. Maybe it's true."

Jake's voice? In her head?

She pulled the covers up to her eyes. Then, peeking over the soft blanket's edge, gave the room a once-over. No Jake. But she was certain he'd spoken to her. Just the way she'd heard his voice at the fund-raiser last night, before he actually appeared.

Maybe Jake wanted to be with her now, but couldn't. Like he explained in the dream.

"To be together," she repeated. "Us, Jake? How can that be?" A painful sadness bore down on her. There was no possible way on Earth that they'd ever be together. Not as man and woman.

"If you really exist, that is." Maybe I'm too far gone to understand what's real and what isn't anymore. Can a crazy person realize they're crazy?

"I have Chandler's lawyer hinting I'm in big trouble. I have total strangers holding guns to my back, to my face, telling me my life's over if I don't sign an agreement to sell my business for peanuts. And I have Jake calling to me from the hereafter."

She reached over and picked up her wristwatch from the nightstand. Six o'clock. Her mouth twitched with a smile, not from enjoyment, but from a wry, unsettling feeling in the pit of her stomach.

"Maybe I'm as broken as the watch," she mused. "Maybe it's time to pack it all in and give up."

Chapter Nine

Walking down the street toward Ray's, Scarlett squinted at the drab sky and shivered. It reminded her of the skies in purgatory and their endless shades of gray. At least she knew that behind the layer of dirty air above, the sun shone valiantly, trying its best to lighten this late March morning. But in purgatory, what lay beyond the gray ceiling?

"Chicken Little?" inquired a husky voice behind her.

She jumped slightly at the unexpected intrusion. Her gaze dropped to Enrique's twinkling hazel eyes as he fell in step with her.

"You think the sky is falling?" He squinted at the heavens with mock seriousness.

"Only on my head, nobody else's."

He looked back down at her, his eyes now somber. "What's the problem, Little One?"

The kindness in his voice threatened to unravel her carefully constructed "I'm okay" facade. Today was day two of Chandler's five-day threat—could she keep her sanity together these next three days? Despite her anxiety, she knew she had to keep working, keep trying to live a relatively normal life. Small acts of normalcy—getting up, going to work—helped maintain some mental equilibrium.

"Nothing," she tried to say lightheartedly, but her voice cracked. She ducked her head and fished in her purse for her keys. She had Detective Ramsey on her side. And half the LAPD, it seemed. No, she didn't need to vent her woes about Chandler to her friends. With her struggling business, all she needed was for them to tell a few of their friends, and for them to tell a few more. Business was slacking off as it was—confiding in even one person would be like sending written invitations to stay away.

"Nothing?" repeated Enrique.

His concern undermined her already shaky resolve. She continued to search through her purse while blinking back a tear. No time for that now. Self-pity was a luxury. She had a business to save.

And her life.

Her fingers wound around the plastic figurine that was attached to the key chain. The feel of the miniature object was reassuring. Strange as it seemed, its concreteness reminded her that this moment was real, and the next moment would be the same. Moment by moment, minute by minute, hour by hour, she had the strength to make it through these next few days.

Finally extracting the keys, she looked up in time to see Enrique's confused look.

"What's that?" he pointed at her key chain.

She held it up, letting the plastic figure dangle for his inspection. "James Dean. Dressed as his character Jim Stark in *Rebel Without a Cause*." She looked at the two-inch-high character dressed in a leather jacket and jeans. For an eerie moment, she imagined it winked at her.

It? Slowing her pace, she held the object closer and squinted at its face. If she wasn't mistaken, it looked more like Jake than James Dean.

He winked again.

Startled, she snapped her fingers closed around it and looked up quickly at Enrique.

"When I gassed my car this morning, I saw it for sale with the other knick-knacks next to the cash register," she began babbling. "Three ninety-nine. I splurged. After all, how many women get to carry Jake in their purse?"

Enrique tilted his head and cast a befuddled look at Scarlett. "I thought you said James Dean."

"James Dean. Yes. Correct."

"But you said 'Jake.' "

"I said 'Jake'?" She heard her voice slide up an octave. She squeezed the slick plastic object tighter. "James. I meant James." She stopped in front of Ray's. "I have to open up now. Nice seeing you."

Enrique halted, a perplexed look on his face.

" 'Jake' was a slip of the tongue," she explained again.

"No, not the little man." Enrique waved his hand slightly as though to erase the misunderstanding. "Why are you using your key?"

She paused, wondering why he'd ask something so obvious. "To open Ray's," she said slowly, flicking her wrist over her shoulder and pointing with the key at Ray's front door.

"But . . . it's open."

How could it be open when I'm the one who opens it?

A twinge of instinct told her the world was once again askew. Without lowering her hand that still pointed at the front door, she gradually turned her head.

Ray's front door was wide open.

Her jaw dropped in surprise. "Wha-what is that door doing op-open?"

Her gaze glued to the gaping entrance, she heard Enrique's voice behind her. "I thought you had opened early when I walked by an hour ago." He mumbled something under his breath, then continued. "Now I think about it, your lights weren't on. No chop-chops. No scents of coffee. Of course you weren't there."

"Right. No chop-chops," she said flatly. She knew exactly what Enrique meant. Chop-chops referred to her daily ritual of chopping pounds of onions.

She took a faulty step forward, like someone stepping onto thin ice. Then she halted. No, she didn't want to walk in there. The open door was undoubtedly another warning.

A trickle of cold slid down her backbone.

Something lay in wait for her. She knew, like a sixth sense, that Chandler's evil had touched her beloved

Ray's once again. Did another thug wait inside, ready to pounce on her? Had the door blown open, blowing his cover as well? Was he inside, anxiously waiting, desperate to finish his business and escape?

Enrique's callused hand touched her elbow. She jerked and gulped back a hoarse scream.

"Like a jumping bean," chided Enrique good-naturedly. He patted her arm, then shuffled past her and peeked in the opened doorway. His white-haired head slowly pivoted from left to right as he did a scan of the inside. Then he shrugged and looked back at her. "Looks like home away from home to me."

He came back and put a fatherly arm around her shoulders. "Next time, pull the door shut tight when you lock up." He mimed how to do it, as though she didn't understand what "shut tight" meant. "Then you don't come to work the next morning and find some thief has stolen all your salt shakers in the night." He chuckled softly and gave her a hearty squeeze. "Look, there's your *policia,* watching over you like guardian angels."

Scarlett watched as a squad car cruised by. A hand waved out the window. Enrique waved back.

"They probably did not see the door slightly open last night because of no light." With his free hand, he motioned at the streetlight outside Ray's. "One street globe. Not enough to see open doors at night."

"Streetlight," Scarlett corrected.

"Yes, we need more."

"No, you said globe, so I said light because . . . oh never mind. We agree. Come on. Two sets of eyes are better than one. With my luck, it's some down-on-his-luck restaurateur who broke in and stole not only my salt shakers, but all my napkin holders as well."

The silly patter with Enrique, the hazy sunlight, the patrolling police car, all worked to ease her discomfort. Plus, on reflection, she had closed early last night because she was anxious to get to the fund-raiser on time. It made sense that disrupting her usual schedule, combined with her rush to get home and get dressed, she'd been sloppy and forgotten to lock up. Her nightly routine was so well ingrained after all these years, it was hard to believe she'd forget something that basic, yet that's obviously what had happened.

They walked in together, Enrique close at her side. She quickly scanned the right wall. The *Wizard of Oz* plates were all there. And Charlie the teddy bear sat at his usual lopsided angle, his orange tummy protruding over his chubby legs. She jerked her head to the left. Over the cash register sat the antique radio.

She expelled a long pent-up breath. More than anything in Ray's, she valued these things because they reminded her of her mother. She was pretty lucky that none of them had been taken, considering the open door was an invitation to do some five-fingered discount shopping.

"Anything missing?" asked Enrique. He was playfully tickling Charlie's toes. Her insides twinged as she remembered her mother doing exactly the same thing to the bear's furry feet.

"So far, so good," she answered, looking away.

She flicked on the overhead light. Beyond the shiny L-shaped white countertop, she saw the room's objects eerily reflected as gray misshapen blobs in the refrigerator's polished stainless steel door.

"At least I remembered to clean the place, considering how flustered I was to get home, dressed, and over to the fund-raiser." She gave the entire room a last once-over. "Everything's in its place. Nobody took anything."

Enrique had sauntered behind the counter, where he was opening cupboards and checking supplies. "If anything was missing, it wouldn't be by anyone in this neighborhood, Little One. We're family."

She crossed to the front window and flipped over the Open/Closed sign. "Kids from other neighborhoods hang out in Venice, though. It'd be tempting to enter a door left wide open."

"Ay, you don't have your mother's trust." Enrique stood and stretched his back, then ambled back around the counter to his favorite stool. It creaked as he sat down.

His words hit an emotional bull's eye. Her mom had been the core of this community. Family, Scarlett corrected herself. Because that's what the community became over the years. An extended family.

She, on the other hand, had never been a family member. She had always been elsewhere—at the mall, on the beach—hanging out with her buddies. It saddened her, more and more these days, to realize how much she had missed out on growing up. Had her adolescent selfishness prevented her from enjoying this tightly knit Venice community and its extended family atmosphere?

Or was her reluctance to accept the comfort and support the community offered more entrenched in her past, like her father's abandonment?

She gave her head a shake. Too many things to think about. "Coffee, Enrique?"

"Nah, I have to go."

"Someplace special?" She lifted the apron from its hook. When there was no response, she turned her head.

Enrique stood at attention, his body posture stiff. There was something in his eyes she had never seen before.

"Something wrong, Enrique?"

His mustache twitched before he spoke. "*Nada.* Nothing. I need to go see . . . a friend."

He said the word "friend" with such meaning, it gave her pause. "Friend?" she repeated, knowing full well this was none of her business.

He seemed to find a crack in the counter's Formica top immensely interesting. He traced its path with his thick index finger. When he reached the end, he looked up and shrugged nonchalantly. "Doris."

Was that a twinkle in his eye? She fought the urge to burst into a grin. *He's definitely sweet on Doris.* When he stopped to check out her place, he must have been on his way to court his new girlfriend.

Scarlett tied the apron around her waist. "Want to take her some pie?"

After a beat, he waved one hand in the air. "No. You're busy. I'll pick up some later, maybe."

But the hopeful look on his face melted her heart. She vaguely remembered that he'd been some type of military man. A merchant marine? *Probably has his monthly government checks budgeted down to the penny. Difficult to treat a sweetheart on a tight pension.*

"I insist," Scarlett said as she crossed to the refrigerator. "Only a piece or two left from yesterday. You take it and enjoy it with Doris."

A few minutes later, Scarlett watched Enrique through the plate-glass window as he ambled down the sidewalk, a covered pie tin in his hands. He dipped his head and mouthed "*gracias*" before he walked out of her sight.

She crossed behind the counter to start her onion chopping chores when a cool salty breeze wafted through the room. On the side of the sink, several loose napkins fluttered slightly. Scarlett glanced over her shoulder at the front door. Closed. Where had the breeze come from?

She ventured to the back of Ray's and through the doorway behind the refrigerator that led to the small alcove where she kept her garbage cans. The alcove had two doors: one to the storage room, the other to the alley behind Ray's.

Through this last door, sunlight spilled into the normally dark alcove.

She stumbled forward several steps. Straining her neck, she peeked into the alcove.

The back door was wide open, offering a view of the parking lot behind Ray's.

She combed a stray hair off her forehead, skimming away dots of cold sweat at the same time.

When she and Enrique had made their rounds this morning, she hadn't bothered to come back here because she only opened this door once a week—on Tuesday mornings, garbage pickup day.

Today was Thursday.

Holding her breath, she eyed the back door. Constructed of thick wood, it required a solid shove to open. Even then it refused to stay open unless she propped a garbage can against it.

Yet the door was wide open, without the benefit of any obvious support. How?

A fly flew through the opening, its incessant drone overpowering the silence. As she stood, debating what step to take next, the high-pitched hum grew louder and louder until it mimicked a buzz saw.

Gritting her teeth, she descended the two concrete steps that led to the parking lot. Flattening her palm against the door, she leaned forward and craned her neck around the edge to see—

Something brushed against her ankles.

She screamed. Her feet stumbled off the back step. Grasping for the doorknob, she missed. With clumsy, lurching steps, she staggered into the sunshine and grasped the warm metal pole of an iron fence that bordered the parking lot. Stabilizing herself, she saw a black shadow zigzag across the asphalt, veer a sharp right, and scramble underneath a parked car.

Adrenaline surged through her veins. For a split second, she thought it was one of the shadow creatures that had attacked Jake. One of the black butterflies.

She panted breaths of heated air. *There are no black butterflies here. This is Earth, not purgatory.*

Her glance flicked back to the car. Whatever had

scurried past now blended with the shadows underneath it.

Don't let your imagination get the best of you. It had to be a cat.

She released her death grip on the fence and inhaled deeply, filling her lungs with sea-misted air. Time to investigate the mystery of why the door remained open.

Moments later, she stood behind the door, perplexed. A white rope, looped around the outside handle, ran toward the metal bar of a neighboring back window where it terminated in a bold knot. Both knots were similar in that part of the rope coiled in a circle from the knot. It struck her as odd that someone would tie a rope like that.

Stranger than that, why would someone tie her back door open?

"I always lock the back door," she muttered as her fingers ran along the taut, sinewy rope. Locking the back door after bringing in the garbage every Tuesday was a ritual drilled into her since she'd begun helping her mom run Ray's seventeen years ago.

But then, she had been careless with the front door. Had she failed to lock up the back door as well? She could have sworn she checked it last night before she left . . . and it had been securely locked.

Or maybe she didn't remember any such thing. Par for the course with her Tilt-A-Whirl mental state these days.

Yet, someone had obviously forced open the door. No fantasy there. She saw it. Felt the ribbed rope. Although how did they get the door open in the first place? There were no obvious signs of forced entry—just like with the front door.

But more confusing, why did they tie open the door? If someone had wanted to steal something large, like her refrigerator, it would make sense to keep the back door open. But nothing large had been stolen.

She shivered despite the heat. *I better call Detective Ramsey.*

He wasn't in, so she described what had happened to the sergeant who answered the phone. Within ten minutes, a police car pulled up in front of Ray's. The first to enter was a trim policewoman with a tightly woven blond braid that fell in a stiff line down her back. She walked as though she had a board wedged between her shoulder blades. Lumbering behind her was tall, gangly cop who looked familiar. Then Scarlett remembered. George.

The policewoman spoke first. "You had a break-in?" Her no-nonsense, monotone delivery made Scarlett wonder how many hundreds of times this policewoman had repeated the very same words.

Scarlett had been chopping onions until they arrived. It calmed her to do something repetitive and mindless. She crossed from behind the counter and answered the question as she walked toward them. "Yes. Last night. The front door was open when I arrived this morning. They also tied the back door open."

George stood next to the policewoman. "They?" His features dropped, as though this moment was the saddest in his life. Then Scarlett remembered he always had that permanent basset-hound look.

"Tied open the back door?" he continued, as though he hadn't heard her right the first time.

"Yes, that's right." His doggy-sad eyes glanced at the knife in her hands. "Did you cut the rope?"

She looked down at the butcher knife, suddenly self-conscious. "No. The sergeant I spoke to said not to remove or touch anything."

"Could you show us this back door?" asked the policewoman crisply.

"Certainly." Scarlett set the knife down on the counter and walked toward the back of Ray's while wiping her hands on her apron. "Follow me," she called over her shoulder.

After showing them the knot, and explaining how the back door was always locked, Scarlett watched as they checked the cord and mumbled between themselves. Finally, George walked a few feet away and scanned the parking lot with his sorrowful gaze while Ms. Braid jotted down some notes.

"Have either of you spoken with Detective Ramsey?" asked Scarlett.

Braid didn't bother to look up. "No. Why?"

"He's in charge of my case."

"What case is that?"

Did it have a name? The Shoot-and-Torment-Scarlett-Ray Case, Scarlett felt like saying. *Haven't you heard of it?* Instead, she took a calming breath and said, "I've been having . . . troubles with my business. Detective Ramsey knows the particulars."

"You've had other break-ins?" Braid raised her gaze a notch without interrupting her scribbling.

"Not exactly, but—"

George was back from his parking lot patrol. "Ms. Ray has had some problems with thugs. We've been patrolling her business and home for several days now."

"I wasn't aware of other details." Braid jotted something else down.

"I was shot three weeks ago," explained Scarlett. "And accosted one night after work—the guy had a gun, I'm certain. Plus, he told me I have five days or he'll come back. Guess I'm down to four now . . . oh jeez. Four. Then today my front door was open when I got to work and my back door was tied open, obviously new warnings . . ." *I'm babbling. I sound like a crisis freak reciting her top ten life threats.*

Braid looked up, her face showing zero reaction. "Earlier you said you'd probably forgotten to lock up properly last night."

"Yes, I know I said that." Scarlett had conveniently forgotten that she muttered something to that effect when she first showed them the rope. Damn, Robo-Braid had a memory like a computer. "It's a possibility, yet I *remember* checking the back door. Besides, he—" Scarlett stopped herself from saying "Chandler." The lawyer's nasty phone call made it clear Scarlett could be legally punished for claiming Kenneth Chandler had made threats on her life. "The people who're stalking me are dead serious. Detective Ramsey knows all about this. I'll get in touch with him."

Braid's eyebrow arched ever so slightly.

Scarlett had the distinct impression Braid didn't believe one word she said. What was happening to her was *real.* She was sick to death of always being on the defensive, trying to explain.

She turned and headed back into Ray's.

When she stepped up the back porch stairs, her gaze landed on a pair of snakeskin boots. She gasped, then clamped her lips shut so as not to alert the police standing only a few feet behind her.

Jake.

She released a nervous breath. "You scared me," she whispered.

He stood in the alcove, his arms braced against both sides of the open door. His face was in shadow, but sunlight poured over the rest of him. It struck Scarlett that she'd never seen Jake in daylight before.

The jacket, normally a whiskey color indoors, seemed to absorb the sunshine and reflect a buttery hue. Inside the open jacket, he wore a simple white tee shirt. Just like her James Dean figurine. The resemblance was uncanny.

Jake shifted his weight slightly. The crucifix around his neck sparkled with light. Not the reflection of sunlight, but small bursts of glitter. Like a miniature fireworks display.

She didn't feel frightened at the sight. If anything, she felt mesmerized. "Your cross—"

"I'd be careful talking to me," he interrupted. From the tilt of his chin, she realized he was looking over her shoulder. "The cops are probably fifteen feet behind you." He stretched his neck as though to get a better look. With his movement, she heard the soft crunch of his jacket's leather. "They could overhear you, although they seem pretty engrossed in their own discussion right now," he said in a whispered aside.

"Why are you whispering?" she said under her breath.

"Because you are." A dimple came to life on his cheek as he smiled.

A rush of heat filled her face as she realized her retort should have been thought, not spoken. She pressed her lips together and stared into the shadow where his eyes should be.

In a good mood, are we? She found herself smiling, enjoying this moment of intimacy with Jake. Behind her, she heard George's baritone voice discussing something with Braid's no-nonsense monotone one.

Jake crooked his finger, indicating she should follow him. Turning, he led her back into Ray's.

His jeans made a coarse swishing sound as he walked. She dropped her gaze. Through the snug denim, she detected the rippling of muscles when he walked. And walk he did. Each step was a sensual undulation of thigh and . . .

"Ahem."

She jerked her head up. Over his shoulder, Jake tossed a look at her that said she'd been caught in the act. One corner of his lip curled into a smile and he winked. "I'm surprised at you, Scarlett. You're in the middle of a crisis and you're thinking of—"

"Let's not spell it out, okay?" She propped one hip against a stool and crossed her arms underneath her breasts. "I'm stressed. Bogeymen are everywhere. My mind . . . wandered."

Jake's eyes twinkled with mirth. "Yeah, and we both

know where it wandered to. My my, Miss Ray. I do believe you were checking me out."

She was going to make up an excuse, but what would be the use? He read her mind anyway. "Sorry about the mental detour."

"I'm not." He took a step toward her and touched the tip of her nose with his forefinger. "We can't stay on this discussion because those cops are going to walk in any minute. Plus . . ." But he didn't finish the thought. Instead, he paced a few steps, then turned back to her. Hitching his thumb in the direction of the police, he continued, "I don't think Dagwood and Blondie believe you. They think kids played a prank on you, but I don't think so. Whoever tied that knot knew what they were doing." Jake sidled onto a stool and lowered her a knowing look. He edged one elbow onto the counter and looked around the room.

"Nothing was taken," she answered to his scan of the room. "I already checked."

Following his gaze, hers alighted on the kitchen wall clock. "Look at the time!" she blurted, jumping to attention.

Briskly, she went behind the counter, opened a cupboard, and grabbed a few coffee filters. "I have lunch customers in less than an hour. If I don't start working, there'll be nothing to serve but sides of mayo and relish."

She began scooping the dark coarse grinds into the filters, stacking them on top of each other. Embroiled in her lunchtime preparations, she didn't hear George reenter until he spoke.

"Got a knife under that counter?"

She looked up and blew a hair out of her eyes. George stood on the other side of the counter. Without his realizing it, he stood so close to where Jake sat on his stool that their bodies nearly touched.

It took her a moment to remember that she did indeed have a knife right under the counter. The butcher knife she'd hidden after she got shot. She retrieved it from its resting place. "This do?"

George's eyebrows lifted in mild surprise. "I said knife, not machete." He took it carefully from her. "Crime scene officers are here. They're dusting for fingerprints, taking a few pictures. When they're finished, I'll cut the cord so you can get that back door shut and locked." He eyed the blade, then looked up and met her eyes. "What do you use this for?"

She made a concentrated effort to ignore Jake. No easy task, considering he was leaning close to the knife, checking it out along with George. Now both of them stared at her, waiting for her answer. She focused all her attention on George.

"Good for chopping cabbages," she said a little too loudly. Avoiding Jake's eyes and pretending only George was in the room was disconcerting.

A confused look crossed both George and Jake's faces. Scarlett swore it swept first across Jake's, then passed on to the policeman's. The oddity almost made her laugh.

"I used to make cabbage soup. Buckets of it, in fact. All that chopping got to me, though. Pounds of onions each week tests one's sanity. Add to that bushels of cabbages and I nearly went out of my mind. I was even starting to dream about chopping." She made a downward slicing motion with her hands, as though that would clarify what she had said.

"I thought . . . restaurants had appliances to do that. What do you call them?" George closed one eye and thought. "Oh yeah. Cuisinarts."

She secretly thanked him for referring to her business as a "restaurant." "I have a great Cuisinart sitting under the sink, but it broke the day after its warranty expired. When this mess is over, and my business is back up, I'm gonna save enough to fix it. Top of my list." Then I'll fix the window. Then my watch. Her running list of repairs was growing.

"Knives in your purse. Machetes under the counter . . ." George's scowl deepened. "What else you got hidden in this place?"

The way he looked at her gave her the willies. What did he think she was? A one-woman knife-wielding vigilante? Charlene Bronson?

"I'll have coffee ready when you get back," she said as George started toward the back door.

"What's wrong?" asked Jake.

She waited until George was safely out of hearing distance before she answered. "How did he know about the knife under the counter?" she prompted.

"Why shouldn't you have a knife under the counter? This is a kitchen, after all." Jake flashed her a bemused look.

"That's not it. He knew I had hidden a knife under the counter."

"I don't get it. How could a guy look at a knife and know it's hidden in just the place you always put it?"

She started to toss some onions on her wooden cutting board. Stopping, she whirled around, an onion firmly in her clutch. "That's it! Who keeps a butcher knife with the towels? My utensil drawer"—she yanked open a drawer on the opposite side of the counter—"contains all my knives, spatulas, and other assorted kitchen paraphernalia." She shut the drawer and narrowed her eyes at Jake. "But he specifically said 'under the counter.' He knew it was under the counter."

Jake raked a hand through his hair as he looked away, then back. "Are you saying he's a knife-psychic? Think he bends forks too?"

"This is hardly the time for levity."

Jake straightened his shoulders and met her gaze. "Then I'll be serious. You're worrying about the wrong thing. Whoever tied open your back door is up to no good, not the cop who asks for a knife to cut the cord."

"But what if the cop was the one who tied open the back door? With squad cars patrolling my place night and day, who's going to take special notice if a squad car lingers a few minutes too long? Chandler's a powerful guy—maybe he has some people in the LAPD on his payroll, and he's using them to terrorize me."

A shadow crossed Jake's face. "Chandler's powerful, but . . ." He gave his head a small shake. "You're wasting your energy thinking a cop's out to do you in, Red."

Am I growing paranoid? she wondered. *Is everyone a suspect now because my life is so out of control?*

Jake leaned over the counter and tapped her hand. His warm touch pulled her back from the troublesome thoughts. "Hey, don't doubt yourself because of Chandler. Finish making the coffee and leave the worrying for later."

Jake watched as she lifted a full filter into the coffeemaker's bowl and flipped the start switch. She'd lost weight these last few days. She seemed like a nervous hummingbird, the way she darted around the narrow kitchen. What was she living on lately? Adrenaline? If he wasn't constantly being tugged back into purgatory, he could stay here and make her eat a decent meal now and then. If he was around more, he'd make sure she ate more than those damn bowls of cottage cheese and fruit.

Around more? The thought made his chest ache. Like a hand squeezing his heart. *You're never gonna be around more. You're lucky you're still sitting on this stool, watching her. Being with her. Because whenever you want more—whenever you start to think of her as a woman—you're yanked back to—*

He made himself draw a deep breath. *No. Think about the door, the police, Chandler, anything but wanting a life with her.*

Think about anything else but your need for her.

She fluttered past and he caught himself eyeing the curve of her breasts and the way her waist cinched and flared slightly into softly rounded hips.

He dropped his head into his hands. *Stop it.* He rubbed his forehead with his fingers and listened to the trickling coffee as it dripped into the coffee pot. The brew's fresh-roasted scent wound its way around him, taunting his Earthly memories. He remembered hanging out in a place just like this years ago. When he was human. A waitress who splashed coffee in his cup and teased him for dressing like a dandy. Yeah, that had been another life. Definitely.

And now he was . . . ?

He couldn't finish that thought because he didn't know. But it had scared the hell out of him when the black butterflies attacked him. All this time in purgatory, they had avoided him. Darted and veered away from him. Then, last night—last night in Earthly terms—they had gathered their forces and overwhelmed him, as though they had the power, or the command, to do so.

He raised his head slightly and watched Scarlett's slim fingers select an onion and slice it expertly in half. In purgatory, he had thought of her, called to her, and she had come. She ran to him despite the forces that convened to destroy him. She overcame her fear to touch him, to send that stream of love into him. And he thought he had the power to save Scarlett from harm?

Think again, Big Man. She saved you from Hell itself.

Scarlett swiveled her pencil-thin body toward Jake. "Coffee?" But her eyes looked past him. Instantly, a worried look creased her face and she pursed her lips.

George and the policewoman entered from the back of the room. "All done," said George. "Department got their pictures, dusted for fingerprints, then left. They'll see if they can make a positive ID."

"And if they don't?" questioned Scarlett.

"We'll question your neighbors," said Braid. "Maybe someone heard or saw something unusual or suspicious."

Hardly, thought Scarlett. Chandler's scared so many businesses off this block, who's left within a hundred feet of Ray's to hear anything suspicious at night?

She motioned to the nearly full coffee pot. "Some coffee before you go?"

George nodded. "That'd be great. Thanks."

He sank down on a stool several seats down from Jake and plunked the knife on the counter. "Bulky knots. Hard to cut through. Whoever Christmas-wrapped your back door must've been an Eagle Scout."

He took a steaming mug from Scarlett and blew on it. The policewoman shook her head "no" when Scarlett offered her a cup.

"Eagle Scout? I don't think this neighborhood has any," Scarlett observed.

George swallowed a mouthful of the brew before speaking. "I think it was kids playing pranks. That or somebody wanted the refrigerator—but after getting the back door open, something scared them off."

"Yeah, I guess somebody might have wanted the refrigerator," conceded Scarlett. "Or Chandler wants to frighten me . . ." She could have kicked herself. Any such statements were legal fodder, according to Chandler's lawyer. What crime had she just committed? Character defamation?

"I believe your allegations are being considered," said Braid, an edge to her voice.

Scarlett met the policewoman's icy blue gaze. "Allegations?" Something inside Scarlett snapped. "Being shot point-blank is hardly an allegation. Neither is being pronounced clinically dead. Or having a gun poked in your ribs."

She was vaguely aware that Jake had leaned across the counter toward her. She felt his warm grip circle her wrist in warning. Shifting her gaze slightly, she caught a plea in his eyes. His voice reverberated in her head. "Not now."

Her body shook. Not with fear, but with rage.

Again she heard Jake's voice. "Don't push it, Scarlett."

His grip hurt. She glared at him. *Don't push what? You heard what she said. "Allegations" my foot. As though the threats on my life are . . . are . . .*

George slurped his coffee, distracting Scarlett. She glanced over. Behind him, the policewoman's eyes glittered, as though she had stumbled upon some prize.

Was that it? Braid knew about Scarlett's "allegations" against Chandler. Could Braid even be a witness—a paid witness—for Chandler?

"Take it easy, Scarlett. They're trying to do their job," scolded Jake.

The lid blew. She heard her own voice before she could stop it. "You butt out of this. First they act like a tied-open door is some kind of kids' prank. Then they bait me about Chandler, knowing he'll take legal action if I accuse him of the truth."

Jake's brown eyes sparked a message she couldn't decipher. He raised a warning finger.

"Don't point at me," she snapped.

He made a slicing gesture across his throat and shook his head before sinking back down onto his stool.

It felt as though an elevator had plummeted twenty floors inside her stomach. She'd messed up. Big time.

Wide-eyed, she pivoted her head and looked at the cops. Four eyes stared back at her as though she were the Creature from the Black Lagoon.

"Think fast," coached Jake from the sidelines.

She cleared her throat. "I'm talking," she said with as much authority as she could muster. "I'm talking to what you think is an empty stool."

"And you worried about Braid being some kind of secret spy for Chandler," muttered Jake. "I bet she heard you're a little cuckoo down at the station, Red, and now you're gonna have to prove you're not."

Scarlett raised her eyebrows and motioned toward Jake's seat. "Well, yes, I know it's empty. I just happen to like to speak loudly sometimes, and I didn't want to speak directly to you because I'm too loud and it would hurt your ears." I'm in this deep, might as well keep going.

She raised her voice. "See? See how loud this is?"

George fumbled with his cup, nearly dropping it. "Why are you yelling?"

"Not yelling. Talking normally. This is my normal range."

Jake winced. "Volume," he corrected.

"Volume," she said quickly. "That's why I turned my head before and talked to that empty stool. To spare you hearing problems later in life."

Braid adjusted the gun belt around her hips. "We have to go. I believe you're safe now." She shifted a knowing look at George.

He gave the "empty" stool a second look before standing up. Unbeknownst to him, Jake twiddled his fingers in an Oliver Hardy greeting, which caused Scarlett to laugh.

George sighed heavily as he turned his forlorn-looking face toward Scarlett. "Are you going to be all right, Ms. Ray?"

She tried to look serious, but another laugh erupted. She couldn't stop it—everything seemed so silly. Invisible men. Tied-open doors. Even the way Braid tried to out-macho George. "Fine, fine," Scarlett managed to say before she burst into another rash of giggles. "Sorry. It's the stress. I'll be better. Really."

Jake quirked an eyebrow at her with a what-do-you-think-you're-doing look.

It only made her laugh harder.

"I think we should go," announced Braid to no one in particular. "File our report."

Jake was laughing now too. As Braid whisked past, he pulled his hair back into a mock ponytail and put a simpering look on his face that rivaled the one on the policewoman's.

Scarlett had wrapped her arms around her waist with the sole purpose of pinching herself so as not to laugh. But watching Jake's antics brought on a fresh avalanche of giggles.

George gave Scarlett a pitying look, then reached in his pocket and extracted a quarter. This he placed next to the coffee cup before he left.

"A tip?" squealed Scarlett. She had to turn around, the racking laughter impeding her ability to breathe. She gulped breaths of air between side-splitting laughs.

Ten minutes later she and Jake weren't so jovial anymore. Sitting on a stool next to him, she gazed at their reflections in the mirror over the kitchen sink.

"We look pretty unhappy," she commented. It was true. The only thing perky about her face was the chaos of red curls that framed it. Jake now looked sadder than the basset-hound cop.

"We blew it, Red."

"What got into us?"

He shrugged. "Too much of a bad thing? Something had to give."

"Your impersonation of Robo-Policewoman was very good. I never knew you were funny."

"I never knew you had a decibel problem."

She smiled. "Don't get me laughing again. I nearly lost it back there."

"Nearly? I'd say definitely. You definitely lost it."

She sank her face into her hands. "They're filing a report at this very moment that says I'm crazy."

"Certifiable."

She looked up. "Are they? Can you read their minds? See them in that tunnel-movie of yours?"

He gave her an exasperated look. "Who do you think I am? David Copperfield of the Otherworld? No, I can't read their thoughts or see what they're doing. Besides, the movie screen is in purgatory, not here."

"So it's only my thoughts you can hear?"

"Well, yours and your cat's. And other animals."

"George looks like a basset hound."

"Animal looks don't count."

She leaned her head back and gave Jake a long approving gaze. "You're okay, you know that? I like a man with a sense of humor."

"And I like a woman with a little spunk."

A long silence fell between them.

"I called you a man."

Jake's eyebrow arched slightly. "Around you, that's how I feel."

"Are we in this deeper than—"

"We should be? Yes."

Scarlett tapped her finger on the counter, debating how to say what was on her mind. "Don't listen to my thoughts for a minute, okay? I want to think about what I want to say without you getting a sneak preview."

Jake nodded and looked out the window.

Scarlett gazed at the back of his head and the long waves of his deep brown hair. It struck her that his hair was longer than she remembered. He was lean, but built. She eyed the expanse of his shoulders underneath the leather jacket. She wanted to slip her fingers underneath that jacket, inside his tee shirt, and touch his bare skin. She imagined the swell of his chest muscles. The ridged indentations of his stomach. He was real. Had to be real. She smelled his scent from where she sat. Sandalwood. And musky, the way she liked a man to smell.

She touched his hair and curled a silky strand around her finger. "You feel real."

"I am real. More real than I've ever been."

He turned and gathered her in his arms, holding her tightly. So tightly, she felt the rhythm of his breath, the hardness of his chest against hers.

"Scarlett, this is agony for me." His words were husky, choked. "I never expected to want more than escape from my world. But being with you, near you, I find myself wanting—"

"Shh." She cradled his head with her hands. His pain ripped at her, tore her apart. The words "a life together" floated through her mind. . . .

"We'll never have a life together," he whispered hoarsely.

Her entire body trembled as she sought the words, the answers. "This is a life," she began hesitantly.

"This is a half-existence."

"It's all we have."

"Or will ever have."

They clung to each other like two shipwrecked souls. Their lips found each other and they kissed. Leaning into her, Jake engulfed her in his embrace and they teetered slightly. Scarlett braced herself with one hand against the counter, an act that made her body arch toward Jake and press against him in all the right places.

With a sound like a growl, Jake gathered her in his arms and nuzzled his face deep in her hair, against her neck. As his roughened cheek pressed against her own, she vaguely realized he was no longer clean shaven.

"You smell like roses," he murmured, his breath singeing her ear.

Rivers of heat coarsed through her body and she gasped when his lips lingered at the base of her throat, as though seeking her invitation to go further.

Suddenly, he reared his head back and stared at her with feverish eyes. "Scarlett, I want to stay."

She answered him by raising her lips and tasting his mouth. As his tongue flicked the inside of her lip and his hands crushed her into an embrace, Scarlett experienced a flush of passion that burned through her entire body. When he pulled back again, the desire in his shimmering eyes told her he wanted her as much as she wanted him.

"If this is all we have, I'll take it," he whispered huskily. "Give me your love before God takes it away."

Chapter Ten

Panting, Scarlett pulled her mouth free from Jake's and met his smoldering gaze.

His dark brown eyes hypnotized her. Staring into their mahogany depths, she swore they slowly spun, the colors changing. Chestnut to copper to amber. The swirling pigments flashed specks of gold and silver. But when his eyes finally shone like mirrors, she flinched. The last time she'd looked into his metallic gaze, she'd seen the man who shot her.

Jake gripped her shoulders. "Don't be afraid."

She closed her eyes against the image. Her breathing grew louder, seeming to fill the room. In the darkness of her mind, all she saw were Jake's silvered eyes. What nightmare would they replay? What terrifying reenactment would rock her world again?

"Please," she whispered, clutching Jake's jacket. "I can't . . . see that man again."

"Trust me. I would never hurt you."

Even without his words, she knew Jake's intentions because his emotions had reached her—just as they had so many times before. But this time was different. Instead of experiencing only his feelings, something that included them both was happening. His ardor stroked her face like dozens of feathers. The soft, tickling sensation subdued her fears.

And made her experience him as a man.

"Look at me, Scarlett." His rich deep voice wrapped around her like sable.

Slowly, she obeyed.

His silvered eyes bore into her from beneath a forehead fringed with dark curls. Even if she wanted to, she couldn't look away. It was as though he were willing her to stare into their brilliance, to be overcome, as well as to overcome her own reluctance.

They grew larger. And larger. She was only vaguely aware of her breathing. Of the room.

"Come into my mind, Scarlett," she heard Jake say as though from far away.

Her breath caught in her throat as her body lurched at an angle. The walls of Ray's vaporized into a vast, airy blue. Below her, a silvery lake filled the landscape. Her heart pounded as she plummeted toward the sparkling waters.

She gasped upon impact, somehow expecting the stun of icy water.

But instead, the mirrored surface gave way to her

body like a down cushion that molded and supported her effortlessly. She sank farther, aware of an internal comfort—a peace—that seemed to come from the enveloping softness. In the distance she heard the faint tinkling of wind chimes.

Then the whiteness evaporated and she found herself soaring like a bird through endless blue, as though she'd passed through a cloud into an azure sky.

As far as she could see, shimmering currents rippled from her body's flight, the undulating waves tinged with glistening pinks and golds. Refreshing breezes caressed her face. She felt giddy with freedom. Every nerve of her body tingled, and she realized she felt more alive than she had in a long time.

"Jake?" She nearly laughed from sheer joy as she swept and dipped like a bird in flight. "Where are you?"

"Above you."

Above? How could she tell what was above or below?

She twisted her body and realized she was no longer flying, but now floating in this surreal world. She waved her hand, the way a swimmer might in water. Rose-hued ripples rolled from the movement.

"Up here, Scarlett."

She lifted her gaze.

Jake hovered above her, his long hair floating around his face, the strands lifting with the breeze. As their eyes met, the line of his mouth softened and he smiled.

Instinctively, she smiled back. Then she almost laughed at the absurdity of it all, the two of them floating in this weightless Shangri-la. As though they had fallen through the looking glass of purgatory's skies and into heaven itself.

She eyed him from head to toe. Silver-edged clouds covered most of him except his head and bare feet.

No snakeskin boots?

Her gaze inched back up. Protruding through a frothy cumulus was a bare arm. Toned and sprinkled with dark hair. She closed her eyes and listened to the sudden thundering of her heart. No boots? No leather jacket?

Chances were there were also no jeans.

"Scarlett."

The deep resonant bass sent a shock wave through her. She'd often felt Jake's emotions before, but this time they were potent, like a charged storm ready to unleash its power. She inhaled sharply. Sandalwood. Its scent intoxicating, masculine. It was all happening so fast. Was she ready to take Jake as a lover? She didn't even know if he was a man.

Was she crossing an invisible line that meant her sanity was finally breaking?

She opened her eyes slightly. Through her curtain of dark lashes, she gazed at the planes of his face. The angular jaw. The strong line of his nose. His full, well-formed mouth.

She licked her lips and imagined how it would feel to know him intimately. To taste his sweat. Touch his bare skin. She yearned for it. *Ached* for it. Did it matter anymore what was real and what was not?

She needed to be with him as a woman.

He reached out, his fingertips lightly touching her shoulder and traveling past the sensitive curve of her neck to the hollow of her cheek. His touch burned a path across her flesh. When his forefinger traced her lips, she thought she'd been kissed by fire.

"You have a beautiful body," he murmured huskily, his voice heavy with sensual intent.

She glanced down. Frothy clouds clung to her, their wispy blankets not concealing the fact that she was naked. A hot blush crept up her neck. Partially because Jake's eyes were seeing her body for the first time. But mostly from the surging need that now fired her body.

God, she wanted him.

As though in response, he stretched slightly, the movement causing his cloud-garments to billow and glisten. Ripples of color emanated from his movements—bands of blue, turquoise, indigo. They lapped seductively against her body and for a fleeting moment, she swore they were his fingers brushing across her skin.

He moved closer and his mouth covered hers. With an electrifying flick of his tongue, he parted her lips. The hot pressure of Jake's mouth churned wild yearnings within her and she ardently returned his kiss. His tongue plunged inside. Tasting, teasing her. A small animal-like noise found life in her throat, answered by Jake's low growl of need.

She ripped her mouth away, panting, her chest heaving as she tried to catch her breath. In her peripheral vision, she saw waves of color roll from her body's movement, the colors deepening from pink to coral.

Jake clasped her hips and drew her back to him.

Pressed against him, she felt his rigid need against her. This was no fantasy. Jake was all male. She shuddered with delight, acutely aware of the craving that had haunted her since she'd first seen him.

"Ah, Scarlett." He gently held her, enjoying the view of her lithe body. Slim ankles and firm calves that swelled into nicely toned thighs. A feathery cloud still draped provocatively across her torso, firing his imagination. He caught a flash of bare midriff, and the rounded underside of a breast. Small, firm breasts that would fit snugly into a man's palm.

He groaned. Could he stand the fierce sweetness of possessing her?

"Thank you, God," he murmured under his breath, "for letting me love her as a man." Hot tears stung his eyes, but he felt no shame. After years of purgatory, he had this glorious gift of freedom, and Scarlett to share it with.

Droplets fell on her face. A salty tear touched her lips. Meeting Jake's gaze, she saw the shimmering emotion in his eyes.

"Give me your love," he said.

She pressed her hand flat against the bulge of his pectoral muscle, relishing the feel of his taut skin and curling chest hair. Her fingers trailed across something cool and ridged. Dropping her gaze, she spied his crucifix.

It took her by surprise. While before it had appeared dull and tarnished, now it gleamed with a metallic brilliance that reminded her of his silvered eyes.

But before she could contemplate this further, Jake clasped her hand and moved it over his heart. She felt its racing beat, matching her own quickening pulse. His fingers intertwined with her hair and he urged her face forward.

"I want to kiss you again," he said, teasing her with a touch of his damp lips.

But he didn't.

Instead, he nestled close and slowly, maddeningly, trailed his finger across her mouth. Oversensitizing every nerve until she thought she'd go mad.

Did he need to know this was what she wanted? Was he asking permission? *Yes, Jake*. To make her answer even clearer, she shifted her body and layered her legs with his. The satiny intermingling of their naked bodies heightened her sexual urgency.

"Touch me," she demanded softly. Impatiently.

He slid his hands down to cover her breasts. Just as he'd imagined, they fit nicely. He pressed his mouth against the pulsating hollow at the base of her throat and felt her heartbeat against his lips. The aroma of roses swirled through the air.

She arched her back, and he massaged her breasts with slow, rhythmic circles. Warm breezes, laced with ribbons of fuscia and purple, swirled around their bodies. When she moaned, the threads flashed ruby.

He dropped one hand and brushed off the last lather of cloud that clung to her upper thigh. Stifling a growl, his gaze roamed the length of her naked body. He trailed his fingers along her rib cage, circled her belly button, then traced the triangle between her legs before moving back to her breasts. As their peaks hardened in his palms, an excruciating thrill seared through him.

How many times had he dreamed of just this moment while imprisoned in purgatory . . .

Purgatory.

He wanted to make love to her slowly, to savor every moment, but a niggling fear tormented him.

I'll be pulled away again, like the other times I desired her.

He hugged her close. "No," he whispered urgently.

"What?" mumbled Scarlett.

He turned his head and caught the sultry need in her gaze. Had he ever looked into the eyes of a woman like this before on Earth? Had he ever, as a man, seen another's soul as he did now?

"Nothing," he assured her. This time was precious, every moment meant for their love only. With all his will, he'd spirited them to the only piece of heaven he knew—a sacred corner of his mind. His retreat when he didn't think he could bear purgatory any longer.

"Jake."

She said his name with such profound longing that he held stock-still, afraid to do or say anything that might shatter the moment's sweetness. Closing his eyes, he promised himself to always remember the sound of his name from her lips. The memory of her voice would see him through difficult times ahead. . . .

Time. Precious time. Don't waste these moments.

He pulled her close. Her sinewy, firm body was warm and inviting. His hands roved along the curve of her spine and cupped the soft roundness of her bottom. She sighed, her breath singeing his neck. Sizzling need ripped through him. "I want to please you," he murmured. "I want to give you love to last a lifetime."

Waves of heat enveloped her. In Jake's embrace, she felt sheltered, safe, as though she'd wandered forever looking for this very refuge. It felt right being in his arms.

Wherever his body touched hers, fires scorched her skin. He said her name over and over like a litany as his head moved between her breasts and he caught one of her nipples with his lips. He tugged gently and she gasped.

She trembled as his fingers slipped between her legs and entered her. Waves of hot need engulfed her, the building pleasure bordering on agony. The sky burned fiery red. She shuddered. Jake's expert hands now moved in an increasing rhythm. The fire within her blazed. She ached for release.

"I want you inside me," she begged, clutching him as a teasing spasm rocked her body.

The surrounding sky flashed with oranges, golds, and crimsons as she swung her leg over his molded thigh and eased herself onto his hardness.

He'd never seen a more glorious sight than Scarlett. Arched over him, she threw her head back and slowly rotated her hips. He reached up and fondled her breasts, teasing the rosy buds with his fingertips. She panted, her partially opened eyes glistening. Her body trembled. The tousle of red curls shimmered red and copper with her body's movements, their colors mimicking the crimson backdrop.

He squeezed his eyes shut as he sank deeply into her. The pleasure was so exquisite it was nearly painful. A burning need consumed every nerve of his being, yet he didn't want this ecstacy to end. Not until Scarlett . . .

She thrust her head back and cried out. Her orgasm

tightened around him, the tremors massaging him. He dug his fingers into her buttocks and pulled her down, thrusting harder, harder, again and again, fighting his own need, until his peaking pleasure could no longer be contained.

"God, thank you," he cried.

Leaning against the counter, Scarlett stared wide-eyed at Jake. He stood before her in his leather jacket and jeans, just as he had before . . . before . . .

"What happened?" she asked breathlessly. Absent-mindedly, she touched her chest. Her cotton blouse was moist with perspiration.

Jake shifted his shoulders and leaned toward her. With his movement, a faint mauve line rippled through the air. She quivered, remembering the currents their bodies had triggered in . . .

Had they really made love?

Where had they been?

"In my mind," answered Jake.

She met his steady gaze. Those dark, chocolate-brown eyes had been the portal to another land. . . .

She gave her head a slight shake and glanced over her shoulder at the clock on the wall. The time hadn't changed.

Or had time stood still?

When she looked back he began to fade, his image blending with the air.

"Jake, wait," she beckoned. But he was nearly gone. For an instant, she swore she saw a faint outline, as though someone had traced his silhouette on a frosty window.

"Jake, please stay." The thought of being abandoned filled her with a brutal, haunting pain. "I need you."

Fragments of colors appeared. A flash of brown at his hairline. A spark of light where his crucifix hung. A shade of beige across his jaw. She reached out, but when she touched his image, the pigments rippled in spreading waves as though her fingers had penetrated a water's surface.

"Stay with me," she pleaded. Whenever she needed him most, something tore him from her life. Some powerful force that seemed bent on destroying their fleeting happiness.

Or maybe it wasn't Jake slipping away, but her mind. She stared at the feeble outline that wavered in the air before her like a hesitant ghost. She released an anguished sigh. "Even if you're some figment of my imagination, you're all I have." Her confession took her by surprise. Other than her mother, no one had ever been that crucial.

A sudden surge of heat burned her cheeks and forehead, as though she faced a burning sun.

In front of her, Jake's eyes sparkled to life. Warm, brown. His face filled in and she watched, mesmerized, as he spoke to her.

"I want to be with you. But it's pulling me back—"

He blurred, as though she were looking at him through a veil of rain. At the same moment, she was struck with an intense yearning. His yearning. His emotions. They rocked her with their ferocity. He needed her, just as she needed him.

Gradually, he faded. . . .

Instinctively, she grabbed at where he would be standing, but her fingers grasped only empty air. "What can I do?" she cried.

His head turned slightly. Like a hologram, it hovered, three-dimensional, before her.

"Jake," she whispered, opening her hands palm up to him. "With all my being, I will you to stay. If love saved you in purgatory, love can hold you to Earth."

A flash of light nearly blinded her. Then, like magic, Jake stood before her. Real. Alive. She touched his face, his chest. A sob of joy ripped loose and she laughed and cried at the same time. "You're back. I'm not crazy—I see you, feel you. You really exist." She felt intoxicated with his return, with their being together. "I can will you back. You don't have to leave, ever again."

His warm hands cupped her face and he smiled sadly. "Your will can only do so much, Scarlett. Being pulled back to purgatory has to do with me, not you." He lowered his voice, its somber tone chilling her exuberance. "I'm only starting to understand."

She clutched his jacket, its texture supple under her fingers. A thread of sandalwood intertwined with the leather's tannic scent. "You're real, Jake. I can feel you." She said it as much for herself as for him. Her fingers curled tighter and the leather crinkled. "You don't have to go. There's no reason to go. We can be—"

The pained expression in his eyes stopped her from saying more. He couldn't say it, but she knew. There was something that always had the power to tear them apart.

"When I want you," Jake began. He frowned and seemed to mull over how to phrase it. Then his eyes bore into hers and he drew close. "It has to do with my needing you as a man. . . ."

She strained to hear, but his voice diminished until it sounded like someone speaking from far away.

The outer tendrils of his hair faded from molasses to a light golden tinge. His jacket melted into a pool of toffee-hued air. Then all of him dissolved into nothingness.

Her hands remained in the air, the fingers tightly curled. Holding nothing. "Jake, why did you give up?"

Silence was her only answer.

She dropped her hands, her eyes still focused on the spot where he had stood. The gut-wrenching memory of her father's abandonment momentarily surfaced, then shrank back into some mental cubbyhole, leaving her feeling more alone than ever.

Or was she? An uncomfortable tingling, like a warning, ran down her spine.

She glanced around the room, half expecting some freakish entity to be laughing at her. An entity that delighted in destroying the happiness they tried to claim. "It's not fair," she whispered in a broken voice. She eyed the empty room, waiting for the demon to taunt her. "You're punishing us for wanting each other."

A plane buzzed overhead. Teenagers' laughter trickled from down the block. Outside Ray's zoomed the grinding squeal of a skateboard.

But inside her heart, she felt alone. Very alone.

She gave herself a mental shake. "Hardly the time

for self-pity. If I don't get ready, I'll have customers and no food." She started to check her wristwatch, but stopped herself.

"Habit," she mumbled. She strapped it on every morning without remembering that it no longer worked. How many times did she have to see the little hand on the six before she'd learn? Giving her head a small shake, she glanced at the wall clock. She had a good half hour before the regular lunch customers arrived.

As she stacked buns and turned on the grill, she thought aimlessly of when her watch had last shown the correct time. It definitely worked that first night she saw Jake. In fact, it had worked for weeks, months before that.

"Coincidence," she mumbled under her breath as she lifted a bag of onions onto the counter. The more she thought about it, the more certain she was that the watch had stopped working after that first meeting. Had that first surreal encounter broken it?

She whacked at an onion. "You're losing it, Scarlett. Next you'll decide he also broke your Cusinart."

The front door creaked open behind her. "Little One?"

She tossed a look over her shoulder, her eyes stinging from the onions. Enrique stood in the doorway, backlit by sunshine.

He stepped inside, shutting the door gently behind him. "You alone?"

"Probably." She put down her knife and wiped her eye with the tip of her apron. When she looked up, she saw Enrique more clearly. He was looking around, confused.

"Yes. I'm alone," she said.

"I need to talk," he said huskily. The way he staggered over to a stool made Scarlett wonder if he'd been drinking. He sank onto a seat and crossed his arms in front of him, resting his elbows on the counter.

She waited, but he didn't say anything. He stared off in the distance, his hazel eyes nearly hidden by his sagging lids. "I'll have a cup of that coffee," he finally said.

"Sure." She poured him a cup and set it in front of him.

He took a gulp. "It's Doris."

"Did you break up?" It was the first thought that popped into her mind. Seeing the quizzical look on his face, she wished she had used common sense and not spoken so quickly.

"I wish it were as simple as that." He took another sip and grimaced. "Needs more of a kick." He raised the coffee cup slightly to indicate his meaning.

"Milk?"

"Whiskey."

She leaned against the counter and patted his weathered hand. "That bad, huh?"

"You don't know the half." He buried his face in the coffee mug again and took another sip.

"Half of it."

"Eh?"

"Half of it. I don't know the half of it."

His bushy eyebrows pressed together. "I know. That's what I said."

The English lesson could wait. "So what's the problem?"

His eyes grew watery and he gazed around the room, avoiding looking at her. "Roger."

"Doris's son?"

"Sí." A tear poised at the corner of his eye, threatening to spill over. Enrique scratched his cheek, nonchalantly wiping away the tear in the process.

Poor old man. Probably had no one to turn to. No real family. Or none that he'd ever mentioned. Besides Doris, her kids, and Scarlett, he had no one with whom he could talk about his worries. And if the problem lay with Doris or her family, that left her.

Turning to me. Just the way locals used to turn to her mom. The realization tugged at her heart. Like mother, like daughter.

Scarlett grabbed the coffee pot and poured her friend another cup. "Did you eat breakfast?" Something her mom would have said. How many times had she seen her first nuture someone's physical needs, then tackle the emotional ones?

"Pie."

She rolled her eyes in mock exasperation. "You only had pie for breakfast?"

"A bite or two. Left the rest for Doris."

"That's not enough for a growing boy like you," teased Scarlett. "Let me see what I got here . . ."

"Growing boy," repeated Enrique, followed by a low, throaty chuckle. "Growing the wrong way, though. Sideways."

Scarlett rummaged in her refrigerator and found a few eggs and a wedge of cantaloupe—enough to make an impromptu breakfast. She prepared scrambled eggs with jalapeño—Enrique insisted on the chili pepper addition—with a side of hamburger-bun toast.

Twenty minutes later, Enrique pushed away the plate now smeared with remnants of egg. He patted his stomach and nodded his approval. *"Delicioso."*

"My pleasure. Now, tell me about Roger."

Enrique's brow wrinkled with worry as he dabbed at his moustache with a napkin. "He was jumped by a gang last night."

"Is he all right?"

"Yes. Broken lip. Bruised ribs. Nothing serious busted." Enrique made a quick sign of the cross. "He didn't have to go to the hospital."

She picked up his plate and set it in the dirty-dish bin under the counter. "Where did this happen?"

"Outside his apartment—you know, a block over. He swears he never saw the boys before. But they knew him. Called him by name."

She wiped the counter in an aimless motion, her mind elsewere. "Boys? They were boys?"

"Roger said."

With the weighted pause, Scarlett looked up and caught Enrique looking at her, an odd expression on his face. "It was dark. Maybe Roger didn't see so good," he said in a low, hoarse voice. His hand trembled as he wiped his eyebrow. "I wish I knew more, Little One. But I don't."

Scarlett felt torn between hurt and rage. Hurt that her old friend Enrique was suffering. He loved Doris's son like his own, she was certain of that. Yet Enrique was an old man, unable to defend those he cared most about. It must demoralize him, a former merchant marine, to be unable to protect those he loved.

Instinctively, she knew this was the handiwork of Chandler's thugs.

She felt rage. Unadulterated, boiling-temperature rage, that he was now hurting innocent people as a ploy to force Scarlett's hand. He was encroaching, circling her neighborhood like a coyote eyeing a chicken coop. But why harm Doris's son? How did Chandler even know Roger?

Chills skittered down her arms, giving her goosebumps. "I'm scared, Enrique. Scared for all of us."

After a beat, Enrique answered. "*Si*. For all of us."

Something in Enrique's voice made her turn and look at him. His face had that same unfathomable expression she had noticed earlier. It hit her that although he was always there for her, they had never weathered a crisis together. And being an "old school" gentleman, he would never voice his emotions. Or fears.

She lay her hand on top of his brown, wrinkled one. "Enrique, we'll see this through together. We're a community, a family. Just like you said." She bit her bottom lip, wondering if she dared say more. "I don't think less of you because . . . because you weren't there to protect Roger."

He ducked his head, cutting off further eye contact. She wondered if she'd gone too far. Maybe she shouldn't have said anything. But when she started to remove her hand, he clasped it tightly. Without looking up, he said in a gravelly voice, "You and I both know . . ."

She waited. And watched his head quiver with obvious emotion, the white hair on the top trembling.

Slowly, he looked up, his hazel eyes clouded over as though he didn't see her. "We both know Chandler is—"

She slapped her hand against the counter, surprising Enrique as much as herself. It was as though she couldn't contain her inner turmoil anymore.

"We can't give into our fears." She swallowed back the break she heard in her voice. She had to be strong. For herself. For Enrique. For the community.

She inhaled deeply, determined to finish what she had to say. "We *can't* give in to Chandler."

Chapter Eleven

"Hello."

"Whoajeez!" Scarlett slammed a salt shaker on the counter. Cleaning up alone after lunch, she hadn't expected to hear a soft female voice behind her. Doris's "hello" was more shocking than if someone had tossed an ice cube down her top.

Doris edged her round frame through the slightly opened door. "Sorry, child. It's just me. Your 'other mother,' remember?"

After the rush of adrenaline Scarlett suddenly felt exhausted. "Didn't hear anyone come in," she said weakly.

"So I gather."

Scarlett gestured limply toward a stool. "Now that I've had my scare for the hour, take a seat." She tried to say it airily, but the slight tremble in her voice gave her away. Truth was, she was always on edge. Always afraid of Chandler's next move. "Get you something? Cola?" She started to head around the counter when she realized Doris hadn't budged.

Of course. Scarlett was so preoccupied with her own life, she'd forgotten about Doris's son Roger.

"I'm—" Scarlett stopped. How to best say she was sorry he had been hurt? Guilt tightened its hold on her like an unwelcome embrace. If she had signed Chandler's agreement, he wouldn't have attacked someone innocent, like Doris's son.

Scarlett raised her hands in a helpless gesture, but words escaped her. "I'm so very—"

"I know." Doris shrugged in resignation and expelled a weighted sigh. "I know," she repeated, her voice nearly inaudible.

An awkward silence filled the space between them.

Scarlett searched Doris's face. Even though the woman was nearing sixty, she'd always had a youthful appearance. Now she looked as though she'd aged ten years in the last twenty-four hours. New lines splayed from her eyes. Her mouth sagged.

"Roger was hanging out with the wrong crowd," Doris suddenly confessed, as though continuing an ongoing internal conversation. "Can't tell you how many times I've watched the sun come up, worrying if he'd ever get his life in order." She gave her head a shake. "Just like his daddy."

Guilt washed over Scarlett. Chandler *had* to be behind this. If she hadn't been so obstinate about holding on to Ray's, nobody would've been hurt. "Doris, it's because of me—"

Doris cut her off with an exasperated wave of her hand. "It's not something I wanted people to know. Kids today, it's tough. A neighborhood like this lacks strong role models. How many years have I been unemployed? Judyl lives out of her car with her boy, Sun. You were shot . . ." She smiled apologetically and shook her head. "Sorry."

"No, it's okay." Now wasn't the time to bring up Chandler. Doris was traumatized with Roger's near tragedy. It would only add to her stress if Scarlett confessed her fears. "What can I do for you, Doris?"

The older woman's lips twitched into a feeble smile. "I just needed a friend, child. Needed to vent."

For the second time that day, Scarlett realized people were turning to her. Just as they had to her mother. *I'm more my mother's daughter than I ever realized.*

"And I also need a favor," Doris added. She blinked her small brown eyes, as though what she were asking was far too much.

"Shoot." Scarlett winced comically. "No, don't shoot. I've already been through that."

Doris looked stricken, then sputtered a nervous laugh. "You can joke about that? Good for you, child. You may look frail on the outside, but inside, you're made of iron." She laid her hand on her ample bosom and fingered a crucifix. Scarlett's eyes were drawn to the silver pendant, which reminded her of Jake's. . . .

"I have my grandson and his friend with me today," Doris began hesitantly.

Scarlett tore her gaze from the dangling cross to Doris's face. "Uh, yes?" she answered, unsure exactly what Doris had just said.

"I need to be with Roger when he goes to the police station. . . ." Doris's voice trailed off and she raised her eyebrows in a question. "But the kids. They'd get in the way. And . . . I wondered if you'd be willing to babysit."

"Sure." *How many kids?* She didn't want to admit she hadn't been listening. "Sure, bring 'em in. I'd love to babysit." She couldn't believe her own ears. Only last week she'd have fumed at being saddled with kids and invented a hundred excuses why they would only be underfoot.

"They're two good boys—"

Two. Great. *Absolutely* manageable. Scarlett wiggled her eyebrows. "I like 'em bad."

Doris squealed a laugh. "Scarlett, if your mama could hear you now." Her smile broadened, momentarily erasing the tension in her face.

"She probably does." *Jake definitely does.*

While Doris went to retrieve the boys, Scarlett noticed something out of the corner of her eye. Next to the cash register, specks of color began to vibrate like sparkles of light across water. Blues, reds, yellows. Bright, shiny dots that fluttered as though a breeze blew across them.

The sequins of light wavered for a moment, then increased their tempo as though they gyrated to some invisible beat. She blinked. Now they were swimming, the vibrant colors bleeding into each other.

Sandalwood filled the air.

Pop.

The colors flared, then shrank back into . . .

Jake.

Scarlett eased a stream of air through her pursed lips. "You sure know how to make an entrance."

They looked at each other for a long moment. But before either could say anything, a commotion at the front door announced Doris's arrival.

She scooted two little boys inside, who were playfully punching each other and laughing. They looked to be around five or six. "Ramon," said Doris.

The little boy she addressed continued to punch his buddy.

"Ramon," she repeated in a louder voice, patting the little boy's curly black hair. His wide brown eyes looked at her.

"This is Ramon," Doris said, giving Scarlett a meaningful look that said "Watch out for this rascal."

"And Geronimo." She patted the other boy's straight blond hair.

"Geronimo?" repeated Scarlett.

He stuck out his bottom lip and glowered at her.

Doris clucked something and the little boy instantly looked sheepish.

"He likes to be called Jerry. My fault," said Doris. She looked back at the boys. "Now behave yourselves, hear? Aunt Scarlett is working—she doesn't have time to sit on you."

Jerry scrunched up his face. "Why does she want to sit on us?"

Scarlett pressed her lips together to hold back a laugh. "Want some hamburgers?" She motioned for Doris to leave.

"I'll be back in a few hours," mouthed Doris behind the kids' heads.

Scarlett nodded. "C'mon over here, guys. I'll show you how the best hamburgers in L.A. are made."

Jake watched Scarlett as she poured sodas for both kids, and plied their goodwill with bags of potato chips and make-your-own burgers. They slathered ketchup and relish all over the patties. And the counter. And their jackets.

Scarlett was busy wiping a dribble of relish off Ramon's jacket while giving instruction to Jerry on how to remove a stubborn cap from a mustard jar.

"You'd make a good mom," Jake said suddenly.

Scarlett jerked her head in his direction, but caught herself before answering out loud. *How would you know?*

"Can see it. You're good with kids." He flashed her a cocky smile. "Good with big kids too."

His glistening brown eyes darkened into a smoldering gaze. That same look he had when they'd made love. Heat tickled her insides at the memories of their shared passion.

She quickly looked down, all consumed with the mustard cap.

"Did I speak out of line?" Jake asked.

She gulped a breath of air, acutely aware of his eyes watching her every move. If they continued with this conversation, Jake would disappear. Isn't that what he had told her? That desiring her was a one-way ticket to purgatory?

She switched gears. "Good with kids? Hey, these are potential customers. I'm cultivating future Ray's hamburger eaters."

The little boys stopped their chewing and laughing

and planted two pairs of eyes on Scarlett. It took her a moment to realize she'd spoken out loud. She back-stroked mentally, remembering what she'd said. "Isn't that right?" she asked them in a high-pitched voice. "You're future Ray's hamburger eaters."

Jerry squinted at Ramon in some quirky little-kid silent language. Then they both resumed their giggling and eating.

"Good save," Jake acknowledged to Scarlett with a wink.

But his cheer faded into what she could only construe as a wistful look when his gaze returned to Jerry. "This wild man here reminds me of myself as a young boy," Jake began in a somber tone. "Happy to be 'hanging' with my pal, eatin' a burger. Pretending the pretty lady was my mom." He reached over and patted Jerry on the head.

The little boy glanced up, his face skewered with confusion at seeing nothing. A playful punch from Ramon redirected his attention back to their mealtime fun.

He felt you. Scarlett was in awe at what had just transpired. *Does that happen often?* She had images of Jake strolling invisibly down a street, touching and tapping people who looked around, but saw nothing.

"Sometimes people sense me," he answered. "Usually it's when someone needs . . . needs an 'intervention'—you know, when a person desperately wants something to extinguish their unhappiness. Children are different, though. They're sensitized to other dimensions."

She remembered Chandler's wife and the surprised

look on her face when Jake had stood "within" her. Had she been unhappy?

Scarlett ran her fingers along the Formica counter's cool edge, wondering how to phrase her next question—and realizing belatedly that it didn't matter because Jake heard her every thought anyway.

What did you mean by the "pretty mom" comment?

Jake's shoulders sagged noticeably as he looked away. "Hardly matters now."

She heard the edge in his words, but had to know. *You said you'd imagine a lady to be your mom. Were you—*

"Momless. Yes." He had cut her off with a distinct surliness.

"I didn't mean to pry. It's just that I know so little about your former life. Your family. The fact you didn't have a—"

He cut her off again. "Bingo. You win. My family life is a source of pain for me. Forty Earth years later, it still hurts to remember certain things. Now can we end this discussion?"

A chilling breeze swirled around her, bringing with it an acute distress that cut to her heart. She felt his hurt at having once been horribly betrayed. And his hurt at never experiencing the love of a family. *His* family.

The feelings were gone now, the chilling breeze replaced by the room's comfortable temperature. Jake's chin rested on his hands, his gaze cemented to something on the countertop. His hair hung lankly around his face like a dark shroud.

"Sorry," she mumbled and grabbed a grill brush

from a hook. Although she had carefully cleaned the grill area after lunch, she began scrubbing it anew with a ferocious burst of energy. He had the nerve to *brood* when he had started this damn conversation? Didn't he think she knew how it felt to be Momless herself?

"Men," she muttered under her breath. She'd never known a "normal" one, that was for sure. From her dad to Neanderthal Bob to Mr. Now-You-See-Me-Now-You-Don't. Either they were *in* trouble, or troubled. And when they weren't self-absorbed with their own self-important worlds, they brooded.

Like ghost-man—over there, pouting. He was upset because they had touched on a sensitive subject in his past? Brother, he had it easy, because he could *vaporize* when the going got tough. God, what she'd give for a back door on this life. An exit when Chandler turned up the heat. But no. She was stuck in this body and had to play by life's rules.

Which meant every day she was a living, breathing target for Chandler.

A drop of sweat plopped on the metal border of her grill and she attacked it savagely with her brush.

Something warm slid around her shoulders. She jumped back with a stifled shriek, tripping over her own feet. Regaining her balance, she clutched her chest and stared at Jake.

"You scared me!" she said, gulping air between words. "You shouldn't sneak up like that."

He swept a hand through his hair and grinned sheepishly. "I'm not like the others," he said softly.

Her breaths were more even now. Realizing she still clutched her grill brush to her chest, she tossed it over her shoulder onto the back counter. Ignoring its clattering descent, she instead concentrated on Jake. "Okay, where were we? You're not like *what?*"

"The others. Your dad. Neanderthal . . ." His brows flinched as he seemed to search his memory. "Stan? Egbert?"

"Neanderthal Bob," she said flatly, correcting him. "Egbert? You think I'd be caught dead dating an Egbert?" She affected an insulted stance, but the mischevious glint in Jake's dangerously sexy eyes made her smile. "You trying to tease me out of my bad mood?"

"Maybe." He took a step toward her. His fingers circled her waist. Leaning his face near hers, he whispered into her hair, "But then, you seem like the type to date a science nerd. Spend your time collecting bugs. Reading to each other from the encyclopedia." He nuzzled her ear, his hot breath tickling her skin. "What have you done to me, Red? I'm more a man each day. I need you. Desire you . . ."

She dropped her head to the side, stifling a small groan when his lips trailed a sensual path down her neck. "You're going to be pulled back," she murmured.

"Red, didn't anyone tell you it's rude to interrupt?" he teased.

Closing her eyes, she inhaled deeply as his hot mouth nibbled on her earlobe.

"And for your birthday," he whispered huskily before planting a strategic kiss at the hollow of her neck. "Instead of jewels, you'd ask for a chemistry set."

She giggled.

Other little voices giggled with her. For a moment,

Scarlett felt like Dorothy surrounded by Munchkins.

She popped open her eyes. Over Jake's shoulder, she spied Ramon and Jerry watching her with with the rapt interest kids usually reserve for cartoons.

"You're silly!" squealed Ramon.

Jerry nodded with great exaggeration, the motion causing his straight blond hair to shake violently. "Silly!" he agreed.

"I forgot we have company," murmured Scarlett, holding her lips in a stiff line as though practicing ventriloquy.

Jake pulled away and rubbed the side of his face in an embarrassed gesture. "Oops." He strolled out from behind the grill with forced nonchalance while wagging a finger at her. "No more talking. They're gonna tell someone about the hamburger lady who talks to herself, you know."

She started to nod, then caught herself. *Right. Thoughts only.*

Cracking her face with the biggest, fakest grin she could muster, she planted herself in front of the still-giggling boys. "Silly me. You're right."

Ramon laughed, his missing baby teeth making his smile look like black-and-white piano keys. "How do you make an egg burp?"

"Huh?" answered Scarlett.

"Egbert," coached Jake from his seat on the sidelines.

"Oh, Egbert!" She flashed another overly enthusiastic smile at the boys. "That's right, I said 'Egbert,' didn't I? That's because . . . I like to make up silly games . . . about eggs." She swiveled a half-turn and marched toward a small display of cupcakes and cookies behind the register. "How about some yummy goodies?"

Ramon and Jerry clapped and yelped as she lay the sugar-laden booty in front of them.

Bribing kids with sugar? Still think I'd make a good mom?

It took every ounce of self control not to join in Jake's outburst of laughter. "Every child's dream come true!"

I have to work. No more silliness. She tossed Jake an amused glance as she crossed to the refrigerator and opened the large stainless-steel door. On the top shelf were packages of hamburger meat, each weighted in equal proportions. Typically, two packages met lunch's needs. Three, dinner's. She reached in and grabbed two, which she expertly juggled under one arm. With her free hand, she yanked out the third.

While tossing her bundles onto the counter, she shoved the refrigerator door closed with her foot. She unwrapped one of the packages and tossed the block of hamburger onto a wooden board. Yanking off hunks of the meat, she began slapping it into patties.

Ramon gurgled a laugh through a mouthful of cupcake. "She's spanking the meat."

Scarlett untied the next package and pulled back the wrapping. Her mouth dropped open, but all that came out was a raspy sound.

Lying in the middle of the paper was a dead cat.

She swallowed chunks of air, unable to speak. Rooted to the spot, she gaped at the black-and-white matted fur.

Cloudy eyes stared back at her.

"Rhett," she finally croaked. Her trembling fingers touched the stiff fur. "Rhett."

"Go stand by the front door," Jake ordered the boys. "Now!" Scampering feet did as they were told.

As her fingers grew icy, she wondered why the boys obeyed his command. *Had they heard him?*

Darkness crowded her vision's edges. The world collapsed onto her shoulders and she felt herself slipping, slipping . . .

Her knees crumbled. The floor rushed toward her.

Hands grabbed her.

The last thing she remembered was the tannic scent of Jake's jacket as he held her close.

Detective Ramsey rubbed the end of his pen against his forehead. In the background, the two little boys ran in circles playing tag.

"A cat?"

She clutched her hands together to stop their shaking. "Yes."

His gaze roamed over to the refrigerator. "In there?"

"Yes," she whispered, following his glance. "At first I thought it was my cat Rhett."

He waited a beat. "But it wasn't?"

"No. Rhett has splotches of white on his tail and paws." She indicated the general proximity, as though she were a feline.

"You're *certain* this cat isn't yours?"

She shivered as chills skittered up and down her back. "Yes." The image of the poor dead cat materialized in her mind again and she cringed. It had looked so pathetic lying there. Only when she had dared to look more carefully had she noticed its solid black tail. She had felt relieved and sick at the same time. "Yes, I'm certain."

"Don't do anything with it. We'll want fingerprints."

She swallowed back a sour taste. "Keep it in my refrigerator?"

"Better than out on the counter," he answered drolly. "I want you to close up early so some of my guys can check this place out."

"I'm not going to be able to make my bills this month if I keep losing business. I'll close tonight, but I *must* open tomorrow morning. No later than ten."

"No problem."

"And the cat . . ."

Ramsey raised his head.

Scarlett cleared her throat. "Can you please take it to the Humane Society tonight when you're through? I can't stand the thought of the poor thing . . ." She couldn't finish.

"Yeah. No problem." He tucked his pen into his jacket's inner pocket. "Kids say a man was here when you found the cat."

It took her a moment to realize what that meant.

She looked over at the boys as they ran and tagged each other.

They'd seen Jake?

She swerved her gaze back to Ramsey. "No. Yes. I mean, people are always dropping by. I can't keep track of my customers."

Ramsey looked up at the ceiling as though something was written there. "Kids say the two of you talked while they played. When you screamed, the man told them to move away. Then he ran behind the counter and caught you." He looked back down and scratched his neck. "You don't remember that?"

"I don't, really. Guess I was in shock." *I'm lying and he sees it.*

"Switchboard says it was a man who placed the call from Ray's."

Jake makes phone calls? "I'm clueless, detective. Sorry." She rubbed her knuckle against her bottom lip. "A good Samaritan, maybe?" she said thoughtfully. "When I got shot, a passerby called nine-one-one. . . ." Her voice trailed off. Had the "passerby" been Jake?

A *harump* sound interrupted her thoughts and she looked up sharply. "I think you're fudging the truth, Ms. Ray." Ramsey said it with all the tact of a heat-seeking missle.

"That's ridiculous," she sputtered. "Why would I do that?"

He cut her a come-off-it look. "Police think you have imaginary playmates. Kids say you have a boyfriend. You trying to run something past me?"

"Like—?"

"Like maybe you and your boyfriend had a lover's squabble the night he shot you, and you're pinning it on Chandler to get the boyfriend off the hook."

"That's ridic—"

"Like maybe you're pretending to talk to invisible people so the court will find you insane should you take matters into your own hands and shoot Chandler yourself."

"*That's* insane, not me—"

"Like maybe you and the boyfriend are in cahoots. Pin enough slime on wealthy Chandler and he'll settle out of court just to keep his reputation intact. Hefty settlement could improve your life. . . ." He looked around. "Remodel this place. Put in a real restaurant, like you've always dreamed about."

Hot tears welled in her eyes. "I'd never, *ever,* do any of those despicable things. How dare you accuse me." She swallowed hard, determined not to cry. "And the things I told you about wanting a restaurant someday—it's not fair that you throw that in my face. Especially since I'm innocent of all those concocted stories of yours."

His gray eyes lost their edge. "Not mine. Other cops."

"What's that supposed to mean?"

"It's not Chandler who has to defend his reputation. You've got to defend yours. Rumors are flying, none of them in your favor."

She hit her fist on the countertop. "Chandler's doing that. Don't you see? He wants to ruin me, one way or another. He's the one starting the stories. He wants to destroy *me*."

Ramsey hoisted his big frame off the stool. "I believe you, kid. Really do. Wish it wasn't all uphill for you."

"What can I do? I won't give up. I can't give up. This is all I have."

"Give me a reliable witness. Like that boyfriend who was here when you found the cat."

"There wasn't anyone here."

"Both kids mentioned him."

"You're grilling five-year-olds?"

Ramsey pointed his square index finger at her. "I have kids of my own. I talked to them as a buddy, not a mean ol' detective. What they said is for my ears only, unless you're willing to produce this guy."

"There's no guy."

"Okay. Then do me a favor."

"What?"

"Stop conversing with invisible people when the police are here. It's not helping your case at all."

She couldn't deny that one. George and Braid had both seen her talking to Jake. "I've been . . . stressed. Sometimes I talk to myself."

"Well, take more vitamin C or something. Cut down on the stress." He tweaked her nose. "I got a daughter close to your age—you remind me of her. She's a little goofy sometimes too."

"Too? Thanks a lot."

"Nuthin' wrong with goofy. Except when people start to think you have nuts and bolts instead of brains. So, for now, put a lid on your inner child or whoever you're talking to."

She had to smile despite herself. Inner child? What psycho-babble radio show did Detective Ramsey listen to while he toodled around town in his police unit?

"Lid's on," she promised.

Chapter Twelve

"Frankly, my kitty, I do give a damn."

Scarlett cuddled Rhett and kissed him lightly on his furry black-and-white head. He struggled a little in her arms, as though to say, "Enough of this lovey stuff."

She pecked him again. "You don't understand, Mr. Rhett. When I saw that poor frozen . . ." She couldn't finish. Her insides caved in whenever she thought about opening that package and seeing the dead cat.

She trembled and hugged Rhett closer. He mewed, then succumbed to the adoration and rubbed his chin against her chenille robe.

She'd obeyed Ramsey's strict instructions to close Ray's until tomorrow morning. Now home for an hour, she'd spent the entire time either smothering Rhett with attention or pacing her living room, worrying how far Chandler would go to get his way.

How much further could he go in three days?

Surges of anxiety, like measured doses of fear, had been shooting through her all afternoon. Another one hit, and she set Rhett in the center of her armchair and resumed pacing.

"Why pick a cat that looks like Rhett?" she said to the empty room for the umpteenth time. "Why didn't they—" Hugging her arms around her stomach, she eyed her cat. Oblivious to her consternation, he lolled on his back in what looked to be an incredibly uncomfortable position.

Despite her anxiety, Scarlett found herself smiling. "You have no idea you almost starred in a film-noir refrigerator mystery, do you?"

He twitched an ear in response.

Whoever killed that cat knew it looked like Rhett, which meant that person—another of Chandler's thugs, no doubt—had *seen* her cat. She flicked her gaze at the kitchen window. Had he peered in while she was at work? A queasiness unsettled her stomach. If he had been close enough to see Rhett, why not just kill him instead of a look-alike?

It was a sick catch-22.

She shuddered and walked stiffly into the kitchen. Flicking open the cabinet above the stove, her gaze zeroed in on her stash of cigarettes. She licked her lips. She could taste the tobacco, smell its smoke.

Damn it. She needed nicotine.

She arched an eyebrow and glanced at the ceiling. "One, Mom. Just one measly cigarette. I've had a hard day. Someone tied open the back door. Then Jake whisked me into never-never land and we—well, I won't go into that. And then I found a dead cat in my refrigerator. With a lineup like that, don't you think I deserve a reward?" She plucked the box from its niche. "Yes, I knew you'd agree."

After shaking out one white cylinder, she raised it to her nose and inhaled. The tobacco scent went straight to her head.

She grabbed a matchbook and tore off a stick. She started to light it, then exhaled heavily. "What am I doing?" The image of Ray Milland in *The Lost Weekend* flared in her mind—the alcoholic who hid a bottle in the lamp, just in case he needed an emergency drink.

"I've got to stop tormenting myself." She crumpled the box with her hand. "And answering for Mom—I've certainly taken poetic license there." She tossed the crushed box and cigarette into the trash, then went back into the living room.

Rhett was now cleaning himself, one leg stretched high at an odd angle. "How about a vacation, Rhett? A few days in someone else's home where you'll be safe." She clamped her lips together, saddened that someone might intentionally hurt her cat. Hurt? *Kill.*

The thought numbed her.

One more death will push me over the edge.

Over the edge. Was that Chandler's tactic? If she was deemed mentally incompetent, he could instigate legal maneuvers to wrest away her business. Then he'd get what he wanted, finally. The block in Venice would be his to renovate and sell, making real estate megabucks in the process.

And she'd be left with nothing.

Except her memories.

Tears stung her eyes, rolled slowly down her cheeks, and plopped silently onto the collar of her robe. She didn't hold back, not this time. Giving in to her pain and fears, she let herself have a good cry.

Standing in his dimension, Jake watched the gigantic screen that had materialized before him. Pictured there was Scarlett, huddled on a corner of the sofa in her living room, her head in her hands. Her thin shoulders shook as the sobs grew in intensity.

It tore at his gut to see her in such pain. "Let me go," he said to the gray void that surrounded him. "She needs me."

A black butterfly spiraled overhead, as though delighting in Jake's agony. He clenched his fists. "What's the purpose of her being my destiny if I can't be with her?"

His words echoed around him.

Can't be with her.

Can't be with her.

The repeated message hurt more than if someone stabbed him over and over. He shoved his palms flat against his ears. "No," he yelled. "I won't let you win!"

He concentrated on his breathing and willed himself to remain calm. He wasn't going to get out of this predicament by lashing out in anger. No, he had to rationally think of a way to escape and be with Scarlett.

His entire being was tightly strung, like a bow ready to let his soul fly. He took several steps toward the screen, his arms outstretched. "Let me go to her. I can't bear watching her like this."

Something fluttered near him. He swiped absently at

it, presuming it to be a black butterfly. Then it felt as though fingers ruffled his hair. Yet no one was near—in fact, he'd never seen another soul in purgatory except for Scarlett.

The invisible hand drifted down the side of his face, past his shoulder, and stopped over his heart. He looked down, astounded to see nothing, yet he *felt* it. It pressed against his chest, pushing into him a terrible sadness that made his heart ache.

Scarlett's sadness.

He jerked his head up and watched her on the screen. No mistake, the sadness was from *her*. Sensing Scarlett's emotions so clearly had never before happened while he was here in purgatory. Only when he'd been on Earth, in close proximity to her. What was happening to him? To them? Their worlds had been veering closer lately, sometimes seeming to overlap.

It gave him hope that he could connect with her.

"Scarlett," he called out. "I'm here. You're not alone."

She looked up. Her huge eyes, greener than he ever remembered, searched the room around her. She appeared so innocent and guileless—life wasn't fair to let someone like Scarlett be Chandler's prey.

"I hope you can hear me." He remembered the words she had used to pull him back, momentarily, from purgatory. "With all my being, I *will* you to hear me." He paused, waiting for a response, but there was none. "I won't let you go through this alone. I may not be able to be at your side, but I promise you that you are not alone. At the very least, my thoughts are with you. *Will* be with you, even after you're no longer my destiny.

And my heart—" His voice broke and he realized he was shaking. "My heart," he repeated softly, "is forever yours."

Had she heard him? Her head sank back down, and she covered her face with trembling hands.

He slammed a fist into his palm and glared at the skies. "What can I do, what can I think so you'll let me go? I'm not some caged animal that you let out for good behavior. I'm a man!" He strode in a large circle, unable to contain his fury. "If I promise not to touch her? Promise not to want her? Is that it?"

He scanned purgatory's dome, feeling more alone than he ever had before in this endless tomb. Panting, he stopped his frantic walking and stared at the image of Scarlett. The window to her world tormented him. He could see her, but his hands were tied to help her.

"I thought God was compassion," he said flatly.

In the distance he heard the faint roar of wind. The ever-present gale that moaned ceaselessly through this land.

He leaned back and opened his arms. "I want her. Is that a sin?" Emotions ripped him apart. He sank to his knees and bellowed his rage against a captor who denied him the only happiness he'd ever known.

The phone rang, startling Scarlett.

She snuffled back her tears and stared at it. With her luck it would be Chandler's lawyer, the last person in this world—or any other—she wanted to talk to right now. Next to the last person, she corrected herself. Chandler was at the bottom of the list.

It rang again.

She flicked her wrist, stared at the time, and groaned. When would she remember her watch was broken? She glanced out the window. Dark. Must be close to seven. Long past lawyer's office hours. Safe to answer.

She caught the phone midring. "Hello?"

"You have a cold?" asked Doris after a beat.

"No." She tightened the sash around her robe, purposely avoiding any explanation.

"Ray's is closed."

She knew what Doris was really asking. "I'm okay."

Another beat of silence. "You alone?" In the background little boys laughed and yelped.

"Yes, but it sounds like you're not," answered Scarlett, a hint of amusement in her words. "Are Ramon and Geronimo playing twenty-four-hour tag?"

Doris chuckled. "They're going for the Guinness World Record, what can I say?" She cleared her throat. "Hey, listen, we worry about you. Ramon said the police were in Ray's again."

"They drop by sometimes. You know, since the shooting." Not that she wanted to sound blasé, but Scarlett sensed she had to start keeping a tight lid on what was going on. Like now, some gut-level instinct told her to skip the dead cat story. Doris was an old friend—her mother's best friend—but right now Scarlett didn't trust anybody.

"Ramon said you fainted."

That Ramon was a Hollywood gossip columnist in the making. "Hadn't eaten. Got weak."

"Enrique told me you fed him, but you forgot about yourself? That does it. I'm bringing over some stew."

"I'm going to bed soon."

"I'll spoon-feed you while you sleep."

"I'm not hungry."

"No, you'd rather pass out instead. Be there in ten minutes."

A crisp click ended the conversation.

Scarlett set the receiver back in its cradle, fighting a flicker of anger at her sanctuary being invaded after such a difficult day. "Chill out, Scarlett. Doris is your 'other mother,' remember? So what are you thinking? That she kills cats on the side and wraps them up like hamburger meat? Or worse, uses them to make stew?" She laughed dryly. "If you stop trusting everybody, what's left?"

She picked a magazine off the floor and tossed it onto the coffee table.

It wasn't that she didn't trust Doris with the truth. It was that whoever had broken into Ray's and deposited the cat was either one of Chandler's thugs or someone who knew her Rhett. One of Chandler's thugs would have killed Rhett with no qualms.

So it had to be someone close to her.

Scarlett picked up a wadded paper towel from the top of the bookcase and carried it into the kitchen. Hadn't the police said the back door showed no signs of a violent entry?

She placed her toe against the bottom right corner of the cabinet under the sink. One well-placed toe-nudge and the door sprung wide open. Scarlett tossed the paper into the trash and started to kick the door closed again when her eyes widened.

"So that's it!" She snapped her fingers as a light went on in her head. "Our trick for opening the back door when we forgot our key! Who'd you show that to, Mom? Because I never revealed our secret to anyone."

Leaning against the sink, she tried to remember if she'd ever seen her mom show anyone their door-opening maneuver. But no memories surfaced. She tapped her foot and thought about her mother's friends. "Who did you trust so completely?"

Whoever it was, that person was now a traitor.

She shivered, sickened at the thought of being close to someone who would willingly kill a cat and wrap it up as a sadistic gift. All to frighten her.

She turned on the tap and let it run over the dishes. Against the backdrop of trickling water, her mind wandered over the locals. "Judyl wouldn't hurt a turnip, much less a human being. And Doris is Mother Earth herself—she's incapable of cruelty."

But what if Doris learned the back door secret years ago, and told her son Roger?

Scarlett grabbed a scouring pad and scraped dried food off one of the plates. "How can I be thinking that about Roger? He cried when I got shot. He loved my mother. He would never do anything to hurt me."

But he can't find a job and he's hanging out with gangs. Maybe he's desperate enough to negotiate a deal with Chandler. What had her mother once said? "Desperate people do desperate things"?

She dug harder at the plate, as though she could clean away her incriminating thoughts.

"It would kill Enrique to know Roger would stoop that low. Enrique's courting Doris, probably wants to marry her and share their golden years together. Doris's kids are like his own. If Enrique suspected anything, he'd put a stop to it, pronto."

She rinsed the plate and set it on the counter. *Desperate people . . . Judyl's raising a son in near-poverty conditions. A mother's desperation could override her ethics.*

She cut off the water with a yank of her wrist. "What am I doing?" she half-whispered. "Judging my friends? Maybe I'm the desperate one for condemning innocent people."

A thump on the door made her jump. She stilled her beating heart with several deep breaths. *Don't panic. It's only Doris with dinner.*

"Coming," she yelled.

Ripping off a paper towel, she dried her hands on the way to the door. Suddenly aware that she'd bypassed lunch, her stomach growled at the thought of hot, savory stew.

But when she opened the door, all that greeted her was a passing breeze, bringing with it a hint of honeysuckle. Looking down the sidewalk, she saw no one.

Had she imagined someone knocking? The evening breezes were growing in intensity. Maybe a tree limb had thumped the side of the house.

She started to close the door when she spied the package.

Small and square, it sat in the middle of her small concrete porch. Carefully wrapped in brown butcher paper and twine, it struck her as odd that the sparsely papered box had a very carefully constructed bow.

Her scalp prickled.

Rhett.

She spun around and tore back into the house. "Rhett!"

She ran into the living room. Whirling in a circle, she scanned the tops of the bookcase and TV. No cat. In her urgency to get to the kitchen, she tripped over the coffee table and stumbled several steps. Flailing madly, she landed against a kitchen chair, grabbed hold, and stopped herself from completing a nose-dive to the floor.

Clutching the chair's back, she drew a shaky breath. Her mind felt numb, unable to cope with the possibility that some pervert had found Rhett and . . .

A mew interrupted her thoughts.

"Rhett?" She looked around.

Over the top of the refrigerator, a furry black-and-white head peeked at her with sleepy eyes.

She giggled, the sound unsteady. Like her mind. "Oh, my God, Rhett. If you only knew the small hell I just suffered."

Rhett yawned, stretched his back, and curled back into snooze position.

"Guess you told me." She straightened, then flicked a glance over her shoulder at the still-open front door. So if Rhett was okay, what sadistic "gift" was in the package this time? And how had the package gotten on her doorstep?

She ran halfway down her walk and searched the street. No one. A car's motor droned in the distance—maybe the person had thrown it while driving by? Despite the cool night air, beads of perspiration dotted her brow. She wiped at them and walked back to the porch, hesitating in front of the package.

Leave it where it is.

She stepped over it and went inside. Closing and locking the door, she stood in the middle of her living room, panting as though she'd run a great distance. What she'd give for Jake to appear now. To help her through this latest crisis. "I need you," she whispered to the empty room.

Outside, leaves rustled with a passing breeze.

Alone. When I need you most. She didn't know whether to feel angry at him or sorrowful for both of them.

Shaking away her thoughts, she headed for the phone. *Better call Ramsey. Let him know there's been another special delivery.*

She was two steps from the phone when sharp raps sounded.

"Open up, this pot's heavy, child."

Relief flooded Scarlett as she crossed back to the door and opened it.

"Dinner," Doris chimed. She gripped a blackened pot by its handles. "And mail." She dipped her chin toward her feet. "Nearly stepped on it."

Scarlett took the pot from Doris, gesturing with her head for Doris to follow her inside.

"Oh, and forget the package. I'll get it later." Scarlett had tried to effect nonchalance, but her words sounded wooden, fake.

"Child, you leave your mail outside where anyone can take it?" Doris muttered something under her breath. "Guess I'll have to play mailwoman *and* chef tonight."

Scarlett plunked the container on the kitchen

counter. "I can't believe you carried this heavy pot—could have put some in a bowl, you know. . . ." Her mouth went into automatic babble, but her eyes and mind were cemented to the package Doris had set on the table.

"Next time I'll bring over a helping on a paper plate, just so's you don't carry on so. Lord Almighty, you'd think I had carried in a couch. . . ."

Scarlett stood, frozen, in front of the package, oblivious to Doris's banter. She envisioned another dead animal, its murky eyes staring at her. Blaming her. She fought a rush of dizziness. "I have to call the police," she said breathlessly, her words nearly inaudible. "The package—"

Doris was instantly at her side. "Child, child, you're whiter than a sheet." She draped a large comforting arm around Scarlett. "Poor thing, you're shaking. I had no idea you were doing so badly. I'm gonna get some of this stew in you—then you'll feel better." She bustled away. A cabinet creaked open. "I remember your mama kept salt up here. . . ."

Scarlett's teeth chattered from a sudden chill.

Doris looked over her shoulder. "I heard that. Louder than castanets. Put a sweater on before you catch cold." She went back to rummaging through the spice bottles. "Don't get sick or Doris'll move in and take care of you."

Scarlett walked mechanically into the living room and picked up the phone receiver. After punching in the police number she'd now memorized, she asked for Detective Ramsey.

While waiting for him to answer, she listened to the

sounds of Doris in the kitchen. Bittersweet memories surfaced. Her mother making them a midnight snack after work. Her mother making a quick cup of coffee before she'd leave to open Ray's.

It was also in the kitchen that Scarlett had found her. Lying on the kitchen floor. Aneurysm, they called it. "She never felt any pain," one doctor had promised.

"Ramsey here."

"S-scarlett." She swallowed back a lump in her throat, not wanting to fall apart again. "A package was on my doorstep."

"You home?"

"Yes."

"They patched the call to my home. It'll take a few minutes, but I'll be there."

Scarlett ducked into the bathroom and splashed some cold water on her face. After all her crying, she knew she looked like hell. If Ramsey brought officers with him, she didn't want to appear like some sort of madwoman. Olivia de Havilland in *The Snake Pit* came to mind. Maybe a dash of lipstick would help her look more like a member of the human race.

Swinging open the medicine cabinet, she eyed a pack of cigarettes strategically hidden behind a metal container of Band-Aids. "I'd forgotten about those," she mumbled, grabbing the box and slam-dunking it into the trash.

Finding a tube of lipstick, she shut the mirror door and met herself, face-to-face. "God, I look I've been bled by leeches." She slathered pink on her lips, then rubbed a little into her cheeks. Then she plastered a smile on her face—it looked fairly genuine in the mirror, anyway—and walked back to the kitchen.

Doris was holding the package up for Scarlett's inspection. "What's inside?" Holding it by the twine's loopy bow, the box rotated slowly.

"Put it down," Scarlett said quickly.

Doris flashed her a bewildered look, then set the box back on the table. "Scarlett, honey, I'm worried about you. Ever since we lost your mama, you've been working double-time at Ray's. Plus all the problems you've been having . . ." She gave Scarlett a somber stare that said they both knew what she meant.

Holding her breath, Scarlett stared at the box, half expecting a trickle of blood to seep through. "You're right. Haven't been myself lately. Sorry if I'm acting edgy."

"Forget it," Doris said sweetly as she picked up a spoon and began stirring the pot. The tangy aroma of spices and beef curled through the kitchen. "Is that a gift from your beau?"

It took Scarlett a moment to realize Doris was referring to the box. "Beau?"

"Ramon said you had a boyfriend at work with you today."

She tightened her clutch on the chair. So the little guy had seen Jake? She hadn't been sure whether or not to believe Ramsey. "What did Ramon say about him?"

"You know kids. He giggled something about a boyfriend, but preferred his train set to further conversation." Doris's eyes twinkled as she ladled a hefty portion of the stew into a bowl. "Our little Scarlett finally has a beau. I bet he's out of this world, eh?"

Scarlett laughed nervously. *Oh, if you only knew.*

In his world, Jake contemplated the black specks. Fragments of evil. *They're keeping their distance. Whatever compelled them to attack me is over.*

But an uneasiness lurked in his mind. Something had changed in his world, and not for the better. He now sensed that purgatory had turned against him. Maybe it was ready to dispose of him. Is that why he'd never seen any other being in purgatory—except when he willed Scarlett here? Was it timed to destroy its sole inhabitant if that poor soul failed God's tests? He was beginning to suspect the test had nothing to do with a destiny.

Did it have something to do with his last life?

Was his test to rectify past wrongs by confronting his nemesis, Chandler?

The specks converged into one black mass that swirled in a dizzying circle, then broke apart into hundreds of free-floating fragments.

Chandler. The black specks vibrated like scum on boiling water. *They're reacting to my thoughts?* The swimming dots settled back down into their hovering patterns.

He made a concerted effort to shoot his thoughts at them again. He shouted the single word in his head. *Chandler.*

This time the black butterflies flew together, like pieces of iron drawn by a powerful magnet. They formed a square, eerily sharp at its corners. The huge object began to rotate. Round and round, spinning faster and faster.

The square finally dissolved into hundreds of tiny black dots that flitted here and there.

Jake turned and began walking into nowhere. It seemed he had spent years, ages, eternities, doing this. Walking and thinking. The screen, the porthole into Earth, was now gone. As it did every time, it disappeared on whim, leaving Jake alienated from further contact with Scarlett.

He shrugged into his jacket, wondering why he felt colder than he ever had before. The chill crept down to his very core. He looked back at the floating black butterflies. They seemed so innocent now, fluttering about in this no-man's land.

Except they would annihilate him if he didn't resolve his own destiny. He was now certain of this.

He shuddered. The cold permeated him entirely, as though he'd been submerged in icy water.

"Can I enter the Earth's plane and confront Chandler?" he asked himself. "If so, I'll warn him to stay away from Scarlett." *Warn him? Think again, Jake. The man stirs martinis with threats. What can I say or do to get him to back off?*

He shoved his hands in his pockets and marched along, viewing the eternity of gray under his feet. "What if I play 'ghost' and frighten him?"

He stopped, pleased with this line of thinking. "Yes. Frighten him. Scare the living hell out of him." He looked up at the pewter sky. A black butterfly skittered past, trailed by another. "God, are you listening? If I'm your lost angel, can I play bad ghost without recrimination?"

He didn't expect an answer, and he didn't get one.

"Okay, I'll give it a shot." He looked off into the gray and willed a link to Chandler. In his peripheral vision, he saw the butterflies go crazy with motion. They swerved and plummeted in different shapes as Jake concentrated on his archenemy.

"Chandler," he called.

He waited, focusing his thoughts on the man who wanted to destroy Scarlett.

"Chandler," he yelled.

The screen materialized, filled with fuzzy shapes. Jake stared at the moving patterns, trying to decipher the blurred images. The stray scent of smoke assaulted his nose.

Chandler, he willed. *Chandler.*

The images focused. Chandler sat at a dinner table. Across from him sat his wife, the woman Jake had merged with. She looked gaunt, frightened.

I've got to get in there. Jake channeled all his energy into that single thought. *Get in there.* He felt the tremors that precipitated his entering the Earthly dimension. *In there.*

His body shook with the intensity of his emotions. He glanced at his hands and watched them meld with the gray. I'm leaving here, he thought. Entering Chandler's world.

Every cell of his being vibrated at a rapid rate. Jake gritted his teeth. It had never been this difficult to make the passage, but he refused to release his goal. "Chandler," he whispered through gritted teeth.

He had to pass through.

He had to save Scarlett.

Searing pain, like thousands of pinpricks, attacked his skin. More excruciating than anything he'd ever felt before. They grew in intensity until they felt like stabs that sliced through to his gut. He doubled over and grabbed his stomach, feeling the urge to retch.

Never, never had he suffered such human agony in this realm.

Fighting for breath, he tipped his head up.

The screen was gone.

He hadn't made it.

Blood still roared in his ears from the exertion. "You won't let me get close to Chandler, but you let him get close to Scarlett." Rage tightened his throat. "What kind of God allows Chandler's evil to hurt her while preventing me from saving her?"

"Goodnight, Doris. Thanks again." Scarlett waved as Doris's round body sashayed down her walk.

Doris fluttered her hand over her shoulder. "Don't do anything I wouldn't do," she teased.

Scarlett smiled halfheartedly. She'd led Doris to think the package was from her beau to avert suspicion. Closing the door, she leaned against it, exhausted. Her tummy ached from gobbling two bowls of stew. Consuming hot food in ten minutes flat had left the roof of her mouth feeling permanently raw. It was the only way she knew to get rid of Doris before Ramsey arrived. She didn't want her to witness the detective, and possibly other officers, investigating the package. Conversations about the dead cat were inevitable, and Scarlett didn't want Doris's innocent conversations with others revealing that Chandler's devious scare tactics had worked.

"Chandler's not going to have that satisfaction." She headed for the phone, feeling twenty pounds heavier. "Scaring me into signing. I'm my mother's daughter—I'm made of stronger stuff than that."

She dialed the Venice police again. The sergeant on duty said he'd check on what was holding up Detective Ramsey.

After hanging up, she sank into her armchair. No way would she sit at the kitchen table and stare down that treacherous gift.

Br-r-ring.

Startled by the suddenness of his return call, she lunged for the phone. Probably phoning from his car, affirming he was on his way.

"Detective Ramsey?"

A raspy chuckle was followed by a chilling beat of silence. "Get my package?"

Chapter Thirteen

She opened her mouth to speak, but panic tightened her throat.

"You got my package," he repeated. Not a question this time—obviously her silence had told him she'd received it. She broke out in a cold sweat. The craggy voice was familiar.

"Only have three more days, doll." He laughed, the sound harsh and joyless.

Doll. The man who shot her had called her that. Now Chandler has his thugs calling her, *threatening* her, at home? A rush of anger overwhelmed her fear. Like an unwanted insect, Chandler had invaded her life, personally and professionally, to torment her. Her fury intensified. At him. And at herself for allowing it.

"How dare you," she began, grinding out the words.

A sharp click told her he'd hung up.

Holding the receiver at arm's length, she shook the phone in frustration. "Brave, aren't you, to hang up when you're not getting your way." She slammed the receiver back in its cradle.

Drumming her fingers against the chair's padded armrest, she told herself not to dwell on Chandler's malicious harassment—she had to take constructive action, not dwell on the negative.

But his henchman's words refused to stop echoing in her head. "Only have three more days, doll."

Three days. Like she needed the reminder. Every hour, every minute, she knew exactly which day it was in Chandler's five-day threat. Sometimes she felt like a walking time bomb.

She rubbed the sudden goosebumps on her arms. Chandler was bent on making each of the remaining days a living hell unless she signed.

Br-r-ring.

She jumped and stared at the phone in horror, as though it might transmute into a beast before her very eyes.

Br-r-ring.

Damn that bastard—making her a victim in her home. Afraid to answer her own phone. That's what he wanted, to be her jailer. Well, she'd play this game *her* way.

Snatching the receiver, she held it to her ear without speaking, listening to the hissing silence. *Hard to deliver your threats when you don't know if it's me. How do you like not being in control, Mr. Thug?*

But the static continued, grating on her nerves.

It struck her that maybe this wasn't such a smart

move, after all, playing phone bluff. *But if I hang up, he knows I'm scared.* Her fingers, moistened with sweat, gripped the receiver tighter.

"Ms. Ray? You there?"

Relief swamped her as she switched hands and held the phone to her other ear. "Detective Ramsey," she said breathlessly, wiping her palm on her robe. "Oh God, I'm so glad it's you."

"Just wanted to let you know I'm on my way. It took me longer than I expected to get away."

All business. He had no idea what she'd just been through. Yet his gruffness was reassuring. *Real.* "Thanks"—she paused and gulped a breath of air—"for calling to let me know."

Thirty minutes later the detective towered before her, his bulky frame disproportionate to her living room. Like someone had parked a tank in a compact car space. Dressed in faded brown polyester slacks and his signature rayon jacket, she could tell he'd been at home when he got the call. Probably enjoying an evening off, as evidenced by the patchy five-o'clock shadow on his massive jowls.

He had never looked better to her.

He scratched his chin and looked around the room. "Where is it?"

"Refrigerator."

"Again?" He snarled something unintelligible and rubbed his eyes with his thumbs. "Another dead—?"

"Don't know. Didn't open it. It might have been, well, you know, and I—" She heard herself rambling, but couldn't control it. Her tongue was now in the driver's seat while her mind sat shotgun. She waved a hand toward the kitchen. "Put it in the fridge. No, freezer. Next to the ice cream. Oh God, I'll never eat Rocky Road again. . . ."

He looked toward the kitchen and his body stiffened. Then, in one large movement, his arm swept down and he clamped her elbow under his. "Come on, we're leaving," he instructed, propelling her toward the door.

She stumbled alongside his giant gait. "Where are we going?" Miraculously, they both squeezed through her front door at the same time.

"Move," he ordered. "We're getting in my car."

She balked. Or tried to. But it was like dragging your heels while attached to a speeding train. "What's going on—?"

He had already opened the passenger door to a Pinto that looked as though it had traversed several war zones. "Get in," he barked, shoving her not too politely. She fell in like a sack of laundry just before the door slammed. By the time she scrambled to a sitting position, Ramsey had started the engine and they were peeling away from the curb.

She swiped hair out of her eyes. "What in the hell is this about?" A ghastly mixture of grease and cigarettes assaulted her nose and she sneezed.

"Seat belt." Ramsey was punching in numbers on his cellular phone. "Now," he ordered, stabbing his square-tipped index finger at her.

A prickling sensation chilled the back of her neck.

Ramsey's the traitor.

Why hadn't she seen it before? All along she'd thought it was one of her friends who knew her cat, Rhett. Someone who had known her mother well, who would have known the secret of opening the back door. But it was Ramsey. Of course. He'd been to her place and seen her cat. And wouldn't a detective have all kinds of tricks for breaking into locked doors?

Where was he taking her now? To Chandler?

Get out! She had to get out!

She yanked on the handle and threw her weight against the door. It fell open, her body with it. Grappling with the door handle, chilling wind exploded into her mouth. Below her, the asphalt was a black blur.

Something grabbed her pant leg and jerked her halfway back into the car. She kicked, but Ramsey's hold was like a trap.

"What the—" Ramsey spat a stream of expletives as they struggled. With one hand anchoring her calf, he turned the wheel. As the car swerved toward the curb, a tree trunk rushed toward her face.

"Tree-e-e-e-e-e," she screamed.

The car jerked to the left, missing the trunk by a foot or more, and slammed to a nerve-jangling stop.

Scarlett tumbled into a heap on the floor. Dazed, she lay there, her legs splayed in a most unladylike position. The stench of grease was worse on the floorboard. She wrinkled her nose and fought another sneeze.

Ramsey picked up the fallen cellular phone and squinted at her with a "what the hell?" look. "Sorry, Sam," he said into the phone. "Hit a bump in the road. Uh, she thought we were hitting a tree. Yeah, that's what she was screaming." He unzipped his jacket partway and stretched his neck, never taking his eyes off Scarlett. "As I was saying, might be a bomb. Yeah. Let me confirm." He lowered his gaze to her. "What's your address?"

Bomb? She had tried to escape when he was saving her life? "2120 Waterloo," she answered meekly.

As Ramsey repeated the address into the phone, she unfolded her body and sat back on the seat. Carefully, she pulled her door shut with a discrete click and slumped against the seat, fighting an avalanche of utter humiliation. She stared at the moon, which looked more like a smudge through the dirty windshield.

Probably how Ramsey saw her now—like some kind of a blotch on humanity after that asinine stunt she'd pulled.

Bump in the road? He could have said I tried to jump from the car—and fueled more station rumors that I'm ready for basket-weaving classes. Nope, he covered for me.

I don't deserve his kindness, she thought, indulging herself in a well-earned moment of self-pity. She cringed and sank deeper into the seat.

"Yeah, about a block away," Ramsey continued. "I'll take her to that Denny's on Washington Boulevard. Right. Have my phone with me." Ramsey pushed a button and tossed the phone on the seat next to him.

Slowly, he rolled down his window. A breeze drifted in, sweetening the car's odor with a flowery scent. Finally, in a voice emptied of emotion, he said, "You're a real handful."

"Sorry," she mumbled. A bird twittered outside, mocking her no doubt.

"Trying out for Hollywood Stunt School?"

She fought a smile and chanced a look in his direction. Even in the filtered moonlight, she caught a glint in his eye. "I thought—"

He cut her off. "I was abducting you?"

She nodded, grateful he didn't see the hot flush crawling up her neck.

He tapped his fingers on the steering wheel. "Let me get this straight. You called me, right? On my night off, I might add. I slip my son a twenty to use his car—mine's in the shop—to race across L.A. to help you."

So that's why he's driving this junk heap, she thought.

The front seat creaked as Ramsey shifted his weight. "You found a box on your doorstep. Chandler's been threatening your life. Doesn't take an Einstein to put two and two together. The package might be a bomb. I rush you to my car and we drive away." He expelled a deep breath and scratched his chin. "Except you decide to jump from my moving car, as though a possible bomb threat isn't enough of a thrill for one night."

She nodded, feeling like a little girl being chastised.

He started the car and eased back onto the road. "Yep. My idea of a night off. Thwarting bomb threats and practicing highway heroics."

Ten minutes later, they were huddled in a booth at Denny's. Ramsey had ordered banana cream pie à la mode. Scarlett couldn't fathom the idea of eating even a cracker after devouring two bowls of stew in record time. Plus, images of the refrigerator door bursting open in a loud, crashing explosion made her stomach twist and turn like a rollicking roller coaster.

"I could have been responsible for Doris's death," she mumbled. The realization numbed her. "And

Rhett—" Her voice cracked. "He's still in the house."

Ramsey patted her hand. "It's okay, kid. I asked that the cat be removed. It'll be safe, I promise."

She looked up into Ramsey's protective gaze and had the childish wish that he was her dad.

The waitress slid the piece of pie in front of Ramsey. Scarlett's stew-filled stomach did a triple gainer at the fat wedge of gooey yellow and white.

"Wanna bite?" asked Ramsey, lifting his fork.

"No thanks." As Ramsey ate Scarlett told him about the menacing phone call she had received right before he called.

Ramsey nodded his head and listened as he finished off his pie. When nothing was left on the plate but a few crust crumbs, his phone chirped. Scarlett's heart doubled its tempo as she watched him extend the portable phone's antenna and answer. He nodded at the caller's words, said good-bye, and shoved the antenna back down.

"Well?" she asked, her heart smashing against her ribs.

"You have some explaining to do," was all he answered.

As they walked down the sidewalk to her house, Detective Ramsey took off his jacket and threw it over Scarlett's shivering shoulders. Tumbling winds swayed the juniper bushes that edged her property and blew chills over the scattered police officers and bystanders that covered a wide radius around her home.

"I have a sweater on," she insisted.

"You call that pink strip of fluff a sweater? Keep the jacket."

They turned down her front walk. Shadows moved behind the kitchen curtains, reminding her of her mom's silhouette on the nights she'd come home late.

She pulled Ramsey's jacket tighter around her and brought the collar up to her chin. Nuzzling her face into its warmth, she caught a faint whiff of his after-shave. The familiar scent offered a small security to her whirling thoughts.

Just as they stepped onto the porch, the front door opened. A man dressed in what looked to be a space suit raised a warning hand.

"This is Ms. Ray," announced Ramsey. He put a protective arm around Scarlett's shoulders and ushered her inside.

Inside, Scarlett blinked at the sudden light. She scanned the room's coziness, grateful that the bomb threat had been bogus. At least Ramsey had told her that on the way over, although she was clueless as to why she needed to explain anything.

Ramsey crossed immediately to another man dressed like an astronaut and they began talking in lowered tones. The man handed something to Ramsey. After a few moments, he turned and waggled his forefinger in a "come here" gesture to Scarlett.

She crossed to them, shedding the jacket in the process. The room was uncomfortably warm, as though someone had turned up its temperature.

Closer now, she saw a piece of paper in Ramsey's hand.

He held it out to her. "This mean something to you?"

She took it and read the writing, neatly scripted on a piece of ivory parchment paper.

Thank you for your generous contribution to Home Meals. Your five-thousand-dollar gift will be used to buy meals for needy families in the Los Angeles area. Remember, this gift is tax deductible.

She squinted and reread the message. Looking up at Ramsey and the other policeman, she stuttered, "I-is this a joke? This couldn't be to me."

The policeman's square face remained expressionless as he held up an envelope with her name written in neat calligraphy. Ms. Scarlett Ray.

Ramsey jerked his thumb toward the open cardboard box on the table. Next to it lay the brown paper and string. "The acknowledgment was in the envelope. Both were in there."

She held up the paper and frowned. Then looked at the box, dumbfounded. "Why not simply mail the envelope? It doesn't make sense—"

There had been a distinct thump when the package hit her door. Plus when she had picked it up, it had been heavy, not light.

"There was a rock taped to the bottom of the box," answered the policeman, as though he had read her thoughts.

She mouthed the word "rock," her thoughts scrambling through possible reasons why someone would tape a rock inside the box. To make her think it was another cat?

Or was it easier to *throw* if . . .

"You giving five-thousand-dollar donations these days?" asked Ramsey, interrupting her reverie.

"Are you crazy?" she snapped. "I need my Cuisinart, bedroom window, and watch repaired. If a bomb had been in that box, I might have needed my house rebuilt. And if I had any money left over after that, I'd go out and hire me the biggest and meanest lawyer I could find to squash Chandler."

Ramsey and the policeman exchanged a look.

"To defend me against Chandler," she corrected softly. The piece of paper fluttered as her hand shook. *Great. I've defamed Chandler again in front of witnesses.* She looked at Ramsey and talked with as much calmness as she could muster. "Can't you check with Home Meals and see if they know what's behind this? Someone had to have picked up this certificate. Someone affiliated with Chandler, no doubt."

"We'll call and verify tomorrow," answered Ramsey. "But for now, does it mean anything to you?"

"I worked at a Home Meals fund-raiser." She hesitated, wondering if she should add the rest. "I had a . . . slight run-in with Chandler there." It was public knowledge; she might as well be honest. Besides, Chandler might have complained to the police about her behavior that night—wouldn't this make her seem more believable—more sane—to be forthright?

The policeman nodded to Ramsey and walked over to another group of officers across the room.

"*Slight* run-in?" questioned Ramsey. She didn't miss the droll twist he gave to "slight."

"Okay. Big. Major. I'm sure it's documented by now in the society pages."

Ramsey gently took his jacket from her and extracted his notepad from a pocket. "You didn't mention this before."

She expelled a gust of air. "No. There's been a lot of other things going on."

He shot her an indignant look and lowered his voice. "Run-ins with Chandler aren't 'things.' Doesn't help me do my job if you hold back information."

Over Ramsey's bulky shoulder, she saw the just-departed officer laughing with several other policemen. They glanced at her and she swore they wore matching smirks.

"Oh, God," she muttered. "Another Scarlett Ray crazy tale is making the rounds. Hamburger Lady Claims Bomb Threat. City Block Emptied for Thank-You Note." She emitted a low groan. "Call the psychiatric ward and reserve me a room, would you?"

Ramsey twisted around and pointed his pen at the officers. "That's enough. Party's over." His words reverberated through the room like a lion's roar.

Within minutes the place emptied.

Shutting the front door after the last exiting officer, Ramsey ambled back across the living room and sank onto one end of the couch. He started to put his feet on the coffee table, but caught himself.

"You're the only one who believes me," mumbled Scarlett, fighting a surge of self-pity.

"Well, the thank-you note crisis doesn't exactly help your case. Probably should also let you know that the crime lab only found one set of fingerprints in the back of Ray's. Yours."

"You mean, whoever tied open the back door wiped off all his fingerprints?" She slumped into her armchair with a groan. "So what does that mean? The police now think I tied open my own back door? Why would I do something crazy like that? Do they think I made up the phone call earlier too?"

Ramsey ignored the questions. "It's late. Let's wrap up business. Let's quickly review your evening one more time. What happened after you left the fund—"

A knock sounded. "I'll get it," he insisted, groaning a little as stood.

When he opened the door, a young policeman thrust Rhett into Ramsey's arms, who accepted the feline with much awkwardness, as though the bundle were a newborn babe and not a feline.

"Rhett." Scarlett rushed over to retrieve her beloved pet.

But stopped short.

Crossing her arms, she leveled a look at Ramsey, Rhett, and back again. "Detective," she said in a voice laced with meaning. "How would you like a roommate for a few days?"

Rhett was purring while using Ramsey's massive shoulder as a pillow. Petting the cat's head awkwardly, he answered, "But you need to stay here, close to work. Or so you said when I offered my family's home before."

"Not me." She laughed lightly. "I meant Rhett."

* * *

Judyl wrapped a leaf of lettuce around a pickle. "The *entire* block?"

"That's what it said in the *L.A. Times*," confirmed Doris. She took a sip of cola. "Must have been ten or more families who had to relocate."

"A block? Probably twenty or thirty—"

Scarlett plunked down a jar of mayonnaise. "That does it." She fisted her hands on her hips and narrowed her eyes, hoping her dramatic stance showed she meant business. "Did you two come in here to give me support or rehash the most humiliating experience of my entire life?"

Judyl chomped down on her lettuce sandwich, her big blue eyes staring at Scarlett as though she were a movie in the making. Today Judyl wore a fruit-stenciled curtain that she proudly considered a shawl.

Doris rapidly blinked and cleared her throat to speak. "Sorry. We didn't realize—"

"That one person could cause such a ruckus," cut in Judyl, the words mixing with her chews.

Doris rolled her eyes at Judyl. "That's *not* what I was going to say. She's trying to tell us it was embarrassing enough to have lived through it. She doesn't need us to sit here, retelling it over and over."

"Yeah," concurred Judyl. "She can watch it on the news tonight."

"I said *enough*, you two," chided Scarlett. She rapped on the countertop to divert their attention. "All the families are back in their homes, safe and sound. There was no bomb. All's peachy with the world, okay? Let's move on to another topic."

She turned around and began tidying the grill area.

After a beat, she heard Judyl whisper, "What time did you leave, Doris?"

Doris whispered something back in a hoarse undertone.

I feel like I'm babysitting again, thought Scarlett. But she had to grin. Judyl and Doris had shown up at Ray's first thing that morning, professing undying support. But ever since then they'd been gossiping about the events of last night like it was the biggest news event since Madonna's last boyfriend.

She caught snatches of words. "Box." "Stew." "Boyfriend."

I'm a Hollywood celebrity, mused Scarlett.

But her playful thoughts turned dark when she remembered Chandler's congratulatory note for donating five thousand dollars. The "five" was a cunning twist. By making the contribution that particular amount, Chandler was reminding her she had been given five days to sign the agreement.

Tomorrow was day five.

A trickle of sweat inched down her back.

"Stay cool," she muttered to herself. She flicked a glance out the plate-glass window at the parked police unit. After last night's fiasco, Ramsey had ordered twenty-four-hour surveillance. He had also pulled strings with the telephone company and discovered the menacing call came from a phone booth a block from her home. There was no way to trace the call to Chandler.

Ramsey had also found out that a young, red-haired woman—that's all the sole witness recalled—had donated five grand, *cash*, at the Home Meals office. The receipt was made out to Scarlett Ray.

It didn't matter if Scarlett swore she received the call and didn't donate the money from now until Kingdom Come. She was once again cast in the role of the fool. While Chandler directed the macabre farce.

"Don't worry. I'll think of something to outwit the bastard," had been Ramsey's parting words last night. She had smiled—he didn't realize that holding a pussycat in his arms had severely undermined his macho cop delivery.

She went to the refrigerator and pulled out two packages of meat. The police had already checked them this morning, but her hands still shook as she slowly unwrapped the paper. As she grabbed chunks of the hamburger and molded them into patties, her mind wandered to Jake.

Throughout last night's ordeal, he had never appeared. Not even his voice in her head, which she was certain—fairly certain, anyway—had happened before. By three in the morning, she had been wide awake, thoughts spinning round and round in her head. Was Jake a ghost? An imaginary friend?

Or was she, in fact, suffering psychotic delusions?

She might *think* he's real, but do crazy people know they're crazy?

Her only other witnesses were Ramon and Geronimo, but according to Ramsey, they had only giggled when asked for a description.

So no real proof existed that there was this Jake person. Ghost. Whatever.

Thinking that made her feel empty. Gutted.

* * *

At closing time that night, she stood at the front door of Ray's and flicked off the light switch. "Goodnight, Charlie," she whispered to the shadowed room. Sometimes this was when she missed her mother the most. She could almost hear Alice's lilting voice. "Listen, Charlie's snickering because . . ."

Scarlett quickly shut the door and locked it. Both to Ray's and her memories. Tonight she felt fragile, worn down.

For a moment she stood outside, looking at the Venice sky. A full moon glazed the sky with a pearly glow. Ocean air mixed with the night, a hint of salt intertwined with spring flowers.

A night for lovers.

"Jake?" she whispered. "Can you hear me?"

In the distance, she heard the hum of traffic from the Santa Monica Freeway. A bird flitted by, its wings brushing the air. She glanced down the street at the parked police unit. It was definitely out of earshot, no chance they'd hear her if she tried again.

"Please, be with me. I need you."

A whizzing sound startled her as a kid on his bike careened around the corner. The gangly boy peddled past her, giving her the once-over. "Sure, babe," he yelled over his shoulder. His pubescent voice broke, shooting up an octave on the word "babe." "I dig older broads." Then he laughed, the sound disappearing as he faded into the night.

I call Jake and I get a hormone-driven teenager. She didn't know whether to feel flattered or insulted. "Older broad? I'm not even thirty, and already I'm an older *broad?*" She laughed softly. "That's not how I felt with you, Jake."

For a moment, she thought she saw a form graze the air, its features hazy, as though she viewed it through a mesh screen.

On second look, it was only the threads of moonlight spilling through a tree. A breeze skittered through its leaves, causing gray shapes to flicker across the sidewalk.

Disappointment weighted her thoughts.

"I called, but you didn't come," she muttered as she headed for her car. She felt like a fool, as though she'd been jilted. "Jilted by a ghost?" she mumbled, reaching her car. "Not too many woman can claim that prize."

The black-and-white police car cruised up and slowed to an idle next to her. "Everything okay, Ms. Ray?"

"Fine." Her car keys clattered as she retrieved them from her purse.

"Lock your doors when you get inside."

"Will do," she repeated, feeling artificial in her sweetness. She'd be glad when all this craziness was over and her life was back to normal.

"Another unit is already stationed at your house. We'll follow you home."

The droning voice was familiar. In this night air, she couldn't see George's face, but imagined the teepee eyebrows and the woebegone basset-hound look.

"Just don't tailgate." It was meant as a joke, but George didn't laugh.

"Did you check the back door?"

She stopped and cast a look toward the heavens,

knowing George couldn't see her disgruntled expression. He, like everyone else no doubt, didn't believe for a moment that her back door had been forced open. *But then, they think I'm crazy.*

"Did you lock the back door?" he repeated.

No, I tied it open so I can call you first thing tomorrow. "Yes, it's locked."

Her voice sounded tired and scratchy. The tension, the disbelief, the madness was catching up to her. She opened the car door and slipped inside. The police unit pulled a U-turn and waited behind her.

She twisted the ignition key. Her Honda chugged to life, and she wheeled into the street. The police followed closely. In her rearview mirror, the elongated light fixture attached to the top of the police unit reminded her of a shark's fin.

Hunted by a shark. That's exactly how she felt.

At the corner, she turned right. Rolling down the window, she inhaled deeply the salty sea air. Soon, when all this was over, she'd close up early one day and spend the afternoon in a string bikini, soaking up sun on the beach.

She laughed, remembering her teenage years, most of which were spent frolicking on the sand instead of studying in school. Her mother had weathered Scarlett's rebellious years with stoic grace, even when Scarlett wore black for a solid six months in honor of Boy George.

She passed a wall mural of dolphins and remembered when it had been painted years ago. In fact, right after the mural's completion, she'd had a memorable joyride down this very street. She and her crazy sixteen-year-old friends had slipped the cops by sliding through an intersection at Main, cutting up to Rose, and hiding in one of the apartment complexes on Third.

What I'd give for a joyride again. Free and wild. No cares. No Chandler.

Ahead, the intersection lights at Main changed to yellow.

She felt giddy, like she was sixteen again. Ready to risk it for a moment's freedom. From cops. From her worries.

"What's George gonna do? Arrest me?" She jammed her foot on the gas. "They think I'm crazy anyway." She slid into the intersection and turned the wheel just as the light flashed red. Her car swiveled left onto Main. Gunning it, she glanced in her rearview mirror. The police unit sat, trapped by cross traffic.

A siren burst to life.

George was ready to play cat and mouse.

"Come on, baby," Scarlett coached her Honda. The tires squealed as she made a sharp turn up Rose. The car's back end fishtailed. A loud clunk told her she'd banged against the cement center divider.

I've probably gouged a nice dent into my bumper. She laughed out loud. A dent was a small price to pay for freedom!

She jammed her foot on the gas pedal and raced for Third Avenue. The siren wailed behind her, but she saw no flashing lights in her rearview mirror.

"Looking good." She giggled as she swerved into an apartment complex on Third that she knew had plenty of parking spaces concealed from the street. She drove into one, turned off her lights and motor, and twiddled her fingers toward the diminishing siren. "So long, Georgie."

After several minutes of silence, she restarted the car and headed toward Pico Boulevard.

Sweet freedom.

Stopping at a red light, she watched as a group of kids danced across the crosswalk in front of her. What was that look? Grunge? One of the boys winked.

She winked back.

Not bad for an old broad.

The flirtation brought Jake to mind. What had he said to her? That whenever he desired her, God pulled him away?

The light turned green and she punched the gas pedal. "But my calling for you tonight had nothing to do with *your* desiring me, but *my* need for a friend. Kinda blows your theory, doesn't it, Jake?" Tears blurred her vision and she swiped them away. On her right she saw an X-rated motel that promised racy movies for no extra charge. One of the films was advertised as "Naughty Cherubs."

Scarlett had to laugh despite her tears. "Naughty Cherubs? Think I've *lived* that one." It felt good to laugh, even at herself. She wanted to escape, to breathe—not dwell on her pain.

She headed toward Highway 101, feeling better than she had in a long time. She felt like a bird, soaring free, unencumbered by life's troubles. On her right was the large expanse of the Pacific Ocean—its darkness blending with the night sky. Strings of lights defined the locations of restaurants, homes, and beach parking lots. She snapped on the radio and hummed to the tunes.

The cool, salty air invigorated her skin. She knew her hair was frizzing—at sixteen, she would have been mortified. Tonight, it felt glorious.

She was on a stretch of 101 that spun through the night like an invisible thread. Farther down the road lay the seaside town of Redondo Beach. It would be ten or more minutes before she hit those bright lights. Maybe she'd stop for a cup of coffee, make small conversation with a waitress. She wouldn't be Scarlett Ray, but someone with a simple-sounding name. And life. If asked, she'd say her name was Mary Brown. Yeah, that sounded pretty normal. For a few stolen minutes, she'd be Mary Brown.

A person no one wanted to destroy.

She touched her tongue to her lip and tasted the light film of salt. Waves crashed in the distance. Like drops of captured moonglow, a dotted line of reflectors led her through the darkness.

Light slashed through the car. Glancing in the rearview mirror, she saw a car following too closely, its bright headlights stinging her eyes. She flicked the rearview mirror, dulling the reflection.

"Great. George found me." *And I thought of him as a basset hound. More like a bloodhound.*

The lights flicked high beam, the splash of harsh light making her wince. "Damn, he's right on my tail."

She pressed her foot a little harder on the gas. "This is my big outing, George. What are you going to do? Make me go home at gunpoint?"

Squinting into the mirror, she noticed the roof of the car was smooth. No mounted lights.

No shark.

She edged her foot off the gas and her car slowed a little. *That's no police car. Just another hyper L.A. driver who's in a hurry to get nowhere.*

The lights loomed closer.

Scarlett pulled her foot all the way off the gas. "Get a hint, bub. I'm going to enjoy this drive, so pass me." All day long people drove her with their requests. I want my burger well done. Rare. Extra relish. Hold the relish. This moment, this drive, was all hers. She was tired of taking orders. The car was going to have to pass her.

Thump.

She lurched forward, her fingers losing their grip on the wheel.

Her headlights swerved. The car bounced over raised indentations along the road's edge.

Bump-bump-bump-bump-bump . . .

Her head bobbed and jerked. Pain shot through her lip. A taste of iron flooded her mouth.

She grabbed the wheel and gave it a sharp jerk left.

Her headlights swept strokes of white across a hill on the other side of the road.

I'm going to hit oncoming traffic!

She screamed.

Straighten the car. Get back on the road. She tugged the wheel. The car weaved back into the right lane.

As though nothing had happened, she found herself driving toward Redondo Beach. Just as she'd been doing before.

Her lip throbbed. Touching it, she felt something sticky dribbling down her chin. Blood.

She hunched forward and tightened her grip on the wheel. What had happened?

What about the car behind her?

She glanced into the rearview mirror. The twin lights were small, probably a good quarter mile behind her.

If it wasn't George, then it must be . . .

The matching circles of light were growing larger in her mirror. "Damn." She smashed her foot on the gas. "Go go go," she yelled at her car. She'd stop at the first place in Redondo and call Ramsey. He'd be pissed at her stupidity, but that was the least of her worries right now. . . .

She glanced at the headlights, now bright circles of light in the mirror.

Closer than before.

Crr-aack.

Scarlett's body jerked forward. Her head hit the steering wheel, then snapped back against the head rest. Her hand flailed out and smashed the horn. The loud blast ruptured the air.

Tires screamed.

The stench of rubber.

Her car rumbled threateningly as it again crossed the warning bumps along the road's edge. But instead of riding those bumps as she did before, her car passed over them.

She was heading toward the beach.

Out there in that pitch black, what did Chandler plan?

Get back on the road!

She struggled with the wheel, but something forced her on a different course. Her headlights danced off portions of a fence and the car bucked as she ran over something large.

She screamed and grabbed at the wheel.

Blinding light stung her eyes. In horror, she cut a look behind her. Behind the car's lights, all she saw was a rounded dark hump. Like a faceless monster.

"Stop it!" she screamed.

She was being driven, literally, along the road's shoulder.

She spied another pair of headlights approaching on the far side of the highway. She smashed her fist on the horn. Then hit the horn over and over, hoping the blasts of sound would alert the passing driver.

"Help!" But her cry was swallowed into the night air.

The distant car whizzed past.

She shoved the wheel with all her might. *Get back onto the road. Get back*. The left tires rattled again over the warning bumps, whose tempo increased. The car behind her had sped up.

She was racing toward certain death.

Her hands, slick with sweat, grappled with the wheel. "I don't want to die," she cried out, her words surprising her with their ferocity. "Oh God," she sobbed. "Please, I want to live."

Something warm, like heated liquid, filled her. Her fingers curled around the steering wheel, their hold strong, firm. Her peripheral vision caught flashes of color that seemed to hover next to her. The tinkling of wind chimes filled the car.

She shot a look to her right.

Jake.

The wind whipped his long dark hair around his face, yet he didn't seem to notice. His eyes, black with determination, stared straight ahead. His jaw was grimly set.

In that single moment, Scarlett knew many, many things as his emotions bombarded her. An ache sliced her heart—from his desire to protect her. A chilling agony because he might fail her. Without a doubt, she knew he would sell his soul to defend her.

That he would battle hell itself if it meant saving her.

He leaned closer to her. His thigh pressed against hers as his arm stretched around her shoulder.

Her breath caught in her throat. An internal fire flamed through her torso.

She looked down. His hand passed through her chest, the movement rippling her body as though it were made of water, not flesh. His arm now encased her left arm as his left hand melded with hers.

Was she still holding the wheel, or was it Jake? She swallowed a gasp and looked back at him. He loomed closer until she felt his cheek against hers. The roughness of his skin burned against her; his breath singed her skin. He never broke his concentration, intensely facing what lay ahead, his face dark with purpose.

Ducking her head, she saw that half of her body had melded with Jake's. Like a double-exposed picture.

"Don't be afraid." His voice resounded in her head, deep and sonorous. Then his entire body slid into hers.

A glow filled her, as though every cell of her being had been injected with . . . joy.

Where she saw her legs, she also saw his. Inside, her heart beat at a furious tempo, doing the work of two. She looked again at the steering wheel. Another pair of hands—Jake's now enveloped hers, yet she still saw her own through his.

Surreal, but not in the least fearful, they were now one.

A loud crack exploded through the car.

The world flipped upside down. Her head banged against the headrest. Her stomach lurched as her body strained against the seat belt.

God, the car's rolling.

Her mouth opened in a silent scream as she clutched the steering wheel. The car rotated and lurched; the world appeared like snapshots.

Jake's hands—and hers—on the wheel.

Stars whirling past.

A section of fence.

Stars again.

Crashing, clattering sounds rang in her ears as the car turned over and over. She smelled sandalwood. Sea air. Tasted something metallic. Blood, from her cut lip? Or the taste of fear?

This is it, she thought. *This time, it's really the end.*

In the distance, waves pounded the shore. Slow, rhythmical. Lulling her.

Maybe death wasn't so bad, after all.

"It's not your time."

Jake's voice again. It filled her head, comforting her, reminding her of another voice. . . .

The rocking stopped abruptly. With mild surprise, Scarlett realized she still sat behind the wheel. In front of her, there was nothing but an endless stretch of sand. Above it, the starry sky with its pearlescent moon.

Transfixed by the moon, she stared as it shifted color, its milky glow deepening to amber. Its roundness metamorphosing into a golden door.

The same door she had seen that night she'd been shot.

"It's not your time," repeated the voice in her head.

Jake's voice.

Had it also been Jake's voice that other night? Had he sent her back to Earth?

The moon shrank into a white circle again.

Suddenly she was aware of the motor still chugging. Glancing out her window, she saw the highway to her left. Surprisingly, only ten or so feet away. The car must have rolled along the shoulder. Looking back down at the steering wheel, she watched Jake's hands turn the wheel, her fingers moving with his. The car glided across a short stretch of sand.

Then hit the road with a sharp bump.

Scarlett swallowed hard, tasting again the blood from where she bit her lip. From the open window, she smelled the pungent sea air. Cool breezes rippled through her hair, caressed her face.

She felt as though she'd held her breath forever. Finally, she released a pent-up sob of relief. "Jake, you saved my life." Her throat hurt when she spoke. Vaguely, she remembered her terrified screams before Jake entered the car.

The other car. Was it still there?

Scanning the area, she saw nothing but the sky, sand, and road. The rearview mirror reflected only a rectangle of black. The thug must have driven away after forcing her off the highway and witnessing the car's rolling. Probably hoped she was dead. Or hurt. He'd undoubtedly hightailed it out of there in record time. Chandler's henchmen were very good at not being caught at the scene of the crime.

She was shaken, but not broken. Breathing in deeply, she whispered, "Thank you, Jake."

But when she loosened her grip on the steering wheel, it was only her hands she now saw.

"Jake?" She twisted her body and searched the car.

She was alone.

Chapter Fourteen

Scarlett stumbled into the beach diner and looked around for a pay phone.

A burly short-order cook eyed her from the kitchen serving window. He swatted a small silver-domed bell several times. Each reverberating tinny smack aggravated Scarlett's already frazzled nerves.

"Order up." He didn't speak, he barked. A nervous-looking waitress scurried over, piled her arms with plates, and headed to the back of the restaurant.

He checked out Scarlett. "You lookin' for something?" he asked, rolling a toothpick in his mouth.

"Phone." She faked a smile, not wanting him to think she was desperate. Out of control. Frightened out of her gourd. Right. How many women with cut lips smiled? I probably look like this month's cover girl for *Collision Babes*.

He squinted at her, then lifted a beefy arm and pointed. "Around the corner, next to the bathrooms."

She nodded her thanks and followed the directions he'd given. Past the kitchen, and lodged squarely between Ladies and Gentlemen, the phones were lined up against a graffiti-scribbled wall. She punched in 911 and a composed female voice answered.

"Detective Ramsey," Scarlett croaked into the receiver. She winced slightly. That had been a stupid idea to force a smile. Squeezing lemon juice into her cut would have been less painful.

"Is this an emergency?"

"Yes. Yes. I need Detective Ramsey. *Now*. This is Scarlett Ray." *I sound like a robot trying to talk without moving my lips.*

"One moment. I'm putting you on hold," was followed by an unreassuring clink.

Scarlett caught a glance of herself in the mirrored plate that covered the front of the phone. Her face looked positively gaunt. Her hair stuck out at all angles, giving her the appearance of a copper-headed Medusa. Her eyes, drained of color, looked like two holes in her face. The tear in her lip completed the Woman-Desperado-from-Hell look.

"Ms. Ray?" The dispatcher was back on the line.

"Yes."

"Detective Ramsey is off duty."

"Could you call him at home?" She hadn't had to ask last night to have her call forwarded, but she stopped herself from saying as much. It was imperative she come across as reasonable and sane. "Please," she added, trying to control her voice so it didn't warble.

"What's the problem?"

"I—" What could she say? *One of Chandler's thugs just ran me off the road, but fortunately my ghost-lover-mind-figment saved me by doing a Vulcan-like mind meld, except this was a full-body thing.*

She loosened her death grip on the receiver. It was a losing battle. She drew in a calming breath. "I need to discuss something urgent with him." She congratulated herself on sounding brilliantly sane—this dispatcher wouldn't dare believe any station gossip about the Madwoman of Venice, Scarlett Ray.

"Ms. Ray, this is an *emergency* line. If you wish to make a personal call to Detective Ramsey, please call the LAPD's central switchboard, 555-9786."

"But—"

The woman repeated the number as though she were a machine.

Scarlett muttered her thanks and hung up. Her lips trembled. Her hands shook. A fat tear welled in her eye, but she gritted her teeth and swiped it away. No way would she crumble. Not now.

She started to lift the receiver to call the police, but changed her mind. They thought she was nutso—why bother dealing with them again? No, she'd drive home, explain her Indy 500 escapade to whatever lucky policeman waited for her. Then she'd dig out Ramsey's home number on the card he'd left her and call him.

I need to settle my nerves before tackling that lonely stretch of 101 again. She was certain the thug had bolted—probably back in L.A. by now. But she needed to get a handle on her emotions, on her *sanity*, before sliding behind the wheel again.

She leaned against the wall, suddenly drained of energy. *Jake, I wish you were here. I need you as much now as I did on the road . . . maybe more.*

With a weary sigh, she forced herself to go into the ladies' bathroom where she dabbed at the cut on her lip with a damp paper towel. After splashing some cold water on her face, she felt partially revived. A cup of coffee before hitting the road would give her the extra boost she needed.

After leaving the ladies' room, she walked to the long faux-wood-paneled counter dotted with napkin holders and randomly placed bottles of ketchup. The line of round brown vinyl-covered stools was empty, so she had her pick. She chose one in the middle. It felt safer, even more companionable, to be surrounded by seats on both sides, even if there were no people in them.

Directly across from her, the cook slugged down a glass of water and met her gaze. The smell of fryer grease and sizzling hamburgers reminded her of Ray's. Brotherhood of the Hamburger Joints. She felt oddly at home.

"Traveling?" he asked. She noticed the tattoo on his bicep. It looked like a well-endowed woman wearing a hula skirt.

"Uh, yeah." She didn't want to divulge too much, just in case. Her paranoia, right or wrong, dictated her life these days. She'd even parked behind a Dumpster in the parking lot, in case someone recognized her car and guessed she was inside the restaurant.

"Hungry?" He crossed his arms and leaned his elbows on the service window. The hula dancer's breasts expanded slightly.

"No, I'm just gonna have a cup of coffee." The thought of wrapping her hurt lip around anything turned her off to eating.

He stuck his head out the service window and glanced toward the back of the restaurant. "Wanda's still trying to figure out who got what." He shook his head, obviously disgruntled. Plucking the toothpick from his mouth, he tossed it into a glass that contained other partially chewed wooden sticks. "I'll get your coffee."

He disappeared, then reappeared through a swinging kitchen door on her left. His white apron was splattered with grease and a piece of lettuce hung doggedly onto his stained tee shirt.

"Cream?" He set the coffee mug in front of her. Along with the chicory aroma, a strong male scent also reached her nose. Musky.

"No. Thanks." She chugged a quick sip to avoid his gaze. To her surprise, the cut on her lip fared well. The warm coffee was like a salve.

"You married?"

His bluntness took her by surprise. "Y-yes," she stuttered. She gulped down another mouthful of the warm brew, mainly to hide the telltale lie in her eyes.

Yet in that moment, she knew it was a truth that transcended reality.

She'd never acknowledged it before now, but she was committed to Jake. When had that realization occurred? Back on the road, when their bodies had merged and their hearts had beat as one? When they'd made love? Or when he'd first appeared under the streetlight outside Ray's, and she'd experienced his gut-wrenching emotions, so akin to her own?

Whichever, she was now left with an inner intuition, a *knowing*, that they were soul mates. And that her life was forever changed.

She took another sip of coffee, cupping the mug with her hands and relishing the heat. Jake was always with her. Not physically, necessarily. But in her heart.

"Yes, I'm married," she said with more authority.

All the way home, she marveled at what had transpired in her life.

Scarlett shrank into her armchair, trying to avoid Ramsey's vehement disapproval.

"Even I'm beginning to wonder if you've gone bonkers!" he said, his voice rising to a harsh decibel. Immediately, he raised his hands in an apologetic gesture. "Sorry. Didn't mean to yell." He cast her a look that made her dismally sorry she'd let him down.

She had made it home in record time to find the police—plus an angry Ramsey—waiting outside her home. Like that Alan Ladd movie where the cops had staked out Veronica Lake's apartment. Only Ramsey looked more like Broderick Crawford than Alan Ladd.

And she looked more like Mary Poppins on spin cycle than the luscious Veronica Lake.

She had tried to explain about the hit-and-run incident—pointing to the bent chrome and dented metal on her traumatized Honda as evidence. Not one officer said a word during her show-and-tell. Finally Ramsey cooly stated that she'd been seen fishtailing around

Rose, her car banging against the divider like a pinball racking up more points.

"Your joyride did the cosmetic surgery, not some bad guy," he'd added.

Insult to injury. She scanned the crowd of uniforms, seeing in their faces what they thought of her. Scarlett the hamburger slinger gone bad. The reckless joyrider. The liar. No doubt George the Basset Hound had dutifully recanted her wild escape, complete with the fender-bender incident. They probably thought she'd driven that way after he lost track of her—crashing and bumping into more cement dividers and walls, which explained to them how her car ended up looking like it had been through a war zone.

To try to get them to believe she'd almost been killed would be written off as more lunatic rantings. Mustering any remaining shreds of her dignity, she had turned away and walked into her house.

Twenty minutes later, alone in her living room with Ramsey, he was finally losing steam. He looked at her, the glint in his eyes softening. "Crazy fool-headed kid," he mumbled, shoving his hands into his pockets. "I don't mean to get so damn mad—it's just—"

"It's okay." She hoped that by saying it she would believe it.

He rubbed his thumb along his jaw. "George called the chief—well, they're brothers-in-law, makes sense I guess. Anyway, George blabbed all about the high-speed chase—"

"High speed? I wasn't going over thirty—"

"What if he—or you—had hit a pedestrian or another car?" He scratched the bridge of his nose and stared at the carpet. "I'm yelling again." He looked back at her. "But you don't seem to realize how lucky you are you didn't cause a twelve-car pileup—"

"I'm lucky I'm not dead after what Chandler pulled." She stared down Ramsey, daring him to cut her off. "I was forced off the road, no matter what George—or any of those other blue suits—thinks." She shifted in her chair, her back stiffening with anger. "After losing George, I drove quite sanely, thank you. If I had known Chandler's thug was following me, I'd never have wanted that taste of freedom."

After a long pause, Ramsey said matter-of-factly, "I didn't listen to you, kid. Sorry."

She wanted to continue her diatribe, rub it in harder. But all she could do was wobble her head in agreement. "Yes, that's right. You didn't listen." Her voice had grown childish, hurt. "Outside, all of you looked at me like I was some wayward teenager who went on a wild joyride. Twelve-car pileup? Jeez, who do you think I am? Clint Eastwood in a bra? If so, we're all starring in *Magnum Farce*, thanks to Chandler's manipulations."

She had meant her speech to be serious, and, she hoped, guilt-provoking. But when she hit the Clint Eastwood line, she had definitely undermined her dramatic intentions. Damn it, she still wanted Ramsey to feel guilty for what he'd said to her.

Too late. She caught the flicker of amusement that crossed his features. "Eastwood in a bra?" He pressed his forefinger against the corner of his mouth, as though warning it to not laugh. "Let me guess. Was that what he wore in *Dirty Henrietta*?"

Her well-honed fury dissolved into a rash of giggles. Ramsey joined in with his baritone laughter. For a moment, their shared humor was a greater freedom than those few minutes of her "joyride."

Swiping at a laugh-induced tear, she noticed that Ramsey was now frowning, seemingly stuck on a thought.

She waited a beat to see if he'd explain his change of mood. "What?" she finally prodded. "What's on your mind?"

He turned slightly, avoiding her gaze. "I believe you, even if no one else—" He spun around. "Damn it. I'm the only cop who doesn't think you're one sandwich short—"

"Of a buffet," she finished.

"It's hurting your case. I can't—" But instead of finishing his sentence, he muttered something unintelligible.

He didn't have to explain. She knew Ramsey's hands were tied if the police thought she was certifiable. Casting her gaze at the carpeted floor, she mumbled, "Tomorrow's day five."

Ramsey sighed heavily. "I know."

She looked back up and pinned him with her eyes. "He's going to kill me." She had been trying to be brave, but her flippant comments and thoughts were sorry disguises for her real emotions. Tonight was her last night on the planet Earth. And nothing short of dynamite could shake that feeling from her gut. Somehow Chandler was going to get to her. "I'm scared. Really scared."

Ramsey threw a punch to the air. "Damn that sonofa—" He bit off the rest, turned, and faced her. "Might as well tell you now. The cops have withdrawn their support."

"What?"

"Your stunt tonight was the last straw. Chief gave the word—LAPD services are no longer available to protect—"

"Great. Just great." She didn't know if she wanted to laugh or cry. "I think I'm hysterical," she whispered before slumping back down into her armchair.

"I won't leave you alone." Ramsey's voice had dropped to a formidable coldness. "Can't stay inside your house—department policy—but I'll sleep outside in my car. I promise you'll be safe."

She nodded, grateful for the warming stream of relief that seeped through her. It wasn't enough to diminish the cold in her veins, but it offered hope. Hope that tonight she'd be protected.

He crossed to her phone and, lifting the receiver, said in an aside, "Need to call my wife, tell her what I'm doing."

After he finished the call, he turned and faced her again. "Tomorrow I'll escort you to work. I'll be at Ray's before closing time so I can escort you home again."

"You can't be my full-time bodyguard—you have a real job. Besides, when are you going to sleep?"

"I'm an old hand at catnaps. Besides, tomorrow's my day off—"

"Your day off? What about your family—"

"—And . . ." Ramsey raised his voice to drown her rebuttal. "If I want to be a one-man SWAT team on my day off, that's my damn business and nobody else's. Including yours, young lady."

Scarlett wanted to argue with him, tell him it was stupid to feel that responsible, but the "young lady" caught her by surprise. "You sound like a dad. I feel like I'm being sent to my room."

For a long moment, they held each other's gaze. "I know you're afraid," Ramsey said simply. "But you'll never be alone. I promise you that."

His words, for a fleeting instant, echoed what Jake had once said.

In the darkness of her room, she snuggled under the covers.

Tomorrow was day five. Although she had tried to suppress that thought, it kept popping back up to her consciousness like an answer in a magic eight ball. Day five, the last day of Chandler's threat.

She balled herself into a fetal position, closing in on herself for comfort.

After tomorrow, what? Would Chandler stop pressuring her to sign? Not likely. When she'd brought that concern up to Ramsey tonight, he said not to sweat it—that he'd think of something to thwart Chandler's extortion attempts once and for all. As much as she placed her trust in Ramsey, she had a sickening feeling that one LAPD detective was no match for Kenneth Chandler.

She rolled onto her back and stared out her window at the deep purple hues of night. Along the distant horizon, she watched the shimmering lights of L.A., the never-dying city lights. Tinseltown.

"City of Angels," she said quietly to herself.

It seemed that a piece of the distant lights broke off and rolled toward her window. As it drew closer, she saw its colors more clearly. Dazzling white mixed with pink and yellow.

She leaned up on one elbow and stared. In the beginning when such spectacular light displays occurred, she'd been terrified.

Now she felt hopeful.

"Jake?"

She didn't care if it was her mind creating this dazzling show. Didn't care if he was a supernatural being. A ghost. A figment.

Nothing mattered but to see him, be with him.

The light exploded silently against her window, causing the glass pane to burst into a sheet of flames. She squinted at the brilliance. Her face felt hot, as though a fire burned before her.

Through her narrowed eyes, she detected a human form through the refulgence. One moment it was fiery, glowing—part of the dazzling light show. The next it was a sharp-edged silhouette that separated from the radiance and stepped onto the floor.

A man.

His shoulders were hunched, as though he were burdened with sorrow. The blazing image behind him faded until the window glowed with the barest hint of gold.

"I was almost too late. You might have died," he said, his voice little more than a hoarse whisper.

A breeze wound its way around her, enveloping her with profound regret.

Jake's regret.

"You mean what happened on the highway?" In the window, the lingering spark of gold vanished. She could barely make him out now in the room's darkness. If it wasn't for the trailing scent of sandalwood, she wouldn't have known he was there.

She threw back the covers and got out of bed. The worn wooden floor was cool and smooth underneath her bare feet. After several steps, she reached into the shadows. She felt his leather jacket, its texture buttery to her touch. Tentatively, she moved her hand up to his muscled shoulder, along his neck to his taut jaw.

Continuing upward, she lightly touched his lips and traced their fullness. And the slight indentation above his mouth. Her fingers brushed the stubble along his chin and jaw. At first, hadn't he been clean-shaven?

Now he felt more human.

More male.

She brought her own mouth close. So close, the skin on her face tingled from his warm breaths.

"Hold me," she said in a low tone, unzipping his jacket.

His arms wrapped around her, then pulled her against him. In the dark silence, she pressed her breasts against his chest, seeking his heartbeat with her flesh. It reminded her of when they had been one and their hearts beat in tandem.

For a long moment, they didn't move. Didn't speak. They clung to each other, both knowing any moment he might be pulled back to purgatory.

"Scarlett," he murmured. His hair brushed her cheek. His lips nuzzled against her ear, the heat of his words inflaming her skin. "I know you question yourself. And me." His voice caught and he moaned, a sound filled with pain and yearning. "I've questioned myself as well. But being with you, knowing you, I've never felt as human, as much of a man—"

Standing on tiptoe, she brushed her lips against his. Small fires burned where they touched.

"I don't care," she whispered, "if you're a ghost. If I imagine you." He scattered kisses across her mouth. She leaned back, shuddering a sigh as his lips trailed a smoldering path down her neck. "I don't care because I need you," she added softly.

Cushioning her head with his hands, he silenced her with a kiss. She felt herself go limp as his tongue sought entrance between her lips. Tremors of desire rippled through her.

When Jake pulled away, she gasped. Her body was gorged with need. Blood pounded in her ears. As though from far away, Jake's voice threaded its way into her mind.

"I need you too, Scarlett. God, I need you."

For a moment the world stilled.

Then, like an unleashed storm, he crushed her against him, his lips devouring hers. Working his fingers into her hair, he pulled her harder against him. Entrapping her to his need. His passion chafed her lips and she winced slightly.

He pulled away with a violent movement and held her at arm's length. Through labored breaths, he uttered, "I shouldn't have—"

She reached up, clutched the lapels of his jacket and tugged him back. "I won't let you go," she warned, her lips moving against his as she spoke. "Until I've loved you."

Her scent, faint like roses, intoxicated his senses. Stray moonlight reflected the highlights of bronze and copper in her hair. He swept his hands under her nightgown. God, he felt drunk with the silkiness of her skin. He cupped her breasts, his thumbs teasing the hardened peaks. She moaned, triggering memories of watching her pleasure.

The way her skin flushed from their lovemaking.

The way she looked when she cried his name.

"I need to see you," he murmured, deftly lifting her gown over her head and letting it drop silently to the floor.

He reached over and flicked on her nightlight.

She stood before him naked, her swollen lips slightly open as she panted.

"Take me," she said, her words breathy with desire. "Take me before I lose you."

Scarlett awoke with a jolt and blinked at the darkness. Wrenched from sleep, she was instantly, strangely awake. What time was it? She stretched her neck and peered at the green digital numbers on her clock. Three-thirty. What had made her wake up at this time of the night?

Something rustled.

Her pulse rate doubled. She inhaled a slow stream of air while gliding her gaze across the room, right to left. Through the window, stray moonlight cast a pearly rectangle across her bed. Outside the light's parameters, shadows bunched and hovered like phantom bystanders.

Nothing moved.

Beyond her window, a dog barked. From a neighboring house, a baby cried. Everyday, normal sounds.

My imagination again. She smiled, glad to release the last few moments' anxiety. She didn't have to fret; after all, Ramsey was outside watching over her. All the windows and doors were bolted and locked.

She was safe.

She lay back and snuggled under the warm covers.

Swish.

Her ears burned hot as her hearing sharpened.

Swish. Like a fingernail scratching against corduroy.

Something, someone, was definitely in her room.

Over the edge of the blanket, she peered at the giant black shape that she knew to be her dresser. Had it come from over there? She lay still, not daring to breathe.

Creak. Swish.

Cold sweat dotted her brow. She clutched the blanket with trembling fingers. Ramsey? Had he come back into the house? If so, wouldn't he have turned on the living room light? Or *said* something, so she'd know he was inside and not be afraid?

"Ramsey?" Her voice sounded thin. She took a deep breath and tried again. "Ramsey?"

No answer.

Slowly, slowly, she scanned the room, dissecting the dark shapes. The squares of her bookcase and dresser, the tile-shaped blots of her pictures, the silhouette of her chair. Somewhere within those shady lumps and curves, the sound hid.

Under these circumstances, only one person had access to her.

"Jake?" she whispered. After their heated lovemaking, he had done his usual disappearing act. Torn back to purgatory again. Had he returned? Why didn't he say something?

A shadow peeled off the wall and hovered at the foot of her bed. Round and misshapen, the opposite of Jake's lean silhouette.

Run! Scream!

Her body refused to budge. Her vocal cords froze.

Snap. A whisper of sulfur.

A small flame burned. In its yellow flickering glow, she recognized the beady eyes that glowered at her.

The thug who shot her.

The match fizzled as the flame shrank. Darkness again swallowed the room. He stood on the edge of the patch of moonlight, his form melding with the room's shadows. From the darkness, he chuckled. A raspy sound that made the hairs on her arms stand on end.

"Having a bad dream?" That Brillo pad voice. Unmistakable.

She drew a strained breath. "How did you get in?"

"Doesn't matter."

"Wh-what do you want?"

"Mr. Chandler doesn't like you playing hard to get."

"I'm not—"

"Cut the bull."

"The police are outside. They're patrolling my

house." Her throat, dry with fear, gave her words a raspy edge.

"Since when do cops cater to screwballs?"

It took her a moment to comprehend what was beneath his words. He *knew* the police thought she was crazy.

Chandler has inside ties with the LAPD.

Another match flared. It moved backwards and touched the wick of a candle that sat on her dresser. The candle's flame grew until its glow glazed the man's black, lumpy shape.

He looked like a squat demon at the foot of her bed. The buttery light traced half his face. The rounded cheek. The stubbly chin. The swollen lips that had spat obscenities and blood at her a few weeks ago.

He flicked his wrist and extinguished the match. "Nice touch." He tipped his head to the candle. "For romantic evenings in bed?"

"The police—"

"Shut up." He pulled something from his pocket. "One guy is outside in his car. No other cops, so quit with the threats."

Had he hurt Ramsey? She swallowed back a rising fear, its taste sour in her throat. Ramsey. She wanted to cry out. Beg for mercy. But an inner voice warned her to stay cool. Instinctively she knew this thug craved her fear—probably got excited by it.

"I'll call Chandler in the morning," she said with forced élan. When there was no response, she continued, "I don't want to . . . cause any more . . . problems for Mr. Chandler. I'm ready to sign—"

An obnoxious scent stung Scarlett's nose. She lost

her train of thought as the stench burned through to her brain.

Lighter fluid.

The man lifted the candle and waved it menacingly over the bed. "Let's see . . . do little liars and fire mix?"

Where had he sprayed the lighter fluid? On her bed? She scrunched her legs up to her chest and pressed her body as close to the headboard as possible. "I-I said I'd call." Her voice gave her away. She heard its tremor. Its fear.

He leaned over the bed, lowering the candle toward her bedspread.

"No!" Scarlett bolted upright to a sitting position. "For God's sake, no." Her chest heaved. She gulped for air.

He laughed. A diabolical laugh that bounced off the walls and seemed to reverberate endlessly through the room.

"Stop! Stop! Stop!" she sobbed. Her body convulsed with rampant terror. *Get a hold of yourself. If you give him your power, you're dead.*

She shifted her gaze back to the man. He waved the candle in large sweeping motions over the bed. In his other hand he clutched what had to be a can of lighter fluid.

Which he slowly tipped at her.

"Don't. Please."

"Pretty please?"

He was a sicko. "Pret-pret—"

"Cat got your tongue?" He laughed again. A cruel, gravelly laugh that frightened her more than the physical threats. "Say please for papa. Like a good girl."

She forced the words out through quivering lips. "Pretty. Please."

"There now. Was that so hard?" He twisted around and set the candle back on the dresser. Turning back to her, he shoved the lighter fluid can back into his jacket pocket.

Then nothing. He stood at the foot of her bed, the candlelight licking small shadows on the wall behind him. He was turned toward her, but she saw none of his features—just a dark splotch where his face should be. Yet she knew he was staring at her. Watching her.

He raised something high over his head.

In the feeble yellow light, she saw a thin silver line sparkle along the object's edge. A knife?

In the next instant, he hurled himself onto the bed. The mattress bounced violently.

She shoved aside the covers. *Run! Escape!*

Just as her bare feet hit the cool floor, hot fingers dug into her shoulders and yanked her back.

He shoved her onto the mattress and threw his body on top of hers. His coarse chin grated against the soft skin of her neck and shoulder. His weight nearly suffocated her. She could barely breathe, much less talk. Her stomach revolted at his salty smell and sour breath. She gritted her teeth, fighting the sudden urge to retch.

"You're a pretty girl," he cooed. "Pretty dumb." Against her forehead, she felt something cold. It slipped across her brow like an icicle.

The knife? No, she would have felt the blade.

Something pricked the shell of her ear and she jerked.

"You're a little block of ice, aren't you? Need a man like me to loosen you up."

His bulk pinned her down. If only she could wrench her leg free, she'd kick him where it counted. The icy object caressed her cheek and traveled across her upper lip.

What had he said?

She stifled her erratic breathing and concentrated on what he held in his hand. He'd called her a "block of ice." The sharp tip, the thin cold blade that didn't cut . . .

Her insides caved in. He was trailing an ice pick across her face.

She pressed her lips together, willing herself not to move. Not even an eyelash.

"Chandler wants to finish the business deal tomorrow, doll."

The cold pick now rested against the corner of her mouth. When she didn't respond, he pushed the pick's tip a little harder. It slipped between her lips, its sharp point nestling against her tongue—its point so cold, it seemed to burn a small hole in her flesh. The taste of metal flooded her mouth.

"Yes," she whispered slowly, mouthing the word with great difficulty.

"If I have to come back again, well . . ." He pulled the pick out of her mouth part way, then pumped it lightly with an exaggerated slowness. She pressed her tongue against the back of her mouth as the rest of her body remained stock-still.

He finally pulled the pick all the way out. Inside her mouth, she touched her tongue across the inside corner of her lips—the point of exit—as though reclaiming her body.

Jake. Jake. Help me.

The thug pressed his lips close and whispered against her mouth. She inhaled shallow breaths, each one tainted with his foul stench.

"If I have to come back," he repeated, "the pleasure will be all mine."

She swallowed back the repulsive taste of his kiss. The stubble of his beard ground her skin like sandpaper.

He crawled off the bed. The release of his weight brought fresh air into her lungs, but she dared not breathe too deeply. She was still not out of danger.

He blew out the candle. In the pitch black, she listened for his whereabouts, but heard nothing. The silence unnerved her—the thudding of her pulse mimicked a pounding hammer.

Without moving her head, her eyes cast about her room, searching for any sign of him. Shadows coagulated in eerie shapes, like a host of still-life phantoms. But nothing moved.

Was he gone?

Suddenly a laugh ricocheted through the room. Loud, brash.

Her heart beat with such a sudden force, she thought it would tear loose of her chest.

Retreating footsteps.

Then, silence.

Chapter Fifteen

"Ramsey here." His voice sounded like it had been rolled in gravel.

Scarlett breathed a shaky sigh of relief into the receiver. "It's Scarlett—"

She heard a rustle of movement in the background. "Where are you?" he asked briskly.

"Inside my house."

"Are you in danger?"

"No, it's over."

"Be right in."

She opened the front door a crack and watched Ramsey's large form trundle up the walk. In the moonlight's faint glow, he looked like some kind of giant beast. When he hit the door, she jumped back to get out of the way.

"What the hell's going on?" His voice crackled with

urgency. "Why are we standing in the dark?"

"I was afraid to turn on a light until you were inside." She moved briskly to where she knew the switch was next to the door. Fumbling for a second, she finally found the knob and flicked it. The room blazed into view.

Ramsey squinted. Lines of exhaustion splayed from his eyes. He quickly scanned the room before looking back at her. "What the hell happened? Did you hear a noise?"

"Worse." She tightened the sash of her robe and shivered. It wasn't cold inside, yet she was shaking. Through chattering teeth, she forced out the words, "He ca-came here. The-the . . ."

Outside the wind gusted. A screen rattled. She swung her gaze to the only window in the room—the one in the kitchen—half expecting to see the thug's face pressed against the glass, leering at her.

But through the window she saw only the night's blackness.

"You're white as a ghost," muttered Ramsey.

She tried to focus on his face, but the crazy tilt of the room made it impossible. He was talking, but she couldn't decipher his words through the high-pitched buzz that filled her ears.

"I-I need to sit down." Yet she remained rooted to the spot. Dark splotches danced at the edge of her vision.

Strong hands gripped her shoulders and maneuvered her into an armchair. She sank gratefully into the familiar cushions. The splotches grew, narrowing her vision to the row of buttons down Ramsey's shirt.

"Put your head between your knees," he instructed. His voice sounded from far away. Her head fell forward with an agenda all its own and she stared at the thin strip of green carpet between her feet.

Her thoughts snapped off.

The floor went black.

She blinked. A bright glare stung her eyes. It took her a moment to realize it was the glass ceiling light in her living room.

Ceiling light?

It was familiar. Déjà vu. She had also lain on the floor of Ray's after she'd been . . .

"I've been shot," she mumbled.

"No, you fainted."

She blinked again and glanced down. No stretcher. No oxygen mask. Just Ramsey sitting at her feet, watching her anxiously.

"I fainted?" she asked incredulously.

"You follow orders too well, young lady. I told you to put your head between your knees, not practice diving from a sitting position."

She ran her tongue across her dry lips. "Why didn't you catch me?"

He smirked a half-smile, but she recognized its look of relief. "Thought I could steady you while I called the precinct. My fault. How do you feel?"

"Like somebody replaced my blood with ice water." She shivered a little and started to raise her head.

"Stay put." Ramsey shed his coat and draped it over her.

Half an hour later, she sat huddled in a corner of the couch, nervously watching George and Ramsey at the kitchen table talking in low, muffled tones. She had dreaded the idea of the LAPD being called, but Ramsey said it was imperative they know of this latest threat.

George nodded crisply to Ramsey, shoved back his chair, and stood. Crossing into the living room, he stopped before Scarlett and announced, "Detective Ramsey said the bathroom window had been locked when he left the house. When he returned, he found it open."

She nodded. Only a few hours before, she'd been utterly humiliated in front of George when Ramsey had yelled at her for her "joyride." George was obviously disgusted to be back here, his valuable time whittled away by her most recent dramatic extravaganza.

"Guess he jimmied it open." Being exhausted had its side benefits. She could answer George's pointed questions calmly because she lacked the energy to get riled up.

He flashed her a look she could only guess was mock bewilderment. "Impossible to jimmy a lock like that from the outside. Perhaps you opened it when you used the bathroom?"

Just like what happened at Ray's. An open door means I forgot to lock up, not that somebody broke in. An open window means I opened it, not that someone forced it open. She glanced around George's body to signal for Ramsey's help, but he was on the phone again, absorbed in a conversation. "I did not open the window," she said matter-of-factly, looking back into George's eyes.

"Mind if I have a look around?"

"Sure." She pulled Ramsey's jacket tighter around

her shoulders. Purple hues of morning glazed the kitchen window. Outside, birds were beginning to chirp. The beginning of another day.

The beginning of day five.

Ramsey hung up the phone and glanced at Scarlett. "You should try to get some shut-eye."

"Look who's talking."

Seconds later, George ambled back into the living room from her bedroom. "No signs of forced entry." He glanced at Scarlett, then back to Ramsey. "The wick of the candle is blackened and there is lighter fluid on her bed, but there is no other evidence of the alleged foul play."

She grimaced when she heard him say "alleged." He might as well have said, "The crazy chick is running us in circles again."

Ramsey rubbed his brow and released a long, exhausted breath. "It's been a long night. Why don't you head on back to the station—I'll be there soon to do my report."

After George left, Ramsey and Scarlett stared at each other.

"I'm going to get dressed," mumbled Scarlett, standing. "Thanks for your jacket." She peeled it off while walking toward him. "I couldn't sleep now if I tried. Want to get some coffee?"

He glanced at his watch. "A little past five. Why not? I know a twenty-four-hour doughnut place."

She handed him the jacket. "How come you didn't ask me if I had opened the window?"

"Why would you? For that matter, why would you pour lighter fluid on your own bed?"

She narrowed her eyes. "I am sure George thinks it was one more act by a crazy lady. But like he said, that creep couldn't have opened that window from the outside, so how did he get inside? You're the only one with a key."

"Dunno, kid. Just called the crime lab. They'll be here in an hour to check your place."

"Great. More cops." She sighed heavily as she trudged toward her bedroom. "I'll be out in a minute."

Back in her room, she glanced at the candle, sickened at the memory of the thug's shadowy silhouette.

"How did you get in?" she whispered hoarsely. Her gaze traveled to the window over her bed—cracked, but still locked. The window on her far wall. Also locked. It didn't make sense. She *knew* the bathroom window had been secure when she went to bed.

She walked down the short hallway to the bathroom, thinking to check it for herself. But just before entering the small white-tiled room, she halted.

In front of her, on the wall, she spied a smudge she'd never seen before. As though someone had accidentally rubbed against it. She jerked her head up. The square opening to the attic loomed overhead.

"Ramsey, come here." Her words were half spoken, half yelled. "He hid in the attic. He was . . ." She stifled a cry, stunned by the horrific realization. "We never locked him out. He was here all along."

"Dorothy's Donuts, down Ocean Park two lights, turn left . . ." Scarlett wove her Honda through traffic, repeating Ramsey's instructions to the twenty-four-hour doughnut shop they were meeting at. She'd never heard of the place, but it didn't matter. If Ramsey had said let's go to an all-night German-Ethiopian-taco joint, she'd have gone. It had nothing to do with hunger. She simply needed a place to go. And a friend.

She eased her foot off the gas and coasted down Ocean Park Boulevard. Along the horizon, the Pacific Ocean was a solid gray line, tinged with rose and gold from the rising sun. Gray like purgatory. Rose and gold like hope. She laughed inwardly at her poetic state of mind. *Hope?* "Maybe that's another word for 'destiny,' " she muttered under her breath. Jake always talked about his "destiny." If she had one, it would be to recapture her old life, to have it calm and peaceful again. Just like that distant ocean.

"You'll have that, Scarlett."

Her foot nearly slipped off the gas. Jake's voice? He dared to appear *now* after leaving her alone last night, when she needed him the most? She edged a sideways glance to her right.

He sat hunched in the passenger's seat, his brown eyes darkened with concern. A dark curl fell across his furrowed brow. "I'm sorry," he murmured.

She didn't need to ask what for. If he had tuned in to her thoughts at any point since last night, he knew how abandoned she felt. Abandoned by *him*. Punching the gas pedal, she said with dead calm, "Get out of my life."

She instantly regretted it. It wasn't what she meant. In her heart, she still desired and needed Jake. But in her mind, she couldn't go on like this. Her life provided enough obstacles and pain. Hell, she might not even live past today for all she knew. These struggles were overwhelming her . . . and she couldn't even count on the support of the man she viewed as her "mate." Crazy. Insane.

Although no windows were open, a warm breeze wrapped around her. A feeling of comfort stroked her skin, then suffused her, its aura as hot as sunshine.

Jake's hand brushed her hair, his fingers straying along her jawline. Her skin burned with his touch. "I wanted to be there last night, but—"

"But you couldn't get back to Earth," she responded, her tone flat.

"That's . . ." His voice was nearly inaudible. "That's right."

"So you watched me through that tunnel-vision theater of yours."

"Yes."

She slapped the wheel in disgust. "My life was on the line, and you're watching it in some cosmic movie house?" She jerked the wheel and peeled down an alley. After slamming to a stop, she yanked on the emergency brake and twisted her body to face him.

"What in the hell are you, anyway?" She flung one arm over the back of her seat and leveled a gaze at him, daring him to answer. His expressive eyes, so full of pain, momentarily unnerved her.

"I'm your des—"

"I know that part." *Destiny*. The word refueled her anger. What right did he have to talk about their "destiny" when he—the ghost, the figment, the whatever—left her alone in her bedroom with a creep who could have killed her?

"What in God's name are you? A ghost?" She suddenly felt shaky and unsure of herself. Was she really ready to face this truth?

He shifted in his seat. The faint scent of sandalwood teased the air. "No." He withdrew a flask from his inner jacket pocket and took a long, healthy swig.

"I don't think ghosts drink." She suddenly felt drained of all emotion. "And I don't think you're a figment of my imagination. I'm not that clever." *But maybe I'm that psychotic. Which means, I've fabricated you all along. A phantom boyfriend who abandons me—just like my dad.*

He shrank a little, as though the unspoken verbal barbs had found their marks. "I'm real, Scarlett," he answered, but his words lacked conviction. He downed another drink.

"Real?" she prompted, turning off the ignition key. A heavy silence fell between them as she waited for him to offer her more of an explanation than that.

He gazed out the window. A muscle in his jaw twitched. His hair, darker than usual in this faint morning light, hung in waves, the ends curling below his jacket's collar. It struck her that his hair was longer—had it grown? She gave herself a mental shake. Ridiculous. Ghosts aren't physical beings—their bodies don't mature and change.

"But I have," he answered, still looking out the window. "You've made me . . . human. More human, anyway. I can't explain it either." In the glass's reflection, she saw the faint outline of gaunt, unshaved cheeks. The image of a tormented *man*. Or was that also her imagination?

He fisted his hand and flexed his arm. For a moment,

she wondered if he was going to smash something. Then his hand dropped open and he looked at her, his eyes bleak and tormented. "I always hoped I was an angel."

"What?"

He sighed heavily and started to lift the flask to his lips again. But instead of drinking, he held the container in midair, his gaze staring through the windshield at the gray-hued alley. He dropped the flask back into his jacket pocket. "An angel," he repeated tightly, his eyes meeting hers. He fingered the crucifix around his neck. "I might be an angel. After all, I've never brought evil into your world, only good. My only sin—if it's even that—is that I've been tested as a man. . . ."

She didn't know whether to laugh or cry. She blinked rapidly and looked away. A street person pushed a shopping cart down the alley, the rough sound of metal wheels against asphalt reassuring and *real.*

Unlike what sat next to her. An *angel?*

She snorted a laugh and slapped the seat with her palm. "What kind of angel belts Scotch?" She tried to bite back the rising hysteria inside her, but an uncontrolled giggle erupted anyway. "A well-preserved angel, I'd guess. You . . . left Earth . . . in the fifties, right? Well, you look pretty darn good for an angel nearly half a century old."

Tears mixed with her laughter. She felt confused, torn apart. Thugs. Angels. It was too much to handle. She started to sob, then burst into a crescendo of unsteady laughter.

He leaned forward and opened his arms slightly. Molten light swam down his leather jacket, sparked as it passed his fingertips, then coiled around her. She blinked and suppressed a cry. The two of them were surrounded by a hazy, golden light. Had they been transported into his mind again?

"No, Jake," she mumbled.

"It's not my mind. It's what we are, together. I don't understand, but I know what I *feel*. We belong together, Scarlett."

His warm hands gently pulled her to him, and she willingly sank into his embrace. Under her cheek, she felt the smooth texture of the leather jacket. Its tannic scent reminded her of other times when he'd held her close. That haunting smell of sandalwood flooded her senses, reminded her of the times he'd appeared in her life—times when she didn't think another being in this world really cared.

Burying her face against him, she gasped when his warm lips brushed against her exposed neck. A lock of his silky hair swept across her forehead. *Angel?* Real, physical sensations shuddered through her—how could her mind fabricate his touch, his scent?

As though in response, he tightened his hold on her. In her ear, his warm breath whispered, "Scarlett, I'd fight hell itself to save you. You've got to believe me. I tried to be there last night—I'd never abandon you."

His lips found hers. Warm. Inviting. She greedily returned his kiss, welcoming their passion. Nothing else mattered but that they were together.

In this moment.

And the next.

"Scarlett, I—" He pulled back from her, panting

slightly. Pain flickered in his eyes. Tension radiated from him.

"What is it, Jake?"

"There's something you must know." His words were clipped, tight. His dark eyes seemed to assess her every reaction.

Anxiety trickled, then flooded her veins. Instantly alert, she shoved herself back into her own seat, her eyes never wavering from his. Was this the moment of truth? Did he reveal himself to be evil, not good?

She pressed her flushed cheek to the window's cold glass, numbing herself for what was to come. *First he tells me he's an angel. Then he kisses me like a man.* Back and forth. Fantasy, reality. *I am crazy, aren't I?*

"No, Scarlett," he answered softly. "That's not it. The truth is, I haven't told you everything about me."

His breath caught when she turned her head and gazed at him. Her beauty ignited his senses. He wanted to kiss those lips again, taste their sweetness, indulge himself in their warm wetness. But the murky green of her eyes stopped him. It was like staring into a churning, unsettled sea.

Something within him snapped. Weakened. *Don't hurt her. Don't tell her.*

The golden haze had dimmed. "What, Jake?" She tilted her head, her eyes suddenly doelike.

She looked so fragile. So *trusting*. He couldn't lie to her even if he wanted to. And he couldn't live with himself if he didn't bare his secret. "I don't want you ever to think I've deceived you. . . ."

Her skin tingled with apprehension. "Don't bring me

this close to the truth, then stop," she warned, her voice a hoarse whisper.

The shimmering haze dissipated totally.

"I'm . . ." He released an anguished sigh. "I'm Chandler's brother."

Jake stalked through purgatory, angry at the endless gray and the black butterflies. But especially angry at his last-minute confession to Scarlett.

"What was I thinking?" he growled to the vast endlessness. "That it would explain something? Like what?" He was now yelling at himself. "That I know Chandler better than anyone, and that the man is pure evil?"

He shook his fists at his prison. "I didn't have time to say it!" His words echoed far off, as though he stood on a mountaintop and yelled his wrath to the valley below.

He was consumed with rage.

And panic.

On Earth, this was the day Chandler made good on his threat. And Jake well knew that Chandler kept his word. Fifty years ago, Jake had died after a similar threat by Chandler.

Jake tore through purgatory like a madman. He yelled and pounded at the air. "You wanted me to have this third destiny, but you stacked the chips in your favor. Do what I can for Scarlett, but don't *feel?* Don't be a man? What did you expect from me? To give love, but not to ask for it?"

Everything, everything felt wrong. Doomed.

His anguish rolled up from his gut and exploded in

a long, drawn-out cry. His pain roared through purgatory like a lion's bellow. The black butterflies scattered as though blown apart.

Exhausted by the release, Jake doubled over. His breaths came in agonized pants, as though he'd pushed his body beyond its limits. Drops of sweat rolled down the side of his face. Human sensations. So unlike anything he'd ever felt in this realm.

Had Scarlett humanized him?

"You punish me for wanting her," he said breathlessly, raising his eyes to the gray dome. "But I must save her."

He buried his head in his hands and channeled all his energy to Chandler again. He visualized his brother's face and held it in his mind. He focused on it with a singleness of thought that made the image real, alive.

Squeezing his eyes tighter, he whispered, "Come here. Damn you, come here."

The rush of wings told him the black butterflies were soaring above him, closer than usual. Still he held his thought. "I command you, Chandler. Be here with me. Stand on my ground."

The air vibrated. The world shook. The rustling of wings grew into a giant flapping, but still Jake held on to the mental picture of Chandler. Something sizzled nearby, as though a bolt of electricity had crashed into purgatory.

"Jake."

He opened his eyes.

Before him stood Chandler.

* * *

Scarlett sat alone in her car, staring at the empty passenger seat where Jake had sat only moments ago. After his stunning pronouncement, he had faded into thin air. As though his molecules had lost their life force, he'd simply evaporated into nothingness.

She touched her forehead and absently wove a curl of hair around and around her finger.

Brother?

Had he really said Chandler was his brother?

Or maybe Jake was more than a brother to Chandler. Maybe Jake was the evil spirit of Chandler. Some dark force that masquerades as a fantastical James-Deanish spirit, when in reality it's the heart of evil itself.

Her mind raced back to all the times Jake had seemed to appear for her benefit, to help her. Now she saw too many coincidences when his arrival either preceded or followed some horror. Like the night at the fund-raiser. Who appeared when she finally came face-to-face with Chandler? Jake.

Or the night she was nearly run off the road. Was it really the fault of the car behind them? Or had Jake tried to destroy her along that lonely stretch of highway? Maybe her strong will had saved her, despite Jake's attempt to gain control of the car.

The dead cat. He had been there when she found the dead cat.

Revulsion curdled her stomach and she thought she'd be sick. Had he placed the dead animal for her to find?

She glanced into the rearview mirror, startled at her reflection. Her eyes looked like smudges of charcoal. Her lips a thin, tight line. Her hair like the flame at the end of a matchstick. Unreal. Just like Jake.

"I can't take any more of this madness," she said. "Ghosts, goblins, thugs, packages. It's not worth it. It's just not worth it."

Something tapped on her window and she unloosened a throaty scream.

Falling away from the sound, she scrambled across the front seat to the passenger's side. Behind her, her door clicked open and the early morning chill invaded the car.

"Scarlett?"

She whirled around, her hands poised on the passenger door's handle. "Ramsey," she croaked.

His tired eyes observed her warily. "I waited for you at the doughnut place. When you didn't show I backtracked to find you. Saw your car down this alley." He hesitated. "Saw you talking to yourself . . ." He didn't finish.

She didn't care if he, too, thought she was crazy. Nothing mattered, except to live.

"I don't want to throw dice for my life anymore," she said, pulling herself into a sitting position. "I give up. Chandler can have Ray's."

Chapter Sixteen

"Chandler," murmured Jake, staring at the man who stood before him. His hawkish profile brought back dark memories of the man Jake had once called "brother."

Cocking his head toward Jake, his eyes went from surprise to narrowed disgust. "Why am I here?"

Just like him to be all bluster and balls when he's on the threshold of Hell itself, thought Jake. Primitive urges clashed within him. Part of him wanted to throttle Chandler with his bare hands. "This is for Scarlett," he'd repeat as he watched Chandler slowly die.

If one *could* die in purgatory.

But another part of Jake—the sadder, wiser part—wanted simply to ask *why*. Why had Chandler murdered Jake? Why did he continue to torment Scarlett? He wanted to grab his brother's face and force him to look into the endless gray tomb of purgatory while asking, "What did you think life on Earth was about? Power? Money? *This* is what it's about—this is the eternal ever after. And you blew it."

But instead of doing either, Jake took a step forward and met Chandler's sullen stare. "You probably think you're dreaming."

Chandler smirked. "Nightmares don't frighten me."

"This is hardly a nightmare, old man. This is real."

"Old man?" Chandler laughed, the sound harsh, hollow. "Nearly forgot your favorite nickname for me. Haven't heard that in—"

"Forty years. Forty Earth years, that is. But here, time doesn't apply. I'm locked in the same age as when you murdered me. Whereas you grew old . . . old man."

Chandler's smile drooped. His eyes dulled until they matched the color of the skies. "You deserved it."

Jake looked up at the swirling black butterflies. "Your time's up." Or so he hoped. If Chandler was allowed into purgatory, didn't that indicate the end of his reign of terror? He'd be destroyed. Scarlett would be free. Perhaps that was the fulfillment of Jake's destiny.

At first the black specks vibrated, as though at attention. Then they grew in number until their amassed forces moved like a giant shadow across the sky.

Jake looked back at Chandler, suddenly filled with unexpected pity. "You know, I always wanted to be you." He shook his head in wonderment. "I idolized you. And what was my payback? Murder."

The butterflies were forming shapes over their heads. A solid circle. A large black square. Agitated, they seemed to be working out some pattern, some understanding of the foreigner in their midst.

Chandler glanced up. His eyebrows merged, creating a mesh of crevices in his forehead. "What in the hell—"

"They smell your evil," Jake said simply. "They recognize one of their own."

Chandler curled one side of his mouth in a snide grin. "Evil? How dramatic, little Jake."

The cool monotone delivery hit Jake like a blast of icy air. He hadn't expected to *feel* Chandler's evil. "I was your brother, you son of a bitch."

Chandler shrugged, his face impassive as though they were discussing something trivial. "You died because of your own stupidity."

"In my sleep?"

"It's not my fault you screwed up your life. I gave you a career, the chance to make a better-than-decent living." He raised his chin, an effect that let him stare down his nose at Jake as though he were an insect. "But was that enough? No." Chandler snorted his disgust. "You courted my enemy behind my back—"

"Who? What enemy?"

Chandler's eyes narrowed. "Innocent even in death, eh? Ellis. Stanley Ellis."

"You think I—?"

"I don't *think.* I know. He paid you a hefty sum for certain information. You played Judas, little brother. Sold me for thirty pieces of silver." The line of his mouth turned downward. "Thirty thousand to be exact."

"What information?" After all these years in purgatory, Jake had never known what twisted belief Chandler held against him.

Chandler crossed his arms and lowered a gaze at Jake. "Who my key men were. The deals going down. Ellis went to the police and talked. The things he spilled, only *one* person knew." He pointed a manicured finger at him. "*You* were that person."

"I was your brother." Jake's voice had lowered to a hoarse whisper.

"Foster brother. Not blood."

In life, it had always hurt when Chandler dismissed their familial ties. Jake wasn't prepared for how much it still hurt, even in death. "My mistake. You had *my* loyalty, anyway." A profound sadness weighted his soul as he realized Chandler had never trusted anyone, not even his family. "You think I was the only one who held your secrets?" questioned Jake in a lowered voice. "Clarissa knew everything you did. Names. Places. Even your mistresses. Even after what you put her through, you also had her loyalty." *Which you never deserved.*

Chandler unfolded his arms. "Clarissa has done well by me," he suddenly said, his voice smooth. "Homes all over the world. Cars. Clothes. I gave her everything she ever wanted—she'd never bite the hand that feeds her."

Jake had meant to stress Clarissa's love for Chandler, not set her up in his brother's mind as the possible culprit. Too late. He knew how Chandler's mind worked. Right now he was mentally weighing and analyzing the pieces, rearranging the puzzle. Forming another picture, another target, in his mind.

"Man, you never got it. She *loved* you." Loved him even while fearing his evil. Jake had felt that emotion when he'd merged with her. He'd also felt her immense pain and sorrow. A woman unloved, yet giving love.

Giving love. Without expecting anything back. Something within him stirred, as though he stood on the threshold of *knowing* an answer. But knowing what?

A rushing sound, like wind through a tunnel, distracted him. Looking up, he saw the same eerie pattern the black butterflies had formed before. A square with pointed ends. It began rotating, clockwise, very slowly. It was the same shape before when they had attacked him.

An icy tremor passed through him. What if they attacked both of them this time?

He resisted the urge to back away from his brother, lest he distract the butterflies away from Chandler. He knew he was playing roulette with his "life," but he had to take that chance. For Scarlett's sake.

A sobering thought piggybacked his fear. *Did he care if this was the end?* What was so horrible about ending an eternal prison term, ending this lonely solitude as purgatory's inmate? Maybe what came after "the end" was far better. Or maybe it was nothing. Either way, he'd have something he'd desired—even prayed for. He'd be free from purgatory.

The only thing he'd miss would be Scarlett.

Scarlett.

If the next few seconds were his last, he had to use them to save her.

The butterflies were now a jagged-edged square,

spinning faster and faster. Their high-pitched whirring like a dentist's drill.

Not much time. "Murder is the greatest sin. Your soul is marked."

"Who says?"

Jake shoved his thumb skyward. "They say."

Chandler jerked his head up, his eyes widening at the sight.

The black object was spinning so fast, its edges had blurred. The rushing sound grew until it resembled a thousand voices in a unified scream. It tilted, slowly.

And pressed toward them, moving through the air as though it were solid.

How much time do I have left? Jake thought.

Minutes?

Seconds?

Scarlett. Scarlett.

What if the black specks attacked only him, and Chandler returned to Earth? The thought tore at his gut. He had to save her.

He stumbled forward a step. "Keep your hands off Scarlett," he growled. "Let her live in peace. If you hurt her, I swear to God, I'll return from wherever I am to make your life hell."

The black butterflies, mimicking a giant saw, spun furiously toward Chandler. But when they touched on his head, they seemed to turn to liquid and melt over him, like black sludge. Chandler's hand shot through their spreading ooze, his fingers tense, outstretched. Reaching for help.

The inkiness ran down his hand, then covered it totally.

Jake stared at the black, thrashing form of his brother, horrified at the butterflies' brutality.

The sludge seeped down Chandler's brow. "Help me, damn you," he demanded through twisted lips. The shadowy ooze hovered above the horrified stare in Chandler's eyes.

It was the last look Jake saw.

"Help me!"

Chandler jerked violently against the cold black thickness. "Help," he yelled again.

Someone grabbed his hand. A human touch. Warm, strong. He clutched at the life support.

The darkness lifted.

Bright light stung his eyes. He opened his mouth to cry out again, but his voice had mutated into a strange, craggy sound. Cold sweat soaked the sheets. His heart thundered in his chest.

"It's all right," said a soft voice. "There now, you're all right."

He tossed his gaze to his right. Clarissa hovered over him, gripping his hand.

"Clarissa?" he asked shakily.

He lifted his head. Across his bedroom sat the Louis XVI chair next to his desk. In front of the fireplace, the matching set of cashmere club chairs. Reality. Sweet reality.

Dropping back onto his pillow, he welcomed the familiar silk sheets. *I'm in my bedroom. My bedroom, not Hell.*

He opened his eyes again and blinked painfully. The light burned his eyes. "Turn down the chandelier," he said hoarsely. "But not all the way," he quickly added. He couldn't stand the thought of all that blackness again.

The scent of jasmine, Clarissa's signature perfume, wafted past his nose. "Are you all right, darling?" she asked.

Through slitted eyes, he analyzed her. Even in the shadowy darkness, she looked taut, old. How many years had it been since she'd been in his bedroom?

Her face was riddled with anxiety. What in the hell had happened, anyway?

"I heard you cry out," she answered, obviously reading the question in his eyes.

"What did I say?"

She shook her head. A wisp of hair fell loose and rested against her sunken cheek. "Couldn't tell. I thought . . ."

"What?"

"You seemed to be talking to someone, but I knew you were alone. I worried you were delirious. Ill."

Was that a tear in her eye? It made him nauseous to see her pity. "If I kicked the bucket, you'd be filthy rich."

Her chin trembled. "Is that all you think I care about?"

He didn't answer. "I was talking to someone. Jake." He swallowed back a shiver. "Hell of a nightmare. Get me a Scotch."

He watched her artificially thin body float out of the room. Had what Jake said been true? Clarissa was the only one who knew his secrets? Had she been the Judas, not Jake?

He reached for the phone next to the bed. After punching in a single digit—a computer-stored number—he listened to a remote phone ringing.

"Hello?"

"It's time," was all Chandler said before hanging up.

Judyl sat on a corner stool next to the phone, punching in numbers. "According to the Dream, Ray's continues to exist. Only better. Its next life goes beyond hamburgers."

Scarlett pointed to an empty cardboard box at Judyl's elbow. "Hand me that, would you?" *Beyond hamburgers.* Scarlett bit her lip to suppress a laugh. Only a die-hard vegetarian like Judyl could concoct a story like that. Despite the sadness of this last day at Ray's, her dream story provided an unexpected comic twist.

With the receiver poised at her ear, Judyl continued. "Peoplekind need to band together. We need be one and share the vision."

Scarlett swept a wayward curl out of her eye before flashing her a look. "I'll miss you, Judyl. I've never known anyone who spoke Sixties all the way into the Nineties." But her comment was lost on Judyl, who was already chatting to whoever had answered her call.

Roger, still nursing a black eye, slurped his coffee. "What is this 'vision' thing she keeps speaking about?"

Scarlett wrapped a dish towel around several plates and stacked the bundle into a box. "Something about a dream. Too many bean sprouts before bedtime, I guess." Even though she was in the middle of a crisis, she was grateful to be surrounded by her friends. Chandler wouldn't dare make a move with people around.

Roger chuckled. "I can't believe I'm laughing when today is so grim."

"Yeah, I know that one." She didn't want to think about Jake's confession anymore. It hurt to be left alone after being stunned with such a terrible truth. It was the last time Jake would ever leave her alone, she swore to herself. That insanity was over. Finished.

She jammed a wad of napkins into the side of the box to protect the edge of a plate.

"What's going on here?" cried a female voice. Scarlett looked up. Doris stood in the doorway, her pudgy shoulders sagging. "Child, I must talk to you."

"Talk to me while I pack. Better yet, help me. I want to be out of here by tonight."

Doris crossed with mincing steps to the counter and sat next to her son Roger. Leaning over, she whispered, "I had a dream."

Scarlett sighed dramatically. "Not you too." She straightened her sore back and squinted at her friends. "What did all of you do last night? Read the same science fiction story? This dream stuff has got to end. A joke's a joke." She resumed her packing.

Doris looked perplexed. "Didn't read anything last night, child."

"Then you must have talked to Judyl on the phone this morning." Scarlett motioned to Roger to hand her another box.

"No," said Doris urgently. "I haven't talked to Judyl in several days." She edged closer and whispered, "Anyway, my dream was about you, child. It was in this golden valley. Your mama was there."

Scarlett arched an eyebrow and mumbled an aside to Roger. "Judyl's dream started like that too."

Doris bolted upright, all ears. "It did? And your mama said not to leave, that life would work out?"

"Something like that," Scarlett answered drolly as she yanked open a drawer of utensils. They clattered as she poured the contents into another box.

Judyl slammed down the receiver and announced loudly, "Max had the same vision!"

Scarlett shot Doris and Roger a look. "Who's Max?" When they both stared back at her with matching puzzled expressions, Scarlett said, "Great. Total strangers are dreaming about me."

The rest of the afternoon continued with more testimonials of the Dream as locals convened at Ray's. Scarlett loved her community, but didn't believe a word of it. Even though the dream-story bit was overdoing it, their hearts were in the right place. They wanted her to stay. Some had heard the rumors that Chandler was behind this, but many thought she was packing up because she was the last remaining business on Gabrielle Street. They didn't realize that after seventeen years, Ray's loyal following would always keep her busy making burgers.

But to risk staying open even twenty-four more hours meant courting death. She had no choice but to close.

By five o'clock, exhaustion claimed her. Tired from packing and saying good-byes, she ambled back to the storage room. Behind her, festive laughter and chatter filled the place.

"Like an Irish wake," she thought with sad amusement. Well, if Ray's had to go, what better way?

They won't miss me if I catch a few winks. She stumbled through the storage room boxes and curled up on a sturdy wooden crate in the back. Drawing an old sweater off a hook, she gave it a shake, then bunched it under her head for a pillow.

Just a little snooze, then I'll go back to packing and . . .

She was running through a verdant valley carpeted with flowers. Chirping birds, gloriously green and red, spun lazily through the blue air.

Peace. Incredible peace. She kicked off her shoes and ran barefoot. The spongy grass was cool and wet under her toes. She laughed at the sheer joy of it.

"Everything will work out, Scarlett."

Was that her mother's voice?

Scarlett turned, slowly.

A few feet away stood Alice, her mother. Gone was the graying hair and seasoned face. In her place stood the mother of Scarlett's childhood. Auburn hair hung loosely to Alice's shoulders. Her slim, girlish figure was adorned in a polka-dot dress—the same dress Scarlett remembered her mother wearing to an elementary school performance.

"Mom." Scarlett ran to her and they hugged. "I've missed you so much."

But when she pulled back, it was no longer Alice in her embrace.

It was Jake.

His eyes were sunken, like two dark pools in his face. "I never meant to hurt you," he began.

Pain, heavy as a rock, sank through her. *His* pain.

She knew he was referring to his confession about Chandler. But why did he appear in her dream to tell her?

Or was she dreaming? She looked around at the endless gray. Purgatory?

"Where's my mother? Why am I here?"

A shadow crossed Jake's face as he seemed to contemplate her question. "I thought *you* wanted to come here. I had nothing to do with it this time." He started to say more, but stopped.

She knew what he was wondering. Because she had the same question herself. Had her mother brought them together?

"Is that possible?" she asked breathlessly. She shuddered unexpectedly. Did her mother want them together? For what? Jake was a ghost—or a phantom or whatever—whose human existence was long over. While her own human life teetered on disaster. Possibly death. Under such dire circumstances, why bring two lost souls together?

As she searched the depths of Jake's eyes, impossibly seeking an answer, she became aware of him changing.

No, aging.

As though years had passed instead of seconds, an older Jake suddenly stood before her. Age lined his face and sprinkled his hair with gray, but those dark eyes had that same come-hither twinkle. He kissed her. A sweet kiss, born of years of loving. And a lifetime of sharing.

Impossible. Things they would never have.

Then, like a figure of sand, he crumbled.

She looked at her opened hands that had touched him only moments before. They were now empty, except for a fine granular coating.

Gone? Was he gone?

She rubbed her fingers together. The texture wasn't gritty, but soft. Like soot.

Before, he had always disappeared from Earth, yanked back to purgatory against his will. This time, while in purgatory, he had decomposed into a handful of ashes.

He was gone.

Her heart felt as though it had collapsed into itself. "Jake," she whispered. She curled her fingers closed, protecting the last of him that remained. "Jake."

She bent her head, closing her eyes.

An acrid stench assaulted her nose, jolting her back to consciousness.

Blinking her eyes, she peered into what seemed to be a gray wall. She bolted to a sitting position and stared, wide-eyed. A wall, yes.

Of smoke.

Billows of gray smoke seeped from underneath the storeroom door, filling the room with fumes.

"Fire!" Her voice was raspy, thin. She fell off the crate in her terrified state, then scrambled to her feet. "Help me! Fi—" A coughing fit stopped her. She grabbed her sweater and brought it to her face.

She remembered an extinguisher next to the door, and she stumbled toward it. Smoke obliterated her vision. With outstretched hands, she fumbled forward.

Her toe hit something hard and she nearly fell. *Careful. Lose your cool, and you're dead.* She slid her feet along the floor, maneuvering around objects and boxes.

It's close, no more than ten feet. She groped through the thick smoke. Her eyes smarted, so she kept them squeezed shut. Sweat inched down her face from the rising temperature.

Something crackled.

Flames?

Through slitted lids, she chanced a look into the thick haze.

Distant fingers of yellow and red flickered through the smoke. From the window over the door?

She sucked in a lungful of hot, ashy air. Coughing and gasping, she clutched her sides and tried to quell her spasmodic breathing.

Have the others left, not realizing I'm back here? She fought a surge of anxiety. *Of course they don't realize—I told no one. Call to them. Get help.*

"Help," she screeched hoarsely. Her throat felt raw, painful. She tried to yell again, but her voice was only a breathy shriek.

She dropped to her knees and cupped her sweater to her face. Another wave of panic surged within her. *Stay calm. Find the door.*

It must be no more than five feet ahead. Five feet. Her fingers skimmed along the still-cool concrete floor. Was that a draft of air she felt along the floor?

Close. I'm close.

Thump. Her fingers hit the bottom of the door. It was hot. If she reached up to the metal knob, it would undoubtedly burn her fingers. Should she even try to open it? What if opening it fueled an avalanche of flames?

I have no choice. Either I die engulfed in flames, or I die in the burning storeroom.

She found the handle. Stinging heat burned her fingertips. She withdrew with a yelp of pain.

Can't give up.

She reached forward.

But instead of hot metal, her fingers touched something thick, corded.

Rope?

She fumbled along its knotted texture until she reached the fiery door handle again. Using the end of her sweater as a glove, she grabbed the handle and turned.

Nothing.

Locked.

Impossible. She hadn't locked the door when she came in here.

The cord.

With a sinking sensation, she grabbed the cord and followed it for a foot, maybe more, to where it tied off on a built-in shelf.

I'm locked in the burning storeroom.

I'm dead.

She wanted to cry, but sheer terror overrode all other emotions. What to do? Cut the rope? There were knives in the other room, not back here.

She groped through the smudgy air, her fingers alighting on the rope. Not the taut line, but a loop anchored at the knot. She slipped her hand through the circle of rope, its shape triggering a memory.

The same loop had been in the rope that held open the back door.

She squeezed her fingers around the small noose. Yes, this same knot had been on the package thrown on her doorstep.

And something else. Where?

A stream of sweat beaded on her upper lip and she squeezed her eyes shut against the painful realization.

The same knot had been on Enrique's gift to Doris.

She stifled a sob. *Enrique*.

Her old friend was the traitor.

Chapter Seventeen

Panting against the smoke's stench, Scarlett grabbed the cord with both hands. She couldn't die like this. Slowly suffocating. Scared and alone. Chandler would never have the satisfaction of her dying such a miserable death. Not without a fight.

Sputtering a cough, she summoned all her strength and gave the cord a hard yank. Nothing. Again. Nothing. Gripping the cord tighter, she pulled, every muscle in her body straining. *Give. Give.* Her hands stung as the cord bit into her palms.

It refused to budge.

Exhausted, she slumped to the floor. The fumes were getting the better of her. Hard to breathe. Hard to think. She felt herself sinking. . . .

Through a thin veil of smoke, a man's face appeared. She blinked. *Jake?* The next instant, he disappeared in a veil of sooty vapor. She coughed and reached through the haze, but her fingers only grasped the thick, smudgy air.

I need you, Jake. A tear seeped from her eye. Drowsiness weighed her down. She dropped her hand. She was vaguely aware of herself drifting down. Down to the concrete floor that felt cool and slick under her cheek.

"I'm here, Scarlett." Jake's voice.

She forced open her sleepy eyes and peered into the swirling gray. "Jake?" she croaked. The taste of ash caked her mouth.

Strong arms pulled her close. Within the acrid air, she smelled—imagined?—a hint of sandalwood. The scent rushed to her brain, infusing her with euphoria.

Or was death this seductive?

She no longer felt the floor's coolness against her face. Instead, she now rested against a gauzy material. She grazed the fabric with her fingertips and felt, underneath it, the solidness of Jake's chest. No leather jacket? She opened her eyes slightly. He wore something white, like a toga. It struck her as odd that the material remained pristine despite the floating ash and fiery residue. Dangling over his heart, the crucifix, tarnished before, now sparkled as though chiseled from diamond.

"Thank God you're here," she mumbled, nuzzling closer.

Cool breezes brushed against her. Was that fresh air circulating through the room? She peered over Jake's shoulder to see if someone had finally opened the door, but instead saw a luminous white fan that undulated gently. She shifted her gaze to the right. Another identical fan swept the smoke away with broad movements.

She inhaled deeply, grateful to fill her lungs with refreshing air. Invigorated, she raised her head from Jake's shoulder for a better look.

Those weren't fans. They were . . .

Wings.

Radiant, larger-than-life wings.

Her heart beat with such a tremendous force, she thought it would tear right out of her.

She peered into Jake's face. His dark curls floated in the air, buoyed by the wings' swishing. She started to speak, but stopped. Gone was the haunted, driven look she'd always seen in his face. Now he appeared . . . serene.

Wings. His face. Was she imagining things again?

Too much. Can't think anymore. She sank back into his embrace. *He's here. That's all that matters.* Her fingers clutched the filmy fabric and she folded into him, welcoming his protection.

Carrying her in his arms, he walked toward the door.

"It's tied—" she began, then swallowed a small cry as he stepped *through* the wooden barricade. Cowering against him, she waited for the door's splintered wood to rain on them.

"Don't be afraid, Scarlett," said Jake. "We're on the other side."

She peeked through one opened eye. Sure enough, they now stood outside the storeroom.

Surrounded by roaring flames.

She flinched in horror. Her beloved Ray's was a

wall-to-wall inferno. The end portion of the counter collapsed with a deafening crash.

Jake continued walking. She held onto him, speechless.

Angry, licking flames towered above them. Along the floor, blazing objects were scattered along their path, yet Jake's bare feet walked over them as though he felt nothing.

Bare feet? she thought hazily.

A piece of burning wood tumbled from the ceiling. It scraped against her arm, yet she felt no pain. Amazed, she stared at her bare forearm and elbow. There was not even a sooty smudge where it had touched her.

They had almost reached the front door, which was open. Through it, she saw a mass of people watching the building. In the center stood Doris, holding her son's hand and weeping. Dotted throughout the crowd were police cars, their circling lights splattering people's faces with red. Close to one car, Judyl was gesturing wildly to a policeman.

Jake lowered Scarlett until she stood on the floor facing the opened doorway. "Go to them," he instructed gently.

"I can't leave you here," she countered, turning around. "You'll die."

A slow smile, which seemed at once sad and knowing, creased his face. His dark eyes held hers. "It's my time," he said simply. "And you, dear Scarlett, have the rest of your life to live."

The next thing she knew, she was standing on the sidewalk outside Ray's.

White lights stung her eyes. Someone shoved a microphone in her face.

"How did you escape the fire?"

Past the brightness, she recognized a reporter from the local evening news.

"Hell, this is no time for a goddamn scoop." Detective Ramsey elbowed the reporter out of the way and grabbed Scarlett by the shoulders. "You gutsy kid. You made it."

Scarlett looked back. Her legacy, Ray's, was being devoured by monstrous burning vapors. Yet, in Jake's arms, she had felt no scalding heat, breathed no suffocating smoke.

Jake.

Through the broken plate-glass window, she saw him. He stood within the burning building, engulfed by the conflagration.

"Oh, my God, save him." She struggled to turn back, to run to him, but Ramsey held her firm.

"No one's in there. You were the last one."

"Look!" She pointed, her hand shaking. "For God's sake, he's being consumed alive! Help him!" She fought Ramsey, determined to break free and return to Jake. But her wasted strength was no match for Ramsey's hold.

"No, honey. There's no one." He nodded to a nearby paramedic.

Yellow-and-red flames swirled around Jake. They seemed to burn right through him, yet he remained fixed, staring at Scarlett. An invisible wind blew his hair. Strange. His hair seemed longer. Golden. The same incandescence matched his face, as though he radiated an internal light.

"I've been released." Jake's voice pulsated in her head, the words more clear than if he stood right next to her. "I learned that all that matters is to *give love*. Unconditionally. Its power is in the giving, not the wanting. Although I wanted a life with you—to be a man—nothing is greater than to give love." He paused. "I love you, Scarlett. Take that with you, always."

A fierce, rushing wind tore through her. And with it, an incredible, almost unbearable joy. Teetering, she thought she'd faint from the sensation. She tightened her grip on Ramsey's hand, grounding herself.

I love you, Jake. Did he smile? Breezes, sweetened with sandalwood, fluttered around her. *I love you. I love you.*

Behind him, his wings stretched open to an awesome breadth.

"Come on, honey," coached Ramsey.

"No, no. Don't you see him?" she asked breathlessly. She watched, spellbound, as the mighty wings beat the air. With grand sweeping motions, Jake rose from the fire, through the burning roof, and into the night air.

For an instant, he hovered above the building, his gaze still locked to hers.

Then, over his head opened a funnel of the purest light she'd ever seen. The tinkling of wind chimes and the murmur of sweet, singing voices filled the air.

"Do you hear?" whispered Scarlett, clutching Ramsey.

Jake lifted his gaze. The light bathed his features

with a pearlescent glow. Raising his arms, the magnificent wings swept the air.

The wind chimes diminished.

The funnel narrowed, then faded.

Scarlett stared, awestruck, into the inky sky.

"We're taking you to the hospital," said Ramsey in a low voice. He guided her toward a waiting ambulance.

"Did you see him?" she asked, her voice barely above a whisper.

"Nobody was there, honey. You had a hell of a shock."

"He *was* an angel," she murmured. "Just like he said. He saved me."

Ramsey handed her off to the paramedic, who gently eased Scarlett onto a stretcher. She grabbed Ramsey's hand and pulled him near. "It's true. He saved me."

He searched her face, then patted her reassuringly on the shoulder. "Something happened in there, kid. How you got out alive is a miracle, that's for sure."

Standing at the plate-glass window overlooking Gabrielle Street, Scarlett flicked her wrist and checked the time. The dinner rush would begin in thirty minutes sharp. This was her quiet time. The lull before her nightly customers filled Ray's.

She tapped the face of her watch, remembering how it hadn't worked those few weeks last year when Jake had entered her life. Strangely enough, it had started again after the night of the fire. The night when Jake rose into the sky. . . .

The night she last saw him.

She brushed back her hair, determined not to give in to the sadness. Losing Jake was similar to losing her mom. With both, she had to learn how to move on and live again.

She gave the room one last check. The scattered round tables, covered with peach tablecloths, gave the room a cozy glow. She feared it was a little too cozy, since she'd had to squeeze in three more tables to meet the growing number of reservations. To think she had considered rebuilding the counter as a bar . . . no, it had been the right decision to leave it out for more floor space.

With the insurance settlement, she'd renovated Ray's Hamburgers into Ray's, the restaurant she'd always dreamed of owning. Judyl now managed the kitchen, and did a fine job of it too. With all the vegetarian entrees, Judyl was in her element, although she still scoffed at the occasional lamb or steak dish.

The one main thing they'd agreed upon was no more hamburgers. However, to remind herself of her roots, Scarlett had framed her old spatula and hung it in the kitchen, in homage to Ray's predecessor, Ray's Hamburgers.

Tap tap tap.

Outside, Doris pointed at the newspaper stand. Scarlett nodded. Blasted across the front page was the headline CHANDLER GETS NINETY. Everyone in Los Angeles knew what that meant. The trial had been long and drawn out, but despite Chandler's savvy and well-paid lawyers, the jury had found him guilty of extortion, attempted murder, and a barrage of other legal indictments as more of his victims stepped forward.

Doris smiled and continued walking.

Probably on her way home to her new hubby, thought Scarlett. Doris and Enrique had married after his recent release from prison, thanks to Scarlett's behind-the-scenes negotiating. Under duress, Enrique had complied with Chandler because he had threatened to hurt Doris and her children. When Scarlett had visited Enrique in prison a week after the fire, he had tearfully confessed that he had no idea she was in the storeroom when he had tied the door closed. Grief-stricken, he begged her forgiveness, which she freely gave. Part of Enrique's restitution had been to name and verify the "errands" Chandler ordered.

But it was Chandler's wife who had delivered the lethal blow. She gave the police all kinds of facts about her husband's sordid dealings. She'd made further restitution by providing scholarships and small business grants to the local community. One newspaper article had quoted her as saying she'd seen the "evil" of her husband's ways and wanted to make amends.

Amends. Scarlett looked across the street at the sign "The Alice Ray Center." It felt wonderful every single time she looked at that building. With the money Scarlett had received after selling her story to a movie studio, she had pondered how to give something back to the community that had stood behind her. When she reflected on all the babysitting her mother, and then Scarlett, had done, she knew what the community needed most. A day-care center. In homage to her mother, she'd named it after her.

"We did good, Mom."

Oddly enough she hadn't dreamed of her mother

since the night of the fire. The dream where her mother brought Scarlett and Jake together, before he returned as an angel.

Jake.

A familiar ache constricted her heart. She started to remind herself, again, that with time she'd move on. With time, the pain in her heart would subside. She'd be free to love another. Someone real, someone human. They'd start a family. Share their dreams, their future.

But not in this lifetime.

It was a simple truth. In her heart, she'd always belong to Jake. And if she couldn't be with him, then she'd accept her life as it was. The comfort of her community and her friends would fill the void of not having a husband or children.

Strange, the lessons of life. Whereas Jake's lesson had been to give love, hers had been to accept it. They had both, in a sense, been released. Just not to each other.

Scarlett turned back to the room and made some last-minute adjustments to a vase of flowers.

Music wafted through the room. Odd, she hadn't turned on the CD player yet.

Straightening, she looked around. Lilting, soft music. From where? She listened intently. It came from the wall behind the register. The antique radio? She stared at it and frowned. Impossible. Although it had been salvaged from the fire, its insides were empty. Always had been.

Yet . . .

She reached up and lightly touched the radio's wooden surface. Vibrations tingled her fingertips.

Behind her, the front door swished open.

Slowly, she turned.

Backlit by evening light stood a male figure. Swathed in jeans and a bomber jacket, he leaned jauntily against the door as his dark gaze met hers.

Sandalwood filled the air.

"Scarlett." His voice. Low, husky. Just as she remembered.

"Jake?"

She faltered forward a few steps, then stopped. What was she doing? He wasn't—couldn't—be real. After all her prayers to see him again, maybe this was a trick her mind was playing. . . .

A caressing breeze coiled around her.

Jake held out his hand. "God gave me a choice."

A choice? They were released to each other? She ran and fell into his embrace.

Crushing her in his arms, he sank his face in her hair and inhaled deeply. "Ah, Scarlett, Scarlett."

"Jake, I love you," she cried, her words choked with emotion.

He nuzzled her neck and sighed. "Forever, I love you." He brushed her lips with his own. Tasting her human sweetness again, his restraint collapsed. With a soul-wrenching moan, his mouth eagerly claimed hers.

Breathless from their kiss, she pulled back. He was real. Solid and warm in her arms. Sudden tears burned her eyes. "Forever?"

"Forever," he promised. "It's our destiny."

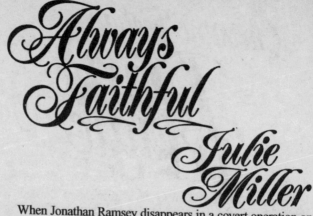

Shadow Of The Hawk
Julie Miller

They looked at each other across the body.

Momentarily stunned, he just stared for a few beats too long. If she'd never seen a violent death, she might be in shock, he reminded himself. Her right hand was bloody, he saw when he could wrench his gaze from her face. She'd touched the victim when she first fell to her knees beside him. Zach lifted his own hand to see that, yeah, his own fingertips were bloody, too. The guy's face was a chunk of raw meat. The hands and arms he'd raised in defense weren't any better.

Recalled by the sound of an approaching siren, he said gently, "There's nothing you can do. The medics will be here any minute."

She looked down, then back up. "He's dead, isn't he?"

"I'm afraid so."

"Why?" she whispered.

"I have no idea."

Dear Reader,

I love to write stories fresh out of the news. Actually, given my law-abiding (possibly even staid) lifestyle, where else would I get my ideas? In this case, the newsworthy drama provides the perfect setup to challenge my hero, who has zero interest in a long-term romantic relationship. After his childhood, how can he trust a woman not to betray him?

If you're a regular reader, you'll recognize where I'm going with this. My stories frequently hinge on the lasting effects of childhood trauma. I firmly believe that our most essential character is formed by the time we leave home at eighteen. Often, way before we leave home.

In *The Closer He Gets*, I have a hero bearing a lifetime of proof that he can't rely on anyone. He returns to his childhood hometown to right a very old wrong, and finds the brother who abandoned him—and a woman under siege after she witnesses a horrendous crime. For the first time, Zach has met a woman he can't walk away from, no matter how much his feelings for her scare him. And in his brother, Bran, he finds another man as damaged by their shared past as he was.

Yep, my kind of story! And, yes, in a flip of the coin, look for Bran Murphy's story, *The Baby He Wanted*, to come in May 2016 from Harlequin Superromance.

Good reading!

Janice

JANICE KAY JOHNSON

The Closer He Gets

ISBN-13: 978-0-373-60948-2

The Closer He Gets

This edition published by arrangement with Harlequin Books S.A.

For questions and comments about the quality of this book, please contact us at CustomerService@Harlequin.com.

Printed in U.S.A.

An author of more than ninety books for children and adults, **Janice Kay Johnson** writes about love and family—about the way generations connect and the power our earliest experiences have on us throughout life. An eight-time finalist for a Romance Writers of America RITA® Award, she won a RITA® Award in 2008 for her Harlequin Superromance novel *Snowbound*. A former librarian, Janice raised two daughters in a small town north of Seattle, Washington.

Books by Janice Kay Johnson

HARLEQUIN SUPERROMANCE

The Baby Agenda
Bone Deep
Finding Her Dad
All That Remains
Making Her Way Home
No Matter What
A Hometown Boy
Anything for Her
Where It May Lead
From This Day On
One Frosty Night
More Than Neighbors
To Love a Cop

Two Daughters

Yesterday's Gone
In Hope's Shadow

The Mysteries of Angel Butte

Bringing Maddie Home
Everywhere She Goes
All a Man Is
Cop by Her Side
This Good Man

A Brother's Word

Between Love and Duty
From Father to Son
The Call of Bravery

SIGNATURE SELECT SAGA

Dead Wrong

Visit the Author Profile page at Harlequin.com.

CHAPTER ONE

BRAN MURPHY WOULD have said he wasn't given to self-reflection. He made one major exception, however. Something like every six months he would feel the pull and next thing he knew he'd be driving slowly by his childhood home instead of parking in his assigned spot at his condo.

This was one of those times, and he had an idea what had provided the impetus today. A couple of months ago he'd decided the time had come to find a wife and start a family. Three weeks ago he'd asked Paige to marry him and she'd agreed. They'd just taken a vacation together to Hawaii. Last night, after they flew into SeaTac, he had dropped her at her place, carrying her suitcase in for her and then gone home alone. He hadn't slept well and had found himself feeling edgy this morning.

What if his desire for a family and the logical way he'd gone about it had started him on a trajectory that would end in a crash landing like the one that had destroyed the not-so-happy family that had lived here in this house?

Maybe every life had a Before and After. Divorce. A death. Another kind of loss that created a divide. His own happened to be a little more violent than most.

Today he sat brooding in his car, remembering a time when his family had been whole. There were signs the family who lived in the house now might be. A kid's bike lay on the lawn, and the barbecue and lawn mower under cover of the carport made him think all-American.

As tense as if he was about to kick in a door to arrest a violent offender, he got out and followed the sidewalk to the corner, turning and going far enough to be able to glimpse the backyard, possible because none of the houses on this block had fences. The neighborhood was holding its own—not upscale but not run-down, either.

He'd put some work into this place before he'd sold it after Dad died. Sometimes he still had trouble believing his father had stayed in this house when he knew the local cops and plenty of the neighbors thought he had killed his own daughter.

And Bran had stayed with him until he'd graduated from high school, using his fists on any kid who dared say anything about Dad or Sheila.

People forgot, of course. The tragedy that fractured his family irrevocably had taken place twenty-four years and eight months ago. Probably he was the only one who ever thought about it.

No, wherever his brother was, he wouldn't be

able to help remembering, either. He'd made a different choice than Bran but would have suffered the same wounds.

Today, seeing how little the house had changed unsettled Bran. As a teenager he'd convinced his father to paint it a pale gray with white and black trim instead of the white it had always been. Wouldn't you know the latest homeowners had gone back to white. Nothing had changed the basic lines of the house. Seeing it today was like stepping through a time warp.

God, he thought, *what makes me think I'm capable of being a husband and father?*

The basics wouldn't have changed inside, either. Two bedrooms downstairs and one up, that one tucked under the eaves with a single window in the small dormer that looked over the front porch. He and his brother had shared it.

From here he could see some boards still clinging drunkenly to a Y high up in the maple that filled the backyard and shed a bounty of leaves every fall. Dad had helped his boys build the tree fort. Bran didn't remember ever going up in it again after Sheila died. He didn't think Zach had, either.

From the tree fort they would have been looking right down at where her body had been found.

What am I doing here?

It was a compulsion. Unresolved issues. He snorted at the thought, however accurate it might be. Open questions ate at him. If Sheila's killer was ever arrested, Bran doubted he'd feel the need to turn down this street again.

A police detective, he knew how to find answers. He'd even worked cold cases.

There were any numbers of problems to prevent him from pursuing this one, however.

To start with, this house—where his little sister had been killed—wasn't in his jurisdiction. The small city of Clear Creek had its own police force, which consisted of a police chief and twenty officers. He worked for the county sheriff's department.

The general ineptitude of the Clear Creek PD back then was problem number two. Unless he'd missed a whole lot, the investigation hadn't gone anywhere. He knew more than his parents ever would have guessed, having eavesdropped on police interviews and even Mom and Dad's whispered arguments in bed. Would evidence even have been saved? If so, carefully enough to allow DNA to be run?

Problem three? Several of the current Clear Creek officers had lived in the area as long as he had and knew Bran's connection to the unsolved case. The way they looked at him when he asked questions made him wonder whether detectives had ever considered him a suspect. He'd been young but not so young he wasn't thinking about sex.

The chilling thought had only recently occurred to him. He'd spent a lot of years refusing to think about the murder at all. Convinced that knowing what really happened wouldn't change a thing for him.

But the twenty-fifth anniversary of Sheila's death was approaching. A lot that had been buried in his psyche had begun crawling out, giving him nightmares.

Who was there to give a damn but him? Zach had been even younger than him when it happened and had probably forgotten more. Bran had no idea, since he hadn't seen his brother in twenty-four years. Anyway, Zach wasn't here in Clear Creek. Bran was.

And Sheila deserved justice. Now that Dad was gone, there was nothing to stop him.

Skin prickling despite the warmth of the sun, he walked back around to the front of the house. He'd swear the cracks on the sidewalk were unchanged, too. Took him right back in time.

HE COULD FEEL the book bag bumping on his back as he headed home. He'd do his homework…later. It was cool having an hour before Sheila and Zach got off, when he became unwillingly responsible for them. Except…that was partly posturing for friends. Really, he and Zach were tight. He couldn't talk to his little brother about girls or these strange, physical urges he was starting to feel, but that was okay. Zach would get there. And Bran loved his little sister. She thought he was a superhero, which felt good—

BRAN BLINKED, MADE a rough sound and ran a hand over his face. Damn. He hadn't expected to flash back like that. If he was going to go back at all, it should be to the night when Sheila was taken from her bed. When—

"Shit," he muttered, getting into his car. Flashing back to the kid he'd been? What good would that do? He had to look at the crime with a cop's ability to be dispassionate. To do that, he needed to get past the memories.

Paige had never said anything to make him think she knew about his past. He sure as hell hadn't told her. Didn't plan to unless it became absolutely necessary. Except for his regular six-month visit to this damn house, he was focused on the future not the past.

As he pulled away from the curb, he took a last look at his childhood home and felt an unexpected pang. How many times had he thought of searching for his brother? Too many. Kids or not, they'd parted as bitterly as their parents had. Chances were they'd pass on the street without even recognizing each other. There was no going back.

Then why am I trying?

A good question. It wasn't as if he believed in

the psychobabble about needing closure or any crap like that.

But he couldn't deny that the tragedy had shaped his life and still hung over him. He would soon be starting a family of his own. He wanted the foundation to be solid, that was all.

ZACH CARTER'S GAZE roved unceasingly as he drove, touching on his rearview mirror every few seconds before scanning for movement on each side of the street. He identified the speed of cars ahead and behind without conscious thought. Although returning to patrol had been an adjustment for him, the instincts were still there. He made constant, automatic judgments.

The man coming out of a garage? Homeowner. The cluster of tattooed young guys clustered around a car with its hood raised? Currently harmless, although the way they all turned as a unit to watch as he passed had him keeping an eye on them in the rearview mirror for another block. Car that swerved and corrected course? A momentarily distracted driver.

He'd been on the job for not quite three weeks. The population of this rural county wasn't large but the square mileage was. Logging trucks still traveled an east-west highway that followed the river deep into the forested foothills of the Cascade Mountain Range. Only one big lumber mill remained in operation, however, which meant logging as an industry was in decline.

The dairy farms he remembered from when he was a kid had mostly disappeared. In fact, the east county communities all had an air of desperation. For Rent, For Sale and Going Out of Business signs were common, boarded-up shop windows even more so. It was beautiful country, but tourism hadn't taken hold. Didn't help that the couple motels he'd spotted were pretty rundown, in keeping with the general atmosphere.

So far, he'd been assigned to patrol the river valley part of the county. Today's route combined new developments, older housing sprawls just outside the city limits of the county seat and farms.

It had been an incredibly mild winter. With it now the first week of April, daffodils were showing hints of bloom and tulips would follow, weeks earlier than usual. He'd seen the fresh green spikes of corn in fields. Peas weren't the big crop they'd been when he was a kid, but were still grown, and strawberries, too.

He'd already discovered that the older neighborhood he'd just turned into was heavily Hispanic. New immigrants and probably some undocumented aliens provided cheap labor for agriculture. He'd been instructed to leave Customs issues to ICE—Immigration and Customs Enforcement—and stick to local law enforcement, which was fine by him.

Whatever his assignment, Zach varied his route every day, trying to learn every byroad. Despite flashes of familiarity, most of it was new to him. What kid paid attention when he was slumped in the backseat of a car?

The stretch of county closer to the freeway had changed the most. Real estate in Seattle and its suburbs was priced beyond a lot of people's means these days, which meant if they wanted to own a home, they bought farther out and resigned themselves to a two-hour-plus round-trip commute to work. Most of the residents of the newer, more upscale developments eating up what had been farmland were commuters. Midday, he could drive up and down the winding streets of any of those developments and hardly see a soul.

In contrast, this neighborhood was what he thought of as in-between: the houses modest but still decently cared for. At least some were owned rather than rented, at a guess. No traffic and the last human he'd seen had been a couple of blocks ago: an old man peering suspiciously from his front porch.

A rack of lights atop a car down the block on a cross street caught his eye. Surprised, Zach made the turn. What was another sheriff's department car doing here? By necessity, patrols didn't have a lot of overlap and he hadn't heard any calls from dispatch that would have sent another deputy out here. Currently empty, the police car was parked on the gravel verge—no sidewalks in this neighborhood. Guy might live here, it occurred to Zach. He'd taken his own lunch break not half an hour ago.

He was still half a block away when he spotted two men arguing. They stood toe-to-toe on a concrete walk leading to the front porch of a small house. Whatever was happening was intense. The one with his back to the street wore the same olive-green uniform as Zach's. Then… What the hell? The deputy pushed the other guy, pulled his arm back and punched.

Oh, shit, Zach thought. No. The cop was using his baton, not his fist. Hammering with it. Blood sprayed.

Zach slammed to a stop and leaped out, now able to hear the snarls, the cries for help.

A good thirty feet away, he broke into a hard run. A woman was tearing across the lawn toward the men from the house beyond, too. She was screaming.

Showing no awareness of anyone else, the deputy threw his baton away and began using his fists instead. "I warned you! Stay away from her. But—" smack "—did you listen?"

"*¡Socorro! ¡Socorro!*" The Hispanic man stumbled back.

Zach caught a glimpse of his face, already battered to a pulp before another fist caught him dead-on and his lights went out.

Time seemed to have slowed. Zach saw what was coming and knew he was too late to stop it. The Hispanic guy toppled back. His head struck the edge of the concrete step. The sound was terrible. A pumpkin being smashed.

One step too late, Zach grabbed the deputy's shoulder and yanked him back. "What the hell are you doing?" he yelled.

The guy staggered, righted himself and lurched around in a fighter's stance. Face crimson with rage, he started to swing at Zach before recognition dawned in his eyes and he stopped himself.

"He went for my gun." He gasped for air. "He went for my gun, goddamn it! I had to defend myself."

Hayes, that was his name. Andrew Hayes. Big, beefy guy starting to go soft. Ugly sense of humor. Zach knew him only from the locker room.

"Oh, my God. Oh, my God." Keening, the woman had dropped to her knees beside the victim, who wasn't moving. "Is he dead? I think he might be dead."

Hayes looked past Zach and said sharply, "Ma'am, you need to back away. This is police business. Return to your house."

She lifted her head to sizzle him with green-gold eyes. "Antonio is harmless. You killed him."

"Ma'am, you need to listen—"

Zach gave him a hard push. "Back off and shut up. Do you hear me?"

That earned him some invectives.

Ignoring him, Zach turned his attention to the victim when, out of the corner of his eye, he saw Hayes lean over to pick up his baton. Swearing, Zach slapped a hand onto the deputy's chest. "Do I have to cuff you?" he asked, voice hard. "You *will* keep back. Don't move. Don't touch. Do you hear me?"

"What the hell? We're on the same side. The asshole grabbed for my weapon! I did what I had to."

"This is now a crime scene. Don't touch anything. Wait."

Zach called for backup and an ambulance. When he saw Hayes take a step toward his vehicle anyway, he snapped, "Do *not* move!"

Then, finally, he crouched beside the fallen man and gently touched his throat.

Oh, damn. The lady with the green-gold eyes was right. Antonio was dead. Zach couldn't even figure out how to administer first aid, the guy's head was such a sickening sight.

The woman and he looked at each other across the body. Momentarily stunned, Zach stared for a few beats too long. Her right hand was bloody, he saw when he could finally wrench his gaze from her face. She'd touched the victim when she'd first fallen to her knees beside him.

Zach lifted his own hand to see that, yeah, his own fingertips were bloody, too.

At the sound of an approaching siren, he said gently, “There’s nothing you can do. The medics will be here any minute.”

She looked down then back up. “He’s dead, isn’t he?”

“I’m afraid so.”

“Why?” she whispered.

“I have no idea.” An ambulance rocketed to a stop in the driveway only a few feet away. Zach stood, circled to her side of the body and held out his hand. “Let’s back off and let them do their job.”

An unmarked police SUV blocked Zach’s car in. Having cut off the siren, the undersheriff himself, a whipcord-thin guy with buzz-cut gray hair, stepped out and started across the lawn. Paul Stokes. He’d been in on the interview when Zach was hired.

“Hayes? What the hell is this?”

The woman still hadn’t moved.

“Please,” Zach said quietly. “I need to talk to people. They’ll want to hear what you saw, too.”

After a moment her head bobbed. She let him pull her to her feet and backed away as medics crouched to conduct an assessment. It wasn’t long before one glanced up and gave his head the faintest of shakes. Zach nodded and walked toward the undersheriff and Andrew Hayes.

Seemingly unaware that his hands were battered and bloody, Hayes was doing all the talking. Zach, eyes narrowed, listened but kept his mouth shut. He'd have his turn. And unless the woman wimped out, there was a second witness.

Unable to help himself, he turned his head. She stood right where he'd left her, shoulders hunched, hugging herself, her stricken gaze fixed on the dead man.

But suddenly, as if she felt a pull, her head turned, too, and her eyes met Zach's. Once again they stared, neither blinking, nothing hidden.

"Deputy Carter," Stokes said sharply.

Zach shook himself, bent his head in acknowledgment to the woman—of what?—and faced his commanding officer.

TESS GRANATH LEANED against the fender of one of the police cars. She had declined the offer to sit in the backseat—behind the wire grille.

"Ms. Granath…or is it 'missus'?" the officer asked.

Not officer, she reminded herself, or even deputy. He had identified himself as a detective. She groped to remember his name. Delancy or Delaney or something like that. He was in his forties, at a guess, and had too many muscles, which meant off the job he lived at the gym.

"Ms. is fine."

"Are you married?"

Tess raised her eyebrows. "How is this relevant to what I saw?"

"Just trying to get some background, ma'am." He paused. "Spouses, what we do for a living, influences our perceptions."

The "ma'am" irritated her, after all that crap about whether she was a Ms. or a Mrs. The use of the word "perceptions" irritated her even more. The event she'd witnessed was straightforward. It had happened too fast for any filters to kick in.

"I'm not married."

"All right then, Mi-izz Granath." He dragged it out, his tone laden with condescension. "You live here close by?"

Since he held her driver's license in his hand, he knew exactly where she lived. She said, "No."

"May I ask your purpose for being here?"

"I was checking on a friend next door who recently had surgery."

"And this friend's name?"

"Lupe Estrada."

"I'm surprised this friend hasn't come out. Given all the commotion and all."

"As I said, she had surgery. Abdominal. She is barely able to get up long enough to go to the bathroom. I stopped by to see if she needed anything because her husband had to work today."

The detective wanted to know if she and Lupe

had been friends for long. Since high school. So that meant Tess might have met some of the neighbors, too. Yes, she had.

"What about the fellow who was involved in this fracas?"

"If by that you mean the man who was just beaten to death? Yes. I knew him to nod at. I wouldn't call him a friend."

"But you know his name."

"Yes. Antonio. Antonio Alvarez, I think."

"So you saw him as a nice guy."

"He seemed pleasant. I understand he lived here with his uncle and a couple of cousins. Antonio is a friend of Lupe's husband, Rey. As I said, I don't—" the word caught in her throat "—didn't know him well."

"All right," he said. "When did you first see him today?"

"I'd left my sweater and handbag in the living room. On my way out, I was reaching for them when I glanced out the window and was surprised to see a police car parked in front of Antonio's house. I could just see him and the deputy, speaking."

"And where were they standing?"

"Antonio had stepped down from the porch. I could see that the conversation was…heated."

"Could you hear what was being said?"

"Not at that point. Only enough to know they

were yelling. The deputy's face was flushed, as if he was angry."

"Now that's quite an assumption, given you don't know him." The detective affected a look of surprise. "Or do you?"

"I do not." And wouldn't want to, she thought grimly.

"Then you have no basis for comparison."

"No, I don't. However—" She lifted her hand when he started to interrupt. "In my experience, a combination of a raised voice and flushed cheeks generally suggests anger in any individual."

It went on that way. He tried hard to persuade her to admit she hadn't seen what had preceded the first blow. But she had. By that time she'd been on the Estradas' front porch with a clear sight line to the two men arguing.

"I was concerned because the police officer was considerably larger than Antonio. His voice and body language were belligerent."

"But your friend Antonio was angry, too."

"As I've said repeatedly, I wouldn't describe him as a friend. It was clear they were arguing about a woman. Just before the first blow was struck, Antonio accused the police officer of hurting her. The deputy told him to stay away from her, pulled his nightstick from his belt, lifted it and swung. That first blow knocked Antonio back a step. The deputy pursued."

Delancy kept circling back to what she'd seen when. "Now, you must have looked away at some point."

She shook her head. "I don't think I so much as blinked. I may have missed something as I bounded down the porch steps, but your deputy was well into the beating by then. The second police car had pulled up and I saw that officer racing toward them even as I ran across the yard." She swallowed. "We were both too late."

"You approached from the left of the two men engaged in the argument."

Since she'd described, ad infinitum, exactly where she was at all times, she said nothing.

"Deputy Hayes wears his service weapon on his right hip. Chances are good you couldn't see it."

She considered and finally agreed that, no, she probably hadn't been able to.

He looked satisfied, thinking he'd made an important point. It wasn't hard to figure out what that was.

Tess continued. "However, if you're suggesting Antonio reached for the weapon, I can tell you that he did not. From where I stood, I *was* able to see his hands. He did not raise them or reach toward the deputy until he tried to cover his face *after* the beating commenced."

God. She sounded like an attorney in court. Had she ever used the word "commenced" before? She kind of doubted it. But she'd never been interviewed by a police detective before, either. Or, in fact, anybody at all who so blatantly disbelieved every word out of her mouth. She'd had angry customers before, but none of them had tried so hard to twist what she said.

He asked more questions that were re-phrasings of ones he'd already asked.

Finally, Tess said, "Detective, I really need to get back to work. You're welcome to contact me later if you need any more information."

She had to ask for her driver's license before he handed it over. The last thing he said was, "You've made one hell of an accusation here, Ms. Granath. I hope you know what you're getting into."

She had started toward her car but a sudden chill raised goose bumps on her arms. She turned around. "Just what is that supposed to mean, Detective Delaney?"

"Delancy. And I think you have a good idea. Deputy Hayes is a sixteen-year veteran of this department. He's well liked and respected. And now here you are, suggesting he killed a man because he was a little annoyed."

"Try furious," she said bitingly. "If you didn't know your Deputy Hayes has an anger-management problem, you should have."

He said something else to her back but she didn't listen and she didn't look at him again.

Tess drove several blocks before she let herself pull over, put the gearshift in Park and rest her forehead against the steering wheel. Her heart raced, her hands shook and she was gasping for breath.

Oh, great. Now *I'm falling apart.*

Because she'd just seen a man killed? Or because she'd just been threatened by a police officer?

A broken laugh escaped her.

Eenie, meenie, miney, moe. God help her, she'd definitely caught a tiger by the toe.

She wanted rather desperately to believe she was overreacting. The detective might have been testing her to find out how strong a witness she'd be. It wasn't as if shutting her up would do any good, considering that other sheriff's deputy had been there, too. She would swear he'd been as appalled as she was. Angry, too.

Tess closed her eyes so she could picture him. Tall, lean, with unruly dark hair, shoving Deputy Hayes and snarling, "Back off and shut up." And he'd said it was now a crime scene.

Her heartbeat picked up again as it occurred to her that he might have been warning the deputy to shut up before he said something they wouldn't want *her* to hear.

But she remembered the way he'd touched Antonio's neck in search of a pulse and then held out a hand to help her to her feet. When she asked why Antonio had had to die, the deputy had said, "I have no idea."

And then there was the way he had looked at her. The way they had looked at each other. He'd been completely in command, except when his very blue eyes had met hers. Then he had let her see that he, too, had been shaken.

Or—God—she was imagining some kind of intense connection and his face hadn't given away anything at all. He hadn't shared the same stunned bewilderment, the same horror and grief she'd felt. She'd seen him talk quietly with whatever superior officer had arrived after the fact, and then he'd driven away in his patrol car. She wasn't sure he'd so much as glanced at her again. He sure hadn't attempted to speak to her before leaving.

It didn't matter. She'd told the truth and she would keep telling it. And even if the sheriff's department didn't want to admit they had a bad apple, they were on the side of law, order and justice, right? That meant the investigator might pressure her, try to sway her testimony, but certainly wouldn't threaten her.

Tess lifted her head from the steering wheel and made a face. No, she wasn't that naïve, but she'd try to have *some* faith in local law enforcement.

Starting with the sheriff's deputy who had run faster than she'd believed possible in his futile effort to save Antonio Alvarez.

CHAPTER TWO

"You haven't been with us very long," Sheriff Brown said kindly, although his eyes were a lot less friendly. "I know you come from a large city police department. Different atmosphere. We don't get much turnover here, and there's a reason. We think of ourselves as one big family. Times of trouble, we stand behind one another."

Zach's primary emotion was disbelief.

His initial, brief interview yesterday with Paul Stokes had been direct, an appropriate opening to a serious investigation. His impression was that the undersheriff had been as disturbed as Zach had been by the situation.

The talk he'd had earlier today with Stokes had been different. The undersheriff had been a little more closed off, his questions sharper, as if he was trying to shake Zach. He had suggested they handle this "incident" internally.

Zach now had a pretty good idea who had been leaning on him.

Sheriff Brown had used the word "incident," too, when he'd made it clear that he wanted it swept under the carpet. Zach was supposed to be the broom.

His disbelief progressed through pissed to full-on fury.

A few minutes ago, as Zach had arrived in answer to the sheriff's summons, Hayes had swaggered out of the office. As they'd passed within a foot of each other, he'd given Zach a look dark enough to lift the hairs on the back of his neck.

"You're right," Zach said calmly now to the sheriff. "My experience is with a considerably larger police force. Professionalism was emphasized." He paused, watching Sheriff Brown's eyes narrow. "What I saw yesterday was a deliberate, brutal beating that led to a death. Maybe Deputy Hayes didn't intend it to go that far. I can't say. But the fact is, it did. What I heard gives me reason to believe the confrontation was over a personal issue, but Hayes was wearing the uniform when he instigated it, and he used his police baton as part of the beating. As far as I'm concerned, that takes him a step over the line from second-degree murder. He shamed law-enforcement officers everywhere."

That hard stare never wavered from Zach's face. Until now, he hadn't made up his mind about the longtime sheriff. In his sixties, George T. Brown was mostly bald and carried forty or fifty pounds too much. His strength was a folksy, reassuring charm that appealed to voters.

Call him a cynic, but from his initial job interviews, Zach had suspected Brown was a figurehead, with the real decisions being made by Stokes, the undersheriff.

Looking into these shrewd, angry eyes now, Zach changed his mind. Brown was no figurehead. And he had to have been leaning heavily on Paul Stokes.

In his short time with the department, Zach had heard some sexist and racist jokes he didn't like. There were only a couple of female deputies on this force. He couldn't help noticing how few Hispanic deputies had been hired, too, considering the county population had to be a third Hispanic. One had risen to sergeant. Otherwise the command structure was Caucasian and male. Ditto for the detectives.

He'd heard the same kind of jokes on his last job, and the hiring of female and ethnic officers had lagged in most police departments. Here in Harris County, part of the problem lay in the fact that so many deputies were long-timers. Change would come, but only as those long-timers retired.

He wondered whether the prevailing attitude might have been a little different if the dead guy had been Caucasian. Say, the son of a local businessman instead of an uneducated farmworker who had turned out to be in this country illegally.

That meant the uncle and brother, presumably

also illegals, had disappeared, unable to demand justice for Antonio.

The sheriff's chair creaked as he leaned back. "Son, I'm going to give you a few days to think about this before you damage the reputation and career of a fellow officer. You go that route, I can't swear anyone will buy in to what you have to say, anyway. Judges, prosecutors, defense attorneys… they all know and respect Andy Hayes. The man is a sixteen-year veteran of this department. You have any idea how many times he's testified in court in those years?"

Zach didn't say a word.

"Nobody knows you." He gestured, as if holding a weight in each hand. One sank while the other rose. "One thing for sure, I can guarantee you won't be real popular in this department if you hold on to what looks a lot like a vendetta. You might find yourself deciding to go back to your big-city department." The last was a drawl barely disguising a sneer.

Zach kept his expression from changing in any way. He held the stare long enough to make it plain he wasn't intimidated and rose from the chair he'd been offered facing the sheriff's desk. "Sir," he said politely, bending his head and walking out of the office.

He knew he was in deep shit, made worse because he was the new guy. A couple other deputies had quietly expressed their support, but a number had urged him to retreat from his "story." Andy Hayes was a fine officer, a good guy. He wouldn't have just beaten a man to death for the hell of it. No, sir. Accidents happened. If the fellow's head hadn't happened to hit that concrete step… Damnedest thing, him stumbling back and falling in just the wrong place. But when a man went for a police officer's gun? Well, he was asking for anything.

Zach was ninety-nine-percent sure Antonio Alvarez had not gone for Andy Hayes's gun. Even if he had, Hayes had dominated the encounter from that moment on. He could have had Alvarez on the ground, cuffed and arrested without breaking a sweat. Zach couldn't think of an excuse in the world for Hayes to have beaten the shit out of the guy. What's more, he had a suspicion Alvarez had been dead before he'd hit the concrete. Maybe he'd only lost consciousness, but he'd looked like a dead man from the instant his head snapped back and his body collapsed like a puppet's with the strings cut.

Nobody wanted to talk about why Hayes had been there in the first place—well out of his patrol sector. They weren't talking about the results of the autopsy, either—if it had even been done yet. As was common in rural counties, the coroner wasn't a physician. Zach wanted to believe he wouldn't cooperate with a cover-up.

No matter at what point Alvarez had died,

going for a police officer's gun was not a crime deserving of the death penalty, not if the officer had the ability to control the situation. Which Hayes unquestionably had.

Zach had no doubt he'd already have been fired if the sheriff hadn't been afraid of the repercussions. Whatever Stokes thought personally, publicly the undersheriff would have to bow to his boss. Right now, they controlled the contacts Zach could talk to. If they cut him loose, they had to know he'd go straight to the press, the county commissioners, activists representing the Latino community.

The killing of an unarmed Hispanic man by a red-neck white deputy had the potential to explode into a scandal of nationwide proportions. The sheriff and undersheriff had to be seeing Ferguson and Pasco in their nightmares.

Too bad no one had had a camera phone, Zach thought grimly.

The good news was that he hadn't been the only witness. It was pretty clear the woman hadn't backed down yet, at least. She hadn't gone to the press, either, but if they pushed too hard, they couldn't stop her.

Zach knew her name now. Teresa Granath. *Ms.* Granath, the detective had said with sarcastic emphasis.

Zach had just come in from patrol. The sheriff's department couldn't afford to lose two of them at the same time and, as was standard practice, Hayes had been placed on administrative leave since a man had died during an altercation.

The incident.

Having finally clocked out, Zach had decided to contact Ms. Granath. He'd been careful yesterday once Stokes had arrived at the scene not to make eye contact with her or to try to speak to her. He didn't want anyone thinking he'd influenced what she had to say. He'd be in trouble if he was seen with her now, but he'd passed the point of caring. He wanted to know how much shit they'd been giving her and whether she could stand up to it. Whether he could depend on her.

He assumed she'd have left her workplace, which he'd learned was a home improvement store. He'd planned to pay it a visit one of these days, anyway, because he was only days from closing on a house that needed work. He'd be out significant money if he lost his job.

But forget the house. If he didn't last on this job, he'd lose the chance to investigate his sister's murder. His jaw was tight as he jumped into his pickup. Damned if he'd give up this easily.

No Teresa Granath appeared in the local phone directory, so, despite the rules against it, he'd accessed DMV records to find her. She lived within the city limits of Clear Creek, which would reduce the likelihood of anyone from the sheriff's department happening to drive by and see his Silverado parked out front.

Just to be on the safe side, he left it a block away. The neighborhood consisted of nice family homes, ramblers and some split-levels. Most probably dated to the 1980s. Hers was a rambler, not a big place but in good shape, with a white picket fence and flowerbeds. She or someone she lived with was a gardener. The concrete walkway passed under an arch covered by rose canes unfurling green leaves.

If she was home, her car was in the garage. He rang the doorbell and waited…

He frowned and glanced toward the front window. Unfortunately the wood blinds were drawn.

At the sound of the door opening he turned back sharply. The sight of her disturbed him, renewing the strange bond they'd formed yesterday when they'd looked at each other over the dead body.

This time he was able to assess her, although no physical evaluation would tell him how strong an ally she'd be. As a man, he did like what he saw.

She was pretty, with beautiful hazel eyes and a cute bump on the bridge of her nose. A few freckles gave her a girl-next-door look—except that she had a sexy mouth. The hair he'd vaguely thought of as brown was actually glossy and caramel-colored.

Otherwise…she was tall for a woman. Five ten

or even eleven, and slim. He'd have said skinny except she did have curves. They were subtle but plenty female. And long legs. Damn, it was no wonder she'd crossed that lawn so fast.

"Deputy," she said, her voice just a little husky.

"Ms. Granath."

Her mouth curved. "Your detective really wanted me to be a miss or a missus. 'Ms.' seemed to disturb his sense of order."

Zach chuckled, although her smile along with those really fine legs stirred his body in uncomfortable ways. He reined it in. "This area seems to be lagging a little behind the times."

She made a face. "I've noticed. Please, come in."

He followed her in and waited while she closed the door.

"Why don't you come on back to the kitchen?" she suggested. "I was working on dinner."

"I'll try to make it brief, then. I, uh, just wanted to make sure you're being treated decently."

He was distracted as they went by the glimpses he had into her living room, what looked like a library and home office and a dining room. He was impressed. She must have had some serious work done.

He doubted floors in a house of this era had originally been hardwood, for example. The molding could have been from a 1920's cottage, the effect enhanced by wood blinds either white-painted or warm-maple-stained throughout and a French door that led from an eating area out to the back garden. Kitchen cabinets had a cottage look, too.

The stained maple was the same color as her hair, he couldn't help noticing.

Countertops had been tiled in a bold red picked up by the display of antique stoneware on a shelf above the upper cabinets.

And, damn, something smelled good.

"You're a gardener," he said, gazing out at a backyard that, like the front, wasn't very big but was bound to be a profusion of cottage-garden bloom in another couple months. There was color even now, mostly from daffodils and crocuses and a shrub with vivid yellow blooms. She seemed to have a lot of rosebushes.

"I am," she agreed. "It's my hobby. I especially love antique roses. There are moments I wish I had a way bigger yard so I could grow more of them, but I remind myself how much maintenance what I have takes. I don't want gardening to quit being fun and start being work."

"I know what you mean," he agreed. "I just bought a fixer-upper to flip."

She raised her eyebrows in surprise.

"I've remodeled a couple before," he explained, "and made a decent profit when I sold them."

"Really." After adjusting the heat on a stove burner, she leaned back against the counter. "You know I'm in the home improvement business." She waved at the bar stools. "Have a seat."

Because he wanted to ease into his real purpose, he asked a few questions and learned she didn't just work at Fabulous Interiors, she and a partner owned it. Her area of specialty was window treatment and ceramic tile. Her partner, flooring. The partner was a man—she called him Greg—but Zach couldn't get a feel for whether the relationship was business-like, friendship or romantic.

He was irritated at himself for even wondering.

"What got you started flipping houses?" she asked. Pretty obviously, she was sounding him out the same way he was her.

So, okay, he could give a little.

"I had a stepfather who was a contractor." Actually the stepfather whose name he'd taken. "I worked for him summers during high school and college. That's not what I wanted to do for a living, but I enjoy working with my hands." He shrugged. "It's a good hobby."

She glanced ruefully toward her garden. "Except you actually make money at your hobby."

He had to laugh. "Mostly. When too many problems don't turn a house into a sinkhole." After a pause he asked, "Are you a local?" This was edging a little closer to what he really needed to know. *How woven into the fabric of this com-*

munity are you? Can I depend on you not to buckle under the pressure?

He hoped she hadn't noticed his stomach rumbling. He'd try to get out of here before he embarrassed himself.

"Yes and no. I graduated from high school here, but left for college. I came back three years ago because my dad is in poor health. Mom is gone…and I thought he needed me." She huffed. "Not that he agrees. He's determined to stay in his house. And although he finally let me hire someone to do the housework, he still insists on doing too much."

"Heart?"

"Stroke." Grief shadowed her face. "It's probably just a matter of time before he has another one."

"I'm sorry," he said gently.

"Thank you." She turned back to the stove, giving something a stir before turning off the burner and pulling the pan off. This time, when she turned to face him, her expression was resolute. "You didn't come to exchange gardening and home improvement tips."

"No." Zach moved his shoulders a little to ease the tension. "The department wants the 'incident' never to have happened. The two of us are an inconvenience."

"I've noticed." Her tone was dry. "Should your

department be investigating when it's one of their own officers accused of a crime?"

"No," Zach said bluntly. "My guess is some of the pressure is being applied now in the hope the department doesn't have to hand off the investigation to someone else. Which, in my opinion, should have happened immediately."

"Well, it definitely hasn't been. Detective Delaney—excuse me, Delancy—grilled me two ways from Sunday. And then he stopped by the store again today. He seems to think if he keeps circling back, I'll either change my story or he'll get me to admit that Antonio and I were having a torrid affair and I'm lying through my teeth because—who knows?—I'm protecting his memory. I haven't a clue."

He nodded. "Ms. Granath, I won't ask you what you've told him, and I'm not going to tell you what I've said, either. It's easy to be subconsciously influenced once you share what you saw with other witnesses."

She nodded. "That makes sense. Please, call me Tess. You're Deputy Carter?"

"Zach Carter."

Her gaze became challenging. "Are you here to lean on me a little, too? Point out how much damage I'm doing to an upstanding officer's career?"

One side of his mouth tipped up. "Never crossed my mind. I will tell you that Andrew Hayes is an ass."

Her carefree laugh came out of the blue, considering what they'd been discussing. "In that case, unless you're expected home for dinner, you're welcome to share mine. It's chicken in a wine sauce on brown rice."

"It smells amazing." Damn, he had to swallow his saliva. "Are you sure you have enough?"

Eyes hinting at amusement, she said, "Positive."

He asked where he could wash up and she sent him to a half-bathroom connected to a small laundry and mudroom.

Tess had produced a salad by the time he returned to the kitchen. She'd set the small table by the French doors rather than the larger one in the dining room. Bright red tulips in a simple white pitcher sat in the middle of the table. A few petals had fallen.

"These were already in bloom?" he said in surprise.

"Oh, I doubt it. I assume they were forced. Truthfully, I bought the bouquet at the grocery store. I spoil myself by buying some occasionally through the winter. I grow daffodils and tulips, but not enough for cutting."

They served themselves then looked at each other across the table. "I guess I kind of stuck you with company, didn't I?" he said ruefully.

Smiling, she shook her head. "I wouldn't have invited Deputy Hayes to stay for dinner if he'd dropped by. *Or* Detective Delancy." Her green-gold eyes met his. "Do you know him very well?"

"No. I'm new with the sheriff's department. I haven't even finished my third week. I moved up from Portland."

"What brought you away from the city?"

Zach hesitated. He should have thanked her for the invitation but then declined. He'd have to make it clear to her before he left that they needed to keep their distance from here on out—at least, until the review and trial. And that could be a very long, drawn-out process. Just the prosecutor's decision to file charges—or not—could be six months or more away.

He was attracted to her, but shutting down anything like that wouldn't be a problem. Yeah, they had some interests in common, but didn't share anything close to the same underlying motivations. He liked turning a dump into a house, but not because he was creating a home for himself the way she obviously had.

As far as women went, he enjoyed sex, but only when it came with no strings. Nothing in his life to this point had made him even distantly imagine himself ever getting married. He rarely had a relationship—if you could call it that—that lasted longer than a couple months.

An alliance was what they were building, one that would ensure justice was done.

"I lived here in Clear Creek until I was nine,"

he said abruptly. "Then my parents split up and…" He shrugged. "I've gotten to an age when I needed to figure some things out." *Like who raped my little sister and then strangled her.*

"Oh." Tess's expression softened. He was pretty sure she wasn't thinking anything close to what had happened. "Do you still have…? I mean, are your parents alive?"

"My mother is. My father…" Another shrug. "No idea."

She went still with a bite suspended halfway to her mouth. "You mean you didn't see him after the divorce?"

"No. He went one way, Mom the other." Although he could have kept seeing his father, that decision had been allowed to be his.

Her eyes searched his. After a moment she said, "I'm sorry."

Jaw tight, he nodded.

She started eating again and kept her gaze on the table, which made him feel like a jerk.

"What about you? Any other family to help you with your father?"

"A brother, but he's in Alaska. In a pinch he'd fly down to help with moving Dad or cleaning out his house but, you know, it's hard for him to get away and expensive to make the trip."

Zach nodded, feeling awkward again. "Ah… Antonio. Was he a friend?"

"I thought we weren't going to talk about him."

"I'll stay away from anything you saw. I would like to know if they're going to be able to trip you up by claiming you're not an impartial witness."

"No," she said flatly. "That detective tried. I knew Antonio's name only because Lupe waved and said hello a couple times when we were coming or going. I nodded and smiled at him a few more times. I don't even know if he spoke English."

"Do you speak Spanish?"

"As someone who took it in high school, which was way too many years ago. My vocabulary has increased because we get customers in the store who don't speak very good English. But all I'm capable of are broken sentences in a lousy accent. Oh, and I don't remember anything I learned about verb tenses. I've actually been thinking of either buying a set of language tapes or taking a class at the community college."

"Lupe speaks English, I take it?"

Tess smiled. "Lupe and I went to high school together. They let her take fourth-year Spanish, which totally destroyed the bell curve. Of course, she pointed out that the rest of us got to take English, which wasn't any more fair to her."

Zach laughed then looked down at his empty plate. "This was great. Thank you."

"There's a dab more if you have room."

A polite man would say no. "Uh…"

She dished it up and he polished it off.

"I'm afraid I don't have any dessert to offer," Tess said. "But if you'd like a cup of coffee…?"

He would have loved a cup of coffee. And maybe to see her smile a few more times. Which meant it was past time he left.

"Thank you, but I'd better be going." He hesitated. "I shouldn't have come at all. I won't ask you to lie, but it would be better if nobody knows we've talked."

"If you're parked out in front…"

"I'm not."

Her eyes widened. "Do you want to sneak out the back and hop over the fence?"

"I'd probably trample on whatever you have growing out there, tear my pants on the fence and discover your next-door-neighbor has a Doberman."

Tess chuckled. "No Doberman, but the rest sounds possible."

"Let me give you my phone number in case you run into trouble."

She nodded and jotted it down. He hoped she'd put it in her phone. She would probably never need it, but…the stand they had taken was infuriating a dangerous man.

She walked him to the door. "I'm glad you were there," he said. "With two of us speaking out, we may be able to force the department to hold Hayes accountable."

She offered her hand. "If you hadn't been there, I'd have lost all faith in the police. So thank you."

They shook, her hand fine-boned and a little cool to the touch. He opened the front door to find that dusk would enable him to depart unseen. He'd pass through the circle of light from only one streetlamp. No sheriff's department cruiser lurked. "I'll hope to see you in court," he said politely. *And not until then.*

She'd retreated as obviously as he had. Like his tone, her smile was courteous and no more. "Don't forget Fabulous Interiors when you get to that stage on your house."

"I won't." He took the porch steps two at a time and moved with long strides to the sidewalk and down the street. Behind him he heard the quiet sound of her door closing.

SUNDAY, TESS VISITED Lupe again, giving only a single, shuddering glance at the small house next door. That was enough to tell her nobody had cleaned up the blood that had dried on the step and the concrete walk. Had the police ever even put up that yellow crime scene tape? If so, it was gone. Probably the landlord would eventually slosh soapy water and wash Antonio's lifeblood off into the unkempt lawn.

It bothered Tess to know that everything Antonio and his relatives owned had been left behind, too, to be thrown away or given to a thrift store. Unless neighbors knew where his uncle and cousins had gone and helped them reclaim their possessions. Tess rather hoped so. She was tempted to ask if Lupe knew, but didn't want to put her on the spot.

Lupe and Rey wanted to know what the police had said and what they'd asked Tess. She was even more conscious of the tension from Rey. He wasn't hostile, but his usual wariness around her had been better disguised by civility. Lupe kept stealing quick, nervous peeks at him.

Tess made her excuses and left sooner than she'd planned.

She felt both angry and disturbed all evening. Reading about tragedies like Antonio's death was one thing, seeing it in too vivid color was another. And the police response was just as unnerving. Her simple faith in her friendly local cops had been shattered.

Except for Zach Carter, of course, who'd made it clear he'd be keeping his distance.

She was a little bit sorry about that. He was a sexy man who also had integrity *and* construction skills. It was hard not to wonder whether he might have been interested in her under other circumstances.

Well, chances were she wouldn't see him again until they both appeared in court—if that happened.

MONDAY MORNING SHE had parked in her usual spot in the alley behind the store and rounded the Dumpster before seeing the piece of paper pinned to the plain back door of Fabulous Interiors. That was odd. A message from one of their installers?

Ten feet away, she froze, clenching the straps of her handbag in a white-knuckled grip. In livid red marker, someone had printed BACK OFF BITCH OR ELSE.

Deep breaths, she told herself. Sticks and stones. Really, as threats went, this was high-school caliber. Immature and not specific.

But when she blinked, she saw Andrew Hayes's face, flushed with uncontrollable rage. His fists flew. Blood spattered. Antonio's head snapped back and he fell.

Deputy Hayes might be immature, but he was big and muscular and violent. And *she* was a threat to him.

Oh, God. Oh, God.

Fear seized her until she shook, but a rising anger gradually enabled her to move again. What she should do was call 911, wait for a Clear Creek PD officer to arrive and then let *him* talk to Detective Delancy.

What she did was take the piece of paper between her thumb and forefinger and carefully peel it off the door along with the packing tape that had been used to hold it in place. She then returned to her car. The sheriff's department wasn't ten minutes away. Before she put the car in gear she called Greg, told him she would be about half an hour late and asked if he could open.

"I might be five minutes late, but no more," he said. "Is something wrong?"

"Yes, but I'll tell you about it when I get there."

She parked in a visitor spot in front of the sheriff's department that, along with county offices like the assessor's, was attached to the county courthouse. After carefully picking up the piece of paper with the same two fingers in the same place, she stalked inside.

Going straight to the counter, she glared at the officer behind it. "I want to see Detective Delancy. Now."

He looked twitchy, so her glare must have been effective. "Uh… I don't know if he's in or free to speak with you right now, but I'll find out. Your name?"

She told him.

"Thank you, ma'am. If he isn't in yet, I'm sure another detective is—"

"I want him." She must have looked as mad as she felt, because he hurriedly picked up his phone and held a low-voiced conversation coupled with darted glances at her and the piece of paper she was holding in front of her as if it was a soiled diaper.

"You can go on back," he told her, indicating a door at the end of the counter.

Just as she reached it, she heard a lock disengage.

She wasn't impressed by the detective bullpen, if that's what this was, she thought as she stepped through the door.

There was something like ten desks, each with a computer. A bank of file cabinets suggested not all records were computerized. Besides Delancy, the only other two people present were a middle-aged man and a younger one half a head taller. Both turned to look at her when she entered, but her eyes never left Detective Delancy's as he rose from behind one of the desks.

"Ms. Granath."

Gee, he'd gotten it right.

"This—" she thrust the paper at him "—was waiting for me when I arrived at work this morning."

He grabbed her wrist and turned it so he could read the threat. "It would have been better if you hadn't touched it."

"I was very careful to touch it only on the one corner. But, really, what idiot doesn't know how not to leave fingerprints? Especially since this was very likely left by a police officer." Her voice had been rising. She let the paper flutter onto his desktop.

"That's a serious allegation..."

"Yes, it is. Murder is a serious crime, Detective. It does not seem unreasonable of me to assume Deputy Hayes or one of his friends is responsible for this."

Out of the corner of her eye she was aware that the other two men had taken a few steps closer. What did they think—she was going to pull out a gun and start blasting?

Delancy gestured. "Please have a seat, Ms. Granath."

"I don't have time. I need to get to work. All I have to tell you is that this was taped to the back door of my business when I arrived this morning."

He frowned. "That's within the city limits."

"Yes, it is. But we both know this has to do with Antonio Alvarez's death and my insistence on being honest about what I saw."

"There's nothing that specific here." His eyebrows rose. "You might even have an unhappy customer."

"I am not currently involved in collecting on a debt. Otherwise, unhappy customers want faster service. They are annoyed because an installer failed to show or was late. The absolute *last* thing they want is for me to back off."

"Now, Ms. Granath, you're getting pretty riled

over something that may be entirely unrelated to the events you witnessed."

She stared hard at him then shook her head. "Maybe what I should be asking is how close *you* are to Deputy Hayes."

He stiffened. "Your implication is offensive."

"*This* is offensive. And I'm here to tell you I won't be backing off. Feel free to spread the word. And, oh, by the way? I'll be going to the press if this investigation isn't taken over really soon by another agency that has some semblance of impartiality."

She spun on her heel and walked out, both exhilarated by the electric crackle of her anger and a little bit afraid because she might as well have waved a red cape.

Come and get me.

CHAPTER THREE

ZACH WAS DRAGGING by the time he parked his patrol car and walked into headquarters to log out. Given that this was the first day of his work-week—Tuesday through Saturday—he had no excuse for being so beat.

He'd issued half a dozen speeding tickets today, one failure to yield right of way, a couple of warnings, had responded to two reports of stolen items, one of which he suspected was an insurance scam, and had administered first aid to a child choking on a gumball at a convenience store. An average day, except that he'd been aware of some hostile stares in the Hispanic neighborhoods. He hoped it had occurred to his boss that whitewashing the beating would be, politically speaking, a really bad move.

Like it or not, this was going to play out as a big, bad, white cop killing a defenseless, younger, physically less imposing immigrant. That they were quarreling over a woman and skin color might have been irrelevant? Not nearly as sensational.

Mood grim, Zach was striding toward the exit

when he glanced down a short hall that connected to the county offices and saw a man approaching. An automatic assessment took in the badge and holstered handgun at the man's belt. A detective he hadn't yet met?

The guy froze between one step and the next, just as Zach did the same. He felt as if he'd walked into a sliding-glass door.

Breathing hard, all he could do was stare. This could not be… But the eyes were his. The height, the build. Not the face. This man's was craggier, rougher. His hair was a dark russet.

He'd been a redhead as a boy.

"Bran."

"Zach?" His brother shook his head. "It can't be you."

"Why not?"

"Someone mentioned the name of the new guy."

"You mean me. I was adopted along the way. I'm Zach Carter now."

"Jesus." Bran dragged his hand through his hair. "What are you doing here?"

"What are *you* doing here?"

Zach's brother grimaced. "Dad and I never moved. I left for college, worked for Seattle PD for a few years…but this feels like home."

"Dad *stayed*?" Zach gaped at Bran, trying to take that in. "Didn't he know what everyone thought?"

"Not everyone," Bran said sharply. Then he let out a long breath. "Sure he knew. But you can't have forgotten how stubborn he was. People could think whatever the hell they wanted."

"Man, this is unreal."

"You can say that again."

Neither of them had moved or did anything to initiate what was bound to be an awkward hug. And yet, part of what Zach felt was something so unrecognizable it took a minute for him to label it as joy. His brother, here in front of him. A cop, too.

He hadn't forgotten the vast wash of hurt, though. This was the big brother who had abandoned him.

"You didn't answer my question," Bran said suddenly. "Why come back to Clear Creek?"

"Sheila. Why else?"

This was so bizarre Zach had trouble taking it in. He felt too much. He was thrilled but angry, too, even if he knew that was childish. And still… stunned.

As, in a completely different way, he'd been in that odd moment when his eyes had first met Tess Granath's.

"Wow." Bran gave something like a laugh. "Your shift over?"

"Yes. You?"

"Yeah, I took a recent vacation. Payroll got confused." He indicated the door behind him with a gesture. "I had to clear it up. Uh…any chance you're free? We could go get a drink. Have dinner."

"I am." He thought quickly. "You know The Creek?"

"Sure. Decent burgers and not a cop hangout."

They walked out together, which Zach found to be surreal. He hadn't seen this brother in twenty-four years. Never thought he would again, even though he'd worshipped Bran. He smiled sardonically at the thought because they'd fought, too. Zach had resented knowing his brother was in charge when Mom and Dad weren't home. He wasn't *that* much older. Sometimes Zach got almost mad enough to tell about the *Playboy* magazine Bran had under his mattress. But of course he never would have. Mostly, it was him and Bran against the world. And taking care of Sheila.

Until…nobody took care of her.

And then it wasn't him and Bran together. He'd have sworn he'd grown past the hurt but discovered he hadn't. Even so…

He's here now. Unbelievable.

"I drive the Silverado." He gestured.

"This is mine." Bran stopped by a sleek, obviously restored classic Camaro. The only thing it had in common with Zach's pickup was that both were black.

"This is a beauty." Zach circled it. "What year?"

"A '73."

"You do the work yourself?"

"With some help. I really wanted one of these when I was a teenager. Took me a few years to get one."

A memory surfaced. "You had a picture of one on your bulletin board."

God, Bran's grin was familiar. "A pinup," he said.

Zach narrowed his eyes. "In place of one of the naked women in that *Playboy*."

"You knew about—?" Bran gave an incredulous laugh. "This is really something."

"Yeah, it is." What, Zach wasn't sure. He lifted a hand and strode the rest of the way to his pickup. That did not require him to assume a pretzel shape to get behind the wheel, was good for hauling construction materials and was just as cool, in his opinion.

He found himself smiling. Okay, almost as cool. He wouldn't turn down the Camaro. Although Bran must have sunk one hell of a lot of money into it.

Ten minutes later his brother parked right next to him in front of the tavern. This early, they found most of the booths empty when they walked in. Two men sat on stools at the bar, one at each end. Neither even looked to see who'd come in. Zach didn't hear any crack of a cue striking a ball from the billiards room.

He ordered a pitcher and then slid into a booth,

Bran across from him. For what had to be two or three minutes, they just looked at each other.

Bran had changed and yet he hadn't. Zach wouldn't have expected to recognize him at first glance, but he hadn't had a moment's doubt. His brother had grown into the nose and jaw and too big feet and hands Zach remembered. But in the important ways, he was the same.

"Your hair got darker."

Bran grunted and rubbed a hand over his jaw. "My stubble has more red than my hair does." He was making as thorough a survey. "You were a shrimp. I thought you might take after Mom."

"I stayed a shrimp through middle school. No, later than that." He'd fought a lot of battles to prove that small didn't mean weak, but now he shrugged. "I had a growth spurt when I was fifteen. Seemed like an inch a month there for a while."

Bran laughed but it didn't last long. His face showed the same incredulity Zach still felt. "Mom alive?"

Tensing, Zach said, "Yeah." This was a sensitive subject, but he wasn't going to cover up, either. "On her fifth marriage, I think."

"You think?"

"I keep my distance."

His brother nodded. "Which one adopted you?"

"Number three. Lowell Carter. He was a good guy. The marriage only lasted four years, but he and I have stayed in touch. I worked for him summers during high school and then during college, too, after the divorce." He hesitated. "Dad?"

Bran shook his head. "He died last year."

Dead? Zach shook his head in shock.

"He was only sixty-two," Bran continued, "but he had cancer. He tried to quit smoking a few times, but it never took. I, uh, wrote to the last address he had for Mom, but it came back."

"We moved a lot," Zach said even as he absorbed the news that his father was dead. There'd be no reunion. He was surprised to feel grief despite everything. He guessed he shouldn't be. Even abused kids continued to love their parents, and he hadn't been abused.

Dad's death was a setback to his investigation, too. There'd be no chance to ask the hard questions now, although he hadn't yet figured out how to ask your own father whether he'd committed an unspeakable crime. But he would have found a way.

If he'd come back five years ago, Dad would still have been here. Two years ago.

I wasn't ready. Didn't have the skills to tackle an investigation this challenging.

He shut down the niggling doubt in his pat explanation. Exploring subterranean fears held no appeal.

A curvy blonde squeezed into jeans that were too tight for her and button-up Western-style shirt delivered their pitcher and glasses and appeared a little miffed at their disinterest. They both ordered burgers and fries.

"You married?" Bran asked.

Zach shook his head. "Are you?"

"Engaged. Paige is a nurse in Mount Vernon. She's kept her apartment so far."

"One of you will have to commute."

"She's watching for openings at the hospital here in town." Bran didn't sound very interested. "Where are you living?"

Zach told him about the house he was buying.

"You're planning to stay?" His brother sounded surprised.

"That wasn't my plan." *Wasn't?* Isn't.

"What was?"

"Like I said. Look into Sheila's death. Make some money on the house. Get answers, get out of here."

"And now?"

Zach took a long swallow of beer. "Still the same, except I'm not making myself popular on the job. The sheriff would really like to see me gone."

Big brother leaned back with a frown. "Why?"

"Because I saw another deputy beat a guy to death the other day."

"Right. Damn. You're the new guy," Bran said slowly. "There's a second witness, too. A woman."

"That's right. I think she'll stay the distance."

Bran smiled. "Going by what I saw, I'd put money on it."

"What you saw?"

"She came in yesterday morning. Nobody told you?"

Zach shook his head. "I'm off Sunday and Monday."

"According to her, a threat was taped to the back door of her business. Instead of calling the city PD, she ripped it off the door and blew in, insisting she wanted Detective Delancy or nobody. Who's a jackass," he added as an aside. "She slapped it on his desk and as good as said Hayes wrote it. Said our department had no business investigating one of our own. That woman had fire in her eyes."

Zach groaned.

"Then she told Delancy no threat would make her back off, and he could take it to the bank. Or words to that effect."

Why hadn't she called him? Damn it, he'd given her his number.

"What did it say? The threat?"

"'Back off bitch or else.' No comma. Red marker, slashed on the paper."

"Sounds like Hayes, all right," Zach growled.

Bran contemplated him. "I take it your stand is unpopular."

He huffed out a laugh then nodded toward their approaching waitress. "Here comes dinner."

A couple of Harleys pulled up outside. Zach didn't recognize either of the black-leather-clad bikers who took a turn around the Camaro before coming in and straddling stools at the bar, not seemingly bothered that two cops occupied a booth. Bran stayed relaxed, but was watchful, too.

Zach had swallowed a couple of bites before his brother asked, "Are you sure about what you saw?"

He set down the burger. "You doubting me?"

If so, this was going to be a real short family reunion.

Bran scowled. "I don't know you. What I heard is that a Hispanic guy went for Hayes's weapon and they scuffled. He went down, hit his head on a concrete step and died. I'm asking what *you* saw."

That was fair enough. It still took Zach an effort to unlock his jaw. He took a swallow of beer and started talking.

Eyes sharp, a couple of lines furrowing his brow, Bran never looked away from his face. At the end he said, "So you can't swear this Alvarez didn't go for the deputy's weapon."

"No, but the woman had a different angle. I'm hoping she knows." He shrugged irritably. "Either way, Hayes had complete control from the minute I arrived. Alvarez was unarmed. Hayes could have had him on the ground and cuffed at any time. Instead he hammered him."

"He's on leave."

"Yep. Because the 'incident' did result in a death," Zach said with curled lip.

"You're getting the feeling the department wants to soft-pedal it?"

"Oh, yeah. Because they think of themselves as one big family. In times of trouble, they stand behind one another. That's a quote from the sheriff, by the way. Me, I wouldn't understand that, coming from the big city the way I do." He grimaced. "Stokes seems okay, but he's bending to pressure."

"What big city?"

"Portland, Oregon."

Bran nodded acknowledgment. "Nothing like being the new guy and stirring up trouble."

"Oh, yeah," he said again. "But Ms. Granath is right. This investigation can't stay in-house. Does the sheriff really think the two of us are just going to go away and the department can bury the whole thing along with the body?"

Still with that frown, which might be permanent, Bran swirled some fries in ketchup and ate them before saying, "I don't know. I'll keep an ear to the ground."

What was that supposed to mean? I'm on your

side? I'll mull it over? Or he wasn't taking a stand of any kind but felt he had to say something?

Zach resumed eating.

It had to be a couple of minutes before Zach asked, "Have you tried looking into Sheila's murder?"

"Off and on. No one wants to talk to me. My last name is Murphy." He shrugged. "A couple of the detectives were around then and know who I am."

"Nolte?" The name rose from Zach's subconscious, surprising him.

"You remember the cops' names? You weren't very old."

He frowned, dredging his memory, finally having to shake his head. "Only his. Because of the actor."

"Except he wasn't Nick," Bran added.

"Last name's all I remember."

"It's Darren. But he has retired to Arizona. I tried to get access to records through Scott Wiegand, the other one I remember interviewing Mom and Dad. I didn't get the feeling he cares much if they ever close the case."

"I always wondered how much investigation they actually did."

"DNA wasn't on their register then." Bran dumped salt on his fries. "I kind of get the feeling it still isn't. I asked if they'd thought about testing her nightgown, but he mumbled something about no budget."

Zach straightened. "They still have her nightgown?"

"I don't know. The fact that he didn't want to talk about it gives me a bad feeling."

"Shit." Zach brooded for a minute. "What *did* you find out?"

"Nothing. He shut me down."

"You know they both thought Dad did it. They just couldn't prove it."

"That's bullshit," Bran snapped.

The two men locked eyes.

"Is it?" Zach asked.

"You're seriously asking?" His brother was pissed. "What would make you think something like that? You knew Dad!"

Zach glared. "Who do you think did it? Came in our house without breaking a window, got Sheila outside without her so much as screaming? Tell me that."

"One of Mom's many lovers," his brother said bitterly. "She might have handed out keys as often as she spread her legs."

Zach wanted to take offense but their mother had liked to pick up men. A little thing like a wedding ring on her finger didn't stop her.

Another thought occurred to him. "That's why you went with Dad."

"I tried to tell you. You wouldn't believe me."

"She was my mother!"

Turned heads told him he'd let his voice rise. As if he cared.

"She was a slut," his brother said flatly.

"Dad lied to the investigators."

Bran jerked back. "What?"

"He claimed he slept the night through. He didn't. I heard footsteps…and he took a piss. Then I thought I heard the back door." The memory haunted him. But he'd been a kid, barely nine. Maybe he'd dreamed it. Fallen back asleep after hearing his dad get up to use the john. Awakened again when the killer carried Sheila out. "He got up sometimes at night and went outside for a smoke." Mom hadn't let him smoke inside.

"You didn't say anything."

"He was my dad. I didn't want to think…" He rolled his shoulders to release the tension. "But I did, anyway. And as an adult? A cop? Yeah, I think."

"You're wrong." Bran reached for his wallet, pulled out two twenties, tossed them on the table and slid out of the booth. He looked down at Zach. "And I'll prove it." Then he walked away.

He'd blamed Mom. Told Zach he hated her. No wonder he'd never written back to her and refused to come to the phone when she'd called him.

Zach hadn't had the guts to say no when Dad called him. Mostly he'd mumbled and made the conversations so useless and awkward, the calls had come further and further apart until they'd ceased altogether.

It was Bran he'd refused to talk to at all. Zach had called it pride, then. Now, stupidity was the word that came to mind. In his hurt, he'd severed the ties that meant the most to him. Whatever happened with their parents, he and Bran could have stayed in touch. Continued to be brothers. Now…who knew?

Zach pushed his plate away but reached for his glass and drained it, his thoughts reverting to the quarrel that had stood between them then and, apparently, still did. Bran held Mom responsible for the tragedy.

Me? I blamed Dad. He lied. No matter what, he was supposed to keep us safe. Sheila's bedroom was right next to Mom and Dad's. How could he not *have heard somebody grabbing her, carrying her outside, raping her right there in the backyard? Unless…*

A harsh sound escaped him. He had loved his brother more than anyone else in the world. As if he'd time traveled, the devastation he'd felt when Bran had decided to go with Dad was new again. As painful in its own way as the one glimpse he'd had of his sister's body before he'd backed into the house and yelled for his parents.

He could still close his eyes and hear his mother's screams.

Dad had gone terribly silent and so angry everyone in the house had tiptoed around him. There'd been raised voices behind Mom and Dad's bedroom door. Mom might not have actually accused Dad, Zach didn't know. But their eyes had told the story. They had held each other responsible.

When Bran had told him about the men their mother saw during the day when Dad was at work, Zach had refused to believe him. He remembered Mom's screams—and Dad's lie.

So nothing had changed, he thought wearily. Bran and he had made their choices back then and they weren't about to unmake them. Bran, at least, had an agenda—to prove their father's innocence. Zach just wanted answers.

Working together apparently wasn't an option.

It would be interesting to see whether Bran admitted on the job to having a relationship with the pariah in the department.

TESS WAS FUMING when she finally let herself out and locked the back door of Fabulous Interiors on Wednesday afternoon. She didn't care what Todd Berry's excuse was this time. She was so done with him. This was the third time in just over a month he'd failed to show up to do a job without having so much as called. She had gone out herself in his place to install tile today, which she hadn't dressed for. She had no doubt the splotch of mortar on her blouse was permanent. The things she'd intended to accomplish today had gone undone. And, of course, she had to go back out to the Lacombes' house tomorrow to spread the grout.

And, blast it, she *liked* installing tile. When she didn't have a long list of other things that needed to be done. This was why the store relied on contract installers.

Of which she now had one fewer to call on.

Keys in hand, she reached her car, parked in its usual spot beside the big green Dumpster. She cringed every week when she heard the garbage truck drop the container back into place. *Please don't let them miss.* So far, so good.

Then she saw her front tire and whimpered. Oh, crap. All she needed was a flat. A slow leak? Maybe she'd driven over a nail…

Heart pounding, she walked around her car. All four tires were flat. Slashed.

She made another circle, looking for a note or another kind of message. But apparently the slashed tires *were* the message.

Tess called 911, then a local towing company. And, finally, she scrolled her contacts until she found Deputy Zach Carter's number, which she'd added right after he'd left her house last Thursday despite her certainty she would never need to use it.

Please let him answer. She desperately wanted to hear his deep, calm voice.

He answered on the third ring with an urgent, "Tess?"

She sagged in relief. "You recognized my number?"

"I put it in my phone," he told her without apology. "Is something wrong?"

"Yes. Um, Monday morning, someone taped a nasty note to the back door of my business."

"I heard about that."

"Just now, I locked up and was about to get in my car to go home. But, gee, what do I find? All four tires have been slashed."

"Are you parked on the street?" His voice had changed indefinably. Became cop.

"No, the alley. All the downtown merchants do. The street parking is for customers."

"Are you alone?"

Suddenly wary, she turned to look up and down the alley. "I don't see anyone else."

"Go back inside," he ordered. "I'll be there in five."

"No, I've already called 911 and for a tow truck. One of them will show up anytime."

"You're vulnerable, Tess." The tension in his voice got to her. "Don't wait out there alone."

"Okay, now you're scaring me," she told him, hurrying back across the alley. Thank God she still had her keys out.

Then she heard an engine and looked to see the tow truck lumbering toward her.

"Tess?" Zach said. "Are you there?"

She slumped against the shop door, willing her pulse to slow. "Yes. Yes, I'm okay. The tow truck is here. You don't need to come."

"I'm already on my way." He was gone.

She dropped her phone back into her handbag and smiled wryly at the muscular young guy hopping out of the tow truck. "Am I glad to see you."

"I get that a lot," he said with a grin.

She told him they were waiting for the police and then discussed options. He could load her car and take it to the tire store or he could go pick up four tires for her and change them here. Of course, she'd still have to take her car in for an alignment, but she could wait until tomorrow. Deciding on choice number two, she called Les Schwab and explained, agreed on the best tires for her car and gave the man her credit card number.

By that time a shiny black pickup had pulled into the alley behind the tow truck, and Zach had jumped out and started toward her, his gaze locked on her face. His intensity made it impossible to look away.

Tess was embarrassed by the rush of relief she felt. It wasn't as if she had been assaulted or even that she'd been waiting alone. But until this minute, she hadn't felt safe. Her knees seemed about to give out. The awareness she felt for Zach as a man—tall, lean, strong and purposeful—didn't help.

Reaching her, Zach murmured, "Tess," then finally turned to the tow truck driver and exchanged a few words. With a deep rumble, the truck departed.

"Still no police?" Zach asked, frowning.

"No. I've only had to call them once before, when we had a break-in. It took them half an hour that time, but it wasn't an emergency. I mean, the guy was long gone."

"This one presumably is, too, but I want to look around."

He circled the Dumpster and went as far as each end of the alley, scanning the pavement as well as each side, pulling himself up a couple of times to look over fences. He returned, shaking his head. "Nothing."

"What would you expect to find?"

He grunted. "Nothing. But you never know. The CCPD officer should look in the Dumpster to make sure our guy didn't toss the knife."

"Oh, sure," she scoffed. "With fingerprints intact."

His grin softened his usually bleak expression. His sharp blue eyes searched hers. "You okay?"

She'd crossed her arms tightly, Tess realized. Holding herself together. "I'm a little freaked," she admitted.

"This is going to cost you, too."

"My insurance might cover part of it. I'll study the policy when I get home. If not—" Thank goodness for the indignation that made the fear recede. "Damn it, I bought a full set of new tires in November."

Zach crouched beside one of her front tires, inspecting the slash and giving her an excellent view of his broad back with the olive-green shirt taut across it. "Nobody will be fixing these, that's for sure." He rose with an athletic ease she envied and faced her. "No note?"

Tess shook her head. "I assumed this was the 'or else.'"

His eyes were very intense. "Or only the beginning. This kind of harassment may continue."

She couldn't help a small shiver. "What about you? Have you had anything like this happen?"

"Not yet." His jaw muscles knotted. "I was given a few days' grace to think about whether I want to rock the boat. I'm expecting to have another sit-down with the sheriff any day. The closest to a threat that's come my way so far is being told I won't be very popular with my fellow deputies if I insist on bringing Hayes down."

Oh, heavens—her muscles were tightening and she wanted to retreat a step. "You've been worrying about whether I'd back down, but it's more likely you will."

"No." There was no give in the one word, but his expression revealed his troubled state of mind.

"The police culture does push us to support one another, and there's good reason for that. We do a tough job. We have to be able to trust fellow officers. Civilians don't always understand why we react the way we do...the split-second decisions we make. And we're human. We make mistakes. This...was different."

Watching him, Tess felt a burning in her eyes and sinuses. Yes, her first instinct had been right. This was a good man. She could trust him.

She took a shaky breath. "Okay. Thank you."

"You didn't call me about the note."

"It made me mad, but I considered it petty. This is different." In so many ways. What scared her most was that whoever had done this damage must have used a knife, and probably not a wimpy little pocketknife. This wasn't just property damage. It was an escalation of the threat. Those deep slashes repeated the threat in an ugly way.

Or else.

At the sound of a car turning into the alley, they both turned. Tess relaxed to see the rack of lights atop the white police car that she knew would have a blue stripe down each side.

Then Zach focused on her again, the intensity burning in his eyes. "Tess, if anything else happens, however petty it seems, call me."

"But...you implied we should keep contact to a minimum. You didn't want us to be seen together."

She couldn't miss the determination in the hard lines of his face.

"This campaign to silence you trumps that. Promise me, Tess."

Unable to tear her eyes from his, she finally nodded. "I promise," she whispered. "But you have to let me know if they threaten you, too. Okay?"

"Deal."

A door slammed behind him. Zach turned but rested a warm, reassuring hand on her back.

Safe, she thought, letting herself lean just a little. For now.

CHAPTER FOUR

AT THE TITLE company Zach shook hands and accepted congratulations along with a sheaf of papers, many copies bearing his signature. He also took possession of two keys—and a bank mortgage. Despite her big, practiced smile, his Realtor looked as if she felt a little bit sorry for him.

He considered himself lucky to have been approved for the mortgage given the condition of the house. It really was a dump. The appraiser had expressed serious reservations. However, the structure was essentially solid. The wiring had been redone at one point. There was an undertone in the appraiser's report suggesting she was mildly surprised to have found something positive to say. The plumbing, however, was vintage, to put it kindly.

Nothing in the report was news to Zach. He had a good eye and enough experience to make a realistic evaluation. He'd looked at half a dozen houses when he'd first arrived in town, and passed on the others because of cracked foundations, walls or floors seriously out of plumb, or rot that wasn't limited to the roof. His gut told him this one was redeemable. His inner eye could see the end result: a charming 1940's era bungalow.

He had climbed up himself to evaluate the roof, which was emerald-green with moss. He'd been reminded of pictures he'd seen of sod roofs in Scandinavia. When he scraped aside the moss in several places and poked a screwdriver into the cedar shakes, he hadn't been surprised to find them squishy.

That made a new roof number one on his agenda. As always, he intended to do much of the work himself, but would have to hire some help. That was a drawback to starting over in a new town. He didn't yet have any friends he could coerce into giving up a weekend or two to sling shingles.

From the land title company, he drove straight to the house. He wanted to walk through and decide whether he could actually live in the place starting May first, only a couple weeks from now. Otherwise he'd have to keep his current apartment for another month.

Doing that might be smart, but he went by the "penny saved, penny earned" philosophy. Plus, once he got started, he liked to work late into the night when he felt restless. There were plenty of jobs that didn't have to be done all in one go. He could strip and refinish the wood floors or molding, install new interior doors or tile when he had an hour or two. Living-in would be more convenient.

Parking in the driveway, he smiled crookedly. An objective observer would probably think he was nuts. The bright green roof, peeling paint and sagging porch didn't make a good impression. A couple of the windows had broken panes, which was no big deal as he would be replacing all the windows anyway.

Demolishing the porch would be a good, early job, he decided. He could build a new one on his own, no problem, and it would provide a nice facelift. A more generous porch with room for a couple of Adirondack chairs or a glider would attract potential buyers when the time came, too.

He circled the house first, making mental notes. Fence around the backyard was a teardown. Back stoop was history, too, except for the concrete pad and couple of steps.

That looked just like the ones leading from the back door of his childhood home.

He tried to shake off the whisper of memory even as he tipped his head back to look up into the big maple tree. He'd come damn close to walking away because of that tree.

In the future, some dad might help his kids build a tree house, he thought, eyeing an ideal broad branch. He and Bran had had a lot of fun in the one Dad had built with them, until that hideous morning.

A fence had enclosed the backyard of the house where he'd grown up, although he recalled it being ramshackle. When he'd gone by his childhood home on his second day back in Clear Creek, he'd noticed the fence was gone. If the yard had been open to the neighboring ones back then, would Sheila's killer have dared attack her right there under the maple tree, only feet from the back door?

He might have stuffed her in the trunk and driven her elsewhere, Zach reminded himself.

The fact he'd…assaulted…and killed her steps from what proved to be an unlocked door was one of the reasons the cops had suspected Michael Murphy. It felt too bold for a stranger to have dared. Zach's mother slept like a log. Zach had a distant memory of his father teasing her, saying she'd handled the middle-of-the-night breast-feeding of all three of their babies without even knowing she was doing it.

Zach swore aloud. Maybe he *shouldn't* have bought this house. Hell, returning to Clear Creek at all had probably been a mistake. Investigating his little sister's murder was one thing, but he sure as hell didn't need to be hammered by memories.

His long strides took him around to the front of the house again.

Different house, he reminded himself. Different time.

"That man said 'shit,'" a high, childish voice declared. "You heard, too, didn't you, Dylan?"

"I heard," a boy replied.

Zach turned to see two kids standing just on their side of the property line, apparently having popped out of their own fenced backyard to get a look at the man who'd said a bad word.

The little girl looked maybe five or six. Blond hair straggled out of lopsided braids that wouldn't last much longer. Her brother, who appeared more curious than shocked, had to be nine or ten. Much the same ages Sheila and Zach had been when—

He blocked that thought, forcing himself to nod. "Hi."

"Somebody already bought that house," the boy said, jaw jutting.

Zach smiled. "I know. I'm the one who bought it."

"Really?" He eyed the structure dubiously. "Mom says probably someone will tear it down."

"Nope. I plan to fix it up." He, too, eyed the house. "New roof first."

"Jessie 'n me kind of like that one. Dad says it looks like one of the greens at Pebble Beach." He sounded uncertain what that meant. "It's better than *our* lawn."

"It is pretty, in a way," Zach conceded. "Unfortunately moss isn't very good for the wood it's growing on. The roof is rotting."

"Jessie?" an alarmed woman called from the children's backyard. "Dylan? Where are you? Who are you talking to?"

The woman rushed through the open gate, not

stopping until she had one hand on each of her kids. "You *know* you aren't supposed to talk to strangers," she scolded them before saying to Zach, "May I ask what you're doing on this property?"

"I'm your new neighbor," he said, smiling. "I'm afraid your kids heard me, uh—"

"He said a bad word," her daughter announced.

He grimaced. "I did."

The mother relaxed enough to chuckle. "Well, it wouldn't have been the first time. When the lawn mower won't start, their father gets a little vocal."

He laughed. "I'm Zach Carter. I'm a deputy with the sheriff's department. I just closed on the house today."

She stepped past her children and held out a hand. "I'm Karen Thompson, this is Jessie and Dylan, and my husband is Dean. He's a heating contractor." Her gaze stole past him to the roof. "Are you actually going to *live* here?"

"I am. As I was telling Jessie and Dylan, replacing the roof is my first job. I'm hoping I might get it done before the end of the month, which would mean I could move in." He grinned at the kids. "It wouldn't be so good if I'm living here when it doesn't have a roof at all."

The girl stared at him in apparent fascination. "What if it *rained*?"

"And it rains around here a lot."

"Dean knows all kinds of contractors and subcontractors," Karen said. "If you want recommendations, I'm sure he'd be glad to help."

Zach nodded. "I may do that, although, to tell you the truth, I plan to do most of the work myself."

"Really?" She looked politely incredulous. "Even the roof?"

"I'm afraid I will need help with the roof," he admitted ruefully.

A minute later, having exchanged phone numbers, he let himself in the front door of his new home. Standing in the middle of the bare living room with its scarred floors, dirty walls with holes in them and a fireplace with mortar crumbling between the bricks, Zach had a thought. He knew one other person here in Clear Creek who could probably recommend contractors and construction workers with various skills.

What better excuse to stop to talk to Tess Granath?

He'd vowed to stay away from her.

It worried him to know he was going to be reckless enough to do it anyway.

TESS TILTED HER head to one side, studying her newly arranged display of sample ceramic tiles. She had just added a line of sculpted tiles she really liked. The manufacturer did custom work, too. She didn't get a lot of customers who could afford the custom route, but once in a while…

"Tess, someone to see you," Greg called.

"I'm back in tile!"

Aside from the window displays, which included wallpaper, tile and window treatments, the front of the store and most of the square footage was given to samples of wood, laminate and vinyl flooring as well as carpet. One wall was devoted to blinds and other window treatments. Tiles were displayed in a large nook tucked behind the office area, and wallpaper books filled their own room. Customers serious about selecting wallpaper could spend hours back there, leafing through books.

She turned, a welcoming smile pinned into place. When a tall, lean man appeared, she did a double-take.

"Zach."

He was impressive in his uniform, but no less so in well-worn jeans that hugged the long muscles of his thighs, athletic shoes and a long-sleeved, black, crewneck T-shirt. Each time she saw him, she was startled anew at the vivid blue of his eyes. His aura of intensity wasn't softened by his friendly smile. He had tamped down the desolation, or maybe only aloneness, she'd seen before. Only shadows remained.

"Nice place," he said. His gaze having taken her in thoroughly, he scanned the display. "Hey,

I like these." He headed straight for the new tiles, picking up one with beautifully detailed leaves and a rustic bronze glaze. He flipped it over, saw the price and winced. "Well, that's not happening."

Tess couldn't help herself. She automatically went into sales mode. "You could use them sparingly, sprinkled among plain tiles of the same color. I sometimes think the effect is even better."

Zach set the one he held back in its place and shoved his hands into the pockets of his jeans, the smile more in his eyes now than on his lips. "I'll keep that in mind. First things first. The roof, then the plumbing. Not to mention the fixtures, faucets and cabinets."

"The roof?"

He grimaced. "My new nine-year-old neighbor told me today that his dad says it's more velvety than the greens at Pebble Beach."

"That bad, huh?"

"Yep. Actually, I stopped by because I got to thinking you might be able to recommend some contractors or just plain laborers. I'll probably need help at several stages."

"Beginning with the roof." Tess smiled. "Already met your neighbors, huh?"

"The mom and two kids on one side. I said a bad word and managed to shock the little girl."

Tess laughed. "I didn't know kids could be shocked anymore." She nodded toward a doorway. "Come on into my office. I'll dig up some names for you."

She stopped on the way to introduce him to Greg. As tall as Zach but lanky, with a likable quality that helped with business, Greg had celebrated his fortieth birthday in January. After blowing out the candles, he had insisted with complete confidence that he didn't look a day over thirty. He'd just grinned and run his hand over his receding hairline when his wife giggled.

He and Zach shook hands and assessed each other, the way men did, after which Zach followed her into her cramped office, thereby shrinking it further. It was something of a relief to squeeze between her desk and one of too many metal filing cabinets to sink into a chair.

"I see you dazzle your customers with your clever use of a small space," he commented with an undertone of amusement.

Tess gave him a look. "I don't let most customers see my office."

He just laughed.

She reached for her card file. "Do you need skilled roofers or just day laborers?"

He sat across from her, stretching out his long legs comfortably and crossing them at the ankles. "Maybe some of both. I'm a decent roofer, but I don't want to be the only one who knows what I'm doing. On the other hand, a beefy guy or two to heft bundles of shingles up a ladder to the roof would be welcome, too."

She thought he had plenty of muscle to do the job. Afraid she might be blushing, Tess concentrated on flipping through the cards, jotting down a name and number when an appropriate one jumped out at her.

Very conscious of him watching, she asked, "Is it still tense for you at work?"

"You could say that." His voice was more clipped than it had been. "I haven't heard from you. I've been hoping that meant you haven't had any more unpleasant surprises."

It had been five very long days since he'd rushed to her rescue in the alley.

Now, she used a finger to keep her place and met his eyes. "There haven't been. But I admit I've been extra cautious every time I open a door or find myself alone for a minute."

Zach frowned. "Are you ever alone here?"

"Of course I am!" she snapped. Okay, overreaction. "The back door is always locked except when we're accepting deliveries. But my partner and I each go out to homes on a regular basis. Seeing the space allows us to make better recommendations. As time allows, we do the measurements, too, and occasionally even installation. Me more often than Greg," she added. "I'm not a big fan of installing blinds, although I can do it, but I'm a whiz with wallpaper and I actually enjoy laying tile."

"Another thing to keep in mind," he said with a hint of a smile.

"I could be persuaded." She raised her eyebrows. "Wallpaper, too?"

"Probably not. Isn't it women who like flowers on the walls?"

"Pinstripes are available." Tess wrinkled her nose. "There's such a thing as wallpaper covered with hunters in camo, carrying rifles and dead ducks. And, of course, the requisite Irish setters."

He laughed. "Sounds perfect for the dining room."

"Wallpaper is a good way to dress up an otherwise pedestrian bathroom," she began then made a face. "Sorry. It gets to be a habit. Um…" With an effort she focused again on the card file. When she came to one, she pulled it out and dropped it in the wastebasket beside her desk. Seeing Zach's silent query, she explained, "He has a no-show problem. Three strikes and you're out with me."

"I'm not real patient with that particular character flaw, either."

Finally she handed him a piece of notepaper on which she'd written ten names and phone numbers as well as specialties.

He scanned them. "Thanks. I'll make some calls right away. I closed on the house today and

I'm hoping to be able to move in before the end of the month."

"It's livable?"

His sudden grin took her breath away. "Depends on your standards. I don't mind sort of camping out for a while."

"Do you have furniture?" she asked, curious.

"I have some stuff in storage in Portland. I'll probably send for it. It's pretty limited, though." He shrugged. "Bed, recliner, TV. My books and music, some DVDs."

"Cinder-blocks and boards?" she teased.

His laugh cut grooves in his cheeks. "I'm a little past that stage, but I admit I've been rootless. When you know you're going to move often, acquiring furniture that has to be hauled along with you lacks some appeal."

Tess really wanted to ask why he chose to remain rootless. It seemed especially odd considering his hobby was turning derelict houses into beautiful homes.

The two of them were virtual strangers, she reminded herself. The fact that he didn't feel like a stranger could be explained by the shocking experience they'd shared. Followed by another experience that would have been more traumatic if he hadn't come the moment she'd called.

As she'd known he would. But...how?

Tess didn't think she'd been brooding that long,

but Zach's eyes narrowed slightly. His expression had changed, too, becoming guarded.

"Um…" She groped for something to say. "Well, I hope those names are useful. I can probably think of some others if you get desperate."

"Thank you, Tess." He rose and stood looking down at her for longer than was comfortable, his thoughts unreadable. "Keep being cautious," he said at last. "I have a feeling my deadline for reconsidering will be up tomorrow morning when I walk in the door to begin a new workweek."

That meant that, like her, he had Sundays and Mondays off, Tess assumed.

She stood, too, hoping she'd feel less vulnerable when he wasn't towering over her as much. "You'll be careful, too, won't you?"

His expression softened. "I'm a tough nut to crack."

That meant he thought he was too tough for anyone to challenge.

"Have you insured your new house yet?" she said with sudden urgency.

Looking surprised, he said, "Actually, the bank required it."

"Oh. Of course, they would."

"Some would say that burning down my new house would be doing me a favor."

He wasn't taking her seriously. Tess wanted to shake him.

"Deputy Hayes is big and mean, and *he's* a cop, too. You're not invincible."

"If something happens to me, investigators would look at him right away."

"But from what you've said, he has friends." Tess couldn't dismiss this sudden conviction that he was in danger. Hayes had to feel special rage for Zach, who was supposed to back him, not turn on him.

"Hey." Zach's voice was suddenly deeper, a little husky. His mouth tipped up on one side. "You're worried about me."

She frowned. "Of course I'm worried about you! And you're not taking me seriously, are you?"

"Yeah, actually, I am." His smile disappeared, an odd expression replacing it. His voice became huskier, halting. "I think…if we weren't under scrutiny, I'd ask you to dinner."

Something a lot more complicated replaced her frustration. "I…thank you." It came out as a whisper.

His gaze briefly lowered to her mouth then lifted. "Just out of curiosity." That husky note was still there. "What would you have said?"

"Yes." Her knees gave out and she plunked back down onto her old chair. "I already invited you to dinner, remember?"

Satisfaction curved his mouth. "Good reminder.

And now I'd better get out of here before I do something I shouldn't."

He was gone before she could open her mouth to ask something stupid. Because she knew what he'd had in mind.

And if her knees were weak just because he looked at her that way, Tess couldn't imagine how she'd feel if he actually kissed her.

But then she remembered what he'd said about being rootless. "When you know you're going to move often..."

Tess made a face. Maybe it was just as well he hadn't really asked. She'd reached an age where she was beginning to wonder whether she'd ever meet a guy interested in permanence. She wanted a family.

Zach didn't even want furniture to encumber him.

Well, the issue wouldn't arise. It could take forever until Andrew Hayes was convicted at trial. She'd read about trials starting, when she'd forgotten the details of the original crime because it had taken place as much as two or three years before. What if the deputy was never arrested? Or was exonerated? Would Zach be able to stay on in Harris County, a renegade in the sheriff's department?

He was already considered a renegade, she felt sure, and because he was so new on the job, he'd have nobody to back him up.

Being honest about what he'd seen, standing up for what he knew was right, had the potential to cost him a whole lot more than it would her. Knowing that scared her even as it increased her resolve to armor herself against his appeal. She hated the idea of not seeing him again…but knew it would be a whole lot healthier for her if she didn't.

ZACH'S PHONE DIDN'T ring often these days. A few friends had called to give him a hard time about his move to a Washington State backwater, all wanting to know if he was ready to throw in the towel and come back to Portland yet. He expected those calls to become more infrequent. A couple of the guys he'd worked with would stay good friends.

Otherwise he only had an occasional work-related call. None yet from Bran, but then, they hadn't exchanged numbers. What with Zach's couple of days off, they hadn't crossed paths, either.

So when his phone rang as he was debating whether to have another piece of pizza or not, his first thought was that it could be the new neighbor, Dean Thompson, calling to fulfill his wife's promise of useful names.

Wait. What if Tess was in trouble again?

He groaned when he saw the displayed name—Mom—and even considered not answering. But, shit, they didn't talk often, and he did love her even if he harbored a whole lot of anger toward her, too.

He wondered if he could get away with not telling her about his latest move and the reason for it.

"Hey," he said. "Haven't heard from you in a while."

"You could call me, too," his mother complained.

"I know, I know. I stay busy, that's all. Uh, what's up with you? Things going okay with—" he had to think to come up with his current stepfather's name "—Henry?"

Mom's last husband had been ten years younger than her. This one was ten years older.

"He's driving me crazy," she said fretfully. "He's retired, you know. All he does is follow me around. I have to lie about where I'm going just to get away from him for an hour!"

What was new about that? Zach wondered cynically. Hadn't she always lied to her husbands when she was running around on them? Although she'd get to an age where she'd lose interest in having multiple sexual partners, wouldn't she?

"Maybe he needs some new hobbies," Zach suggested diplomatically.

"The man doesn't have *any*." She paused. "He used to play golf but he herniated a disk in his back so that's out. He's like...like a new puppy! I don't know if I can stand it."

Husband number five was history. He just didn't know it yet. Poor Henry, Zach thought.

"I just bought a new house," he offered, to get off the subject of his soon-to-be-ex stepfather.

"I suppose it's another one of your dumps," his mother said with a sigh.

"Yep, and this is a good one." He described the house at length and everything wrong with it, hoping he'd bore her and she wouldn't ask for his new address. "I haven't moved in yet," he added hastily.

"I assume it's in Portland?"

Zach hesitated, wanting to lie but knowing eventually he'd have to come clean with her. And then he thought about Bran. Her son. *God.* What would she say if he told her he and his brother had had dinner and beers together the other day? That Dad was dead? Would she care?

"Zach?"

"Just trying to think of how to tell you this," he said finally.

"This?"

"I took a job in Clear Creek. With the county sheriff's department, not the Clear Creek PD. The house I bought is here in town. It's… I don't know, ten blocks from where we lived."

Where we lived. That was as euphemistic as saying, *He passed on.*

The silence extended so long he wondered if she'd hung up on him.

"Why would you do something like that?" she whispered.

He rubbed the back of his neck. "You know it's coming up on twenty-five years."

"Of course I know!" his mother cried. "Do you think I forget for one minute?"

Sometimes he wondered. Aside from dragging him along every time she'd ditched another husband, she hadn't been a bad mother. But maybe that was because he'd made sure he was never any bother. That lesson had been hammered into him by seeing repeatedly what happened when boyfriends or husbands began to annoy her. Or bore her. Or become too preoccupied with work or anything else but her. It was a hard thing to think about your own mother, but he'd come to doubt she was able to feel emotion of any real depth.

"It eats at me," he explained. "I want answers, Mom. I'm here to get them." Zach knew he sounded implacable and didn't care.

"How could you possibly find out anything after all this time?"

He frowned, bothered by something in her voice. Did she hope he *wouldn't* find any answers?

"I need to try." He closed his eyes. "Mom, Bran is here."

Her "What?" was so soft he barely caught it.

"Turns out he and Dad never moved away. Bran is a cop, too. A detective with the sheriff's department."

"I never dreamed..."

"You knew they were still in the house at first."

"Because it would take time to sell!" she cried. "The way everyone looked at your father, how could he bear to stay all these years?"

"Bran said Dad was too stubborn to go. He thought he'd look as if he was running away. So he just kept staring 'em down."

Her voice got even smaller. "Have you seen him?"

"He's dead, Mom." It felt awkward to say, even if he didn't know whether she'd care. "Lung cancer. Bran says he never quit smoking."

"Of course he didn't!" she snapped, sounding more like herself. But her tone became tentative when she asked, "Do you think if I flew up, Bran would be willing to see me?"

Taken aback he said, "I...have no idea." Why did she even want to renew a relationship with the son she'd let go? Yeah, Bran had been a butt, but she could have put her foot down and said, "I'm your mother and you'll spend vacations with me whether you like it or not."

Of course, Dad could have said the same thing to Zach. Neither parent, he'd been long aware, had behaved like the adults they theoretically were. For each, the hurt of being rejected by a son must have been one too many blows. Zach had seen his brother as in league with his father and rejected them together. It was no surprise if Mom had felt the same way, or if Dad's bitterness spread to include Zach.

What an unholy mess, he thought bleakly.

We shouldn't have been asked to choose. We shouldn't have been allowed *to choose.* Maybe he wouldn't be as screwed up now if he hadn't lost his father and brother.

"Will you ask him?" she begged.

He let out a breath, not seeing an alternative. "Yeah. When I see him again. I don't know when that will be, Mom. Our...meeting didn't end on a great note. We both remembered why we hadn't seen each other in twenty-five years."

That silenced her.

They ended up talking for a few more minutes, exchanging small news, the kind neither would remember five minutes from now, but it served as a decompression.

Only at the end did she say "Please" again, with the result that he reiterated a promise he knew he'd regret.

CHAPTER FIVE

THE STENCH WAS UNBELIEVABLE. Zach wasn't two feet into the locker room at work when his eyes started to water. Jesus, it smelled like something—or somebody—had died in here and been left to decompose. No wonder the room was empty at an hour when deputies tended to hang out and trade jokes before taking on the stress of their day.

Oh, hell, he thought between one step and the next. Sure as shit, everyone else knew whose locker stunk and why.

His muscles tightened, making him battle ready even though it was a waste of adrenaline. He stopped in front of his locker, his stomach churning. He didn't look forward to seeing what was in there.

Was anybody watching for the fun of seeing his reaction? Zach didn't as much as turn his head. He wouldn't give them the satisfaction. He sure as hell would be making a formal complaint, though. If Hayes and his asshole friends thought they could terrorize him with impunity, they were in for a surprise.

Making sure absolutely nothing showed on his face, he dialed his combination.

With a clang, he opened the door and gazed at the rotting obscenity lying on the bottom of the locker. It was…a rabbit. He thought. He refused to as much as gag, even at the sight of the maggots.

Instead he calmly closed the door, whirled the dial and walked directly to the patrol sergeant's office, making no eye contact on the way. He'd be lucky if one of his molars didn't crack.

At his knock Luis Perez called, "Come in." The minute he saw Zach, he grimaced. "This have something to do with that god-awful stench?"

"Which everybody has just been ignoring? For how long?"

"I'm told it appeared this morning." Perez sighed and pushed back from his desk. "We both know who this message came from, although he probably didn't deliver it in person. But I suppose I'd better come take a look."

"The smell is worse than the morgue during an autopsy," Zach warned.

The middle-aged sergeant grunted. He didn't pay any more attention to deputies who happened to be loitering than Zach did.

Despite the stink, Perez's face stayed utterly impassive. He waited while Zach opened the locker, contemplated the rotting creature inside and said, "I want pictures."

"Fine." Zach slammed the locker again. "Looks like I'll be a little late getting out on patrol."

"You shouldn't have to clean it up," Perez said, sounding more human.

"Yeah? Who's going to? Andrew Hayes?" Anger vibrated in Zach's voice.

The sergeant grimaced.

"I'll do it," Zach said shortly, "once there's documentation."

Turned out Perez was pretty good with a camera. Zach wondered if he was afraid something would happen to those pictures for some mysterious reason if an evidence technician took them. Everyone was subject to pressure.

Zach snapped on latex gloves and grabbed a couple of plastic garbage bags.

He was bending over to slide one of them around the carcass, gagging despite his determination not to, when behind him someone said sharply, "Son of a bitch!"

Zach recognized the voice. He turned slowly to see his brother, obviously breathing through his mouth. Zach stepped to one side and gestured with a flourish.

Bran's expression hardened.

Seeing his distaste improved Zach's mood marginally. At least his brother hadn't been part of this.

"Lucky you got here in time to view the latest warning," Zach said, turning back to his task.

By the time he got the damn thing in the bag, he was swallowing bile. Mumbling obscenities beneath his breath, he was surprised to turn to find Bran standing at his elbow, holding out a roll of paper towels and a spray bottle.

Zach nodded his thanks and went to work scrubbing. Finally done, he wordlessly carried the whole mess, double-bagged, out to the Dumpster. When he returned, Bran was waiting, leaning with one shoulder against a locker. He didn't say anything as Zach took everything out of his locker and closed it.

Then Zach said grimly, "If you'll excuse me, I need to get to work."

He hoped the vile stench hung around for days. He'd made a decision: he wouldn't be using a locker again.

BRAN WAS PLENTY pissed when he stalked into the detective bullpen. The simmer heated to a full, rolling boil when he saw a smirking Rich Delancy leaning back in his desk chair, feet stacked on his desk, hands clasped behind his head. "You might want to avoid the locker room," he suggested.

"Been there." Bran stopped right beside Delancy's desk. "Was there something funny about it I missed?" he asked coldly.

"Where's your sense of humor? You know that saying about payback being sweet?" The idiot laughed. "Sometimes it stinks to the high heavens."

In a quick, violent motion, Bran knocked the bastard's feet off the desk. Delancy's chair fell backward, thumping against the desk behind him.

He roared to his feet. "What the—?"

Another detective jumped up. "Cool off! For God's sake, we don't brawl on the job."

Bran speared him with an icy look. "Usually we don't commit murder on the job, either, and assume we'll get away with it because, hey, we're all good ol' boys, aren't we?"

Neither of the two men he was facing moved. Out of the corner of his eye, Bran was aware that their lieutenant had stepped out of his office.

The smart thing would be to go sit at his desk. He didn't know the man his little brother had become well enough to step out on a limb for him. His brain was telling him to think this through before he shot off his mouth any more than he already had.

Maybe the sickening taste in his mouth left from the fetid odor in the locker room had short-circuited his common sense. He didn't know. Because he kept staring hard at Rich Delancy, his fingers curled into fists. "Have you ever really looked at my face?"

His fellow detective's complete bafflement was obvious. "I don't know what you're talking about."

"Maybe I should say, 'Have you taken a good look at Deputy Carter's face?'"

The transformation in Delancy's expression was slow but shock did arrive. "Hell. Are you trying to tell us…you're *related*?"

"That would be my brother who is refusing to let Andy Hayes kill an unarmed guy because he felt like it. So here's how it is. I have no sense of humor where this kind of shit is concerned. Do you hear me?"

Delancy had the sense to shuffle back a step. "Come on, it was a prank, that's all."

Bran forced himself to stand down physically. He relaxed his shoulders with an effort. "The really funny part," he said, "is that any stuff in a locker in that room is going to stink for a good long while. Me, I don't use my locker." He walked to his desk, sat and turned on his computer, ignoring the other three men in the room.

Somehow, though, he wasn't surprised when ten minutes later his lieutenant tapped him on the shoulder and said, "In my office. Now."

ZACH WAS CALLED in to Stokes's office at the end of the day.

Knocking on the door, he braced himself.

"Come in." The undersheriff looked tired and irritable. "Sit down, Deputy."

Zach sat, feeling unpleasantly like a rebellious teenager being called to account.

"I take it you're determined to put a fellow deputy and this entire department under scrutiny."

"Not the entire department," Zach objected. "The department as a whole looks good or bad only in how it responds to Deputy Hayes's violent behavior."

"He is adamant that the other man went for his gun and he was responding appropriately."

"I've had a suspect lunge for my gun. I didn't kill him. What about you? Ever had it happen?"

Stokes's mouth tightened. "Your fellow witness threatened to create a public uproar if we don't bring in outside investigators."

So he had no intention of discussing his personal experience with similar "incidents."

"Not *my*." Zach leaned a little on the word. "I'd never set eyes on the woman until we looked at each other over Antonio Alvarez's body."

Stokes bent his head in acknowledgment. He picked up a pen but began fiddling with it rather than using it to make a note.

"Since you're new to the department, you may not be aware that we are part of a multi-county special investigation unit. I have, in fact, arranged to transfer the investigation to that unit. It's my understanding that, in this case, detectives from Stimson will handle it."

Stimson, a county away, was one of the bigger cities in this rural corner of Washington State. Zach had heard good things about the police chief, a man named Duncan MacLachlan.

He nodded but figured it would be smart to keep his mouth shut.

"You will be contacted by a member of the special unit and make yourself available to be interviewed. I trust you will remember what uniform you wear and confine your observations to the incident in question."

In other words, don't criticize the department.

"My interest is seeing justice served," he said. "You can't say I haven't been professional."

"No," the undersheriff conceded, "I can't. Just between you and me, we should have handed off this investigation sooner. If Deputy Hayes is a bad apple, we need to know that."

Zach tried to hide his surprise. He felt sure Stokes wasn't expressing an opinion Sheriff Brown shared, which meant he was putting some trust in Zach. In his own quiet way, he was saying that he supported Zach's determination not to back down. In doing so, he also restored some of Zach's pride in the uniform he wore.

"Thank you, sir," he said.

Stokes nodded. "You may go, Deputy Carter."

THE CAMARO WAS already parked outside the tavern when Zach arrived. He pulled in right beside it and walked into the Creek.

At almost six-thirty, the place was busier than the last time they'd been here. Bran had already claimed a booth in the corner and a pitcher of beer sat on the table along with two glasses. Zach scanned the room. No one he knew. Relaxing slightly, he slid in across from his brother.

He poured for himself then sat back and studied Bran. "What inspired this?"

Bran's eyebrows rose. "You're my brother."

"You seemed to have mixed feelings about that the last time we talked."

Bran was shaking his head even before Zach finished. "Not about you. It was Sheila, Mom, Dad. Everything spilled over."

Zach understood that. "Mom called yesterday."

Glass halfway to his mouth, Bran went completely still for a few seconds. Then he took a long swallow before setting the glass down. "You implied you don't have much contact."

Zach shrugged. "We talk every few months. I don't know why she called this time."

"Did she know you moved back to Clear Creek?"

"Not until I told her." His gaze met his brother's. "She was even less happy when I told her why." He paused. "And then I mentioned that you were here. Oh, yeah, and that Dad died last year."

Bran's fingers tightened on his glass, but his other hand was out of sight beneath the table and he succeeded in appearing almost bored. "Yeah? Was she interested?"

"In Dad dying? Not all that much. In you? Yes. She wants to fly up here to see you."

"No." It was flat. Final.

He shrugged. "I asked."

After a minute his brother's shoulders sagged. "Crap. She won't just show up, will she?"

Zach thought about it. "I don't know. She sounded…like it really matters to her. So… maybe."

"Why?"

Zach had been asking himself the same question. "She did try. I remember her crying once after hanging up the phone because you wouldn't talk to her."

"After I saw her in bed with—" His shoulders moved. "It was like our bright and cheerful mommy was a veil and I could see through it. She made me sick. Once it occurred to me one of her men might have snatched Sheila, I didn't want anything to do with her." He grunted. "And how long did she *try*? A few months?"

"More like a year." This, now that he thought about it, was surprisingly persistent. His mother craved affection, attention, given as extravagantly as possible. If it flagged…she sought it elsewhere. Really sustaining a relationship with her oldest child would have meant she had to do all the giving, with barely a hope that someday he might again reciprocate.

That would have required depths she didn't possess.

Loyalty to her, despite her failings, kept him

from sharing what he was thinking with his brother. Instead, conscious of Bran watching him, Zach said after a minute, "Dad didn't do any better."

Bran obviously struggled with this, but at last he let out a long breath. "If you'd given him the chance…"

Zach looked his brother in the eye. "If you'd given her a chance…"

Bran's laugh didn't hold a lot of amusement. "At least we each got one of them."

In retrospect Zach thought Bran had had the better deal. He'd ended up with stability. To Zach, the whole concept of love and commitment was a joke. The breakup of his parents had been only the first blow. Any belief he'd retained had eroded as his mother dragged him along in her wake. He had been foolish enough to let himself get attached to the first couple of stepfathers and even a stepsister; he'd let himself make friends in his new schools. Once his mother left Lowell Carter because she *loved* someone else, Zach had quit trying. He would have said he'd forgotten how to grow attached to someone.

Funny now to find the bond with his brother might have endured.

Of course, Bran had had to keep living in a house that must have felt haunted and withstand the stares of people who had judged his father. That wouldn't have been any picnic, either.

Bran growled an obscenity. "Keep telling her no."

Understanding, Zach nodded.

A waitress appeared and took their orders. Only when she was gone did he say, "Thanks for helping out this morning."

"You mean, handing you a bottle of cleanser? Big deal."

"It was better than the alternative."

"Which was?"

"Thinking you might have been in on it, too."

Bran stared at him, his blue eyes unnervingly like the ones Zach saw in the mirror every morning. "You're serious?"

"You're part of this department. How do I know where you stand?"

"Not behind any crap like that." Bran clenched his teeth. "Delancy—do you know him?"

"He interviewed me after Hayes killed Antonio Alvarez."

"He thought the dead rabbit was a good joke. I let him know I didn't. While I was at it, I told him we're brothers."

Warmed by the solidarity, Zach warned, "You may be sorry."

"I got an ass-chewing from my lieutenant, who thought I came on too strong." A smile flickered on Bran's face. "I told him it wasn't that strong, not considering that what I really wanted to do was to knock out Delancy's front teeth."

Zach laughed. "I appreciate the thought. More

on Tess Granath's behalf than my own. He really leaned on her."

His brother's smile widened. "Yeah? You should have seen her when she planted her hands on his desk and got in *his* face. The guy was shrinking back. That woman is no pushover."

"No." Zach thought about yesterday in her office and how seriously he'd thought about kissing her. Maybe she'd have slapped his face.

She was the first woman to catch his eye since he arrived in Clear Creek. He liked that she was fiery, too, and gutsy. And smart. And…

You don't always get what you want.

Their food arrived. As he started eating, Zach told his brother about the meeting with the undersheriff.

Bran nodded. "Yeah, the unit gets activated now and again. Last year I investigated a Sauk County deputy accused of soliciting sex from teenage girls—he'd picked them up for things like shoplifting—in exchange for not filing a report."

Zach shook his head. "How'd it come out?"

"His ass is in jail now."

"Good."

After a momentary lull while they both worked on their burgers and fries, Bran asked, "Where are you living?"

Zach told him about the apartment and then about the house and his plans to tackle the roof this coming Sunday and Monday, assuming the weather didn't include a torrential rainfall.

"You lined up help yet?"

"No." Zach stared at him. "Why?"

"I can give you a couple days." He shrugged. "Heck, I can probably round up a couple more guys if you can use them."

"I'm not real popular right now in the department, in case you didn't notice."

Bran shrugged it off. "Not everybody is on Hayes's side. And I have friends who aren't cops."

"I can bring coolers with drinks, maybe order pizzas for lunch."

"We might do better than that." Bran took a big bite of his cheeseburger, chewed and swallowed. "I told you I'm engaged. Paige likes to do things like organize a potluck. A friend of mine is a newlywed, too. He's a firefighter," he added as a seeming aside. "His wife and Paige have hit it off. Let me see if Isaac and Stella are free."

Stunned, Zach set down his burger. "I was going to hire some labor."

"I don't think you'll need to. I helped another buddy re-roof his place. I'll see if he's free, too."

It couldn't be this easy. Bran was acting as if they were family in fact not just in theory. Zach felt a strange ache beneath his breastbone. He resisted the urge to rub it with the heel of his hand.

No, he thought, it wouldn't be as easy as Bran was making it sound. The roofing part, sure, maybe. But neither of them had forgotten the divide between them.

So what? Take what you can get.

"You ordered materials yet?" Bran asked.

"Yesterday." Enthusiasm for his new project had carried him that far. "It's set for delivery Saturday."

Bran nodded and took out his phone, tapping it a couple of times. "You're in luck. Google is optimistic about the weather."

"Thank you." Zach heard the huskiness in his voice. The emotion. "I, uh, didn't expect..."

"What are brothers for?" Bran asked.

Zach half laughed. "I don't actually know."

"I don't have any experience, either, but I think a roofing job qualifies."

Zach lifted his glass. Bran did the same and they tapped rims.

THE RINGING OF her phone brought Tess out of a heavy sleep.

Dad, she thought on a burst of fear, scrambling across the bed toward the nightstand even before her eyes were open.

Please, God, I'm not ready...

The number on the screen was unfamiliar.

She snatched up the phone. "Hello? I mean, this is Tess Granath."

"Did you get our messages?"

Her brain was just fuzzy enough she was still

thinking Dad and strokes. "No. I must not have heard my phone ringing. I'm sorry, I—"

"Listen up, bitch," the man interrupted her. "Here's tonight's message. A knife can slice all kinds of things besides rubber."

Suddenly she felt hot and cold at the same time. *Oh, God. Not Dad.* Between one blink and the next, she was standing in the deserted alley staring at the long slash in her tires. Feeling how utterly alone she was.

And then she was back in her head, listening to the silence. She knew this quality of silence. She'd been cut off.

Really bad choice of words.

A shudder traveled from her nape to her toes. She hurriedly turned off her phone, just in case, then huddled with the covers drawn up to her throat, once again listening.

What if she *wasn't* alone?

Would the police come if she called?

Probably, but then she'd have to walk through the house to let them in. And what would they do but look around, tell her to lock up and then leave?

She could call Zach. *He* would come, and probably stay, too.

Coming to depend on him…would be foolish. He'd be moving on before she knew it.

Plus…what if he was seen leaving her house in the morning? It was a threatening phone call. That was all. She hadn't heard a window break or the creak of a floorboard in the hall. She knew all the doors and windows were locked.

Nonetheless, she slipped out of bed as quietly as she could. She tiptoed to the bedroom door, closed it as fast as she could and pushed the little button that locked it, for all the good that did. Then she grabbed the antique chair she sat on to put on her socks and braced it under the doorknob, checking to make sure there was no give.

Okay, early warning system was in place.

The caller's number would be stored in her phone, although she remembered belatedly that it had had an unfamiliar area code. In every mystery novel or thriller she'd ever read, that meant a throwaway phone.

Nonetheless, she would report the threat to the police first thing in the morning and tell Zach about it, too.

Although...why was she the only one being threatened? Or had Zach not told her everything?

Today, she'd heard from a detective from Stimson who explained that he was part of a special unit taking over the investigation into Antonio's death. He'd scheduled an appointment to talk to her.

Tonight's threat must be related. Hayes and his friends had probably decided scaring her now might make her remember differently.

To hell with them. Anger had supplanted her fear.

She turned on her lamp as a comfort, an adult's

night-light, then pulled the covers around herself again. Restful slumber was not in her near future.

"IF THE CLEAR CREEK police won't do anything, I will." Half dressed and still bare-footed, Zach paced from one end of his apartment to the other. He had so little furniture, nothing got in his way.

This was the third morning in a row Tess had let him know about another middle-of-the-night phone call. He'd insisted she report every single threat to the Clear Creek PD, too.

Hayes and his buddies wanted her to stay nervous. Okay, mission accomplished.

But it had become plain that nervous wasn't enough. She needed to be scared into retracting her original statement when she met next week with the Stimson detective.

This was a campaign of terror and he suspected it was proving more effective than she wanted to admit. She'd been evasive, but Zach doubted she was getting any sleep. How could she, never knowing what time the phone would ring or whether tonight they'd act on the threats?

"What can you do?" she asked dully. "There have been three different numbers. All of them from those stupid cheap phones anyone can buy. Can you magically trace them?"

Frustration choked him. No, he couldn't. Protecting her had somehow become his first priority, but he felt pretty damn useless right now.

"Has the officer you're dealing with informed anyone at the sheriff's department?" he asked.

"Well, he called Detective Clayton first."

Smart man. Clayton was one of the detectives from Stimson.

"But he also talked to Detective Delancy."

Zach grunted. "I'll make sure my sergeant knows." When she called after the first threat, he had told her about the dead rabbit in his locker the previous morning. He hadn't gotten graphic, she didn't need to hear about rotting flesh or maggots. She'd been appalled after hearing the sanitized story and had apologized for bothering him about anything as trivial as a phone threat.

Personally, he was a lot more worried about the increasingly vicious threats on top of her slashed tires. They probably saw her, rightly, as the more vulnerable target. His testimony would be drastically weakened if the second witness suddenly claimed Antonio had gone for the deputy's gun and had kept lunging at him until Hayes finally knocked him to the ground.

His first instinct was to tell her not to answer the damn phone again if she didn't recognize the number. But he had second thoughts. If they couldn't get through to her that way, they'd feel compelled to try something else. A lot of dangerous possibilities fell under the "something else" category.

"Listen." This was impulse, and probably stupid, but he was going with it anyway. "A bunch of people are supposed to show up Sunday and Monday to help me put on a new roof."

"A bunch?" She sounded pleased. "Oh, good. I'd hoped the names I gave you would turn out to be useful."

"I haven't called any of them yet. My brother is local." *My brother.* It felt weird to say, but good, too. "He organized some of his friends."

"You didn't say anything about a brother."

"We've been estranged. I didn't even know he was here in town until we came face-to-face."

"Oh, my."

Zach laughed. "You could say that. Anyway, some women are coming, too. They've planned a potluck. I thought you might enjoy it."

Silence. His pulse kicked up.

"I thought we were trying to avoid being seen together," she said cautiously at last.

"If the threats escalate again, I'm throwing that out the window," he said, making sure she knew he meant it. Funny, when he hadn't even known he was thinking that way. "But I doubt anyone who would report us will be there Sunday, and that's assuming anyone recognizes you. Did I say my brother is with the sheriff's department, too? A couple other deputies are coming, but he says they're good guys. Otherwise, none of his friends have any reason to know what's going on with us."

Whatever that is, he thought, unwilling to lie to himself. His need to keep her safe had nothing to do with his invitation. Or maybe it did. He could relax if she was close, if he could reassure himself of her safety by scanning the yard until he saw her.

"I…"

He held his breath while she hesitated.

Then, "Thank you," she said. "That sounds like fun. I assume the women get to work, too."

Relief rushed over him. Too much relief. "As much or as little as you want."

"Can I bring some food?"

"I'll pass the word for Paige to call you. I'm told she's trying for a balance of hot dishes, desserts and what-have-you." He was a little bemused by that, because what difference did it make what food appeared, as long as there was enough of it? But it must be a woman thing because Tess said, "Oh, good."

He gave her a few more details, asked her to call tomorrow morning whether there was another threat or not so he knew before he started the day that she was okay, and tossed the phone aside. Then he glanced at the clock.

Oh, crap. He really needed to get out the door and he hadn't even shaved yet.

Just as well not to give himself time to think about why he was trying to make his relationship with his fellow witness personal.

TESS HAD TO park a block away. She hadn't expected the size of the crowd she'd seen in the yard and on the roof when she'd driven past.

Apparently she was fashionably late. She locked up and walked to Zach's house, her Crock-Pot heavy in her arms. Her work gloves were balanced on the lid.

The fact that Zach had invited her made her a little bit nervous, but even more excited. The result was butterflies in her stomach.

A pretty brunette crossed the yard to meet her. "Are you Stella or Tess?"

"Tess." She hoisted the Crock-Pot. "Baked beans."

"Yum. Why don't you bring it in the house? The electricity is still on. The men seem confident they won't crash through the ceiling and electrocute themselves on the way down." She flashed a smile as she led the way to the front porch. "I'm Paige, by the way. I'm engaged to Zach's brother."

Geez. Typical man, not to have said who Paige was. Tess picked her way carefully up the obviously rotten steps to the front porch. "I haven't met Bran," she said. "Congratulations on your engagement."

"Thank you." She preened, lifting a hand to display a diamond ring. "Who knew planning for a wedding was practically a full-time job?"

Not Tess.

Paige's forehead crinkled. "It was really odd, the way he had a brother materialize from nowhere."

Intrigued, Tess asked, "You don't believe they are brothers?"

"Oh, they're brothers. You can't mistake it."

Tess lost interest in the other woman the moment she stepped inside. She immediately saw the appeal of the house. Her experienced eye noted that the wood floors—were they maple or sycamore rather than the more common oak?—were in good condition, considering. They badly needed refinishing, but she didn't see any irreparable gouges, water stains or rot.

She mentally listed the jobs that needed to be done. Sandblast the fireplace and replace mortar. Strip paint from the thick slab of wood that formed the mantel. Peering at it more closely, she suspected that Zach would find himself stripping off many layers of paint. But she bet he'd find something interesting under it all. A lot of wallboard would need replacing or patching. Refinish or replace molding.

She and Paige chatted as they went to the kitchen, where she set her Crock-Pot on the counter with relief and plugged it in. "Do you suppose Zach would mind if I wander and check out the rest of the house? I don't know if he told you I'm in the business."

"Real estate?"

"No, remodeling. My partner and I own Fabulous Interiors." She smiled. "In case you ever need new blinds, flooring or tile."

Paige's smile was polite but she didn't appear very interested. "I live in Mount Vernon, and in an apartment, at that. All maintenance is my landlord's obligation, thank goodness."

"When's the wedding?"

"This summer. July twenty-third—" Her head turned at the sound of other voices. "Excuse me. That might be Stella."

"Go ahead."

Instead of inspecting the kitchen more closely, Tess slipped into the hall and poked her head into more rooms. Male voices came from above along with occasional, alarming thuds—bundles of shingles being dropped?—and the tearing sounds of boards being ripped up. Someone was hammering up there, too. The ceiling quivered in one bedroom as she looked up and she hastily withdrew.

The bedrooms were nothing special, but the ceilings were high and some of the molding seemed worth keeping. She liked the proportions. The bathroom? Well…there wasn't much he could do but tear it down to studs.

At the back of the house she found a glassed-in porch that had hookups for a washer and dryer. It was too nice a space to waste on a utility room, she thought, then looked through the windows to the backyard, where the construction activity seemed to be centered. A man stood on one of the two tall ladders propped against the house, visible to her only up to his armpits. As she watched, another man descended the other ladder and dropped lightly to his feet on the grass, his muscles flexing with athletic ease.

Zach.

He stayed where he was, apparently listening to what someone up above was saying. Then his head turned and his eyes locked on her.

For a moment all they did was look at each other. She had that shocking sense of connection just as she'd had that first day over Antonio's battered body. As if the rest of the world blurred and only he remained in focus.

She couldn't let these feelings be any more than trust and professional dependence, even if she was attracted to him. He was still taboo—and she'd be an idiot to forget that he was restoring this house only so he could sell it at a profit and move on.

CHAPTER SIX

WHEN THE CREW took a break for lunch, Zach introduced Tess and Bran. She'd noticed him earlier, thinking that Paige was right—the resemblance was unmistakable. Of a similar height, both men had the same lean, strong builds. Zach's cheekbones and jaw were more sharply honed, Bran's face more roughly sculpted. Tess was unnerved to be faced by two pairs of bright blue eyes.

The most obvious difference was that Bran's hair was a deep auburn instead of brown. His extra years showed in deepened creases on his forehead and at his eyes, too.

She smiled, said the right things and shook hands with him, but had the strange thought that she'd never have been attracted to him even if he did look an awful lot like Zach. He had an air of remoteness that made her suppress a shiver.

The two men appeared comfortable in work boots, faded jeans and T-shirts. Zach had worn a tool belt earlier, too, as comfortably as he did his holster and handgun on his day job. The day wasn't hot, but Tess wouldn't be surprised if some of the men went shirtless by midafternoon. She secretly hoped Zach was one of them.

"We came close to meeting before," Bran surprised her by saying.

"Really? When?"

"I was there the day you roared in to confront Detective Delancy."

Tess involuntarily made a face.

He laughed, although if he was genuinely amused, it didn't show in his chilly blue eyes. "Several of us saw the confrontation. I think you scared him."

"Good. He's a jerk." Suddenly she felt warmth in her cheeks. "Um, I hope he isn't a friend of yours."

"No. We work together."

"I do remember a couple of other men watching. You're the tall one."

That was a silly thing to say. Tess didn't like how he intimidated her.

"Compared to Lieutenant Arnold, yes." He looked past her. "Paige."

His mouth curved into a smile and he slipped an arm around his fiancée, but Tess didn't see any softening of his general mien. Her eyes lingered on him as Paige led him away to solve some dispute over a long-past pickup basketball game.

"What are you thinking?" Zach asked quietly.

She started then forced a smile. "Just curious. You two look a lot alike but..."

"But?"

"I just have a feeling he'd be hard to get to know."

He glanced after his brother, too. "He and I know where each other is coming from."

"Even though you haven't spent much time together in the past few years?"

"Past few?" His tilted smile held no amusement whatsoever. "Try twenty-five. The last time I saw him, I was nine years old and he was twelve."

"What?" She gaped at him. "You're serious? It wasn't just your father you lost touch with?"

"I'm serious. Our parents parted ways, Bran and I each made a choice, and that was it." He shrugged. "Mom and Dad didn't mean it to be that way, but—" His frown was a mere flicker but suggested he hadn't meant to say as much as he had. "By the way, I don't think I thanked you for coming today, Tess. You've been working hard, too."

He could shut down emotions *and* any possible questions like no one she'd ever met. Although Tess had a suspicion his brother was as good at it if not better.

"I thought everyone at this little party was supposed to work," she said lightly.

"Yeah, but some are working harder than others." His gaze flicked again to his brother and the fiancée. Paige's only contribution had been laying out the food and producing paper plates, napkins and plastic cutlery.

"We all have our strengths."

"True."

He stood at ease beside her but had kept at least a couple of feet of separation all day. She had the impression he was making sure no one made the mistake of thinking they were intimate.

That was smart, given the other deputies here today. She had felt a little uneasy earlier when she'd become aware of a man watching her and one of the other women identified him as a cop. There hadn't been anything to object to, but…

Shaking off the niggling unease, she tipped her head back, shading her eyes with her hand. From this angle, she saw fresh boards and the edge of the last row of shingles that had been nailed down. "Are you happy with the progress?" she asked.

"Amazed by it." He shook his head. "I never expected a turnout like this. Most of the guys have worked their butts off, too. We should finish tomorrow, easy."

"So you'll be able to move in."

"Yeah." His eyes glinted with amusement. "You didn't say what you think."

"You mean about the house? I love what I've seen of it. I didn't go upstairs."

"There's not much up there. One decent-size bedroom and a smaller room that might have been a study or, I don't know, nursery or sewing room. I intend to turn it into a second bathroom."

"That's a good idea. I will say, if I were you, I'd tackle the downstairs' bathroom before anything else. Except maybe the front porch."

He laughed. "Before I lose a UPS man through the rotten boards, you mean? And you're right. The porch and bathroom are running neck and neck at the top of my list."

Someone called his name. He waved at the man and bent to pick up his tool belt, fastening it around his waist. "Back to work."

Tess looked around for her heavy gloves. "Me, too." She and a couple of other women had tried to keep up with the debris, hauling everything that wasn't too heavy to the two Dumpsters Zach had rented.

His hand on her arm stopped her. It was the first time he'd touched her today. "I don't know if you can make it tomorrow..." he began, his voice low, velvety-deep.

"Do you want me to come?" She didn't know why but she spoke softly, too.

"Yeah." His eyes were intense. "You don't have to, but..."

"I'll be here." She was almost whispering.

"Good." He cleared his throat. "You can call me in the middle of the night, you know. If anything happens."

"And wake you up, too?"

"I worry about you," he murmured.

The expression in his eyes was so compelling, Tess couldn't look away. She was afraid she swayed toward him.

But suddenly Bran was there, standing between them and the rest of the crew. Glaring at Zach. "Dial it back, bro," he snapped. "Watching out for her is one thing, sleeping with her is another."

Tess's lips shaped the word *What?*

Zach's teeth showed. "We were talking. That's all. And I didn't ask you to chaperone."

"You should have," he snapped. "And if you're not sleeping together, you want to be." He gave Tess a brief glance that was probably supposed to be apologetic but failed in its intent. "Sorry." He scowled again at Zach. "Let's get back to work."

Knowing her face was beet red, Tess slipped away, leaving the two to glower at each other. Oh, God—was that what everyone was thinking? That she and Zach—

Oh, who was she kidding? Isn't that what *she* had been thinking?

But Bran was right. They did need to be careful. Andrew Hayes might get away with beating Antonio to death if what she and Zach had said was cast into doubt because they were seen to be in collusion.

Hayes needed to *pay*, she thought fiercely. That meant…she shouldn't come tomorrow.

She shouldn't have come today, either.

Tess didn't let herself look toward Zach, now climbing one of the ladders. She went back to work, scooping up armfuls of thick moss and damp, pulpy shakes while being cautious about protruding nails and making repeated trips around the corner of the house to the Dumpsters.

If Zach took off his shirt that afternoon, she didn't see him. She couldn't let herself look.

WHAT SHOULD HAVE been satisfaction the next day wasn't. Because Tess wasn't there.

She had called first thing in the morning to let him know there'd been no phoned-in threat last night. He didn't know if that qualified as good news or not.

Then she'd said, "I figure you can do without my limited labor today." Her tone was light but hadn't fooled him. "Your brother was right. We should avoid being seen together."

She'd made the best decision. Zach knew it, but raged at the necessity. He'd enjoyed yesterday, seeing the progress on the house, sure, but also because he'd caught regular glimpses of Tess working her butt off, laughing at jokes or teasing someone else, blushing when he caught her stealing glances at him.

Seeing her genuine enthusiasm for what he was trying to do with the house had energized him, too. This evening, he felt…let down…even though he now had a new roof and maybe some new friends.

He'd been amazed at how many of his crew had showed up for the second day. A few had been missing because, this being Monday, they'd had to work, but two neighbors showed up ready to pitch in, including Dean Thompson from right next door. The boy had helped haul debris, too, and Karen, accompanied by her wide-eyed daughter, had brought over pitchers of lemonade.

But Tess's absence had clouded Zach's mood all day.

Once everyone was gone, he found himself prowling through the house, evaluating it anew. Physically exhausted, he still felt restless. He found himself trying to see it through Tess's eyes.

She was right—the glassed-in porch had potential as a sort of sitting room or casual dining room. It occurred to him that, since it stretched all the way across the back of the house, he could divide it, keeping a small utility room while opening the rest of the space to the kitchen. Yeah, that would work.

Kid's bedroom, he decided, and maybe a study there. Master bedroom could either be upstairs, once the second bathroom was in, or down here. If he were a parent, he'd want his bedroom on the same floor as his children's while they were young.

Even if that sometimes wasn't enough to protect those kids.

Just a pedestal sink and shower in the bathroom upstairs, he decided, maybe open shelves for towels, an in-wall medicine cabinet. Full vanity, sink and tub down. If he could find a claw-footed tub not too far out of his budget it would suit the house. Yeah, but then what about a shower?

In the end all his attempt to distract himself did was bring his thoughts full circle to Tess.

She triggered something in him that he didn't recognize. Zach didn't like it—whatever "it" was. He should be relieved that he had an excuse not to get involved with her. The very fact that he was on edge like this told him he'd be smart to stay away.

Too bad she wasn't already married or at least involved. She wouldn't have had to turn to Zach, then. She probably wouldn't have looked at him the way she did in the first place.

But he didn't like the idea of her with another man. Depending on him to keep her safe. Sleeping with him. Giving him instead of Zach that wide-eyed look and down-deep *knowing.*

"Crap." The word echoed in the empty house. He yanked at his hair until it hurt.

He pulled out his phone. Nothing. That meant she was okay, right?

What if she had made the decision to quit turning to him when something happened? He hadn't liked her tone on the phone that morning, as if she was closing a door. Damn it, she had to know how useless the Clear Creek cops were turning out to be. She wouldn't be stupid enough to shut him out completely, would she?

Maybe he should go by her house.

Maybe he shouldn't.

What would it hurt? He could park a block or so away again. With it dark out, no one would see him make a quick stop by her house. He could make sure she was okay and reinforce his order for her to call him if anything unsettling happened. Promise to keep her informed, too. They were in this together, after all.

He locked up his house but left on porch lights front and back. Next couple of days he'd install a motion-sensitive floodlight on the back of the house and maybe one over the detached garage. Doing some damage to his house would be a logical next step in the campaign to make him back down.

He was going to be damn careful where he parked his pickup from now on, too.

Tonight he'd left it on the same block he had the first time he'd visited Tess, and walked the block to her house knowing he was passing unseen but for the short distance under a streetlight.

Something smelled good in her garden. Inhaling, he decided it was lilac. This was the right time of year, wasn't it? He'd have to plant one in his yard. Not, he reminded himself, that he'd be around long enough to see the new bush reach any size.

He'd already pressed Tess's doorbell when he realized belatedly that an unexpected visitor might frighten her. *Should have called first.*

But then she might have told him not to come.

The porch light came on, momentarily blinding him. Nothing else happened for a minute. Then he heard the snap of the dead bolt and the door swung open.

Tess confronted him with her arms crossed. "What are you doing here?" she asked.

Good question.

"Can I come in?"

She gave an impatient huff of breath but did step back. Zach crossed the threshold and closed the door.

"I worried about you home alone today." Lame, but the best he could come up with.

"I went in to work, even though I'm supposed to be Tuesday through Saturday. You don't really think they'll physically assault me. How will that help Andrew Hayes?"

"He may decide nothing else is working."

She didn't blink for longer than he liked. Finally her shoulders sagged. "You're not being a comfort here."

"No. Sorry. I just want to be sure you keep your guard up."

"Fine." She glared at him. "You could have said that on the phone."

"I didn't like it that you weren't there today." Oh, hell, why had he had to say that?

She retreated a step. "You know your brother was right. Antonio didn't deserve what happened to him. We're the only ones who can give him any kind of justice."

As if he needed the reminder. "If something happens to you, too…"

Looking into her witchy, green-gold eyes was like gazing into a crystal ball at an astonishing scene that was probably an illusion but could be real.

Not for me. But, damn, the temptation was there.

"You're not my keeper." Her voice was soft, almost tremulous.

Oh, no?

Knowing he sounded like a wind-up toy that repeated the same phrase over and over, he still said, "I need to keep you safe."

Tess frowned. "You're not responsible for me being involved in this. You had nothing to do with my presence there. *You* need to stay safe, too." She said that last with passionate urgency.

"You don't understand." *God*, he thought, *do I*?

"What don't I understand?"

Zach shook his head. He couldn't tell her that he didn't think he could live with it if she got hurt. Yeah, part of it was his sense of responsibility but… These unfamiliar things he was feeling confused him, but he couldn't seem to shut them down.

He crossed the small foyer and closed his hands around her upper arms. Tension quivered through her and she stared at him in alarm. He should back off…but he could swear he saw yearning in those amazing eyes, too.

"Tess…" Shouldn't do this. But he was already bending his head. Uncertainty kept the first touch of his lips to hers gentle. He brushed his mouth over hers. She made a sound of surrender and threw her arms around his neck, rising on her toes to meet his mouth more fully.

Her taste was indescribable, sweet and tart at the same time. His thoughts blurred when her body, long, fine-boned, supple and soft in the right places, pressed against his.

He wrapped one hand around the back of her head, his fingers threading strong, silky hair, while he grabbed her butt with his other hand and lifted her. Next thing to desperate, he was devouring her now.

He felt the thump when she came up against a wall. He hadn't even known he'd walked her backward. If only she had on a skirt instead of jeans… He could strip them off, lift her…

He didn't have a condom with him.

Maybe she had some. Or was on birth control.

With a groan, he tore his mouth from hers.

Her eyes had been closed. Slowly her lids lifted until she stared at him, dazed.

"I want you," he said, voice guttural.

Her eyes widened. Then she blinked a couple of times. Her breath shuddered in and out.

"Oh, my God." She stiffened.

Suddenly, instead of yielding woman, he had a bundle of high-tension wires in his arms.

"This is wrong." She squirmed against him.

Blood flow hadn't yet returned to his brain but he still recognized a no when he heard it. In fact, a hell no.

His hands didn't want to leave her but he didn't see a choice. After a moment he made himself step back, releasing her.

"I didn't come here meaning to do that," he said hoarsely.

Her eyes met his again. "Didn't you?"

Zach couldn't swear, even to himself, that it hadn't been in the back of his mind. All he'd known was that he'd needed to see her.

"I don't know," he admitted.

"I think you should go."

"You wanted this, too."

"Of course I did!" Tess cried. "But...*you're* the one who impressed on me how important it is that we keep our distance. What if somebody is watching my house right now and sees you leave? Can you imagine the way we'd be grilled? Suddenly everything we say would be suspect. You know that's true."

He knew.

Zach shook his head and backed up a couple more steps.

"Why are you shaking your head? You've changed your mind?"

"No." He ran a hand over his face, which felt weirdly numb. "It's you. There's something about you."

"You're blaming *me*?" She sounded outraged.

"No. Yes." He was blowing this big time. It was like being stuck on a railroad bridge with nowhere to go and seeing a freight train barreling toward him. The wail of the horn came too late.

"You need to leave." She slipped around him and wrenched open the door. "Please."

"Tess." He could salvage this much. "I'll go if you promise to contact me if they threaten you again. If anything happens at all."

Her chin lowered. "I'll promise, if *you* promise to stay away from me unless something bad enough happens I need you."

"I missed you today," he heard himself say, shocking himself. He hadn't missed anyone since he was a kid. After he and Mom had moved away, there'd been no Sheila, no Bran. No Dad. That first year or so had echoed with emptiness. Loneliness. He hadn't let anyone that close since.

Maybe because of his job, he was usually good

at reading people, but Tess was sometimes an exception. This was one of those times. He had the uncomfortable feeling she was looking deep into him. He was uncomfortably aware of how much he didn't want her to see.

But then she said, "I wanted to be there. I thought about you all day. But you know the right thing to do, Zach."

"Yeah." It came out rough. "I know."

Without looking at her again, he walked past her, out the door. Stopping with his back to her he said, "Promise."

"I promise," she whispered.

He nodded and kept going, glad when he left the pool of porch light for the safety of the darkness. He heard the sound of the door closing and he kept going.

ZACH SAT IN his recliner, the only furniture in his battered living room except for his TV on a stand. Oh, yeah, and the folding wooden TV tray he was currently using as an end table and dining table.

After leaving Tess last night, he'd been in a shitty mood. He'd made the decision to move out of his apartment the next day. At least in the house he'd have ways to vent his restlessness.

Not wanting to test the commitment of any of his new friends, he'd lined up a couple of community college students to help him once he was off work. It hadn't taken them all that long to move his limited belongings.

On the way out, one of them had taken a last, dubious look behind him and said, "You're really going to live here, dude?"

Pretty sad when a broke college student thought your digs were substandard. Although Zach supposed it was possible that particular kid actually drove a BMW and still lived at home with Mom and Dad.

Moving wasn't the only vow he'd made last night. What he needed to do was to refocus. Think about something besides Tess. To channel this prowling sense of urgency, he'd begin the investigation into his sister's murder. That was why he'd moved back here, wasn't it?

So now he dialed the number he'd extracted from another old-timer at the Clear Creek Police Department. A man answered. "Nolte here."

"Sergeant Nolte, my name is Zach Carter."

"Wife said you called. What do you want? I can tell you we're not buying."

"I'm not selling." Zach would have smiled if he hadn't been so tense. "I'm hoping you'll talk to me about a murder you investigated almost twenty-five years ago."

"Sheila Murphy." Darren Nolte was still sharp.

"Yes."

"This isn't Brandon Murphy, is it?" the retired sergeant asked suspiciously.

"No, I'm his younger brother, Zach."

"I thought you said your name was Carter?"

"I ended up adopted by a stepfather."

"Why in hell are you asking questions about this now?" He didn't sound real thrilled with the opportunity to reminisce. "It's too late, son. And what makes you think you'd like anything you learn?"

"I want the truth, whether I like it or not," Zach said flatly. "It's my understanding you think our father killed her."

"That's my best guess." The gruff voice softened, just a little. "Couldn't prove it."

"So I understand. Will you tell me why you focused on him? And who else you looked at?"

After a long pause Nolte said grudgingly, "Suppose it wouldn't hurt." He started talking, picking up steam as he went.

Zach jotted in the notepad he held on his lap. Not very many notes, though. It became clear to him right away that then-detective Nolte had zeroed in on a preferred subject right away.

When Zach asked why, Nolte said, "Best opportunity, and, I got to tell you, I had the feeling he was lying to me then."

He was right. Michael Murphy *had* lied to him. He hadn't slept through the night, the way he'd insisted to investigators he had. Maybe he'd lied because he'd committed a terrible crime. But it was always possible he'd been afraid if the detectives knew he'd been up at any point, they'd be more likely to suspect him. People were stupid that way, Zach had long since discovered.

"I'm assuming you knew that my mother had had affairs," Zach said bluntly.

"You kids knew?" Nolte sounded appalled.

"I didn't at the time. Bran did. He tried to tell me and I accused him of being a liar. But I lived with her for another nine years, you know. She's remarried several times, but she never stays for long."

The sergeant harrumphed. "We knew. She never admitted to it, but we came up with a couple of names. Neighbors and coworkers notice things like that, you know."

"I do. I've been a detective for a couple of years now."

"Have you? Where?"

"Portland. I've taken a job recently with the Harris County Sheriff's Department because I wanted to look into Sheila's death." He looked down to see that he was drilling a hole through several pages with the nib of the pen. Cool as a cucumber, that was him. "Do you remember the names of either of those men?"

"Good God, it's been twenty-five years!"

"Big case and one you never closed. You can't tell me you don't still think about it sometimes."

There was a moment of silence.

"Hell, yeah, I've thought about it. Truth is I

knew one of the men. Kind of shocked me. I'd met his wife, too. Nice lady."

"Did he stay married?"

"I don't know. I didn't have to make any claims, and I didn't have any other reason to see him. At the time, we interviewed him real quietly. She never knew anything about it." He sighed. "Duane Womack. Insurance agent. I guess he handled your parents' auto and homeowner insurance. Mine, too."

"What did he say when you interviewed him?"

"That it was none of our damn business but that he was with his wife. What else? He says he and your mother always met during the day. He'd take a long lunch hour. Being married, neither of them ever tried for an evening date or an overnight."

"Had he met Sheila?"

"A couple of times," he said. Now the sergeant sounded uncomfortable. "Commented she was a pretty little girl."

The hair on the back of Zach's neck prickled.

CHAPTER SEVEN

ZACH MENTALLY REPLAYED what the retired detective had just told him.

One of the men his mother had been seeing on the side had gone out of his way to comment on how pretty a six-year-old girl had been, only days after some sicko had raped and strangled her?

If the investigators had been any kind of cops at all, that should have sent off burning hot flares for them.

"Those were his words? Not yours?" Zach asked carefully, hoping his incredulity wasn't leaking into his tone.

"His," the retired sergeant said. "Bothered me, but people say things like that all the time. 'What a handsome boy!' 'Oh, your daughter is so pretty!' You're reading something into it that isn't there."

"You so sure about that?"

Again there was a momentary silence. "He had two daughters, one a couple years older than your sister, one a little younger," Nolte said. "Best I could do was talk to the older daughter's teachers and have the school counselor sit down with her. There was no suggestion she'd been molested."

In other words, he'd done his job. Above and beyond, even.

"And you took his word for it that he hadn't slipped out of his house that night?"

"No, I managed to run into his wife real casually and say, 'Hey, I thought I saw Duane driving home, middle of the night. Hope there wasn't an emergency.' That kind of thing. She looked completely puzzled and said Duane wasn't a night owl. She couldn't remember the last time he'd been up past eleven. I couldn't find any hint he'd had an inappropriate interest in little girls. What else could I do?"

"Probably nothing." Those prickles hadn't subsided, though. "I might get a little further now, though, in case he was later accused of anything."

"Guess that's true. Twenty-five years ago we couldn't find out everything we ever wanted to know about someone on his Facebook page."

Zach smiled. "I'm willing to bet people were just as dumb."

"Took different forms."

Turned out Nolte remembered the other name, too. Sam Doyle. Sam was a plumber. Zach recalled a plumbing disaster, a pipe broken in the wall behind the shower. The wall had had to be torn out and Dad had replaced the saturated plywood on the bathroom floor and the vinyl. Zach was even able, kind of vaguely, to picture the plumber who had responded. He'd been a young guy, with hair long enough he kept having to push it out of his eyes. Zach had wondered why he didn't cut it. No guarantee he was this Sam Doyle, but what were the odds?

He'd certainly been younger than Zach's mother, who at the time was… Zach had to count back. Thirty-five, he decided. But then, as he'd noticed since, Mom liked men of all ages.

Nolte didn't remember, as well, what Sam Doyle had said, except that he'd been outraged at any suggestion he'd be sexually interested in a girl, far less willing to kill her.

"He'd had girlfriends," the sergeant said. Something in his tone told Zach he was shrugging. "Seemed normal. You know? Again, no hint he could be a pedophile."

"What about neighbors? Older teenage boys who'd have seen Sheila playing outside?"

Nolte and his partner had knocked on doors, asked around, but hadn't come up with anyone of interest.

"Have you asked to see a copy of the police report?" he said a little testily. "All of this would be in it."

"I haven't yet, but Bran did and got the runaround. He wondered if it might have gone missing."

"Huh. If you like, I'll ask for a copy."

"I'd like." Zach set aside his notepad. "Thank you, Sergeant." He gave him his phone number and mailing address, and said if he thought of anything else to please call.

After setting the phone aside, Zach did some concentrated thinking. He needed to tackle this as he would any other investigation. One advantage of having been there was that he remembered a couple of his mother's good friends. Neighbors, too. He'd track down as many people who'd been close to the family as he could. There might have been a pedophile living a block away. The intervening years made investigating a challenge in one way, but in another way they gave him an advantage. He could find out where life had taken all those people. Who had been arrested, convicted, fired from jobs.

His mother could have had other lovers, but the few times he'd tried to talk to her about it, she wouldn't admit to any. Instead she'd wept, as if he was committing the worst kind of betrayal.

There might have been whispers about Dad and other young girls. Would Bran have told him? Zach wondered. Or would people have whispered out of his hearing?

He and his brother could team up and make this go faster...but he found himself speculating on why Bran had never opened a serious investigation, despite being right here in town.

He'd been damn defensive about their father. Because he had a niggling—or even a solidly based—suspicion he'd rather not acknowledge, even to himself?

It was possible.

That meant Zach would go it alone, at least until he felt more trust than he did yet in his brother, the stranger.

FOR ONCE, IT wasn't the sound of her phone ringing that awakened Tess. Straining to hear the faintest sound, she lay utterly still. The drumming of her own heartbeat filled her ears. She was afraid an intruder could hear it from across the room.

Oh, God. What if someone was in the house?

Nobody was in her bedroom, she knew that much. What little light leaked through the blinds was enough for her to make out the chair still braced under the doorknob.

Tap, tap, tap.

Fear felt like an electric shock. She rolled to stare at her window. That had sounded like…fingers tapping.

A hard knock, knock, knock followed against the glass.

She jackknifed to a sitting position, her hand pressed to her mouth to stifle a scream.

Her telephone rang and she couldn't help crying out.

She snatched up the phone, never taking her

eyes off the window. She absolutely did not want to answer.

The closet. She could wedge herself into the corner…

And what? Attack whoever found her there with the highest, sharpest heel she had? Why hadn't she been smart enough to bring something to bed with her that would serve as a weapon?

Ring.

Tap, tap, tap.

Tess sucked in a deep breath. She pressed the screen of her phone. It took every ounce of willpower she possessed to say, with some facsimile of coolness, "This is really tiresome, you know."

"You're meeting with the new cops tomorrow. You're going to be confused. You were so shaken up, you don't remember what you said that first day. This time, you won't lie. You understand, bitch? You better, because we can get to you anytime."

She heard another tap, tap, tap on the window. The scratching sound of something scraping across the glass made her shudder. Her teeth chattered.

Finally, a hard wham made the window vibrate.

She found herself on her feet beside the bed. On the far side of the bed from the window, for what that was worth. She didn't dare open her bedroom door. If one of them was at her window, only a few feet away from her, what if someone else stood, even now, in her hall, waiting for her to burst out?

Despite her promise to Zach, Tess had made the sensible decision not to call him just because there was another threat. The worst that had happened was the slashed tires. She really believed what she'd told him: an assault on her wouldn't achieve anything.

But quaking in the dark of her bedroom, waiting for the glass to shatter, being sensible quit seeming smart.

With her hand shaking, it wasn't easy to find Zach's number, but she managed.

Please answer, please answer. Please, please, please.

"Tess?" He said her name, hard and urgent.

"Somebody is right outside," she whispered. "Rapping on my window. I'm scared."

"Jesus. I'm on my way. Stay on the line with me." Rustling sounds made her think he was throwing on some clothes. A door slammed. Then he asked, "Did you call 911?"

"No." Oh, God. He could probably hear her teeth chattering. "I will."

"Forget it. I'm faster."

"THERE ARE FOOTPRINTS outside your bedroom window, Tess. Broken branches on that shrub, too."

"It's a *viburnum carlesii*."

No big surprise that Zach looked at her as though she was nuts. Who cared what shrub grew beneath her bedroom window?

"It's probably too much to hope he was stupid enough to have had bare hands when he tapped on your window."

"You think it was Andrew Hayes."

He was pacing the length of her living room, his long strides eating up the distance in seconds. Tess had never seen him anything but athletically graceful. Tonight, the way he swung around was jerky. Fury showed in every line of his body.

"I don't know. Would you have heard if the man talking to you on the phone was right outside your bedroom window?"

Tess clutched her completely unsexy fleece bathrobe tightly around her. She had settled in a glider, out of Zach's path. She kept it in motion with one foot on the floor but the rocking was jerkier than normal for her, too. So much adrenaline.

"I think I would have. I mean—" she couldn't help shuddering again "—he couldn't have been ten feet away from me. I've been in my bedroom and heard neighbors talking on the other side of the fence even though my window was closed."

He had paused briefly, his jaw clenching as he noticed her distress. "Then there are at least two of them."

"I told you I'm pretty sure the voices on the phone haven't all been the same."

"Yeah. Shit, Tess. They took a big risk tonight."

"You mean, if I'd called 911 right away and a patrol car happened to be close by." She bent her head. "That's what I should have done, isn't it?"

"Maybe."

He came to crouch in front of her, bracing his forearms on his thighs. He wasn't wearing socks, she saw in some weirdly disconnected part of her brain. He probably hadn't bothered with underwear, either, unless he wore it to bed. She had a feeling he didn't.

"It's a waste of time to ask yourself what you should have done." His blue eyes compelled her. "It all happened fast, didn't it? Maybe took no more than a minute? What are the chances a Clear Creek officer would have arrived that quickly? And, if he had, that he'd have caught anyone?"

"He might have taken off if he'd heard me talking loudly to a 911 dispatcher." Another thought occurred to her. "If I'd already been on the phone, I wouldn't have answered the call."

"I'm not sure that would have been a good idea, Tess." Lines deepened on Zach's forehead. "I've said that before. If they can't terrorize you with a phone call, they'll find another way."

She shivered. "They did."

"Damn it!" He rose fluidly to his feet, pulling her up with him. For the second time tonight she found herself securely enclosed in his arms. For the second time tonight she succumbed to temptation.

When she'd first let him in the door, he'd yanked her into his arms after saying only one word: her name. She had held on for all she was worth. He'd been breathing hard, his heart racing.

This felt just as good. Just as safe. It was spoiled only because Tess hated being the little woman clinging to the manly guy who had come to her rescue.

Until the past couple of weeks, her greatest fear had been of her father having that second stroke she knew was inevitable.

She was the one to hear a car pulling up outside. When she stirred, Zach let her go with what felt like reluctance.

"It might be better if you weren't here," she suggested for a second time.

"You don't think they'll notice the pickup in your driveway?"

"It could be mine," she pointed out.

"They can check DMV records easily enough. No, Tess. We have no reason to hide the fact that you contacted me when the threats started."

She nodded because it was too late anyway. She could hear a heavy tread on her front steps and porch just before the doorbell rang.

Still clutching the robe close, she let the police officer in.

Balding, probably in his early fifties, he wasn't even her height, but was so solidly built Tess guessed he'd be very hard to bring down.

"I'm Officer Parish." His brown eyes took in first Tess then Zach standing protectively behind her.

She held out a hand. "Thank you for coming so quickly. I'm Tess Granath."

Zach was a little slower to offer his hand. "Sheriff's Deputy Zach Carter."

They all went into the living room, where Tess asked if he knew about her previous calls to the Clear Creek PD.

"I've heard. You believe this is connected to the fact that you're a witness to the death of the illegal Mexican."

She bristled. "I fail to see how Antonio Alvarez's country of origin or his lack of paperwork has any relevance to his murder."

"I didn't mean to suggest it does, ma'am. Truth is, I couldn't recall his name. That's all."

Tess relaxed. "I'm sorry. I'm feeling a little defensive." A lot, actually. "And tense," she added. Understatement, anyone?

"Let's start with you telling me what happened tonight," he suggested.

Zach stayed silent, letting her describe the terrifying sequence of noises and threats in her own way.

"Deputy Carter wasn't here when any of this happened?" Officer Parish asked.

"No. I called him because he knows about the other threats. He's…taken it upon himself to protect me."

It bothered Tess that she couldn't tell what Officer Parish was thinking about their relationship. But did it really matter? What the new team of investigators and then the DA thought would matter, but Tess was feeling combative.

She had told Detective Delancy the truth and nothing but the truth. The first time she had ever set eyes on Zach was when she'd seen him leap out of the patrol car and sprint across the lawn toward Hayes in an attempt to prevent him beating Antonio to a bloody pulp. Nobody would be able to prove any different.

Her statement tomorrow when she met with Detective Clayton and his partner from Stimson wouldn't change. She hadn't forgotten a single second of the most horrifying scene she'd ever witnessed. She relived it every night.

She stayed inside when the two men went around the side of the house with flashlights to inspect outside her window. Waiting, Tess had the disorienting realization that she had no idea what time it was. Midnight? Four?

She didn't bother to reach for her phone to check. Even if dawn was hours away, she wouldn't be going back to bed.

Would she ever feel safe in her own bedroom again? Maybe...maybe she should go stay with Dad for a while. Being afraid to stay in her house would be a good excuse. She could take care of him and he could enjoy feeling protective.

Except...what if someone actually *did* break in and her father was hurt? Plus, she'd have to tell him what had been happening. The doctors had recommended he avoid stress.

Her current lifestyle definitely couldn't be described as low-stress, she thought hysterically.

She heard the two men talking as they came in the front door. Officer Parish didn't sit again.

"Someone will be back in daylight to get some pictures," he said. "We'll check your window for fingerprints, too."

Zach walked the officer to the door, locked it behind him and then returned to the living room.

"It's three-thirty. Why don't you go back to bed, Tess?"

"All I'd do is lie there staring at the window."

"I'll be here. No one is getting in this house, and if your phone rings again, I'm answering it."

"What?" She gaped at him. "You can't be seen leaving here in the morning."

"I can and I will." That implacable expression was familiar. "We can talk tomorrow about security measures. In the meantime, you have to be exhausted."

"Adrenaline isn't exactly a sleep aid," Tess said wryly.

"Can I get you something?"

"You mean a sleeping pill? I don't have anything like that." And wouldn't take it if she did. Under the circumstances, the idea of being dead to the world held no appeal.

"I was thinking herbal tea. Cocoa. Wine?"

Tess shook her head. "I'm fine."

After frowning at her for a minute Zach rolled his shoulders, stretched both arms toward the ceiling, groaned and sank onto the sofa. "Okay. I'm still not leaving you alone."

She couldn't bring herself to argue. "Thank you," she said after a minute. "Um, if you want coffee or something—"

He shook his head. "What time's your appointment tomorrow?"

"You mean today, don't you? Eleven. Is yours today, too?

"Two o'clock. I'm kind of hoping the DA will have chosen to involve herself at this stage, too. I know the case has been assigned to Christine Campbell. I checked her out. She's a senior criminal deputy attorney, which means they're pulling out the big guns."

"I don't suppose you've been here long enough to know anyone in the office."

"No. I called Bran. He thinks she's okay, but

working well with local law enforcement agencies isn't necessarily a good indication for us."

"No. But it's not like we get to pick and choose." Tess hesitated. "Will she be the one to make the decision whether to prosecute Hayes?"

He waggled a hand to indicate there was a possibility. "I'm sure she'll consult with her immediate boss, and my guess is something like this will go all the way to the top. The prosecuting attorney is a guy named Troxell. Joseph Troxell. He's up for re-election in November."

"The Hispanic vote has to be really significant in this county."

"It is. I've heard he leans to the conservative side, though."

"A conservative should be strong on law and order," Tess said indignantly. "Not letting a murderer skate!"

"Hey." He smiled crookedly. "I agree with you. I'm just saying he'll be weighing which side brings him an electoral advantage."

"You notice how little coverage there's been in the news so far?"

His mouth tightened. "Oh, yeah."

"If they don't charge that creep, I'm going to raise a huge stink," she told him. "So be prepared."

Zach tipped his head. "I'll be cheering you on."

Her spine stiffened. "But not doing the same?"

"I can't unless I quit my job."

"Because of the way they're pressuring you?"

"No, because individual police officers are not allowed to speak out at will. A designated spokesperson represents the department. The chief or sheriff will be behind the podium for press conferences. Only occasionally is a deputy or detective allowed to answer questions."

Of course he was right. And quitting his job so he could speak out on behalf of Antonio would be a drastic career move.

"I understand," she said.

The silence was almost comfortable. Tess rested her head against the cushion, giving an occasional push with one foot on the floor to keep up a slow rocking. She didn't look at Zach.

"Once we've given our statements tomorrow, there won't be any point in threatening me, will there?" she asked.

"My guess is we'll be interviewed repeatedly. Certainly by the DA if she's not sitting in on tomorrow's meetings. Leading up to trial, if it comes to that, she'll spend more time with both of us, too. Tess…it won't be over until Hayes is convicted." Zach sounded grim. "Witnesses frequently recant before a trial. If he is convicted, his friends will be pissed. It'll be a condemnation not only of him, but of the way they conduct themselves as officers, too. You'd better not go one mile over the speed limit when you're on county roads. The response time might be really slow if you call 911. There are any numbers of ways to make you pay."

She stared at him. "What about you? They obviously think I'm the one likeliest to give way to pressure and change my story. Which I find really insulting, by the way. But if you testify in court against a fellow deputy—"

"Unless there's a major shift in attitude at the sheriff's department, which I don't see as likely, I may as well tender my resignation. I think Portland Police Bureau would hire me again, but I might have trouble getting in anywhere else," he said, echoing her thoughts.

"Wonderful. The deck is kind of stacked against us, isn't it?"

He cocked an eyebrow. "Kind of?"

Tess made a face at him.

His smile was surprisingly relaxed. "Yes. There are consequences to telling an unpopular truth. But you knew that, didn't you?"

"I admit I didn't think it out. I was too mad."

"You and me both." Lines deepened between his dark eyebrows. "Tess, nobody would blame you if you chose not to give a statement tomorrow or…softened what you have to say."

"*I* would blame me," she said sharply.

After a moment he nodded. "Okay. Then let me suggest again that you try to get a few hours of sleep. You want to be at your best tomorrow."

She was surprised to realize that maybe she

could sleep now. In fact, she was suddenly groggy enough she could have nodded off right where she was.

"But what about you?"

"If it's okay with you, I'll stretch out on the couch and catch some shut-eye, too. But don't worry—I sleep lightly."

Tess nodded, stopped the glider and, with a major effort, stood. "I'll get you a pillow and blanket."

"Okay."

He followed her down the hall, watching as she put a pillowcase on a spare pillow. Then he took it from her along with a comforter. His eyes were a brighter blue than should have been possible in the low lighting. Dark stubble shadowed his jaw, tempting her to lift her hand to feel the texture. He glanced toward her bedroom before looking back at her.

The open bedroom door was only a few steps away. Just thinking about bed had her feeling warm enough she wanted to strip off the heavy bathrobe.

Sure, and why not the midthigh-length T-shirt nightgown beneath it?

Warmth pooled low in her belly.

Tess made herself back away. "I hope you get some sleep." Her voice sounded odd to her ears. A little husky maybe.

"Thanks." He cleared his throat. "Sleep tight."

His mouth quirked. "That's what my mother always said."

"Mine, too." Making an awkward sideways step, she bumped the door frame and blushed. Nothing like being a klutz at a moment like this.

Moment like what? she asked herself. She was not, repeat, *not*, inviting him into her bed.

But, oh, she was thinking about it. In fact her whole body hummed with anticipation for something that wasn't going to happen.

"I'll see you in the morning," she said more firmly as she backed into her room and closed the door.

She didn't bother with wedging the chair beneath the doorknob.

CHAPTER EIGHT

SENIOR CRIMINAL DEPUTY ATTORNEY Christine Campbell sat one chair removed from the two male detectives who faced Zach across the table. It was as if she was making the point that she was present only as a bystander.

Her nod as the three introduced themselves was crisp and he sensed annoyance.

Both Stimson detectives had an air of experience. Detective John Clayton was the oldest, probably in his fifties. Lieutenant Niall MacLachlan might be in his early forties. His dark auburn hair was graying at the temples.

Seeing Zach's surprise at his name, he said, "Yes, Chief MacLachlan is my brother."

Zach nodded. The poor guy had probably had to say that a few million times.

It was Lieutenant MacLachlan who asked if he would describe the event in question—cop-speak—from the beginning, as if he hadn't made a previous statement.

Zach began with his glance down the side street and his surprise at seeing another sheriff's department patrol vehicle.

When he finished, it was a moment before anyone said a word.

Then DA Campbell tapped her pen on the table. "I would have preferred to be a part of this investigation from the beginning. May I ask why you retreated from your initial statement, which implied that you believed Deputy Hayes was reacting in response to an attempt to take his weapon?"

He stared at her. "What?"

Her eyes narrowed. "We were given rather sketchy notes regarding your original statement to Undersheriff Stokes, and an equally abbreviated version of your subsequent conversation with Detective Delancy."

"I told both of them exactly what I just told you," he said flatly. "I have felt strongly from the beginning that the investigation needed to be taken over by an impartial party."

"I see."

Did she? "My stance has made me rather unpopular. There has been a certain amount of pressure applied. What sounds like an editing of my original statement may have reflected a belief that I would be obedient enough to back off and let the department handle Antonio Alvarez's death internally." *Cool it*, he told himself. "They were wrong."

Lieutenant MacLachlan said, "I'm sure you're aware that your statement differs on many points from that of Deputy Hayes."

"I assumed as much," he said.

None of the three were easy to read. MacLachlan least of all. Zach had a feeling his apparently relaxed air was very deceptive. Clayton looked as if he didn't believe Zach. DA Campbell…who knew?

"We interviewed Ms. Granath this morning," Detective Clayton commented.

"I knew you were going to," he agreed. He didn't let any tension show on his face or in his body language.

"She mentioned that there have been a number of threats directed at her. She said she got a call last night specifically ordering her to 'become confused.' She was told to forget what she said in her initial statements."

"Did she also tell you that, while she was being told 'they' could get to her anytime, someone was tapping and scratching on her window a few feet from her bed?"

"She did. She says she called you."

No secret what they were getting at.

"Ms. Granath was a stranger to me when we both witnessed Deputy Hayes beating Antonio Alvarez to death. I would have had no reason to pursue an acquaintance with her after that." Thank God he was telling the truth. Later…but that wasn't their business. "However, I won't stand by and allow a witness to be terrorized by members of my own department or anyone else."

"You believe Deputy Hayes himself is involved in this campaign to intimidate Ms. Granath?"

"I do." He made sure his gaze didn't waver. "I also believe friends of his are involved. It's hard to imagine them pursuing these tactics without his encouragement or at least compliance."

"And what makes you think these friends are fellow sheriff's deputies?"

He raised his eyebrows. "The rotting, beheaded rabbit in my locker at the sheriff's department was one clue. Deputy Hayes is still on administrative leave, as I'm sure you know. It would have been tough for anyone not an employee to get in there to start with. The only people who might have been able to watch me dialing my combination to unlock were fellow deputies."

DA Campbell's lashes fluttered a couple of times, suggesting he'd surprised her. The lieutenant looked exceedingly unsurprised.

She picked up her pen and made a note, then lifted her gaze to him. "This is very much a 'he said, she said' case, which is always difficult."

Abruptly pissed, he stared her down. "Fortunately 'he' and 'she' happen to agree."

If he wasn't mistaken, a smile started to form on her lips before she firmed them.

Clayton remarked, "A number of Deputy Hayes's

coworkers have come forward with glowing testimonials of his performance on the job."

"I'm sure they have." With an effort, Zach relaxed his shoulders. "Did any of them happen to mention the several citizen complaints accusing him of unnecessary force?"

MacLachlan spoke up. "I'm sure it goes without saying that we have access to Deputy Hayes's personnel file, including commendations and grievances."

Reassured, Zach nodded toward the paperwork on the table. "I don't suppose Detective Delancy has made any attempt to discover the name of the woman Hayes was warning Antonio away from."

"He isn't convinced that you could have heard anything said between the two men, given that Deputy Hayes had his back to you."

"Deputy Hayes was yelling. And, as it happens, I approached at an angle."

The two detectives perked right up. "Did you?" MacLachlan murmured. He flipped a notebook to a blank page and pushed it across the desk to Zach. "Please draw me a map, to the best of your recollection."

Zach indicated the houses by drawing crude squares, using smaller boxes for where Hayes's patrol car had been parked and where he himself had pulled up. A couple of lines, complete with arrows, showed the directions from which he and

Tess had come completed the picture. Then he passed the notebook back across the table.

MacLachlan studied the sketch and then pushed the notebook to Clayton, who in turn passed it to the DA.

They asked more questions, undoubtedly trying to trip him up. He told her again about Hayes trying to pick up his bloody baton, and how Hayes had ordered Tess to butt out because she was interfering in police business. Zach also reminded them that Hayes had been well out of the area he had been assigned to patrol.

Zach talked until he was hoarse.

In the end, he shook hands all around and left, having no sense which side they would come down on. He had the most faith in the lieutenant, even if he was hard to read. Clayton, he thought, might be more inclined to come down on the side of a longtime deputy who had been fighting off an assault.

It might or might not be a good sign that the DA had chosen to involve herself in these interviews. She was obviously pissed that the prosecutor's office hadn't been immediately informed so that they could have seen the crime scene before the body was removed. What was critical was whether she believed Zach's insistence that his statement had been shaded to suit the department.

It irked him to know he had to stay hands-off from the investigation.

He was especially frustrated, knowing how long this could drag on. Ultimately, the prosecutor's office had to wait until investigators issued a report, and then they'd take their own sweet time in making a decision, especially given the sensitivity of the case. He'd known better than to ask for a possible timeline, but it occurred to him that Tess might have. He'd have to ask her.

He was walking out to his car when his phone rang. He glanced at the name on the screen, winced and muted the phone. This was the second time he'd chosen not to take a call from his mother.

Behind the wheel of his truck, he called Bran instead, expecting to be dumped to voice mail. Instead his brother answered.

"Wondered if you're free for dinner," Zach said. "I have some things to discuss."

Voices in the background told him Bran wasn't alone. But he said, "Sure. Where?"

Zach had found a diner he liked with a broader menu than the tavern's. Bran's agreement was abrupt but unhesitating.

Getting behind the wheel, Zach wondered if this meal would end up cut short the way their first one had, and for the same reason.

TESS'S FATHER SCOWLED at her as she set grocery bags on his kitchen counter. "I have to read about my daughter's troubles in the damn newspaper?"

he said in the voice still a little slurred as an after-effect of the stroke.

She winced. Wonderful. She should have realized he'd find out about the whole mess one way or another.

No, she reminded herself. Not the *whole* mess. The campaign of terror, as she had come to think of it, hadn't made the paper yet.

Abandoning the half-unpacked groceries, she turned to face him. "I didn't want to worry you," she said.

He snorted, expressing his opinion without a word.

"You know what the doctor said," Tess reminded him.

"I don't want to spend what time I have left in some kind of damn cocoon."

Her father didn't swear often. The fact that he'd said damn twice in such a short time told her he was really mad.

She sighed. "Okay. I don't blame you."

Tell him or not?

Watching her unwaveringly, he sat at the kitchen table, still a big, vital man. Seeing him immediately after the stroke had been painful. That a tiny clot of blood could steal his ability to form words, to use his right hand, to walk, had seemed unthinkable.

It hadn't taken her long to realize he was still the same man she had loved and admired for as long as she could remember. His determination to come back from the stroke had been formidable.

He'd begun physical therapy with grim determination. He now swam laps every morning. At first an old friend had driven him to the YMCA. He was now driving himself, in a limited way. And it had been nearly three years.

Maybe, she kept telling herself, the blood thinner really would prevent another stroke. The odds were scary...but he'd beaten them once already.

Dad was all she had left. It had been years since she'd seen her brother more often than every other year for a holiday. Tess doubted she'd see him even that often once their father was gone.

Tess had the sudden, disconcerting thought that Zach reminded her a little of Dad. Zach wasn't a man who would ever accept defeat, either. And he had that same intensely protective nature.

Making up her mind, Tess sat and said, "There's more going on than you've read in the newspaper, Dad. Promise me you won't get upset."

He snorted his opinion of that, too, which made her laugh.

So she told him everything, including the fact that she had a defender.

"Come home," her father said instantly, the way she'd known he would.

"I won't let them drive me out of my house. It might be different if I really thought I was in danger, but hurting me would really backfire for

Deputy Hayes. He's surely smart enough to realize that."

"Get a gun," her father suggested.

"Dad!" Tess stared at him in shock. He was a big proponent of gun control laws.

Unbending, he said, "If you won't protect yourself, come home and I'll do it."

Tess jumped up, came around the table and threw her arms around her father, hugging him hard. "Daddy," she whispered.

His arms came around her, too.

His strong embrace felt almost as good as being held by Zach.

"NOLTE ACTUALLY TALKED to you?" Bran slowly lowered his beer glass to the Formica-topped table.

"He was a little testy at first, but once I got him started, he didn't seem to mind talking." Zach set his laminated menu aside.

"He never returned my phone calls."

"I sneaked under his radar, what with my last name not being Murphy."

His brother didn't look pleased.

"He promised to try to get a copy of the police report, too."

Bran shook his head. "It'll be interesting to see if he comes through."

"It will." Zach paused, turning to be sure no one had quietly slipped into the booth right behind him. Having his back to the room disturbed him, but Bran had arrived first and obviously had the same instincts. At least he'd grabbed the booth at the very back of the diner and, so far, no one else had been seated within earshot. "He gave me the names of a couple of Mom's lovers, too," Zach added, keeping his voice low whether they were alone or not.

Bran met his eyes. "I knew who one of them was. I wasn't sure you'd really want to know."

"I want."

They were interrupted by the middle-aged waitress who appeared vaguely familiar. The mother of someone Zach had gone to school with? But she didn't seem to recognize him, so he let it go. Both men ordered and then waited until she was chatting with a family several booths away before resuming their conversation.

"Who?" he asked.

"You remember Jack Percy? Friend of Dad's?"

Zach had trouble hiding his shock. "You're kidding. *Jack?*"

"Oh, yeah." Bran leaned back in the booth, anger in the rigid set of his jaw. "Dad deserved better than a best friend and a wife who both betrayed him."

Zach shook his head. "Man. I really liked Jack. He never seemed to mind Dad bringing us on fishing trips."

"After I saw him with Mom, I quit going on those trips."

"I remember," Zach said slowly. "It hurt Dad's feelings."

"Not like I could tell him why I didn't want to go."

"So you just looked sullen and said, 'Because I don't feel like it.'"

His brother's face relaxed into a grin. "I was practicing at being a teenager."

Zach laughed but was left oddly unsettled. This was the kind of information that made him feel as if the binoculars he was looking through had just been readjusted, sharpening or possibly distorting a view he'd thought he was already seeing clearly.

"You didn't know," Bran said suddenly. "Nolte didn't give you Jack's name."

"No." Zach hesitated. "The two he admitted to knowing about were Duane Womack, who was apparently Mom and Dad's insurance agent, and a younger guy named Sam Doyle. Him, I remember. He was a plumber. He came out to the house when the pipe broke in the bathroom wall."

"God, I remember that." Bran looked stunned. "He was practically a kid."

Zach nodded. "I've already traced him. He'd have been twenty-one."

"That's sick."

"Mom was a beautiful woman." He thought about that. "Still is, for her age."

His brother appeared to be stuck on the idea of their thirty-five-year-old mother sleeping with a kid only a few years out of high school. His expression suggested he was doing his best to swallow something indigestible. Zach knew how he felt.

Their food arrived. Neither reached for silverware.

"Here's the interesting thing," Zach continued. He'd begun some serious digging in the past couple days. "Duane Womack is ten years older than Mom. He had two daughters, one only a little older than Sheila. Nolte told me he was bothered at the time when Womack commented on how pretty Sheila was."

Bran's gaze sharpened. "*After* she was raped?"

"Yeah, kind of gives you pause, doesn't it? Nolte did a little investigating and came up with nothing to support the idea that Womack was molesting his own kid. He decided the comment was just one of those things people say."

"And it might have been." Although Bran didn't sound convinced.

"Yes, except it turns out Womack's wife left him later, taking the girls with her."

"The man was screwing around on her."

"Uh-huh. But she ended up with sole custody. No visitation."

"Isn't that interesting."

"Yes, it is. I'm going to try to get in touch with

the plumber and with the ex-Mrs. Womack or one of the daughters. I'll follow up on Jack, too, unless you've stayed in touch and know what's up with him." He started eating.

Bran shook his head. "Dad and he stayed friends. Can you believe it?" He ate a couple of fries. "All I know is, he's still married. He and his wife had a couple of kids, but they were enough younger than us I don't really remember them."

Zach frowned, vaguely able to picture Jack carrying a cranky toddler during a backyard cookout.

"There might be something there."

"Let me have him," his brother said. "I've held a grudge for a long time. It would give me pleasure to find out that scumbag is a pedophile, too."

Seeing Bran's expression, Zach tossed aside his reservations. "Go for it. The only thing that bothers me about all three of these guys is that they were sleeping with Mom. I know pedophiles are sometimes married, but that may be partly cover. Do they have affairs with adult women, too?"

"I don't know."

They both concentrated on their meals for a minute.

"I'm surprised you're not focusing your efforts on Dad," Bran said suddenly. "Given your hostility to him."

Zach looked at his brother. "I'm casting a wide

net," he said carefully. "Dad will be caught in it if there's anything there to find."

Anger tightened Bran's face but he kept his mouth shut.

"Nolte still thinks Dad did it."

"Nolte is full of shit."

Zach shrugged and polished off the BLT that he'd ordered along with chili.

"Speaking of sleeping around." That same anger darkened Bran's eyes. "Rumor has it you're spending nights with Tess."

"Now, how did rumor come up with something like that?" Zach said sarcastically.

"Is it true?"

"That I spent last night at her house? Yeah." He didn't even try to hide his anger. "Did rumor tell you she called me at almost 3:00 a.m. because someone was at her bedroom window while someone else phoned to tell her she'd change her story when she talked to the new investigators today or *they* can get to her anytime? Close enough to a direct quote."

"Crap," his brother said quietly.

"Busy night. We invited a Clear Creek officer to spend part of it with us. By the way, he's having photos taken of the footprints under the window and the broken branches in the shrub. Fingerprint technician is doing his thing, too. Did I stay the rest of the night, so she'd have a prayer of getting some sleep?" He pushed away his unfinished chili. "Yes, I did."

Bran squeezed the back of his neck. "You haven't said what you think of the new investigators."

Zach shared his impressions and doubts. "The DA was there, too. Mad because my version of what happened had altered since the initial one. If I'd accused Hayes of wrongdoing from the beginning, she'd have been involved. Now she feels like she's playing catch-up."

"Altered?" Bran said in disbelief.

Zach's temper spiked again. "Edited, apparently."

His brother shook his head. "The threats might stop now that you and Tess have both talked to the Stimson detectives."

Zach gave a short laugh. "You're kidding, right? It's never too late for a witness to develop amnesia."

"You sure she's not making all this up?"

This jolt of anger he didn't try to hide. "You saw her roar in to talk to Delancy. Did that look like someone simply seeking attention?"

Bran grimaced. "Nobody is going after you."

"Except for the beheaded rabbit."

"That could have been a frat-type prank. You're the new guy. Some of the others might have wanted to see if you had a sense of humor."

Zach stared at him in disbelief. "Did anything about that strike you as remotely funny?"

"No, but I heard some people laughing."

"Who?"

"You think I'm going to tell you? All you need to know is it wasn't anybody close to Andy."

"Andy?" This time his laugh held even less humor. "Good friends now, are you?"

"You know better than that."

"Do I?" Zach shifted his weight to pull out his wallet. He tossed a twenty on the table and slid out of the booth. "Glad we had this talk."

When he walked out, he felt more than a little juvenile, but also too mad to go back.

He'd been right about how the evening would end, but wrong about who would do the walking.

IT WAS LATE afternoon on Saturday when Tess ended a phone call and lifted her head to see Zach walking into Fabulous Interiors. Deputy Carter. He was very obviously a cop in his olive-green uniform and badge, his weapon and all kinds of other implements hanging from his belt. He swept the store with an assessing eye that paused briefly on every customer present before his gaze settled on her.

In turn, those customers stared at him.

Hunched at the computer behind Tess, Greg was filling out an order for vast amounts of a hugely expensive textured carpet that was certified green. The house being built, he'd told her, was to be nearly five thousand square feet. There would be hardwood in the entry and dining room, but most of the acres of flooring were going to be carpeted.

Tess rose and smiled. "Deputy Carter. Is this business?"

He stopped on the other side of the counter. "Considering Fabulous Interiors is out of my jurisdiction, no. I'm here to look at tile." He glanced ruefully down at himself. "I was afraid if I went home to change, you'd be closed by the time I got back."

"Let me show you what we have available," she said in her best sales voice. "I can answer any questions, too."

He stopped to exchange a few words with Greg, whose glance at Tess was quizzical. She hadn't said *that* much about Zach, had she?

As soon as she politely could, she led him toward the back of the store.

"Are you serious?" was the first thing she said.

Zach raised expressive, dark eyebrows. "Very. You were right. The bathroom has to be done first. Since I need to gut it—which means no bathroom for me to use for a few days—I want to have materials on hand so I can put it back together as quickly as possible."

"Do you have a shower available at work you can use?"

His mouth twisted. "Yes, but I haven't been real enthusiastic about using the locker room since the one episode. Not sure I like the idea of being alone and naked in the shower room. I think I've seen scenes like that in prison movies."

Tess had to laugh, although she was transfixed by the idea of him naked, water sluicing over his dark hair and long, muscular body.

"I may get a hotel room for a couple days," he continued as he started moving along the rows of display tiles. "Depending on the alternatives." He turned and pinned her with a stare. "Speaking of..."

"Of what?"

"I don't like you being alone."

"I was fine last night." If sleeping in jerky, ten-minute segments could be called fine. She had taken a variety of possible weapons to bed with her, including a marble rolling pin and a butcher knife.

Not that she could, in a million years, imagine stabbing someone.

"I wasn't fine," Zach said. "I drove by your house at midnight and again at around five. Didn't do a lot of sleeping in between."

She stared at him. "Really?"

"Really."

Tess nibbled on her lower lip. "My father wants me to move home."

"Your father, who just had a stroke?"

"Three years ago. He's made an amazing recovery," she said defensively.

Zach shook his head. "Not a good idea."

She looked away from him. "No. I know it isn't." She hesitated. "I have friends…"

"This isn't the kind of trouble you want to bring down on most people."

"Nothing that terrible has happened," she fired back, her argument losing force when she barely stopped herself from finishing with a *yet*.

Zach did it for her. "Yet."

She crossed her arms. "What do *you* suggest I do?"

"Part of me thinks I should stay with you."

Wow. Nice of him to let her hear his deep reluctance.

He shook his head. "Bran told me yesterday that a rumor was already going around about me spending the night at your house."

Her mouth fell open. It was a moment before she could form words. "But…how?" Then she scowled. "Officer Parish."

"I doubt it." His voice wasn't much better than a growl. Zach wasn't a happy man. "I think somebody had to be watching your house."

Goose bumps rose on her flesh, giving her the sensation of invisible fingers moving over her.

Tap, tap, tap.

She didn't have to say anything. Zach swore.

"I'm sorry, Tess. Damn it! I wish they'd come after me."

"No!"

"I'm ready for them."

There he was again, terrifying her with his certainty that he was invincible. Just like her father, who was so sure *he* could protect her even if he was still semi-crippled from the stroke—*and* was on a blood thinner.

"They…they won't go after you the same way," she said. "You know they won't."

Zach tipped his head in a form of acceptance. "You're right, of course."

Suddenly desperate not to be talking about this, she said, "We close in half an hour. If you were serious about looking at tiles, you'd better do it."

He grinned wickedly at her. "Of course, I could go to Home Depot and pick up some plain black and white tiles. Do the classic checkerboard."

"You could." Despite herself, she was smiling. "Have you?"

"Yeah, looked good in one of the houses I flipped. Did glass blocks between the toilet and sink, a shower with etched glass, chrome fixtures. It came out great."

"It sounds like it." And, truthfully, it probably didn't make sense for Zach to buy super high-end materials of any kind for a relatively modest older home he intended to sell once he finished the remodel.

He reached for the tile he'd picked up the last time he was here. "I really like these."

"Anything you buy here will be at cost," she told him.

He turned his head. "Why? You have to make a living."

"You're the guy who comes running, night or day, when I call. It's not like I'm losing anything to order whatever tiles or flooring you want at cost."

"How about cost plus ten percent?"

They negotiated, but he won. Or lost, depending on your point of view. He took out his wallet and removed a piece of paper with measurements. Tess led the way to her office, carrying the sculpted tile and the plain one that worked best with it, and filled out the order form. Concentrating was a challenge with Zach in the straight-backed chair on the other side of the desk from her, his legs outstretched, his gaze never leaving her. She watched as he wrote a check to cover the deposit. He'd come prepared.

"Will you have dinner with me?" he asked suddenly, the words hardly spoken before he looked disconcerted, as if he'd never meant to say any such thing.

Her eyes widened. "You mean...go out?" Where anyone at all could see them together?

"Actually, I thought I'd put dinner together at home."

"Is this part of the Protect Tess program? Or—" She couldn't make herself finish.

But of course he prodded. "Or?"

"I suppose this has to do with you kissing me." *You wanting to get me into bed.*

Now he had the strangest expression. "No," he said slowly. "That isn't what I was thinking. But let's just forget I suggested it."

Even with her alarm bells ringing, she wanted to have dinner with him. Listen to him tell her what he intended to do with his house. Get to know the man who *did* come running every time she needed him.

"If you meant it, I'd like to have dinner with you," she said a little shyly.

He studied her face for a moment before he nodded. The set of his shoulders eased just enough to betray that he hadn't been enjoying what must have felt like rejection. "You'll be glad to know I even have a table and chairs now."

"You went furniture shopping?" If she sounded amazed…well…she was.

"Me? God, no. I stopped at a garage sale."

Her bubble burst. Of course he hadn't bought anything that might be permanent.

Before she could dwell on it, a worry struck her. "What if someone follows me there?"

"*I'll* follow you there." His voice had become steely. "I kind of hope someone does show up on your tail. I'll hang around until closing."

"Actually… I can probably go once I find out whether the customer looking at wallpaper is still here."

He strolled out into the main showroom while Tess stuck her head into the back room. The woman had decided to check out several books and carried them to the counter in front. Tess jotted her name and phone number on the cards and filed them, chatting as she did so.

As soon as the customer had carried her hefty pile out the door, Zach quit pretending interest in carpet samples and planted himself in front of the counter. He turned a now-serious gaze on Tess. "Got your purse? Let's do this."

She hadn't known Greg had popped out of his own small office until his voice came from behind her. "Do what?"

"Oh." She swung around. "I'm cutting out early, if that's okay?"

"You know it is." His gaze went past her to Zach. "I repeat, do what?"

Tess made a face at him. "You know the trouble I'm having. Zach asked me to have dinner at his place and he's going to follow me to be sure no one else does."

"You need an escort home? Damn it, Tess!"

"Zach wants to see if anyone tries to follow me," she said uncomfortably.

"But they already know where you live."

"They" had become one of her least favorite

words, assuming horror movie proportions. She could still picture Andrew Hayes's face, first with his lips drawn back from his teeth as he'd swung his fist over and over, then when he'd tried to resume his cop facade but forgotten his face was flushed a deep purple-red from his killing frenzy. And then there were his bloody hands.

She hated that his confederates were still faceless to her. It was almost creepier to imagine one of them watching her than him.

Zach stayed silent, letting her handle this. Of course, he had no way of knowing how much she'd told her business partner.

"But they might like to be sure that's where I'm going when I leave work," she explained, knowing Greg could tell how disturbed she was.

"I suppose that's true," he said grudgingly, not looking any happier.

"And there's nothing I'd like better than to have a license number to run," Zach interjected, after which he determined where she was parked and which way she'd be emerging from the alley.

"All right. Give me a minute before you go out."

Tess nodded and watched him leave. When she turned around, she found Greg frowning at her.

"Tess, you're welcome to stay with Josie and me until this is resolved."

"And your children?" She shook her head. "Thank you, Greg, but there's no way I want to have something happen that scares the daylights out of Maddy and Dominic."

He raised his hands in acceptance. "Then let your cop take care of you, Tess. Don't get stubborn."

"Stubborn?" she said, trying to lighten the moment. "Me?"

Greg didn't laugh.

She knew his eyes were still on her as she made her way to the back door.

CHAPTER NINE

HAVING TESS HERE, in his house, felt right. He'd had women to dinner and occasionally even to spend the night wherever he was living before, but never thought of them as *belonging.*

Sheer desperation gripped him. No bonds in his life had ever lasted, except for the one with his mother, and that was eroded by bitterness.

His mother might have had nothing to do with Sheila's death. And it was true that even solid marriages often ended after the death of a child. He and Bran, in their misery and stubbornness, had deepened the split.

But Zach had tried again, with his first stepfather and a younger stepsister. Once Mom had announced she was leaving him, packed and taken Zach with her, he'd never seen either again. Her next husband, Lowell, had sensed a boy's need and tried to be a father to him. Mom had taken care of that, too, leaving Zach…numb.

I've been numb ever since, he thought bemusedly. He didn't want to feel attachment for anyone. Inevitably, it resulted in hurt. Mom had been every bit as effective as that crap they gave alcoholics to make them puke when they took a drink.

He shouldn't have invited Tess over. She tugged at him and that made her dangerous. She could make him feel. But he didn't have in him the ability to trust that what other people called love would last. And yet his need to be with her seemed to be more powerful than his fears.

At least the last time she'd been here they'd been surrounded by other people. He hadn't given her a personal tour, so that now a picture of her in every single room was burned into his brain.

Upstairs he watched as she stopped in the middle of the larger room and turned slowly in place.

"This is wonderful. I love all the interesting angles the ceiling forms." She sent him a sly look. "It would be perfect for wallpaper."

It was when she stepped into the smaller room that her face lit with joy. "Oh, Zach! You added a skylight."

"Yep." It was a hell of a lot easier to add a skylight during the roofing process than later.

That's not what he was thinking about now, though.

Something about the late-afternoon light pouring down on her made her scattering of freckles stand out. Because of them, he noticed that small bump on the bridge of her nose, too. Most often, he was too aware of her sexy mouth and riveting eyes to see the girl-next-door quality of the rest of her face. Now, gazing upward, she looked… natural. Real. There was no artificial construct to her unlike—

He frowned.

Unlike his mother, an undeniably beautiful woman, but one who had always used a lot of makeup, hair coloring and styling, clothes, whatever tools she could find to enhance that beauty. Exercise wasn't for its own sake or because it was good for her health. Nope, she saw it as body sculpting.

His mother struck poses. She was beautifully made up before she came to the breakfast table.

His mother didn't let men spend the night until they married her. As he got older and more cynical, Zach had wondered how shocked those husbands were the first time they saw the woman behind the mask.

Tess, he thought, never wore one. And yet she was beautiful.

He'd been silent so long she turned her head in gentle inquiry.

Talk. Distract her. Distract me.

"I'm still debating between putting a large bathroom in here versus a small one and walk-in closet."

Seemingly oblivious to his turmoil, she said promptly, "The closet has my vote. Otherwise you'll almost have to build one tucked under the eaves in the bedroom somehow, but I like the idea of bookcases and a window seat along that wall." She pointed.

The minute she said it, he was sold. He'd had in mind built-in bookcases somewhere, but hadn't thought of a window seat.

In fact, as they finished the tour, she gave Zach several good ideas. She had both an amazing eye and a practical bent. She knew what could be done and how much it would cost to do it. His invitation tonight might not have been so dumb, after all.

This wouldn't be the first time he'd liked a woman he slept with, Zach reflected. That didn't mean anything lasting came of it.

But along with a fervent hope they actually *made* it to bed, Zach was still edgy. The fact that spending time with her had even set him to analyzing his own emotional state wasn't a good sign.

"I'm surprised you didn't buy an old house," he commented as he started on dinner. Cooking gave him an excuse not to look at her—and chicken tacos didn't take long.

Of course, she insisted on helping and was chopping cilantro.

"I thought about it, but I wouldn't have been able to do as much of the work myself as you plan to. I added enough charm to my house to satisfy me." She smirked. "Didn't have to replace the roof or plumbing. Plus, there were no big surprises."

Zach grimaced at that. "My first one, the bathroom looked solid. I was going to replace the vanity, new vinyl flooring. You know, just spruce it up a little. And then I tore up the ancient linoleum to find major rot. Had to gut the whole room *and* replace most of the pipes in the house. Some poor sucker was lucky he and the toilet he was sitting on didn't plummet into the basement one fine morning. Pretty undignified way to die."

Tess giggled. He loved the ripple of sound. His body tightened as he imagined feeling the vibration when she laughed.

While they ate they talked about anything and everything except the way they'd met, Andrew Hayes and the mounting threats. Zach had yet to ask about her meeting with the Stimson detectives and DA, but he saved that, too.

Instead they talked about the little stuff—what they liked to read, the kind of music they listened to, movies that interested them. College, sports they'd played.

The stuff, he realized, that was usually filler for him, a stage required before he could get a woman in bed. He was disconcerted to discover how hungry he was to learn all that Tess was willing to tell him.

Another bad sign.

He failed to head her off before they segued into more personal information. She told him about her mother, who'd died of breast cancer, and he talked about how much, as a kid, he'd idolized his big brother, Bran.

Her gaze softened and her forehead crinkled in perplexity. "Splitting two kids up like your parents did seems wrong. Maybe especially brothers."

"It was our choice." He saw that his harshness had startled her. Damn. He shouldn't have let himself get drawn into this. He didn't talk about Sheila. Not to anyone.

Yeah, but he was back in Clear Creek now.

"There was more to it," he said brusquely, making a decision. "Uh…can I pour you a cup of coffee?"

Her expression suggested she knew he was stalling. "Not yet."

"We had a sister." *Had* was such a powerful word in this context. "Sheila. She was three years younger than me. Bran's three years older. We were evenly spaced." As if that mattered. "When Sheila was six, she was raped and murdered."

Tess's shock was quickly followed by compassion that softened her face. "Oh, Zach."

"I found her body." He still had occasional nightmares about it. "Someone took her out of her bedroom in the middle of the night. She wasn't ten feet from the back porch. Under—" he cleared his throat "—a big maple tree."

His head turned, allowing him to see the backyard through small-paned windows. To where another maple tree shaded the grass. If he'd had any intention of staying in this house, he'd cut the damn tree down.

Haltingly at first, he told Tess the whole story. About the investigation, the obvious suspicion of his father, the angry voices from behind his parents' bedroom door—the only thing that had broken the thick silence that otherwise enveloped their home.

At some point Tess reached across the table and took his hand in hers. A minute later he looked down to see that he was holding on as if that grip was all that kept him from plummeting. No matter how fine her build, she was strong enough to hold on.

"They never made an arrest?"

Tearing his gaze from their linked hands, he shook his head. "Over the years I've wondered how competent the investigation was. Supposedly they didn't get anything useful from trace evidence, which is a little hard to believe."

"That's really why you're here, isn't it?" she said suddenly.

"Yeah. The twenty-five-year anniversary is coming up. It may be hopeless, but answers can sometimes be found even this long after the fact."

"Why did you wait so long?"

Loaded question. He'd balked at directly confronting the possibility that either of his parents was guilty or bore some of the responsibility for something so terrible.

Or maybe he'd only been clinging to the comfort of feeling numb. And no wonder. He wasn't enjoying the reawakening of painful memories.

"I always had the goal of becoming a detective," he told her. That was true enough. "I wanted to know I had the skills to open a cold case."

"So…how are you going about it?"

He made his answer vague, talking in general about investigative methods. Finally he shrugged. "I may hit a dead end, but I have to try."

Tess nodded, but still looked perplexed. "I can see why your sister's murder created a wedge between your parents, but I don't understand what it had to do with you and your brother."

"We were each angry at the other parent. And angry at each other for supporting the wrong parent. Contact just…dwindled." He shrugged. "It happens."

"I suppose so," she said slowly.

"Finding Bran again was…" He finally settled for simple. "Really good. But our relationship isn't easy. I don't know if it ever will be. He gets mad if I even hint that Dad might have done it, and I have trouble understanding how he could have stayed in this area, become a cop and then a detective, and yet never seriously investigated. It's like…" He hesitated.

"He doesn't want to find out what actually happened," she finished for him.

That was his guess, too.

"It means, deep down, he's afraid your dad did do it."

That would be it. And this conversation was over. He pushed back his chair. "I don't know about you, but I could use that cup of coffee now."

She watched him steadily but didn't comment on his retreat. Zach did hate having to let go of her hand. But, damn, as hard as he'd been squeezing, she was lucky he hadn't crunched any bones.

She rose and cleared the table while he started the coffee. He watched out of the corner of his eye as she put leftovers in what containers she could find. The gleam of the kitchen light off her glossy hair kept catching his eye. He'd like to feel it slipping between his fingers while he kissed her. One long step and he could tug her into his arms. Lean back against the counter, maybe, and pull her close. Her long body would align perfectly with—

"There should be enough for your dinner tomorrow night," she said.

He blinked. Enough…? Oh.

"You know you may never find out for sure, don't you?" she said.

Great. Did they have to circle back around to this? Even so, he made himself think about what she'd said. It was true that he'd tried to make himself accept the possibility—no, likelihood—of failure, but he wasn't sure he really had. "I tend to be stubborn. You ask one question at a time and keep asking them." He released a long breath, knowing he was being evasive. "But, yes. Of course, I know."

"If your father did it…"

Her hesitation told him where she was going with this. "Then he took the truth with him to the grave. Is that what you're trying to say?"

Her eyes were big and somber and so damn beautiful. "I suppose."

Best way to get her off the subject would be to kiss her.

Yeah, but he needed to think long and hard about the consequences of starting anything more with her.

"Bran and my father must have talked about it," he argued. "If I can get Bran to open up…"

"But surely he and your father wouldn't have stayed close if he'd made any kind of admission."

"That's true, but maybe Bran deliberately misunderstood something Dad said."

She frowned, thoughtful. "What do *you* think? Looking back, was there anything that bothers you in how he treated your sister?"

He shifted irritably as they sat back down. "Who thinks that way as a kid? You take your parents for granted." He didn't want to answer, because if he'd had faith in his father then, his childhood would have been different. He wouldn't have lost his brother. "No," he said hoarsely. "If he hadn't lied about being up during the night, I never would have thought it was possible he'd do something like that."

She nodded. "It would be a stranger who might need to kill her to keep her quiet, you know. Sad to say, plenty of parents sexually molest their kids and the kids don't tell anyone. And fathers…have plenty of opportunities. Your dad wouldn't have *had* to take her outside in the middle of the night."

Zach stared at her, stunned by her simple logic. As a kid, he wouldn't have had any way of knowing that what she said was true. As an adult… had he still been letting himself *think* like that kid? Could he investigate with his emotions so tangled?

After a minute Tess said tentatively, "Bran could be afraid you're out to prove your dad did it. If you tell him what you just told me, it might help."

He gave a humorless laugh and shook his head. "I was the jerk the last time we talked about this. I like to think I'm a reasonably mature human being. But with him…"

"You fall back to reacting like you did when you were both kids."

She saw a lot more clearly than he did these days. *Or ever?* And…should he worry about the fact that he'd never had this kind of talk with a woman before? *Or anybody?*

Shaking off both thoughts for later consideration, he said ruefully, "Sad but true. We were good friends, but we fought a lot, too." Because it felt necessary to hide the mess he was inside, he grinned crookedly. "No way was I going to let him be the boss of me."

Tess wrinkled her nose even as she laughed, letting him see her as a girl, freckled, almost plain, but...luminous.

"It happens to all of us," she said. "Every once in a while, Dad and I squabble and I realize I'm mad for no good reason at all. I have my triggers and he probably does, too. He has trouble accepting my independence, for one."

Zach nodded. If he ever had a little girl, he might be the same. No, would be the same. He'd be scared to death something would happen to her. A good reason not to have children.

As much to divert himself as her, he said, "I guess Bran and I have a ways to go."

"But you have the chance now," Tess said gently. "I'm sorry you've had to spend so much time protecting me. It's probably kept you from getting as far as you'd hoped with your investigation."

"Sheila died twenty-five years ago. What's a few more days or weeks at this point?"

She looked worried but nodded her acceptance.

"Back to your problem," he said abruptly. It

was past time to remember he was in this to protect her. She wouldn't be here otherwise. "I have an idea, but I'll need your permission."

"An idea?"

"I'd like to install some hidden cameras around your house to try to catch one of these bastards in action."

Tess didn't as much as blink for a minute. "How would you hide them?" she asked.

"You've got a lot of shrubbery out there. Trellises that would be good camouflage. I'm thinking, if your neighbor gives us the okay, of hanging one on his eaves pointed at your bedroom window."

"But at night, would there be enough light to make anything out?"

"They'll have infrared. Wouldn't hurt if you leave on more lights, too. They'd assume they've got you scared. Front and back porch lights, for starters, but maybe a bathroom light or hall light, too. Leave curtains or blinds open on any other windows on that side of the house."

He couldn't blame her for not wanting to plan for another episode like the last one, but she took only a moment to decide before nodding.

"It's a good idea. But if they're watching the house and see you doing the installation..."

"I doubt they're watching the house twenty-four-seven. Tomorrow is Sunday. I can head over to Mt. Vernon or Burlington to buy the cameras."

She nodded.

"Unless you intend to work Monday, I might wait until Tuesday to install them. I can use my lunch break. With you at work, there's no reason for them to be hanging around your place."

"I…was planning to take Monday off. Thank you," she said, holding herself with a dignity that told him how much effort it was costing her. "And let me know what the cameras cost. As soon as I get home, I'll call Chad next door. It might be just as well if I tell him what's been happening, anyway."

"I agree."

"On that note—" she pushed back her chair "—it's time for me to go home."

Zach wanted to beg her to stay. Partly because he hated the idea of her spending even one more night alone, waiting for her phone to ring or the scratch of a branch at her window. Or a whole lot worse.

But, maybe even more, because he wanted to take her to bed.

Except for holding her hand while he told her more than he'd ever told another person about his past, he had managed not to touch Tess. She'd made her feelings about it clear. He felt like a jerk when he caught himself thinking about how he could undermine her resolve.

Besides, tonight was a whack upside the head. He'd peeled himself open for her. He felt raw enough without risking the possibility that sex with her would be as different from anything he'd experienced as tonight's dinner-table conversation had been. Tess threatened his resolve never to fully trust anyone, to never give another person the ability to hurt him. To never even toy with the idea that he was in love.

For an instant he lost the ability to breathe. Because he had the shattering fear that it might already be too late.

And walking away from Tess Granath, even if that's what it took to save himself, was not currently an option.

He stood, too, and said, "I'll follow you home. And walk you in, just to be sure no one else is already waiting for you."

Nothing like feeling the need to scare a woman.

But this one only nodded and said, again, "Thank you," before looking around for her handbag.

TESS SAT IN her car, waiting for Zach. He parked openly in her driveway, got out of his pickup and walked into the garage. He reached for her door handle as she pushed the remote to start the garage door going down.

And, call her a coward, but she let him enter the house first. He'd changed out of his uniform before he'd started dinner, but Tess had seen him tuck a handgun into the waistband at the small of his back before they'd left his house.

He didn't pull it out now, but from the minute he stepped into her kitchen he moved in a silent, purposeful way that was unfamiliar to her. It made her think of a cat stalking prey. He was alert, focused, radiating intensity.

Tess turned on the kitchen light and stood with her back to the island as Zach vanished into the dark living room. It would be smart, or at least reassuring, to start leaving lights on even when she expected to be home before dark, she decided. She imagined how terrifying it would have been to enter the completely dark house alone.

Although she strained to hear his progress, Zach was absolutely quiet. He apparently didn't turn on lights as he went, either. She quit breathing as she listened.

Suddenly the hall light did come on and a moment later he walked back into the kitchen from the dining room, as casual as if he hadn't, only moments before, been ready to take down an intruder.

"No sign of visitors," he reported.

It was embarrassing that she felt compelled to ask… "Did you look in the closets?"

He smiled. "I did. You're a neat freak."

Her chin came up. "It's called being organized."

Oh, God. He'd leave now.

Of course he would leave now, she told herself before saying, "I'll lock up behind you."

Nothing happened last night, she reminded herself. Maybe they'd given up now that she hadn't changed her story.

She'd feel more confident about her theory if Zach felt the same, but he didn't. Unless he planned to install those cameras mostly to reassure her?

Right.

He was quiet until they reached the front door. Then he faced her.

"You know how fast I can get here."

Her heartbeat kicked up a gear. No, the cameras weren't the equivalent of warm milk at bedtime.

She managed what she hoped was a saucy smile. "If you get a speeding ticket, I'll pay it."

Zach grinned. "They'd have to catch me before they could issue a ticket."

Tess rolled her eyes.

His smile died. He didn't move, just stood looking at her. With only the single lamp on in this room, the shadows beneath his cheekbones were pronounced, his eyes dark.

"I don't want to leave you, Tess." His voice was low and gravelly.

"I know," she whispered, and she did. Integrity, common sense, even dignity, felt unimportant compared to this almost painful need she had to touch him, to melt into him.

She was so shaky, if he'd taken even a step toward her, Tess knew she couldn't resist.

But she saw him conduct an internal battle and then back away, nod and leave.

Staring at the closed door, she wanted to cry. Instead she turned the dead bolt then leaned against the door, forehead pressed against the cool surface, and breathed.

ZACH'S EYES SNAPPED OPEN.

He must have dozed off, at last, but his mind cleared instantly.

Metal screamed and glass exploded. Son of a bitch. A car accident—

He was on his feet, yanking on the pants he'd left draped over a chair, wishing his window looked out on the street. He heard the deep rumble of an engine…singular.

Another slam of metal on metal could have been heard two blocks away. More glass exploding, crumbling.

Suddenly he understood. He grabbed his Glock and ran through the house, barefoot, bare-chested. Out the back door, so they wouldn't see him coming.

When he came around the corner of the house, he was momentarily blinded by the headlights of a big pickup or SUV. From his ramshackle detached garage came sounds like a foundry in full production—metal being tortured into twisted shapes by impossible forces.

A voice shouted out a warning, making him realize he had to be silhouetted by the headlights.

Zach yelled, "Police! Don't move!" and ran forward, prepared to fire, but he saw two dark shapes burst from the garage. Seconds later vehicle doors slammed and the pickup—no, it was an SUV—rocketed backward. Someone whooped.

Despite the gravel cutting into his feet, Zach raced out to the street, taking up a stance in the middle of it. But the big, dark vehicle was receding at criminal speed. It had to be going fifty or more in a residential neighborhood.

Lights were coming on up and down the block. He heard voices calling out to him.

"I've called 911," someone said, and he waved his thanks as he made his way more gingerly up the driveway to the garage, holding the gun, barrel down, alongside his thigh now.

The double doors stood open. He stubbed his toe on something and, looking down, realized it was the padlock. Inside, the darkness momentarily defeated his eyes. Swearing viciously under his breath, he felt his way to the light switch.

In the harsh glare, he stared incredulously at what had been his truck.

Every window was shattered. Fenders, doors and roof smashed in. A few steps inside and he could see that the hood had been, as well.

The truck hadn't been alive, but, in that moment, he felt as if it had been. A killing rage rose in him.

Zach kept his back to the neighbors he knew now clustered on his front lawn, because he couldn't let any of them see his face. In the distance, a siren wailed.

He shook with his anger…until something crept from beneath it. A fear so terrible, it wasn't the truck he saw but Tess.

Her body, battered until he barely knew her.

What if…?

Zach bolted for the house.

SHE WOULD *NOT* ANSWER, Tess decided when her phone awakened her from an uneasy sleep. Why give them the satisfaction?

But she fumbled for her phone to see the number displayed. What if it was Dad?

Zach.

Apprehension gripped her as she answered. "Zach?"

"Are you all right?" His voice was hard, urgent, threaded with something that lifted the hair on the back of her neck.

"Yes. Yes. Nothing's happened." Not here. Not to her.

They had gone after Zach instead, she realized.

Clutching the phone, she whispered, "Oh, God. Are *you* hurt?"

"No, not me." He swore. "I shouldn't have called. Scared you."

"Someone is hurt."

"Only my pickup." He'd regained a measure of calm, or was pretending he had. "It's totaled, Tess. There were three of them. I saw them. They cut the padlock off the garage door and took something like steel mauls to my truck. Smashed all the windows, doors, fenders. It's a goner."

"Oh, Zach."

"They blinded me with headlights on high beam. I did see two men run out of the garage and jump into a big-ass SUV. There was already someone behind the wheel. They took off like a shot. I stood there mourning the damn truck and then suddenly I thought…" He went silent.

She knew. "That they might have been here first."

"Yeah," he said hoarsely. "Ah, there's a cop here I need to talk to. Don't go to sleep right away, Tess. Stay alert. They probably went home, but just in case."

He didn't have to say what he was thinking. *I don't have any transportation. Even if you need me, I can't get to you tonight.*

"I'll listen for trouble." She sounded steadier than she felt. "I can call 911 and Chad next door. He told me to if anything else happens."

"Good. Okay."

She sensed he wasn't okay at all. "Do you want me to come over?"

"More than you can imagine," he said quietly, a new tension in his voice. "But, no, Tess. I want you to stay safe where you are. I mean that."

"Will you call me in the morning?"

"I'll do that. You call me if anything makes you the slightest bit nervous. *After* you call 911 and your neighbor. Got that?"

"Yes, sir," she said crisply.

He sounded a little bit amused when he said goodbye, which had been her goal.

Tess sat on the edge of her bed, phone still tight in her hand, and discovered anger had once again supplanted her fear.

CHAPTER TEN

"HAYES HAS A girlfriend who claims he was with her all night," Zach reported grimly.

He had leaned on her doorbell before ten o'clock that morning. It was just as well that Sunday wasn't a working day for either of them. Tess, for one, had a headache. It didn't help that, as Zach seemed so often to do when he was at her house, he was pacing, which meant her head swiveled back and forth to allow her to keep him in sight.

Put her in the stands at Wimbledon and she'd fit right in.

Unfortunately *not* watching him didn't seem to be an alternative. How could she look away from his broad-shouldered, long-legged, lean body in motion? The angles of his face seemed starker than usual today, too, more compelling than ever. She'd never been a big fan of the two-day beard, but had to admit Zach was incredibly sexy with his jaw shadowed by stubble. Obviously he hadn't bothered to shave this morning. Or to comb his hair, either, although the wild dishevelment might have more to do with his habit of thrusting his fingers into it when he was agitated.

With an effort she gathered her thoughts. “Who interviewed his girlfriend? Not Detective Delancy, I hope.”

His mouth tipped up on one side. “No. A detective with the Clear Creek PD. His name is Guy Easley. Seems okay.”

“Oh. That’s right. You live within the city limits.”

“Easley was already up to date on your problems. I was able to give him names of a couple of Hayes’s friends.”

A sense of betrayal balled in her stomach. “You didn’t tell me you know who they are.” What else hadn’t he told her?

“Because they may not be the ones involved in this. Easley expects to have a long list of names by this afternoon. He’s really beating the bushes. Turns out Hayes has a brother, by the way, which I didn’t know. A logger who lives in the area. A couple years younger.”

“He’d have a splitting maul.”

“That’s an easy connection, but the truth is, everybody who burns firewood has one. Which is half or more of the households in the county.”

Of course, he was right. Even her dad doubtless still kept his maul and ax, although he hadn’t split any wood in a few years. Until she’d left home, she’d used both plenty of times herself.

"There are probably other things they could have used to smash your truck," she suggested.

Zach shrugged. "Sure. The butt side of a single-bladed ax would have worked, as well. Against the headlights, all I could see was that they were each carrying something with a long handle, and from the dents we can tell whatever they were swinging had a bigger head than the typical mallet or hammer. No sharp cuts, like the blade of an ax would have made. It had to be metal."

She winced. "Have you talked to your insurance agent?"

"Yeah, he came out first thing this morning. It sounds like I'll be covered, fortunately, but of course I'll lose money. The truck was less than a year old." Frustration tightened his voice.

"I'm sorry."

He stopped to frown. "Not your fault."

"I'm expressing sympathy, not apologizing."

Zach nodded. "Then, thank you." The restlessness still drove him because he started another lap.

"All of his friends will have alibis, too. You know they will."

"Probably, but we may be able to break them. How steadfast will the girlfriend be, for example, when it sinks in that being an accessory to a crime means she'll be in deep shit, too?"

"At least one of the friends helping almost has to be another deputy, right?"

"The dead rabbit might have been a nasty gesture of support for Hayes from someone who wouldn't consider committing an actual crime or threatening a woman who lives alone. Bran tells me a lot of people at work considered the dead rabbit a prank—and a pretty funny one."

Appalled, she stared at him. "And these are your coworkers?"

He didn't say anything, but she could tell he shared her opinion.

He left a few minutes later in his rental car, letting her know he still intended to buy the cameras today as well as to look at pickups even though he would wait until he got the check from the insurance company before buying. Part of his annoyance, she knew, was that he'd also planned to purchase plumbing fixtures today but now would have to pay for delivery if he went ahead.

Unless his brother had a pickup as well as the Camaro he'd driven to the roofing party.

Somehow Tess had a feeling Zach wouldn't be willing to ask for a favor from Bran right now anyway. Their relationship was obviously an uneasy one.

She hadn't much liked Zach's brother, which she was honest enough to know wasn't fair on such brief acquaintance. She'd definitely be keeping her opinions to herself.

Knowing she'd have thrown her housekeeping chores over in a minute if Zach had asked her to go with him, Tess sighed and went to start a load of laundry. Maybe she'd invite Dad to have a late lunch here today. He'd like that better than her taking the makings of a meal to his house. That would just give him an excuse to accuse her of treating him like an invalid, waiting on him hand-and-foot. Her accepting that he was driving fine would salvage his dignity.

IT MIGHT NOT be in his job description, but Bran spent one hell of a lot of time chasing down rumors. This time, though, nobody was paying him for the effort. Whether Zach would be appreciative was an open question.

At the moment Bran was leaning against his Camaro outside the sheriff's department, going for "relaxed, not in any hurry." It was mere chance he'd parked next to Dave Sager's Explorer. He wasn't going to interrogate anyone. Nope. Just ask a couple casual questions during an idle conversation.

"What are you doing here on a Sunday?" the uniformed deputy asked, pointing his remote at his Explorer. The SUV flashed lights and beeped. Dave made the mistake of hesitating, responding to Bran's friendliness.

"Just thought I'd put in a few hours' work." It was a convincing excuse, since Bran often did come in on Sundays, taking advantage of the lack of distractions. Today, the goal was fictional.

In fact, pursuing overheard gossip about a rumor that might or might not be true, he had timed his arrival carefully to be sure he crossed paths with Sager, who he'd known would be exiting the building about now. Bran hadn't even had to check schedules; he'd heard him grumbling about his recent reassignment to the night shift.

He was at least a couple of years older than Bran's thirty-seven. Hard to tell for sure, with his thin, boyish face and wiry, strong body. He was getting a bald patch, though, that he tried to disguise by shaving his head. To the best of Bran's knowledge, he wasn't friends with Andy Hayes, but might be with some of Hayes's friends.

A hint of aggression entering his voice, Dave Sager said, "I hear the new guy is your brother."

"He is," Bran agreed. He went for a tone of mild curiosity. "You see anything of Hayes since he went on leave?" The segue was certainly natural enough.

"Not me, but I hear he's hopping mad."

"Yeah? I guess I haven't talked to any of his friends."

Sager scoffed. "Like they'd talk to you, anyway, once it got around Carter and you are related."

"Why is he mad? Administrative leave is standard after something like this."

"Getting charged with murder isn't, not when a cop is only doing his job."

Bran let his eyebrows climb. "Is that what you think? I don't know, two witnesses both say the attack was unprovoked and brutal."

Sager thrust out his jaw. "I don't know either of them."

"You ever worked directly with Andy?"

Sager's hesitation was telling. "I won't say he doesn't have a temper," he was honest enough to concede.

Bran nodded a greeting at another couple of deputies leaving the building for their vehicles. Neither was within earshot, but he lowered his voice anyway. It was a technique he'd used before, sucking the other person into believing the two of them were exchanging confidences when, in fact, only one of them would be sharing any.

"Between you and me?" he said. "He swaggers around like he's God. I can see him letting his personal feelings bleed over into the job."

Unaware he was being played, Sager lowered his voice, too. "If what I heard is true, he might have done that."

Bran shook his head as if dismayed. "Yeah, I heard something like that, too. I guess that Alvarez got a little too friendly with Hayes's girlfriend."

He was taking a logical leap from the little Zach had overheard as he'd raced to futilely save a man's life. Bran hoped he wasn't way off track.

But the guy didn't even hesitate this time. "Yeah, she's a checker at that little market on Laurel."

"I know the place. Wonder if I've ever seen her there," Bran mused, even though he had stepped foot in the place only once, and that was over two years ago, to ask questions in pursuit of an investigation. Mostly he knew *of* it. A small grocery store, it catered to the surrounding Latino population. Everyone who worked there spoke at least rudimentary Spanish, unlike at the Safeway or Haggen stores.

"She's pretty enough, I guess. Kind of quiet."

"Yeah? I guess Andy wouldn't like a girlfriend who argued with him."

The other deputy gave a bark of laughter. "That's safe to say."

"So she met Antonio at the market?" Bran was prodding.

Sager grimaced. "Way I heard it, Hayes decided to surprise her by picking her up after work and found her lingering in the parking lot with Alvarez. He took a swing then, but the girlfriend found herself some guts and got between them. Alvarez took off." He shrugged. "Guaranteed to piss off Andy."

How many people knew this story and had kept their mouths shut? Bran tried to hide his fury but said, "That's more than I heard. You know, you should tell the special investigators about this.

And maybe the DA. Uh, Christine Campbell, I think."

Sager looked alarmed and backed up a few steps. "I have a wife and kids."

Time to quit pretending. "So it's okay to let the witnesses be terrorized by that asshole and his friends? Damn it, you're a cop."

Maybe he was projecting more menace than he'd intended because Sager talked fast. "I wasn't there. It may not even be true."

Bran straightened, pushing away from his car. "Tell me who you heard it from."

Dave saw the steel in his eyes and shuffled a few more steps back. "You're kidding, right?"

"I won't say where I heard it. I promise."

He hesitated, his basic decency at war with his sense of self-preservation. At least, Bran hoped that's what was happening. Hearing laughter and a shouted goodbye from somewhere near, Bran tensed. It wouldn't be good if anyone interrupted them right now.

Fortunately the voices receded.

Dave groaned, wiped a hand across his face, and said, "Bobby Ketchum and Todd Vance were talking in the locker room. I don't think they saw me."

Ketchum, Bran knew, was tight with Andy Hayes. He'd have thought better of Todd Vance, but didn't really know him.

"There are times we have to back each other

when civilians don't understand what came down," Bran said, "but this isn't anything like that. Wearing a badge shouldn't give us immunity when we kill a guy because of a personal beef."

"No." Dave grimaced. "I know you're right. But there's been a lot of talk, a lot of pressure. The brass thinks a conviction would make the department look bad."

"A cover-up makes us look a hell of a lot worse."

Sweat beaded on Dave's forehead despite the day being in the low sixties. "Jesus," he muttered. "Why did I ever tell you anything?"

"I said I wouldn't name you and I meant it."

He glared at Bran. "I'm holding you to that."

He leaped into his vehicle, undoubtedly regretting that he'd stopped to talk to Bran at all, especially right when the shift was changing and a lot of people could have seen them. Everyone assumed Bran and Zach were close.

If only they all knew, Bran thought sourly. So far, every step forward was followed by two back.

His fault as much as Zach's, he knew, even if he was less sure how to fix it.

What surprised him was how much he wanted to fix the relationship with his brother. Having Zach walk back into his life had shifted something in him. Whether Bran liked him or not was irrelevant.

He gave a short laugh. Truth was he and his brother were too damn much alike.

Waiting until he saw the Explorer speed out of the parking lot before he got into his Camaro, Bran mulled over how he'd tell MacLachlan and company what he'd learned without admitting he'd been asking questions.

MONDAY MORNING, ZACH stood to the side and watched as the tow truck backed up to his garage. A police photographer had already come out and taken a few dozen pictures from every angle. Detective Easley had given his permission to have the battered Silverado hauled to the wrecking yard, where it would be parted out.

Just the thought curdled Zach's stomach.

He sure wasn't in the mood for a visit from Bran, but damned if that wasn't his Camaro pulling up to the curb.

Zach's brother got out, raising his brows as he looked at the tow truck. "Something wrong with your pickup?" he asked, cutting across the patchy lawn.

"You could say that."

With an irritated glance, Bran walked right past him, circling the tow truck to see into the garage. On the threshold, Bran came to a dead stop. He stared for what had to be a couple minutes before turning around.

"What the hell—?"

"I had visitors last night. Three of them. They

beat the shit out of my truck and then ran when I came out."

"You saw them?"

"Unfortunately not well enough to identify them. One guy never got out of the SUV. The other two were carrying some kind of long-handled tools. Maybe mauls."

Bran nodded.

"I had my Glock with me. I've never wanted to shoot someone so bad." That excited whoop had told him they'd had fun here in his garage.

"I can see why," his brother surprised him by saying. He hesitated, obviously something was on his mind. "I've been asking around," he said finally. "I heard something you need to know."

Zach watched as, with whining gears and a clank, the tow truck driver began to attach the pickup. "What's that?"

"Apparently, Hayes's confrontation with Alvarez was the second of two parts. The way I hear it, the evening before—" His gaze went past Zach. "Oh, damn."

Zach turned to see an older pickup slamming to a stop right behind Bran's black Camaro. A man leaped out and stormed toward them.

It took Zach a moment to bring into focus someone he hadn't seen in twenty-five years. Dark blond hair had become white. His face was fleshier, his nose had some broken veins that made Zach wonder if he was a heavy drinker. His skin looked leathery. His body had thickened.

But—damn—he was unmistakably Jack Percy, who was now in his sixties. And in a rage, from the look of it.

He got right in Bran's face, not even glancing at Zach. "You son of a bitch, you've been asking questions about me. You couldn't have the decency to talk to me? You had to go behind my back?" Spittle sprayed Bran, who didn't as much as flinch. "I was good to you when you were a kid. If you're suggesting what I think you are—"

"Good to me?" In disgust, Bran wiped his forearm across his face. "You call sneaking into my mother's bed behind Dad's back being *good* to our family?" He'd started low but ended up yelling.

Zach was vaguely aware the tow truck guy had stopped work to gape at the scene being enacted on the lawn. But he couldn't tear his gaze from Jack Percy's stunned expression.

"What would make you say that?" Jack asked. He might still have been going for belligerent, but his voice faltered.

Bran looked as hot under the collar as Zach had yet seen him. He snarled, "I walked in on you, in my parents' bedroom. You were both so busy, you didn't even see me."

Jack took a cautious step back. His Adam's apple bobbed. "Your mom came on to me, not the other way around."

Bran leaned in, his hands balled into fists at his sides. "And that made it okay? Is that what you're saying?"

"Ah..."

"You son of a bitch. Do you have any idea how much I wanted to tell Dad?"

A nerve beneath Jack's eye twitched. "Why didn't you?"

Bran huffed out a breath then turned his back on their father's old friend. He walked in a small circle before facing him again. "I would have if my parents hadn't split up anyway." He shook his head. "But don't you dare blame her. You were on top."

Jack's face worked. He was actually afraid, Zach realized. And maybe he should be. Bran had stored up even more hostility than Zach had realized, maybe because he'd had to keep his mouth shut while seeing the friendship endure between Dad and this man.

Jack looked sidelong at Zach as if suddenly becoming aware someone else was there. His expression of dawning shock gave Zach, at least, some satisfaction.

"Zach? Is that you?"

"It's me." He didn't elaborate.

"What the—?" Jack's gaze darted from one brother to the other.

"Do you want to know why I've been asking

questions?" Bran had a grip on his temper again. His voice had become silky.

Jack didn't say anything. He didn't have to.

"What I'd really like to know is whether you thought Sheila was as pretty as Mom. Whether you had a taste for little girls. Maybe you still do. What do you say, Jack?"

There was a frozen moment during which Jack processed what Bran had just suggested.

Then, with an angry roar, he flung himself forward, a big fist swinging for Bran's face.

Zach stepped toward them, but Bran had already blocked the punch and stuck out his foot, sending their father's old friend crashing to the ground.

Then Bran planted that same foot on his back and put some weight on it as he bent forward. "Want to try that again, Jack?"

The older man's face flushed dark red. He didn't move, but his glare could have lit the coals in a grill.

"Answer me, Jack. Did you ever even *think* about what it would be like with my little sister?"

"No! Goddamn it, no! That's sick. I'd never…" His body sagged.

"But you'd betray your wife and your best friend both," Bran said with contempt.

Jack's Adam's apple bobbed. "Your mom…she was so beautiful. I never thought I could have a woman who looked like her. I let it go to my head, but it's not like I really had her anyway. Her interest didn't last very long, you know. She moved right along." Old hurt was in his voice. But something else, too.

Bran removed the foot he'd had planted on Jack Percy's back. His eyes briefly met Zach's, his naked torment visible.

Lip curled, Zach looked down at the piece of shit lying on his lawn. "I suppose you felt real bad after."

"I always wondered if Michael knew," Jack mumbled. "And Janet—" He choked. "I hope to God she doesn't. I'm lucky to have a good woman like her. I just… I went crazy there for a while."

Nothing he said suggested real remorse, Zach couldn't help noticing.

"Get up," Bran snapped.

Jack pushed himself awkwardly to his hands and knees, then by degrees to his feet. Grass stained his canvas carpenter pants. He brushed at his shirtfront. At last he lifted his shamed gaze to Bran and Zach, now standing shoulder to shoulder.

"Hate me for what I did, but nothing in the world would have made me hurt Sheila. She was the sweetest kid—" He swallowed. "And I got to say one more thing. All that talk about your dad…" He shook his head. "He'd no more have done something like that than I would have. You kids were everything to him. What happened to her broke him. His job was to keep her safe. He could never understand how he didn't hear the back door opening and closing. Why didn't she scream? Call for her daddy? And what if she had and he didn't hear? Do you know how many million times he asked himself that? His little girl dying that way, him losing her, and then his wife and his youngest boy, too." He looked at Bran. "He hid the worst of it from you, but it about killed him. I guess maybe it did, in the end."

"I think it did, too," Bran said quietly.

In that moment Zach would have given anything to have come back to Clear Creek before Dad died. To have been able to say, *I missed you.* And *I love you, Dad.*

But he also knew he'd never be satisfied until he had his answers. Monsters were good at hiding in plain sight. Families were the last to guess.

When neither brother said anything, Jack nodded, turned and shambled away. Bran and Zach watched him get into that old pickup, start it and drive away without ever once looking back.

"Shit," Bran said under his breath. He bent his head and pinched his nose so hard between his thumb and forefinger, Zach would have sworn he heard cartilage creak.

Zach couldn't think of a single thing to say.

He met the tow truck driver's stare and waited

until the guy's face reddened and he went back to work. Then Zach laid a hand on his brother's shoulder.

"Come on into the house. At least have a cup of coffee. Or, hell, a beer."

"Yeah." Bran let out a long breath. "Damn. I lost it there. I never do that."

Zach shook his head even though Bran's outburst had jarred him in a way he didn't recognize. "You're entitled once in a while. Anyway, he's the one who took a swing, not you."

Bran only grunted, but he did walk with Zach to the house. As Zach shut the front door, he heard the clank of chains, a mechanical groan and, a minute later, the sound of the tow truck moving slowly down his driveway and into the street.

No reason he should feel as if he'd been turned upside down and shaken.

LATE TUESDAY AFTERNOON, Zach strolled into Fabulous Interiors, once again wearing his uniform. Only Tess was behind the counter, Greg having left to take his seven-year-old daughter to spring soccer practice while his wife chauffeured their son to some other activity. As slow as business had been, Tess had shooed him on his way.

Predictably, Zach frowned after taking a look around. "Are you here alone?"

"For the moment."

"I guess you can't help it," he conceded, not sounding happy.

She smiled at his tone. "No, I can't. Anyway, there are businesses on each side. We share a hall and a restroom with the coffee shop. People walk past the front windows often enough, I don't feel all that alone."

He nodded. "I installed the cameras today, but they feed to a receiver I need to put inside your house."

When she asked, he explained that he'd gone with three cameras, one looking at the back of the house and one on each side. All had motion detectors and quality night vision. If something happened, they could watch what the camera had recorded.

"Okay. Um, do you want to follow me home?"

"I'd rather nobody sees me arrive. I'll come over after dark. Don't turn your front porch light on. I won't use the doorbell, I'll knock."

"Three times?"

He cocked an eyebrow, not amused.

No surprise, he waited until she had closed the shop. The last thing she did was let him out the front.

His knock didn't come until almost nine. Days were stretching now, in early May, with sunset at eight-thirty or later already. A box under his arm, he slipped inside the moment she opened the door. He'd changed to all black—chinos and a long-sleeved T-shirt with boots.

Didn't it figure? Black suited him, enhancing his air of danger. He could have been a burglar… no… Tess thought, her grandmother had had a more romantic term. Second-story man.

"Where do you want the receiver set up?" Zach asked.

"That depends. Does it just record, or if I hear something outside, can I watch?"

Zach's smile was wolfish. "You can watch."

"My bedroom, then."

He followed her without comment. By his very presence, he shrank the room and made her acutely conscious of the bed. Thank goodness she'd made it that morning. It looked less suggestive than it would have if disheveled.

Zach set up what looked sort of like a notebook computer. He showed her how to switch from one camera to another.

"I'll go out in back and trigger this one. Stay here so you can tell me if it works."

Barely a minute after he disappeared, the screen brightened to a sort of greenish hue and there he was, walking into the middle of the yard, looking directly into the camera then returning to the back door. The camera hadn't yet lapsed into stand-by mode when he reappeared.

"It worked?"

"Yes." She couldn't take her eyes off the screen, which abruptly went dark.

"How's the picture? Could you recognize me?"

"Yes." Tess shook herself slightly. "This is weird. I never imagined..."

"You'd need any kind of home security system?"

After a moment she nodded.

"Better safe than sorry. And, I've got to tell you, I'd really like to catch these bastards on camera."

She finally raised her gaze to meet his. "Did you install any of these at your house?"

"I did. I wish like hell I'd done it Saturday."

"My father would say you're shutting the barn door..."

"After the horses are all out?" His smile was a little crooked. "My dad used to say that, too."

They stood there looking at each other for a minute, the bed assuming larger and larger proportions in Tess's peripheral vision.

She had to get him out of there. This man could break her heart.

"Would you like a cup of coffee before you go?" There. That was pleasant but impersonal.

Something flickered in his eyes but he only said, "Sure."

As she started the coffee, she asked whether he was ready to begin work on his bathroom.

"I've put it off until I get a new truck. Tackling

the porch, too, since that involves hauling lumber. I started stripping the living room floor instead, just for fun."

"*Is* it fun?"

He grinned. "Nope. Stuff stinks, which means the whole house stinks. Sanding isn't one of my favorite jobs, either. Using a big, upright sander is like riding a motorcycle over cobblestones. It wants to throw you off real bad."

Tess laughed. "Do you own one?"

"Nah, they're cheap to rent. I might strip a couple of rooms before I do rent the sander, though." He stretched his legs out. "The empty bedrooms, for sure. Might as well make it worth it."

They talked a little more about the logistics. He didn't want to finish the hall and have the new finish damaged while he was hauling the fixtures into the bathroom, for example. It was like building a tower with blocks. They had to be in exactly the right order.

Tess felt sure his mind wasn't a hundred percent on the conversation any more than hers was.

Finally she couldn't stand it. She set a mug of coffee in front of him and said, "I get the feeling there's something you don't want to tell me."

He grimaced. "Yeah, I've been debating. It's not bad," he said hastily, seeing her alarm. "Like I told you the first time we talked, in a way it's better if you don't know too much." He shook her head at her expression. "The fact you've been threatened and the sheriff's department is pretending it isn't happening throws all the rules out the window, though, as far as I'm concerned."

If he'd said otherwise, she would have gotten mad. As it was, she took her seat across the table from him and just waited, aware of apprehension.

"Apparently, Bran has been asking questions."

"You didn't know he was?"

Zach shook his head. "We've had enough conflict, this…kinda surprised me, to be honest."

And pleased him, which made him uneasy, if Tess was any judge. Typical man, not sure how to react to the softer emotions.

"Anyway—" The way Bran had heard it, Zach told her, was that Hayes and Antonio had had a near-fight the evening before the scene she'd witnessed. One the deputy's girlfriend had seen and kept silent about.

"Are you going to try to talk to her?" she asked.

He shook his head. "I can't. I'm a witness, not an investigator in this case. I've already called Lieutenant MacLachlan and told him what I heard without admitting who told me."

"Wouldn't it have been better coming from Bran?"

"No, he's gone out on a limb here. To step into someone else's investigation without being invited…" He shook his head.

Tess made a face. "I guess that makes sense."

Zach laughed. "I'll tell Bran you approve."

"You do that."

He laughed again. "Feisty woman."

"Am I?" She looked away from him. "Lately, I feel like all I do is cower and call you to rescue me."

"You're not a cop," he said flatly. "I am. What are you going to do, buy a gun? Any idea how to use one? What if you shot someone who never had any intention of hurting you?"

"I didn't say I wanted to buy a gun. I just don't like feeling helpless."

"I know you don't." His voice was suddenly, impossibly, gentle. He pushed his chair back from the table but didn't rise. Instead he held out a hand to her. "Tess?" The gentleness remained but a new huskiness was there. "I say let's throw out all the rules."

CHAPTER ELEVEN

HE COULDN'T BELIEVE those words had come out of his mouth. That he'd just suggested they break the rules together. And yet…nothing on earth would have made him take them back.

Zach waited, his hand outstretched to Tess.

When she stood and started around the table, relief and something more powerful threw his heart into a new rhythm. Her approach was cautious, but he saw enough in her eyes to be sure she was as drawn to him as he was to her—and as worried about it. In his fear that she'd change her mind, he quit even breathing in an attempt to look as unthreatening as possible.

And then she took the last, hesitant step and laid her slim, cool hand in his. As air rushed into his lungs he tugged her forward. With a small cry, she dropped onto his lap, threw her free arm around his neck and pressed her mouth to his.

The kiss was clumsy, their noses bumped, he even tasted a hint of blood when his teeth scraped the inner flesh of his lip. But urgency rose in him as hot and fast as it had in her. He banded her with his arms and tilted his head to change the angle at which their mouths met. His tongue plunged deep, until he wrenched back enough control to stroke her tongue more deliberately, a sensual dance she met.

As they kissed, Tess's back arched, pressing one breast against his chest, shifting her weight on his thighs until he had to grab her hips and reposition her to allow for his erection.

He'd never been so ready so fast. He squeezed her butt, wrapped her hip with his hand and kneaded, moved down her thigh then slid up. The heat and dampness he felt even through denim went to his head.

Even so, kissing her was enough for now, which would alarm him if he let it. But he loved her taste, her answering pleasure, the small sounds she made, too much to tear his mouth away. His lust was contained by an unfamiliar tenderness that heightened all his senses.

He suddenly realized they might not make it to a bed if he didn't move *now.* For their first time, the kitchen table wasn't right. With a groan, Zach lifted her and set her on her feet, shoved the chair back hard enough to make it rock, and stood.

"Bedroom," he said hoarsely.

Her dazed look, showing incomprehension, went to his head, too. Or maybe not; his thinking had regressed to the primitive.

"Yes," she whispered. "Yes."

Zach hustled her out of the kitchen and down

the hall. He didn't turn on the overhead light in her bedroom, only the lamp beside the bed. He unceremoniously yanked back the covers and then went to work on her clothes. He wanted desperately to see her.

She wriggled a little to help him peel her shirt over her head, exposing a simple, white cotton bra. Zach liked it. He'd never been a fan of satin and stiff lace and wires. He cupped both her breasts, squeezing gently, feeling her nipples peak beneath the cotton, watching her eyes dilate as she stared down at his hands on her.

Then, patience abruptly gone, he unhooked the bra and was working on the button and zipper of her jeans before it hit the floor.

He had to crouch in front of her to pull jeans and panties over her feet. The position was excruciating in one way, but in another... She was gorgeous, long-legged, long-waisted, the curve of her hips luscious.

Enthralled, he dropped to his knees and nuzzled the caramel-brown curls that stood out against the white sweep of her belly. He inhaled, breathing in her scent as if it was a distillation of *her*. He could get drunk on her, he thought. Maybe he already was.

Was this why he couldn't resist her? Basic chemistry?

No. It was her eyes that had fascinated him first, the swirl of green and gold, the way they so often betrayed what she was thinking… The jut of her chin when she was angry… Her courage, integrity.

Her smile.

Her long, long legs.

"You're beautiful," he said thickly, pulling back so he could wrap his hands around her ankles, stroke and explore his way upward. He found the sensitive places that made her jerk and breathe harder, the unbelievably soft skin behind her knees and on her inner thighs. The way she radiated heat the higher he got.

Tess bent her head to watch him, her eyes dilated, her lips slightly parted, her color high. Her fingertips rested on his shoulders. When he reached her warm, damp center, he wanted to press his lips to her, but, damn, he didn't have it in him to play.

Making a ragged sound, he rose to a crouch and untied his boots so he could kick them off as he stood. Tess reached for him with urgency that matched his, yanking his T-shirt over his head then flattening her hands on his chest. She explored, her strong fingers kneading, tangling in his chest hair, delicately pausing at his nipples.

Zach's backup pistol clunked down on the bedside stand. He'd never stripped faster. He tumbled Tess back onto the bed and went after her mouth even as he positioned himself between her thighs.

Her legs wrapped around him and he started to push into her before his brain flashed a red light.

Swearing, he stopped, pulled out.

"What are you doing?" Tess exclaimed. "Stop!" Her legs tightened around his waist.

"Condom."

She whimpered but released him. He grabbed the packet he'd taken from his pocket before he'd tossed his pants aside. In disbelief, he saw his hands shaking as he sheathed himself.

Worry about it later.

He pushed back into her, and her back arched in a long, luxurious spasm. Tess uttered little cries and held on to him with her arms and legs. They had a brief fight as he retreated, but then she surrendered to the rhythm, slow at first because… God, the tight clasp of her body felt so good he wanted to do this forever, then faster and faster because he couldn't help himself.

Her fingernails dug into him at the exact moment he felt her small muscles begin to contract around him. She cried out his name. Zach reached down, grabbed her hips and drove hard, closing his eyes and gritting his teeth as his own orgasm roared through him. The pleasure went on and on, until he was wrung dry, and aware of some sharp emotion beneath his breastbone. It was an uncanny feeling, as though he'd received an injury without noticing.

Something else he'd think about later. He collapsed on her, knowing he was too heavy but unable to persuade his muscles to obey. Breathing was all he could manage.

But when he finally made the effort to roll… Tess wouldn't let him.

"Stay," she whispered. "Don't go."

The not-quite-painful sensation in his chest sharpened.

ZACH LEFT BEFORE DAWN.

Tess's sleep had been so deep, she'd felt drugged when she became groggily aware that he was gently moving her arms and legs to free himself. She seemed to float higher on the mattress when he got out of bed and reached down onto the floor.

For clothes, she realized. All their clothes must be down there, mixed.

He picked up and discarded what must be hers, then dressed quickly. Her eyes had adjusted enough for her to see when he reached for his handgun.

"You're leaving," she mumbled, oh so brilliantly.

Zach sat on the edge of the bed, planted a hand on each side of her shoulders and bent to kiss her. He took his time, but had himself so thoroughly in control, Tess knew he couldn't be persuaded to come back to bed.

"Trying not to be obvious," he murmured.

She frowned. "I thought we were throwing out the rules."

"Doesn't mean we have to tell everyone else we did."

"Oh." Tess wasn't sure that made sense, but arguing about it was pointless when he was so obviously determined to go.

"I have to shower, shave and change before work, too." He nuzzled her cheek and sat up. "I'll call."

Dark against not-quite-as-dark, he left. A moment later she heard the front door open and close softly.

Instead of brooding, she set her alarm and tumbled back into sleep—better sleep than she'd had in weeks, because Zach had been here most of the night and because of the cameras he'd installed.

Tess was in the shower at her usual time in the morning when she realized how amazing she felt. Champagne-in-her-veins, two-double-back-flips amazing. The thought made her laugh and she ended up swallowing water.

As if. Tess Granath, elementary-school giraffe, couldn't in a million years have been a gymnast. She had dreaded the gymnastics units in PE. The only varsity sport she'd participated in had been basketball, her junior and senior years, after she'd finally gained control of her body.

With the spring in her step this morning, maybe she'd surprise herself, she thought in amusement.

Actually, she reflected, grabbing her purse to go out the door, she was already surprised. Sex had never made her feel nearly this good before.

On impulse she called Lupe Estrada and asked if she could take her out to lunch. She hadn't seen her in a couple of weeks and Lupe had been subdued even then.

Lupe was quiet today, too, even once they arrived at the pizza parlor. Lupe had always loved pizza, but Rey scoffed at it.

She'd gone back to work doing tailoring for the dry-cleaning business, she said, but made a face. Laying her hands over her stomach, she said, "Every time I feel a twinge, I think it's happened again." She'd told Tess how excruciating the kink in her intestines had been, and worried because even the doctors didn't seem to know why it sometimes happened. And, of course, the surgeon had had to cut muscles to go in, which would also be slow healing.

In answer to Tess's questions, she admitted that once she was fully healed, she hoped to get pregnant. Then she might have to take in sewing instead of going out to work.

Lupe was a beautiful woman, petite and curvaceous with glossy, wavy, black hair down to her hips, who hadn't married until she was nearly thirty.

Rey had never seemed comfortable with Tess, which had limited the two women's friendship.

Mostly, they got together when he wasn't around. Her best guess was that he was ashamed not to be fluent in English, even though he hadn't moved to the United States until he was a young man. She'd seen him flush when he made a mistake. But when she tried out her Spanish on him, he had looked at her with a stony face and said, "I speak English."

Typical male ego, she'd thought at the time.

Lupe claimed not to have heard anything about the other men Antonio had lived with. "I don't think any of them were home to see what happened," she said. "I don't know why *he* was home during the day like that."

"I was on my lunch break, so he might have been, too."

Their number was called and Tess jumped up to get the pizza. They both dished up slices.

Into a silence Tess said, "Have you heard that the investigation has been taken over by two detectives from Stimson? I gave my statement to them last week. The deputy prosecuting attorney was there, too."

Quiet for a minute, Lupe at last said softly, "I heard someone say you'd changed your mind about what you saw."

Tess's shock was supplanted by anger. "Who?"

Lupe's very dark eyes skittered from hers. "It was...people talking where I work. Out in front, customers. I didn't know them."

"Did you believe them?"

"Of course not! But Rey said he heard the same, so I thought I should tell you."

"Did he believe it?"

"He doesn't know you the way I do. I told him you'd stand up for what's right."

Maybe the time had come to just ask. "I've... had the impression he doesn't like me."

"That's not true!" Lupe exclaimed with more spirit, her head lifted. "He just worries that you're not Catholic and you have so much more money... That you might look down on us."

Tess wasn't sure she could take another bite. She set the pizza down.

Lupe frowned. "You have to understand. He's still constantly asked to prove he's a citizen. He's made to feel stupid. I think he's embarrassed because I finished high school and he didn't. And you—you have a college degree and own your own business."

"You don't feel that way, do you?"

"No!" Lupe declared indignantly, her color high. She bit her lip. "Sometimes I'm a little bit jealous."

"You could have gone to college." With her grades and family background, she might have even gotten a full ride.

Lupe made a face. "You know my parents didn't let me. They needed me to start working, to bring in money for the family. They never understood..."

"How much more you could have made if you'd gone on with school."

She nodded, her dark hair swinging, but then shrugged. "I'm lucky because I like to sew. I didn't really want a career, anyway. You know how much I want children. A big family."

"I do, too," Tess said softly. "I've met a man—"

Lupe wanted to know all about him. Tess told her what she could without revealing the part Zach played in the ongoing investigation. "He's been protecting me from the threats I've been receiving. But I don't think he's ready to get married or start a family." She tried to smile. "So, you see, you're lucky to have Rey."

"I'll tell him you said so." Lupe patted her hand. "He thinks you look down on him because he's only a farm worker."

"Isn't he a foreman?"

"Yes, but still he goes out to the fields every day. He takes orders. He could lose his job anytime."

Tess snorted. "I can't be fired, but I could end up losing the store. If a Home Depot or Lowe's opens here in the county, so people didn't have to drive as far to get to one, it would do in my business. Not many of us can afford to be smug."

"That's true," Lupe said thoughtfully.

"Will you ask Rey who said that, about me changing my mind? Whether someone has been spreading a lie or whether people were just shrugging and saying, 'Oh, she'll say what they want her to, you know she will'?"

Lupe nodded.

Conversation became easier after that. Tess had to accept that Rey might never relax around her, but that didn't mean she and Lupe couldn't stay friends. Maybe they'd cleared the air today, at least.

Driving away after dropping Lupe off at the dry cleaner, Tess found herself angrier than ever about Antonio's death. Despite knowing he didn't dare attract the attention of authorities, he had still been courageous enough to try to defend a woman.

Andrew Hayes needed to pay.

ZACH WAS ON the car lot when his phone rang. Crap. His mother. He'd been dodging her calls for ages. He'd told her Bran wasn't ready to see her, but obviously she wasn't about to accept no for an answer.

Tough shit, he thought. *He* had a little trouble accepting her persistence. He couldn't remember the last time she'd even mentioned Bran. She hadn't tried very hard at all to hold on to him, yet now, suddenly, she wanted to envelop him in her arms?

But he couldn't forget his regret that he hadn't reconnected with Dad before he died. So he waved off an approaching salesman and took the call.

"And here I thought you were ignoring me." Forget hello.

Reluctantly smiling, he said, "I was."

"You're lucky I didn't buy an airline ticket and show up on your doorstep."

"How would you find my doorstep?" he pointed out, the smile still tugging at his mouth.

"You told me where you're working."

He cringed at the idea of his mommy walking into the sheriff's department asking for her son. No, worse: asking for her *sons*, plural. And Bran would be likelier than Zach to actually be there.

"Mom, don't do that. Don't put him on the spot."

"What could he do but talk to me?"

"He could stare right through you then turn and walk away." And Zach could see him doing it, no problem. "He's not a boy anymore, Mom. He's—God—heading toward forty."

"Thirty-seven." Her sharpness betrayed hurt that surprised Zach. "Do you think I don't remember?"

He stared blindly at the sticker showing features and price in the window of a Ford F-150.

"No," he said. "I know you do." That, he had to admit, was a surprise.

"Then what am I supposed to do?" she asked. No, begged.

"Wait," he told her. "One reconciliation at a time is enough."

All he heard was silence. It extended long enough he thought the call might have been dropped.

"Mom?"

"You've made your point," she snapped.

He'd swear she sounded…different.

Had she been crying? he wondered, stunned. For all her breaks with lovers and husbands, he hadn't seen her cry since those long-ago weeks after Sheila's death.

"Mom?"

"Please call me if there's any chance."

"Yeah." He cleared his throat. "Yeah, I'll do that, Mom."

She didn't even say goodbye, she was just gone, leaving him wondering if he knew her as well as he had always believed he did.

He suddenly saw himself introducing Tess and his mother. What would they think of each other? He'd have to give Tess some advance warnings and…

Good God, was he serious? He hadn't even introduced his girlfriends to his mother when he was in high school and still lived at home. He'd gone out of his way *not* to let any of them cross paths with her.

Nothing could have made him more uncomfortably aware that Tess was different.

He should have set up the damn receiver and gone home last night.

But then he'd have missed the best night of his life. They'd made love three times. But for some reason today what he found himself thinking about was how satisfying it had felt to hold her. He didn't like having a woman cling to him. So why was it that when Tess snuggled, it felt instead like both trust and comfort, given and received?

He made a muffled sound and went to meet the salesman politely hovering a few vehicles away.

He'd intended to buy another Silverado, which would have been his third, but surprised himself by buying the F-150. Black, of course, he liked black. Something he and Bran apparently had in common.

As an option he took one with a truck bed liner already installed and drove straight off the lot to Lowe's to pick up the shower, toilet and sink he'd chosen. He found the vanity he had custom ordered was in, as well, and just got everything in.

Tomorrow, he had a new garage door being delivered, a lot sturdier than the original. Automatic, which would be nice, too, but it was the security he especially wanted.

What worried Zach was the likelihood Hayes and company wouldn't repeat themselves. He had already done enough work on the house that he would be seriously pissed if they burned it down even if his homeowner's policy did cover it.

But he was more worried about Tess, less able to defend herself or her home. He didn't like believing a fellow cop would go beyond threats, but Zach had begun to believe Hayes had lost any sense of honor he'd once possessed. What if, at some point, he and his buddies decided a dead witness who'd already given a damaging statement was still better than a live witness who wouldn't back down and would be damned persuasive if she ever got in front of a jury?

It continued to chafe that he didn't know what MacLachlan and Clayton were doing and whether they'd learned anything new. If they were doing their jobs at all, they had to be making Hayes nervous.

Pulling into his garage, Zach wondered what Tess would say if he invited himself to spend the night again.

IN THE NEXT few days Zach tried to keep his head down and to only be with Tess when it was unlikely anyone would notice. He was fine when he was out on the roads doing his job.

He did his best to follow his usual morning routine: get his head together on his way in to work, think about anything that had gone wrong the day before, any oddity he'd seen that made him want to go back and take another look.

He'd walk himself through possible scenarios, transitioning from being the man who spent his evenings sawing and swinging a hammer, and his nights making love to Tess, into a cop.

He continued his habit of stopping by the records unit and flipping through recent reports of break-ins, auto thefts, whatever, so he had an idea of what to watch for that day.

The preshift briefings should have been equally routine.

Zach tried to step into the room at the last minute so he could stand at the back. Otherwise he'd sit there with his skin crawling, knowing on some deep, primitive level that he was being watched.

Walking in and then leaving, he had to nod at his fellow deputies, including Todd Vance, who had kept his mouth shut to protect a cop who didn't deserve it. Most of the time, Zach kept his expression bland. Only once did he meet his eyes and let Vance see his contempt.

Maybe Antonio had said the wrong thing when Hayes showed up on his doorstep, but Zach didn't think so. He believed Hayes had gone there with every intention of beating the crap out of him, at the very least. Showing him who had the power.

Bobby Ketchum, thank God, didn't work Zach's shift. Bobby, everyone knew, was a friend of Hayes's. He'd have been leaving his current graveyard shift at the right time to have deposited the rabbit in Zach's locker.

Bobby had never been in the locker room at the same time as Zach, which meant there was at least one confederate in the department who'd watched and memorized the combo for Zach's lock. Not knowing who that was could drive him crazy, if he let it.

Half the guys on his shift and a few on other shifts who didn't know him at all had taken a moment to slap his back and say something like, "You hang in there" or "Don't let the bastards get to you." That support—and Tess—was all that kept him going.

Yeah, okay. Bran, too.

He'd just parked Saturday morning and was walking in when he almost bumped into someone coming out the door. Wouldn't you know? Bobby Ketchum, whose face darkened at the sight of him.

"Feel good about destroying a man's career?" he snarled.

"You think a guy who killed an unarmed man because he'd had the nerve to talk to his girlfriend *deserves* to be a cop?" Zach got right in Ketchum's face. "If he's kept on in this department, it will shame everyone else who wears this uniform."

"He's a good cop. Who are you to talk? You're a newbie who doesn't know jack shit!"

"I'm a twelve-year veteran of a major police department. I've seen more violence than you've ever imagined. I spent two years working Homicide—"

"And couldn't cut it." Ketchum's lip curled.

Zach leaned in, his lips pulling back from his teeth. "So, being *Andy's* good friend the way you are, do you get a charge out of terrifying a woman who lives alone? Imagining her shaking in her bed as you threaten her? Or was it you who rapped on her bedroom window? And, hey, did you have a really good time hammering on my truck? Guess you've got to get your fun where you can, 'cuz the prison term you're facing won't be much fun at all."

Ketchum's jaw slackened and he took a step back. "I don't know what you're talking about."

"Don't you?" Zach let his gaze rake the other man head to boots. "I saw the three of you, you know. Couldn't make out faces, but your height, your build…oh, yeah. You were there."

"I was *where*?" This guy was seriously freaked.

Zach had to wonder if Bobby had taken part in the destruction, after all. "Well, here's a tip," he said, "if you weren't there, you might want to find out what Hayes and your other buddies have been up to. Decide if you really think any of them should be carrying a badge and a gun."

"I don't know what you're talking about," Ketchum repeated. His back was pressed to the brick facade of the public safety building.

Zach put his hand on the doorknob. “Guess you’ll find out. I’m sure Detective Easley from CCPD will be in touch. Since your name is on his list of Hayes’s good buddies.” He shook his head, dismissing Ketchum, and opened the door.

A hand caught it before it could start swinging closed. Zach spun to find a detective he’d barely met had come up behind him. He groped for a name.

Something Warner. No, Warring. Chuck Warring? Charlie, he corrected himself.

Warring was the other young detective in the department. Bran hadn’t commented on him one way or the other, but Zach had seen the two coming and going together, as if they had been assigned to work together.

The guy was thin, no more than average height, brown hair cut to regulation length. His badge was hooked to his belt and he was wearing a polo shirt with khaki chinos. He had the kind of face you forgot quickly. But his eyes told Zach he was smart, cynical. He had a cop’s eyes.

And right now a smile warmed his face. “Well, you scared me,” Warring commented.

Zach clasped the back of his neck and squeezed hard, willing the red haze in his vision to subside. “Did you hear the whole conversation?”

“Enough.” The smile died. “Bran has told me some of what’s been going on. I know Ketchum—

I was his field training officer a few years back, before I was promoted. I could be wrong, but I don't see him pulling the kind of crap you've been dealing with."

"Do you see him keeping his mouth shut, even though he knows that the evening before Andy Hayes killed Alvarez they had a mix-up? That logic should tell him Hayes went after Alvarez the next day?"

"I wouldn't have thought so." Warring looked tired suddenly. "But we can all fool ourselves."

Zach couldn't argue with that. He'd damn sure fooled himself when he was a kid that his mom was as pure as the driven snow.

"I don't know him at all," Zach admitted. "I wouldn't have said anything if the first words he's ever spoken to me hadn't been 'Feel good about destroying a man's career?' That kind of rubbed me the wrong way."

"I can see why it would." Warring's head turned, as if he was making sure they were, however briefly, completely alone. "The sheriff is so damn worried that this might screw up his chance of being re-elected, he's stuck his head up his ass. Most of the rest of us are behind you." He nodded as he turned toward the detective bullpen. "I'd better get to my desk."

More surprised than he ought to be, Zach watched him walk away. It seemed he had more allies than he'd known.

Yet somehow they were overshadowed by the faceless men who might not stop at anything to silence two inconvenient witnesses.

CHAPTER TWELVE

LEFT ALONE BRIEFLY, Bran looked around his brother's kitchen. Zach hadn't done a speck of work in here yet. Shifting in his seat at the table, Bran kept catching the tread of his athletic shoe on a separating seam of the ancient linoleum. But there *was* a table, unlike the last time he'd been in the house; a round, oak one that needed refinishing but had potential. A new refrigerator, too, he saw, big and white and out of place.

When Zach returned, Bran nodded at the new appliance even though he wanted to lunge out of his chair and snatch the manila envelope Zach carried in his hand. "I thought you were getting a dishwasher first."

"The refrigerator that came with the house died." Zach glowered. "Do you know how much new ones cost?"

"I've never bought one. They come with the apartment."

"Take my word for it." Zach's expression lightened and he ran his fingers over the tabletop. "But this? It'll be a beauty when I have a chance to work on it. Got it and the chairs at a garage sale on Sunday. It hadn't sold. Can you believe it? I paid peanuts and it's an antique." He shook his head and then tossed the envelope to Bran.

Man, it was actually here in his hands, everything the police department had on Sheila's murder. He could hardly believe it. When Zach had called to tell him it had arrived in the mail, Bran had come straight over. But now, as he shook out the thin sheaf of papers, he said incredulously, "This is *it*? There has to be more."

"You'd think so, wouldn't you?" Across from him, Zach shook his head in matching disbelief. "Look at Nolte's note on top. 'Here you go.' If he thought there should be more, you'd think he would have said something like, 'What the hell? I'll follow up.'"

"Yeah. Damn." Of course there had to be a hitch.

Zach grabbed them each a beer while Bran started reading. It didn't take him long. Ten or fifteen minutes in and he'd at least skimmed every page, which included the first responder's report and the coroner's report. Neither had told him anything he hadn't already known, although his stomach had clenched when he'd read some of it.

> Younger son Zach—nine years old—woke early and decided to go outside. Yelled to rouse parents, who ran outside. Boy had to be sedated.

Bran hadn't forgotten his first sight of Zach's face that morning, but he didn't like to think about it. Zach's shock had been so absolute, he had stared right through Bran, seemingly unaware that tears ran down his cheeks, snot over his upper lip. Bran hadn't been scared until he'd seen his brother and known something unimaginably terrible had happened.

"Nothing about her nightgown," he said, his voice hoarse. "Surely to God they kept it."

Zach's eyes were unfocused right now, too. Seeing another time, another place. "She was naked. The nightgown was underneath her. Like…he spread it on the grass because it was damp."

Considerate of him, Bran thought but didn't say. "There was no semen. The nightgown might not tell us anything."

"He'd have touched it." Zach sounded as if he was strangling.

Bran, too, was having an unusually difficult time separating what they were saying from his memories of Sheila. It was true she'd been pretty. She would have grown into true beauty if she'd had the chance.

But that was the adult looking back. Then, all he'd known was that she was the sweetest kid. Even stuck with more responsibility than he'd wanted for watching over her, Bran had never resented the little girl with the sunny nature. When he remembered her, she was always smiling or giggling. He thanked God he wasn't burdened with the memory of her corpse.

For all that he'd dealt with in the years since, working as a cop, Bran's mind still boggled at the idea of a man seeing a child that age as sexual…and then putting his hands around her neck and killing her because he couldn't afford to let her talk.

"I'll try asking," Zach said.

Bran stared at him without comprehension for a moment. Try asking for what? Then he remembered. He cleared his throat. "Yeah. That would be good. Worse comes to worst… I don't know. Maybe we'll have to hire a lawyer to put them on the spot."

"Or find a journalist who's willing to ask hard questions, maybe wants to follow the working of a cold case."

Bran grunted. He wasn't much of a fan of reporters, having seen too much insensitive and intrusive behavior in the past. But the right one… yeah.

"Worse comes to worst…" Zach agreed.

The two men sat in silence for a minute. Finally, Zach pushed himself up and went to the refrigerator. "Want another?"

"Sure."

Bran accepted the can, pulled the tab and took a long swallow before deciding to change the subject. "It's been a good stretch—what, a week?—

since anything has happened. You think Hayes's group has given up?"

"No." Anger tightened Zach's face, making the bony angles sharper. "God, I hope not."

"What?"

"Think about it. Even if Hayes is charged, it might not be for months. It could take another year for a trial to happen. Tess won't be safe until that son of a bitch has been convicted and the prison doors have slammed shut. Unless—" his hands flattened on the table and he leaned forward, his gaze boring into Bran's "—we catch him and his friends in action, intimidating a witness. If we do that, we can end this."

Bran stared at him, taking in the feral expression he'd never seen before. "You're not afraid for yourself."

"Should I be?"

He laughed, more in disbelief than anything else. "You're in love with her."

Zach didn't look away but he managed to wipe his expression clean. "You don't know what you're talking about."

"This is all about her now."

"It's about Antonio Alvarez."

"You're not seeing her on the sly?"

Guilt flickered in Zach's blue eyes, giving him away. His mouth tightened. "And if I am?"

"What, it's just sex?"

"No, it's—" He swore. "I don't know. You

know I'm not big on the idea of love and happily-ever-after."

It wasn't as if Bran ever imagined himself in love, but he felt something now he finally identified as pity. He'd lost his mother, brother and sister, but he, at least, had stayed in the same house, the same school, kept the same friends. Bran hadn't been yanked into the unfamiliar, Dad had never remarried. Bran had been older than Zach, too, when the split happened.

In contrast, Zach had grown up with constant moves and new schools. His only parent didn't know the meaning of the word "fidelity."

"Did Mom ever even pretend to be in love?" he heard himself ask.

Zach made an indescribable sound masqueraded as a laugh. "You kidding? Of course she does. She falls in love extravagantly. She gets dreamy, girlish, excited. She's made so many mistakes, she says, but *this* is real. Until she gets bored or—" His laugh was harsh. "Who knows with her? Lowell Carter—the guy who gave me his name—he was great. Treated her like a queen. He was a father to me. They stayed married four years, which was her record after Dad. But I think she was screwing around on him a couple years into the marriage. It was hard to watch." He zeroed in on Bran's face. "You're engaged. Aren't you in love?"

Even the question made Bran uneasy. He'd set

himself up for it, after accusing his brother of being in love, though. "I guess not," he said finally. "I don't even know what that feels like. But I want a family. I want a woman I can go home to every day. Kids. Commitment's what counts, not some romantic bullshit."

"I've never even wanted that," Zach said slowly. He had a strange look on his face. "Wife and kids, I mean. After I quit hearing from Dad..." His shoulders jerked. "And, Mom aside, I know too many guys who are divorced. Get to see their kids every other week, if they're lucky. As cops, our odds are even worse than most people's."

"Paige likes her job, too. I don't think she'll mind my hours."

Zach's eyes, which looked eerily like Bran's, could be damn penetrating. "Does *she* know you don't love her?"

"I haven't told her I do." There'd been a few awkward moments when he could tell she was waiting for words he couldn't give her. Bran thought she'd convinced herself he did, which was okay. He'd never walk out on a commitment, which was more than most men could give.

Not feeling anything he could call love? Maybe it should bother him, but it didn't.

In that instant he had a thought that did bother him. What he felt for Zach was tangled, infuriating, but powerful. It might even be love. It was certainly more powerful than what he felt for Paige.

So what? He was thirty-seven years old. If he hadn't stumbled head over heels in love with a woman by now, it wasn't happening.

Bran swallowed the last of his beer and pushed back his chair. Looking down at his brother, he said, "Would a wife and family be so bad?" Before Zach could answer, Bran said, "I'm out of here. Paige wants me to look at silverware and china patterns, believe it or not."

"Better you than me." Zach walked him to the door.

Bran was halfway down the narrow, cracked cement walkway when his brother's voice reached him. "Mom keeps asking."

He didn't even turn his head. "And I'll keep saying no."

"She'll be the grandmother of those kids you're planning."

Bran flipped his brother off but that last shot stayed with him. Paige's dad was okay, but Bran didn't like her mother. Was she to be the only grandmother his children ever knew?

He paused for a minute, car door open, and gazed at Zach's house. His mother, at least, had been likable. He grimaced at that. Too likable, apparently. Bran found it hard to forgive the damage she'd done to Zach. None of which meant she wouldn't be an indulgent grandmother. As a mom, she'd been fun and affectionate. His kids probably *would* like her.

Bran found himself shaking his head. Her cheating had too much to do with making him the man he now was. Letting her back in his life… he couldn't do it.

No was the right answer.

MOSTLY ZACH APPEARED at Tess's after dark, but Sunday night he suggested she come to his house instead. He'd done some work she might like to see, he said. If she hadn't already eaten, he'd cook.

He'd parked to one side of his driveway and left his garage door open, which she took as an invitation. Tess drove in and, as she walked the short distance to the house carrying her tote bag over her shoulder, saw Zach's front door open. He stepped out as the new garage door slid closed behind her.

In the overhead light she saw that the old porch had been torn down and the bones of raw lumber framed a new one. He really had been making progress.

"Got a lot done today," he told her, turning his head to assess his progress. He sounded satisfied. "As long as the skies don't open up, I'll shingle the roof tomorrow and build railings."

"It's wonderful." She'd have to drive by in daylight to better take in the effect, but she had seen enough to know he had an eye for design. "I love wide front porches. I thought about putting one on my house but I'm afraid it would look wrong."

"I plan to hang a porch swing," he said, stepping back to let her in. He added a careless, "Should help sell the house."

A vicious slice of pain told her she hadn't accepted the knowledge that he'd be moving on as well as she'd thought. Or…maybe, deep down inside, she had let herself think he'd change.

"God knows," he continued, oblivious to the blow he'd struck, "*I'm* unlikely ever to use it. I sit on my butt in the patrol car too much of the time as it is."

Somehow she managed to laugh. "You know, it might be good for you to slow down once in a while and rock a little."

He gave her a wicked grin. "I prefer to do my rocking in bed. With you."

Of course, she blushed.

He looked satisfied at that, too.

She admired the new refrigerator he'd bought, which had the freezer compartment on the bottom. It surprised her that he'd spent several hundred dollars extra for a feature like that on an appliance that would be staying with this house. Probably, she thought with another sharp reminder, he considered it a selling feature.

While he dished up dinner, she wandered down the hall to see if he'd started on the bathroom. He hadn't, but when she stuck her head into the two empty bedrooms, she saw that he had stripped the wood floors. Her noise crinkled at a smell she hadn't noticed until now, probably because whatever he was cooking had overcome it.

Dinner was simple: a salad and marinated chicken breasts over rice. While they ate, he told her about the police records he'd received concerning his sister's murder.

"I can't believe there isn't more. What do you want to bet there's a full box stowed somewhere down in the basement?"

"Why would they try to block you?" she asked.

He made a sound in his throat. "My best guess? Some of the old-timers are still around and maybe they know they didn't do what they should have."

"So what will you do next?"

"Apply pressure. Keep looking into the background of everyone I can think of who was around enough to have noticed Sheila *and* known where her bedroom was."

Thinking about that felt like fingers crawling up Tess's spine. "He'd have had to, wouldn't he?" she realized. "He couldn't exactly start flinging open bedroom doors until he found her."

Zach grimaced. "Actually there were only two bedrooms downstairs, my parents' and Sheila's. Plus a bathroom, of course. Zach and I had the room upstairs."

"Like the one in this house?" Did that bother

him? she wondered. How much did this house resemble his childhood home?

"Bigger and open. It was pretty much an unfinished attic with steep stairs. One window." His mouth curved. "Bran and I thought it was cool. Mom especially hated going up there. If we weren't too noisy, we could stay up all night if we felt like it, and be as slobby as we wanted, too."

Tess laughed. Two boys sharing might not have been as congenial a few years later when his brother wanted to sneak girls home to listen to then-popular hard rock but was stuck with his kid brother as a roommate. She decided not to mention that, though, given that he and Bran had never had the chance to find out what happened to their relationship when one was a teenager and the other still a boy.

"We wished we had a bathroom up there, though," he said slowly, betraying his unease with the parallels between his childhood home and this house. Where he would be plumbing in a bathroom upstairs. Another selling point, he'd tell himself, but it had to be more.

They were cleaning up after dinner when Zach's phone rang. He glanced at it where it lay on the kitchen counter and groaned.

"Speak of the devil."

"Your brother?"

"My mother." He wore an odd expression as he frowned at the phone.

"Why don't I give you some privacy?" Tess offered, driven by instinct.

He looked at her, those creases still in his forehead, and she thought he was disconcerted by something.

"That's okay," he said, shaking his head. "I don't mind you hearing anything I say to her." He picked up the phone. "Mom."

Fortunately, Tess couldn't hear his mother's side of the conversation. After a minute Zach said, "I asked again, Mom. He still says no. If you push too hard it's never going to happen."

Tess dried dishes and put them in the cupboards. No dishwasher. Zach had confessed to being irritated enough at having to wash his dishes by hand. He was about to have one installed without waiting until he replaced the cabinets and flooring.

"He's not married, but he is engaged." Pause. "Uh, it must be pretty soon. They went shopping for china today."

"July twenty-third," Tess said softly.

"What?" Zach covered the phone. "Really?"

"Paige told me."

"Huh." He put the phone back to his ear and repeated the date. Then he looked wary. "Yeah, I have a friend here. We just had dinner."

His mother said something.

"Yes, a female friend." Pause. His gaze slid

sidelong to Tess, then away. "Uh, no." He listened again. "You know I would."

No mystery what his mother was going on about: she wanted her son to get married and give her grandchildren. It was classic. And that "no" confirmed Tess's worst fears, sinking like a lead weight into her belly.

"So, how's Henry?" he asked suddenly. He listened, an odd look crossing his face. He said goodbye to his mother a minute later, shaking his head as he set the phone down. "Go figure."

Pretending for all she was worth that she hadn't listened to the conversation and wasn't hurt, Tess replaced the dish towel on its hook. "Go figure what?"

"I thought Henry was history. But she almost sounded fond of him." He gave a short laugh. "Did I tell you he's husband number five?"

"Five? Are you serious?"

His mouth twisted. "Yeah, constancy is not my mother's middle name."

Something told her to step carefully. "I'm sorry."

"My mother cheats on her husbands." Zach sounded disturbingly matter-of-fact. "She always has someone waiting in the wings."

Did he realize he had just explained his rootlessness, his unwillingness to commit to any place or anybody long-term? How easy it would be to hate his mother, a woman who must be impervious to the destruction she had left in her wake.

"Do you have a picture of her?"

His eyebrows went up in surprise, but after a moment he took his wallet from his hip pocket and laid it open on the counter. He removed a picture from a plastic sleeve and handed it to her.

Somehow, Tess wasn't at all surprised to see that his mother was movie-star gorgeous. His spectacular cheekbones and blue eyes had come from her. Not his coloring, though. She had the auburn hair she'd passed to her oldest son and a smile that hadn't quite reached her lips, but could be seen in her eyes. The photo was only shoulders up, but the woman in it looked delicate.

Handing the picture back, Tess suddenly felt tall and gawky.

"She's very beautiful." What else could she say? "It must have been weird, having the kind of mother men were turning to stare at."

Zach carefully replaced the photo and closed his wallet, leaving it on the counter. "I didn't notice when I was a kid. But once I hit adolescence…yeah. I was incredibly embarrassed. I wanted her to put a paper bag over her head before she went out."

Despite the grief squeezing her chest, Tess laughed at his expression, and he reached out and pulled her close. He leaned back against the counter, his feet spread enough that she could stand between his legs.

"Come on," he said, "I was a teenager. Of course she embarrassed me."

Tess made a face at him. "My parents didn't embarrass me. I was too sure *I* was an embarrassment to them."

"Seriously?"

She nodded. "I was this height by the time I was twelve. I towered over my mother, not to mention all the other girls my age and ninety-nine point nine percent of the boys. I was unbelievably skinny. To make matters worse, I developed a couple years later than most of the girls. I thought of myself as a giraffe."

Zach bent his head and rubbed his sandpaper cheek against her cheek. "Spots and all?"

"Oh, God, yes." She laughed again. "Too bad teenagers don't have the perspective to know that someday they'll be laughing about their worst despair."

She felt his chuckle vibrate his chest before she heard it.

"You and I would not have had a steamy romance in seventh grade, I've got to tell you. Or any other kind of romance."

Tess pulled back in mock offense. "Because you didn't like beanpoles?"

"Because the top of my head might have come up to your chin." He pinched her chin lightly.

"I was scrawny and short. It's funny, I'd almost forgotten until Bran reminded me. He said he thought I was taking after Mom."

"She's petite?" Naturally.

"Yep. Dad was a big guy, though." An emotion ghosted through his eyes that might have to do with regrets. "To my surprise and Mom's, though, about my sophomore year in high school, I started to grow. And grow. Forget back-to-school shopping. I needed a new wardrobe quarterly." Amusement colored his deep voice. "Mom grumbled. I was secretly delighted."

"Of course you were. So there you were shooting up at the same age I finally needed a bra."

He squeezed her butt then moved one hand up to cup a breast. "And the results were very nice."

She pressed her lips to his throat, inhaling a scent that was uniquely his. His hair had still been damp from a shower when she'd first arrived. She'd never let herself live in the moment before, but now she held no more illusions. This is all she would have with him. *Then treasure the moments*, she thought fiercely.

"You know," she murmured, "when you tear apart your bathroom, you can shower at my house."

"I am sleeping there a lot of the time anyway."

"I like it when you sleep there," she admitted, then felt a shaft of alarm. Would he take that as a hint that she wanted something more than their existing relationship? Well, so what? she thought defiantly. She did. What she felt was *hers*, whatever the consequences would be.

He'd gone still. Not for long enough to be obvious, but Tess felt it. But then he relaxed, tugging her closer again. And his voice was husky. "I don't usually stay the night with women. But with you… I like it, too." He was silent for a moment. "When you're not there," he said more slowly, "it feels wrong."

Pleasure and anxiety made a peculiar mix, but she felt both. He'd just told her she was different… though he wasn't altogether happy about that.

Tess rested against him, pretending she hadn't noticed. She was struck by the fact that they'd never had the usual talk people who were dating did about prior relationships. Partly, of course, because they hadn't dated. They'd just sort of drifted into sleeping together because he was there to protect her anyway. Once he didn't need to, what would happen?

Tess believed in facing her fears. So it was a little bit of a shock to discover that she was afraid to confront this one. It was bad enough knowing he'd pack up and leave eventually…but what if he lost interest even while he remained here in town?

Which left her two options: scramble back to safety now or enjoy the time she had with him and not dwell on what was ahead.

Making her choice, she tipped her head back and tugged him down into a kiss.

It was no secret that Hayes was enraged to be questioned first by Detective Easley from CCPD, then by the two detectives from the special investigative unit. A couple of people quietly told Zach to watch out for retaliation.

He felt the escalation at work. A hard bump of a shoulder as someone walked past him. Glares, sneers. He found a couple of ugly drawings and block-printed threats in his mail cubby at work.

Thursday, he checked his cubby warily, pulling out what looked like a flier printed on copy paper. He unfolded it and froze. Fury and near-panic pumped through him.

What he held in his hand was a photograph that had been blown up and printed. Clear as could be, Tess, smiling a welcome, was holding her front door open to let him into her house. His head was turned enough that his face, seen in profile, was recognizable. The crosshairs of two gun sights had been drawn in by hand, one targeting his temple, the other the center of Tess's forehead.

His hands trembled as he folded the piece of paper again. He debated skipping Sergeant Perez and going straight to the top, but had just enough self-control to handle this the way he should.

At the rap on the door Perez called, "Come in."

Animosity must be leaking from Zach, because the sergeant let out a long breath and sat back in his chair. "Now what?"

Zach let the piece of paper flutter to the desk blotter. He did not take a seat. He wasn't sure if he was capable of sitting still.

Perez unfolded the paper and looked at the photograph in silence. His eyes were black with anger when he lifted his head. "How'd it get to you?"

Zach told him.

"Don't suppose there's any chance of fingerprints, but whoever he was might have been careless. Say, when he put the paper *in* the printer?" He produced a file folder from a drawer and gently enclosed the newest and best threat.

"What do you intend to do about this?" Zach hoped he sounded more civil than he felt.

"I'll take it to Stokes and, if necessary, Sheriff Brown. They need to put out the word that this is unacceptable and anyone caught pulling this shit will be fired on the spot. As leaders of this department, they have to understand that they set the tone."

"Oh, I think they understand. We both know they *are* setting the tone around here."

"Not Paul."

"No?" Zach's teeth were clenched so hard, it wasn't easy to loosen his jaw enough to speak. "Then Stokes is not trying very hard to convince his boss that his stance is going to backfire. If this keeps up, he can kiss that election goodbye."

Perez's eyes narrowed. "You'll see to it personally?"

"If anything happens to Tess—" His throat closed. "These bastards are going down."

"Watch yourself, Carter. You'll regret it if you lower yourself to this level." He nodded at the photograph.

"I haven't started sending anonymous notes yet. But my temper is getting a little shaky."

"I hear you. Now get out on the road. Don't let this rattle you so you can't do your job."

"I'll do my job." His jaw flexed. "I'll leave you to do yours."

By the time he reached his assigned patrol car, he realized he was damn lucky Perez hadn't called him on insubordination. He must have seen that Zach was vibrating with rage, and understood.

Gripping the steering wheel, he thought, *Tess*. He *couldn't* let her be hurt or killed. The memory of Sheila's naked body, legs sprawled, head twisted horribly to one side, had never left him. What he'd seen in that first horrified moment hadn't softened or blurred in the least with the passing of the years. There'd been an instant of disbelief—that was a doll, not really his sister. The eyes were too blank, the skin too waxy. What would Sheila be doing out here before Mom and

Dad had gotten up? And then his stomach had heaved and he'd begun yelling.

What if he found Tess…? Hunching his shoulders, he shook his head. No. It wasn't happening.

He'd survived the loss of his sister, although he knew it had shaped his life more than he probably let himself recognize. But if Tess, a woman he hadn't even met six weeks ago, was killed, too? If he failed to keep her safe—found her body or even saw it happen…?

A raw, inarticulate sound escaped him.

She had touched him as no one else ever had. He loved his mother, had kept loving his father and Bran, he guessed, but with reservations. He hadn't wanted to ever feel this way about anyone, but he hadn't had any say in it, and now it was too late.

God, he thought, closing his eyes. *I love her.*

And somebody had just threatened to kill her.

CHAPTER THIRTEEN

TESS HAD BARELY arrived home from work Thursday when Zach showed up. He'd called midafternoon and said, "I'll bring a pizza for dinner. Six o'clock."

When she'd stuttered, "Wait…w-why?" all the answer she got was "Later."

Now she peered out cautiously and saw that he had abandoned his usual skulking. His new truck was parked in her drive and, in broad daylight, he was walking up to her door carrying an extra-large pizza box.

His expression was as closed as she'd ever seen it.

"What's wrong?"

He shook his head. "Let's eat. I never stopped for lunch."

Barely vanquishing her curiosity, Tess led the way to the kitchen where she set out plates as Zach tore a couple of paper towels off the roll in lieu of napkins. He chose a bottle of beer she had kept in the refrigerator for him and she poured a glass of white wine.

As they ate, she felt compelled to fill the silence. Or was it to talk him down?

She found herself making a funny story out of the young woman who'd come in to the store to browse wallpaper books, bringing two preschoolers with her.

They'd sat still for about thirty seconds before pulling books from the shelves. Mom didn't seem to notice. That got boring, so they went out into the main showroom, where they hid from each other behind racks of carpet samples. They ran laps.

Mom didn't even seem to notice how many wallpaper books were heaped on the floor. She picked more out and slowly leafed through them, also not noticing that her children had disappeared from the small room.

Tess had the pleasure of seeing some of the tension on Zach's face ease and a smile curl one side of his mouth. "So you got to babysit. Sounds like my job some days."

"Yes, and you want to know the kicker?" Tess was still mad. "I asked if she wanted to borrow any of the books and she said she'd written down the information she needed to price the wallpaper online. She didn't even apologize!"

"Can she order the same wallpapers you sell online for cheaper?"

Tess's mood plummeted. "Probably. They don't

have to pay overhead for a store that can hold a huge selection of samples."

"And a playground," he said almost straight-faced.

She huffed.

He laughed, which helped.

"If she comes again," he said, "I'll bet you won't be anywhere near as nice about her hellions."

"You'd better believe it." Watching as he took his fourth slice of pizza, she judged the time to be right. "Are you going to tell me what had you so grim when you got here?"

He set the pizza down on his plate, wiped his fingers with a paper towel as if to give himself a moment, then met her eyes. "Yeah. I'll tell you."

When he was done, she didn't know what to say. Even what she felt. She discovered she was rubbing goose bumps on her arms. Did that mean she was afraid? Yes, she thought, but it wasn't only that. It was knowing, absolutely for sure, that someone was watching her through a telephoto lens that allowed him to see her as if he was only a few feet away. He had photographed her when she'd had no idea she was being watched.

"I feel violated," she said at last. "My skin is crawling."

Zach watched her. "We knew they were probably keeping an eye on both of us."

"Yes, but—" She shuddered. "This makes it

real. Are they watching all the time? Do I dare glance out my window? And…there's no way to protect myself from a high-powered rifle."

"No." It was the first time she'd ever seen emotions so naked on his face. His fear and frustration turned his voice into a growl and darkened his eyes. "If it were short-term, I'd push you to take a vacation. But this could drag on for a year or more."

"Do you trust this Sergeant Perez to do anything?"

He scrubbed a hand over his face. "Yes. But whether he can get any action out of Brown or Stokes? I don't know."

"What can they do?"

"They could launch a serious investigation."

"Assigning it to whom? Delancy?"

He sighed. "There are some decent investigators in the department. Probably goes without saying that Bran can't work this."

Tess nodded.

"We need the sheriff to get behind changing the culture in the department. To say, 'This isn't acceptable.'" His shrug didn't express a lot of hope.

"So…why does this mean we don't have to sneak around anymore?" Tess asked. "If that's what you're suggesting by showing up when anyone can see you?"

"It got me thinking. Why should we have to?" he countered. "Everybody knows I'm determined to protect you. If that led to a personal relationship, whose business is that but ours?"

"And if a defense attorney tries to imply we're in collusion?"

"We tell the truth. We say the same thing we have from the beginning. We had never met before that day. Never even set eyes on each other, as far as I know. We might not have exchanged a word again unless we met going in or out of the courthouse for Andrew Hayes's trial, if the defendant and his friends hadn't decided to try to pressure you into retracting your statement."

Nice to be reminded he wouldn't have bothered to call her had she not needed a protector.

But…was that true? Tess didn't know. She couldn't forget the way his gaze had burned into hers as they'd looked at each other across Antonio's body. The huskiness in his voice, the gentle quality, when he'd talked to her.

Her chest continued to ache, though, as if she'd strained something, while he talked about the calls he'd made that day to Lieutenant MacLachlan and Detective Easley at CCPD.

"For what good it did. 'We'll look into this.' What kind of bullshit answer is that?"

"What did you think they'd say?" she had to ask.

A nerve twitched beneath his eye, his jaw muscles tightened. Then he gusted out a sigh. "Exactly what they said. What I'd have said in the same situation."

Tess managed a small smile. "Don't you hate having to admit that?"

"Oh, yeah." He laughed, a rusty sound. "I'm like a doctor who has cancer and is suddenly a patient. He knows what should be done but has to put his treatment in someone else's hands."

"And hates every minute of it?"

He grunted his agreement then drained his can of beer, his throat working as he swallowed.

Tess couldn't seem to tear her eyes away. Why should a throat be sexy? But his was.

"I'm sorry I bought the house," Zach said suddenly. "If I was still in the apartment, I'd ask you if I could just move in. I'd be here to protect you and we'd limit the number of targets the perps have."

A constriction around her rib cage threatened her ability to take a breath. She wanted nothing more than to live with him, to come home to him every evening…but not if he was here to stand as her bodyguard.

Only once had she fallen for a guy enough to let him move in with her. It hadn't lasted quite a year. The takeaway for her had been that the deterioration of a relationship was magnified if you lived together—and the hole left after the split was devastating.

And yet she'd have had no hesitation at all in saying yes, if she believed Zach loved her.

He watched her with increased wariness as she sat silent. "I take it that would have been a resounding no," he said wryly.

"No," she said. "I mean, not necessarily. I mean..."

He cocked a dark eyebrow.

"I might have said yes," she finished softly, feeling the heat in her cheeks. "But you do own a house, so...?"

"You're right that I'm afraid to leave it completely empty, but we can't leave your house completely empty, either." He scowled at her as if it was her fault. "And I don't want to leave you alone."

"You've been leaving your house empty a lot at night." Seeing that his interest in pizza had waned, Tess closed the box, thought about standing and putting it in the refrigerator, and decided it could wait.

"I have. I want them to target us here."

"Because of the cameras?"

"Right." He looked older, as if the lines on his face had deepened. "I put in a couple at home, too. But I don't see them vandalizing my house, not if they're capable of learning from their mistakes. They went after my truck and I just got madder."

Subtext: he still thought *she* was the weak link. With a tiny shiver she thought, *And he might be right*. But then she straightened her spine. Damn it, she was just getting madder, too.

"I guess I'm asking if I can mostly move in for the duration." The wariness or at least apprehension had reappeared in the way he looked at her. "I'll probably spend days off working on my house, maybe a couple hours after work some evenings, but I want to be here at night."

Her squeeze of panic was back. "You've already been here most nights." She was talking just a little bit too fast, her voice maybe higher than usual. "And now you're asking permission?"

"I don't want to sneak out before dawn and go home to shower and change clothes," he said. "If I could, uh, at least put some of my stuff in one of your spare rooms."

And his razor on the counter beside her sink, his toothbrush in the holder with hers, his shampoo in the shower…

And he would be in her bed, all night, every night.

Isn't that what she really wanted? Would he really be so passionately worried about her if he didn't feel a whole lot more than a mere sense of responsibility? Maybe this was one of those times when she should just close her eyes and jump.

In full faith a parachute would open, even if she hadn't been wearing one when she'd stepped out of the airplane.

Tess nodded, almost steadily. "Yes, of course.

That's fine. Um, there's probably room for both of us to park in the garage, too. It's not like I have a workbench or anything taking up space."

The signs of his relief were so subtle, she wouldn't have noticed them if she hadn't been looking closely. "Thanks," he said roughly. "As it happens, I threw a duffel bag in the truck."

"Taking me for granted," Tess said way more lightly than she felt.

He smiled. "If you'd been reluctant, you would never have known about the duffel."

She'd stood to put the pizza in the fridge when she stopped dead. "Oh, no. Dad."

Silence behind her.

"Does he have to find out?"

She made herself move again. "I do have him over to dinner sometimes, or I go there."

"I can make myself scarce, as long as he isn't given to dropping by unannounced."

It hurt. He couldn't have said any more clearly that this was *not* the beginning of something important between them. Instead of friends with benefits, it was bodyguard and pro bono client with benefits.

As if she hadn't already known that.

Tess closed the refrigerator and turned to face him. "You don't want him to know you're staying here?" she said, striving to sound unconcerned.

Zach hadn't moved. His eyes were alert on her

face. She had no idea how much he could see. "Do you?" he asked.

What was she going to do, put him on the spot? Not a chance in hell.

She shrugged and said, "Something short-term, it's probably best not to. He's worried about me already. I don't want to freak him out totally."

This time his relief wasn't subtle at all.

That hurt a lot more.

"I'll go get my bag," he said.

"Why don't I open the garage and we can reshuffle vehicles to see if we can't get your truck in, too?"

"I can wait until tomorrow."

"There's no camera out in front, remember."

Zach winced. "Yeah, okay. You're right. Although your driveway is pretty exposed."

"Why take a chance?" Tess was proud of her casual tone.

He came to her, slid a hand beneath her hair and kissed her, so softly, before stepping back. "Then let's do it, oh, wise one."

THE SCENE IN the kitchen left Zach confused. By the end, he hadn't been able to tell what she really wanted or felt, and he wasn't any too sure what he felt, either.

He'd spent the day trying to convince himself that, of course, he wasn't in love with Tess. Things had just been...intense lately. And, yes, protecting her was his first priority. Shouldn't it be? Even thinking about the things associated with love—such as marriage and kids—made him twitchy.

At the same time, if she'd said no way, sorry—

Damn it, he didn't want to think about that, either. He hadn't much liked her off-handed agreement that it would be better if her father never knew about Zach, even if *he'd* been the one who suggested it. That made no sense, he knew.

Of course, if she had insisted on having her dad to dinner to announce the deeply significant change in her life and show off Zach, he might have freaked. Meet the parents? Words to turn a man into a coward.

By the time they managed to squeeze both vehicles into her garage, Zach's tangled emotions had settled in his stomach like a heavy serving of pancakes.

Nothing felt good as they whiled away the evening, pretending this was normal. She did something online. He turned on a baseball game even though he didn't care about either team. He checked for messages and email on his phone. She did a load of laundry.

The change for him came after he shaved for a second time today, cleaned up the whiskers, brushed his teeth, popped his toothbrush in the ceramic holder that was an interesting part of the tile work behind her sink, and took a last look in the mirror. He wore only a pair of pajama pants that sagged low on his hips.

Tess had taken the first turn in the bathroom, emerging while he was still digging his kit out of his duffel. She, too, was wearing pajama bottoms and a thin, white T-shirt that let him see the shadow of her nipples.

She would already be in bed. Waiting for him. As she would be every night from here on out.

For as long as we both shall live.

He frowned at himself in the mirror. No, until she didn't need his protection anymore.

Satisfaction filled him when he turned off the bathroom light and saw her sitting up against a pile of pillows in the pool of light from a bedside lamp. This felt different tonight. More.

He'd shaved here, his toothbrush was here, he'd get dressed in the morning for work here. As if he belonged. Him. A man who hadn't belonged anywhere since he was nine years old.

Zach walked to his side of the bed—yeah, *his*—and climbed in, immediately rolling to face her. "You're beautiful," he murmured, slipping a hand beneath her tee, feeling her muscles tighten. He stroked the silky skin of her midriff in a circular motion. "Why don't you lose a couple of those pillows?"

She reached for the lamp.

"Leave it," he said. "I like to look at you."

Tess hesitated then turned back. She did as he'd

suggested, tossing pillows to the floor, then pulled her T-shirt over her head, leaving her hair ruffled and her breasts bare for his mouth and hands.

Zach made love to her as he'd never made love to a woman in his life. Heat and passion merged with the tenderness and fear for her that burned in his chest. He worshipped her body, not letting her hurry him even though he ached for her. He pushed her to a long, shuddering climax, then had her reaching for him frantically again before he slid into her. He held on to his control, driven by determination to please her ahead of himself, until she shattered around him, pulling him with her.

He'd never felt anything like it, either. Not the intensity of the orgasm or the sense of peace afterward. Mind turned off, body sated, Tess's arms around him. Breathing in her scent, his face turned into her neck, one of his hands still wrapping her hip.

This is what I want, he thought drowsily.

The lamp was still on when he woke a couple of hours later. Tess appeared unconscious. Also irresistibly naked. Zach did turn off the lamp, but then, when she woke, he made love to her again.

Zach timed his arrival for the morning briefing perfectly. The seats were full and a few men stood to the side and at the back. He found a spot against the wall where he could lean.

Several people turned to look past him in surprise. Paul Stokes had just walked in and was striding toward the front of the room. Stiffening, Zach flicked a glance at Sergeant Perez, already half sitting on a table at the front, arms crossed, obviously expecting the undersheriff's arrival.

Uniform crisp, hair razor-cut to a precise length, Stokes faced them in a parade stance. No casual pose for him. "Gentlemen. And ladies." He inclined his head toward the two female deputies who worked Zach's shift. "You are all aware that a man died recently from an apparent beating administered by Deputy Andrew Hayes, who is one of us."

His pause was long enough for Zach to feel some shock at the blunt beginning. No hint that Alvarez's death might have come about accidentally, from his head hitting the concrete step. That made Zach wonder what the coroner knew but hadn't released.

"As you're also aware, according to our tri-county agreement, a special investigation unit is looking into the death to determine whether criminal charges should be filed. Once we have those conclusions, we will discuss whether policy within the department needs to be changed and new training implemented."

The silence was absolute. They all stared at the second-in-command of the department. Waiting. Knowing this wasn't all he'd come to say.

"In the meantime," he continued, his voice hardening, "both witnesses to the altercation between Deputy Hayes and Mr. Alvarez have received threats. One of those witnesses is also a member of this department." He nodded at Zach, their eyes briefly meeting. "I'm sure you all noticed the state of the locker room a few weeks back."

A stir of amusement in the room died as his narrow-eyed glare searched out the sources.

"Three men smashed Deputy Carter's pickup, resulting in the insurance company totaling it and a significant financial loss for him. Ms. Granath, the other witness, has been threatened with notes and phone calls. The tires on her car were slashed. At least one perpetrator terrorized her in the middle of the night at her bedroom window at the same time as she received one of those telephone threats. *This—*" he held up a sheet of paper Zach hadn't noticed he held "—is the latest attempt to silence witnesses who are only trying to describe events as they saw them. *This* is a death threat. It's despicable. It was delivered to Deputy Carter by one of us."

He let them all stare at the photo. "I'm here to tell you that the investigation into Deputy Hayes's blame—or lack of blame—in Mr. Alvarez's death is being conducted as fairly as is possible to achieve. If it turns out Hayes is innocent of wrongdoing, that truth will emerge. If, however, you believe he should be shielded, guilty or not, from the consequences of his actions simply because he's one of us, you're wrong. So wrong you're not worthy of wearing this badge—" he touched the one pinned on his chest pocket "—and don't deserve the trust of the citizens of this county. When we discover who took this photograph and turned it into a death threat, that person will be arrested. If and when we discover who delivered this threat to one of our own *right here in this building*, that person will be arrested. If that person is a sheriff's department employee, he or she will be fired. No recourse."

The room was like a tomb. Zach looked until he saw Todd Vance, sitting toward the back. He seemed to be fascinated by something on the floor.

Stokes swept the room with one last look then gave a formal nod. "Sergeant Perez."

He stepped aside and Perez began the usual report of new alerts. Stokes continued to scan the room as the sergeant talked, his gaze pausing on one face after another. When his eyes met Zach's, he bent his head a bare inch—but Zach thought he was indicating respect.

Or, Zach reflected, it might have been the equivalent of a fencer signaling his readiness before a duel.

Well, there was nothing he could do about it either way, except stick to the truth and protect Tess to the best of his ability.

Zach tried not to look as though he was hurrying when the briefing ended, but he made it out of the door first.

One guy he didn't know well and hadn't especially liked caught up with him in the hall.

"Man, I hadn't heard about all this crap. Hope you know I wouldn't have any part of it. I'm sure most of us wouldn't."

"I assumed as much, but thanks for saying it," Zach returned.

He had to repeat his thanks a few times before he was finally alone behind the wheel of his squad car. The deputies who'd stopped him had seemed genuinely shocked and concerned.

Hayes's best friends in the department, the ones willing to go out on a limb for him, might not work this shift, of course. But Zach felt sure Stokes would deliver the same message to all three briefings.

And then what? Would the perpetrators think twice? Or would they figure they were already screwed if they got caught, so they should carry the plan to its final conclusion?

Whatever that plan was.

Zach started the engine and reached for his sunglasses, ready to start his patrol.

Serve and protect.

ZACH EXCUSED HIMSELF after dinner Friday evening to make a call. Tess was a tiny bit relieved to have some space. Even if she hadn't had doubts about his reasons for moving in, she'd still have some trouble adjusting to living with a man.

It had felt odd to come home, remembering she needed to wedge her car as close to the left wall of the garage as she could while still allowing her enough room to open her door. From then on, she'd found herself listening for Zach's arrival the whole time she was changing clothes and starting dinner. Tonight was the first time ever she heard the garage door opening when she wasn't the one pushing the button on the remote control.

It had taken some digging, but she'd found the second remote and even a new battery for it.

When he came in through the door from the garage and through the utility room to the kitchen, Zach smiled. "You're making dinner already. If I can get here earlier tomorrow night, I'll figure out something. It has to be my turn." He kissed her lightly and kept going toward the bedroom.

Her first impression had been that he'd looked preoccupied and tired until he'd seen her. Tingling from the smile and the kiss, Tess wondered whether she'd been imagining things.

Over dinner he told her about the undersheriff's talk at the morning briefing. "Half a dozen guys have said something about it to me since." Zach shook his head. "So far, they've all been supportive. I think a few of them were embarrassed."

"Do you think Stokes meant what he was saying? Or is he mad because you boxed him in and he had no choice but to speak out?"

Zach seemed to think about that. "He can be a little hard to read. Best guess...he was sincere, but Sheriff Brown is pissed. Stokes is pretty straight-arrow. I don't think he's political enough to condone any of this."

He would have cleaned the kitchen alone if she hadn't insisted on helping. When they were done, he went outside onto the patio to make a call.

Tess set up the ironing board in the kitchen and began one of her least favorite chores. She wondered whether his uniforms had to be dry-cleaned. Being a man, he probably took them to the Laundromat no matter what. Anything not to iron.

She caught glimpses of Zach through the window every time his pacing brought him to the near end of the patio. It was enough for her to see that the conversation was a stormy one.

Tess reminded herself the call wasn't any of her business. And, no, she couldn't ask him about it. He had every right to his privacy.

She saw the moment the call ended. He held out the phone and stared at it. Then, with a violent motion, he shoved it in a pocket of his jeans and thrust his fingers into his hair.

He disappeared from her sight.

It was probably five minutes later when the French door to the dining room opened and closed. Tess carefully slid the iron over a cuff. The steam hissed.

Zach appeared in the kitchen. "My mother," he said curtly.

"You don't have to tell me."

"If you'd rather I don't—"

What could she do but make a face at him? "You know I'm nosy."

He smiled but not very convincingly. "I filed a request for information at the Clear Creek PD during my lunch break today. The one detective who investigated Sheila's death and is still on the job won't return my phone calls."

Absorbing his apparent non sequitur, Tess slipped the blouse on a hanger that she'd suspended from a hook at the end of the upper cabinets. "Why doesn't he want to talk to you?"

"He's probably just being territorial. Maybe thinks the very fact I'm asking questions means I don't believe he did his job."

"You don't."

This time he grinned at her. "You're right. I did think that. Nolte—the retired detective—surprised me a little. He sounded like he'd done everything he could and should. The copy of the reports he forwarded are laughable, though. I have to think there's something they're hiding."

She nodded, still unsure what this had to do with his mother.

"Mom has never been willing to tell me what she knows. I decided I wouldn't take no from her tonight. By God, I want a list from her of what men she had on the side around then."

Tess had picked up the iron again but set it back down in its rack, unable to take her eyes off his face. "Oh, Zach."

His mouth twisted. "Oh, yes. End result is, I don't have a single name I didn't already know, and she thinks I was accusing her of having something to do with Sheila dying." He rolled his shoulders. "I don't know how we can go on from this."

The unhappiness on his face had her sinuses burning. She couldn't *not* go to him. "You'll tell her you love her and eventually she'll understand you're thinking of Sheila." She wrapped her arms around his waist and squeezed.

He grabbed on to her so hard, her face was mashed into his chest. "Oh, God, Tess," Zach said, his voice raw, painful to hear. "I'm glad you're here."

When he finally loosened his hold, it was only to capture her mouth with equal desperation.

Tess barely remembered to unplug the iron before Zach swept her off to the bedroom.

CHAPTER FOURTEEN

We Care Plumbing paid for an ad in the Yellow Pages of the local telephone directory. "When you need us, we're ready to serve you," the ad read. It also featured the photo of a handsome man in a uniform shirt with We Care Plumbing stitched on the chest. He looked earnest and reliable.

Considerably older than Zach's memory of him, but Sam Doyle, no question.

It wasn't a lie to say he needed some plumbing work done, Zach thought, even if hell would freeze over before he'd hire this guy.

"I'd like Mr. Doyle himself," he told the cheerful woman who answered the phone.

They agreed on ten o'clock Monday morning. Zach hadn't expected We Care Plumbing to show up on a Sunday in the absence of an emergency.

Sunday, Tess spent the day working with him at his house. He'd finished the porch earlier in the week and was now set on gutting the bathroom. She alternated between hauling debris out to the Dumpster and staining the porch floorboards and steps. He gave her a last chance to use the bathroom before he turned off the water and removed the toilet, sink and vanity.

Then he went next door and returned with Dean Thompson, trailed by the kid, Dylan. Dean hadn't seemed to mind being asked to help Zach haul out the tub.

He introduced Tess before leading him inside the house.

"Haven't seen much of you this week," Dean commented.

"I'm staying with a friend for the moment, but I'll be here tomorrow. I have a couple plumbers coming in the morning to give me bids. The new fixtures are all sitting in the garage, so I'm set to go once these pipes are replaced."

They each went to one end of the tub but before they could pick it up, Tess stuck her head in the bathroom.

"There's no rot," she said in surprise.

Dean laughed. "I can tell you've remodeled a house or two."

They were both grunting and sweating by the time they got the tub out to the bin. Dean stayed to help carry the new vanity and then the toilet in, setting both down in the bedroom across the hall.

After Dean went home, Zach found Tess wandering around the yard. Envisioning landscaping, she admitted. When he told her he thought there should be a lilac, she agreed and they chose a spot. Since they were both at a good stopping point, they locked up and made a grocery store run before going back to her place.

Zach used the evening to make phone calls, figuring it was a good time to catch people at home. He hadn't yet located Duane Womack, which made him think the guy had left the state. His ex was proving as elusive. Zach wondered if she had remarried and changed her name. He had identified the two daughters, however, and started with them.

The oldest, Andrea, was thirty-two, only two years younger than Zach. The younger sister, Shelby, was twenty-nine. Andrea was a paralegal at a law firm in Everett, a couple counties away. Her sister lived in Bellingham, to the north. Neither was married. That wasn't necessarily unusual these days, but he wondered about it anyway.

Tess had asked if he'd wanted privacy to make his calls, but he'd shaken his head. "Unless I'll be bothering you."

"No. I'll be quiet," she promised. She sat on the sofa reading. Zach sat in the chair facing her.

Andrea answered her phone tersely.

Zach talked fast, telling her he was now a police officer and explaining that his parents had known her father when he was a kid. "My sister, Sheila, was murdered when I was nine."

"I remember," she said slowly. "The principal talked to us at school."

He frowned. "I'd forgotten. Friends told me.

My parents kept me out of school for something like a week." He hesitated. "Were you aware detectives talked to your father about Sheila back then?"

She was silent for quite a while. Zach saw that Tess was watching him, her book open but apparently forgotten on her lap.

"No," Andrea said finally. "I had no idea."

He waited for more. Shouldn't she be asking *why* investigators would have thought her father had anything relevant to offer?

"I haven't been able to locate him. I'm hoping you'd be willing to give me his phone number."

"I'm no longer in touch with him," she said with flat finality.

"Would you be willing to tell me why?"

"That's kind of personal, don't you think?"

He might as well be blunt. "Ms. Womack, I think you can guess what I'm driving at. My sister's murder was never solved. I'm determined to find who was responsible. I'm guessing our elementary school principal didn't tell the assembly that Sheila was raped before being strangled."

He thought he heard a quiet gasp on the other end.

Continuing, he said, "I understand your mother received sole custody of you and your sister after the divorce. That's unusual. Your father was at our house often enough around that time to have seen something of Sheila and to know which bedroom was hers. He might conceivably even have had a key to the house."

He paused but she said nothing.

"Look, I'm a stranger to you. I understand your discomfort with what I'm asking. I can give you some references if you want to check on me before you tell me anything more. I'd also be glad to meet with you."

Her voice was so soft he had to strain to hear her. "What is it you want to know?"

She had to have guessed. He took a breath and asked anyway. "Did he molest you or your sister?"

Before he could finish with the rest of the question—or do you know if he was ever accused of molesting any other little girls?—she answered, "Yes." Voice firmer, she repeated, "Yes, he did. But…not until later. I was almost twelve the first time."

Stunned by feelings more complicated than he would have expected, Zach closed his eyes.

"I'm sorry," he said quietly. "Sorrier than I can say."

"Yes, well…" Her shrug, unseen, could be heard in her voice, as could her bitterness.

"Your sister?" he asked gently.

"Does it matter?" she snapped.

Ripping open someone else's wound was never pleasant. "It does if he started in on her way younger than he did with you."

He waited out a long silence.

"Yes," she said in a muffled voice. "He… molested her, too." *Raped her.* "But not when she was younger. It was the same age as with me. When I found out about Shelby, I told my mother. She took us and left Dad that same day. I felt sick. I could have prevented Shelby from being… I still don't know why I was so sure Mom wouldn't believe me."

"Because he convinced you," he said, almost harshly.

She did nothing but breathe for what had to be a minute, then whispered, "Yes."

It was none of Zach's business but… "How old were you? When you told?"

"Fifteen. I was so afraid." Her shame could still be heard. "But when I found Shelby sobbing and she told me—"

"I understand."

Zach was ashamed of himself, because for his own reasons he'd actually hoped she'd admit to having been molested by her father. Tunnel vision. He hadn't thought of *her.*

Then he paid attention to the uneasiness awakened by what she'd said. "Are you sure about her first time? Your sister's, I mean? When you found her crying?"

"Yes. Why would she lie about that? She was almost exactly the same age I'd been."

"Eleven."

"Yes."

They talked for a few more minutes. Her mother had eventually remarried, she told him, but not until her daughters were grown and gone.

Andrea's hostility didn't reawaken until he asked for her mother's phone number.

"I don't want you bothering her. She had a really hard time. Don't you understand?" She was almost hysterical. "I've already told you more than I probably should. Leave her out of this!"

Realizing there wasn't a thing he could do for her, Zach thanked her for her honesty and let her go.

He wondered if Andrea Womack would sleep at all tonight.

He dropped his phone on the coffee table and met Tess's eyes. She'd closed and set aside her book, and was watching him steadily.

"That son of a bitch," he growled.

"Both daughters," Tess murmured.

"Yep."

"So…it really might have been him."

"Yeah," he said hoarsely.

"How could police back then not *know*?"

"Because he hadn't molested either daughter yet."

Tess somehow radiated compassion and worry both. "Do you think Sheila was…well…his first? That he'd somehow kept himself from touching his own daughters even though he was thinking about sex with children?"

Zach shook his head. "I don't know. What she told me doesn't entirely fit. He went for his daughters when they were entering puberty. Almost twelve years old for both. Sheila was half that age. If he liked girls when they were that young, why didn't he start in on his own two way earlier?"

"Because...what he did to Sheila shocked him?"

"Maybe." He didn't like the doubt he was feeling, but couldn't deny it, either. "It's also possible Andrea lied. She might not want to admit even to herself how long it had been going on." But he remembered Nolte saying he'd talked to her teacher and the school counselor, and had gotten no vibes whatsoever to suggest she was being molested. "Or her sister lied."

"You didn't get the mother's phone number, did you?" Tess asked.

"No, she flipped out. Maybe the stepfather doesn't know the history?"

"Or...there's something she doesn't want her mother telling you," Tess said slowly.

He mulled that over. "I don't know."

"Are you going to call the sister?"

"Yeah, although what do you want to bet big sister is already on the phone with her? Which will mean Shelby won't answer."

"Probably," Tess agreed. She watched him brood for a minute then patted the cushion beside her. "Do you want to come over here?"

"Yeah." He cleared his voice. "I would."

Sunday, after talking to his mother, he had come perilously close to telling Tess that he needed her. Somehow he'd kept the words to himself. Close to saying the same thing now, he held back again. Admitting as much even to himself still scared him.

To think he'd always considered himself even-tempered, not given to a lot of emotion. Maybe in returning to his hometown he had opened his own Pandora's box.

Most of the consequences so far had been unintentional but powerful: meeting Tess, opening a schism in the sheriff's department, coming face-to-face with his long-lost brother.

Now, he might have severed the bonds between him and his mother, who, despite his complicated feelings for her, had been his only remaining family. Tonight, he'd upset a nice woman who might have tucked her memories of sexual abuse safely away until he had prodded them to life again. He was obviously pissing people off at the city police department as well as the county sheriff's department.

I'm a man of talent, he thought wryly.

Of course, if he hadn't come back to town, Tess might have been the only witness to Hayes beating Alvarez to death. Would she have been believed? He didn't like thinking about how much more vulnerable she'd have been to threats if she'd stood alone.

So, unlike Pandora, he'd released some good along with the bad. He seemed to have a brother again. And he had Tess.

Short term, remember?

"SAM DOYLE," THE MAN on the porch said, beaming. He held a clipboard tucked under his arm. "We Care Plumbing. Are you Mr. Carter?"

Oh, yeah, this was him. Still handsome and sporting a goatee. *Which Mom would like.* Dark hair with a little silver at the temples. Lean but solid instead of thin and lanky. Zach's gaze dropped to the wedding ring on his finger.

"I am." Zach let him in but didn't start for the bathroom. "Formerly Zach Murphy. You did a plumbing repair on my parents' house, if I remember correctly."

Doyle's smile fell away and alarm flickered in his gray eyes. He wrinkled his brow, as if searching his memory. "Uh, Murphy. Do they live here in town? I can't seem to recall..."

"I think you do. I'm betting you remember Gayle Murphy with no trouble at all."

The guy had the guts to stand his ground. "What's this about?" he asked.

"This is about my sister's murder and the fact that you'd been around our house a lot by then. Could be my mother even gave you a key."

Doyle's jaw tightened. "No, she didn't. And the only time I ever remember seeing your sister was when I came out to fix that leak."

"But you came back, didn't you?"

To his credit, he held Zach's gaze. "I'm not proud of it, but, yes, I did."

"What did she do, ask you to tea?"

"She set me up, just like you did this morning. Called and asked for me, said she and your dad were thinking about adding another bathroom. They'd been impressed with my competence. And then she came on to me."

Zach stared at him, unblinking.

"I was a twenty-one-year-old kid! Flattered. It scared me a little, thinking she might want to leave your dad for me. I still lived at home," he said, his mouth twisting at the memory of his own immaturity. "But, Gayle…she was like a fairy princess. The most beautiful thing I'd ever seen." His voice was heavy.

Zach's long-held anger deserted him just like that. When he was that age, would he have said no to a beautiful older woman just because she was married? Of course not. Her marriage was her business, he'd have figured. At some point he'd gotten a little more particular, but at twenty-one?

What Mom and Sam Doyle did in bed wasn't the point here.

"What about Sheila? Did she look like a fairy princess, too?" he asked.

"Your sister? Like I said, the only time I ever saw her was that night when the pipes in your house sprang a leak. If not for what happened, I wouldn't even be able to picture her. All I remember is that there were some kids and one of 'em had red hair. Guess that wasn't you."

"My older brother."

He nodded, but his eyes were unfocused, as if he wasn't seeing Zach standing in front of him anymore. "Then I read about what happened to that little girl. I'd, uh, been with your mom only the day before. That made it worse. It got all tangled up in my head. I couldn't figure out why God would have hurt your sister if it was me and your mom He was mad at." His Adam's apple bobbed. "She never called me again, you know."

He was seeing Zach now, pain in his eyes. "I wouldn't have come if she had," he concluded with a simple honesty Zach had to believe.

"You're married?" he asked.

"Yeah. I told Marianne about Gayle and about the worst tragedy this town has ever seen. She's a good person, Marianne is." Doyle shook his head. "I'm sorry for what happened to your family, Mr. Carter."

"Were you aware of whether my mother had other lovers while you were seeing her?" Zach asked.

The man's cheeks heated. "I was only sleeping with her for a couple weeks. Don't know when she'd have had time. Most days we, uh, got together during my lunch break."

"You should know I'm a cop. A deputy with the sheriff's department." Zach made his voice hard. "If you've ever been accused of molesting young girls, or even touching one in a suspicious way, I'll find out."

Clearly affronted, Doyle straightened. "Look all you want. I would never do anything like that. It's disgusting! I have a daughter myself. If some man had ever even *looked* at her that way—" He broke off, breathing hard.

Zach nodded. "I appreciate you talking to me. You have every reason to be mad I got you here under false pretenses."

"Why did you?" He seemed honestly puzzled. "Why didn't you just call to ask me your questions?"

"Most people I want to talk to are dodging me."

"They might have something to hide, but I don't." He raised his eyebrows. "Are we done?"

Some strange impulse seized Zach. "It so happens, I do need a plumber. I understand if you don't want to give me a bid, under the circumstances."

Sam Doyle actually chuckled. "I have a boy in college and a girl who is a senior in high school and has already been accepted to Pacific Lutheran University. Do you know what four years of college costs these days? Got to tell you, what

I couldn't turn down at twenty-one and what I can't turn down now are two different things."

What could Zach do but laugh and lead the way to the bathroom, bare but for corroded pipes?

GREG HAD LEFT for a quick lunch and then on to take measurements for carpet and vinyl installations at a couple different houses, leaving Tess alone for what she'd known would be a good part of the afternoon.

She smiled and called, "Thanks for stopping by," when a couple who'd been studying blinds left at two-thirty. She felt barely a flicker of apprehension at being alone in the store. Except for the creepy photograph left in Zach's mailbox at work, it had been several weeks since she'd so much as had a phone threat.

Given the down time, she wandered the store to study some of the new carpets and vinyl flooring Greg had added. She had to be familiar with all the stock, just as he did.

The bell tinkled when the front door opened and she turned. The happiness she felt when she glimpsed an olive-green uniform was immediately supplanted by apprehension. Something had to be wrong. Why else would Zach stop by in the middle of the afternoon without calling first?

And then she saw that the deputy who had entered wasn't Zach. She didn't recognize this man.

He wasn't any of the cops who'd helped on the roofing party, Tess was sure.

Despite her sudden wariness, she smiled. "May I help you?"

"I'll just look around for a minute," he said, and prowled toward the back of the store.

It wasn't his fault, of course, but he reminded her unpleasantly of Andrew Hayes. He looked as though he spent a lot of time lifting weights to build those muscles and thicken his neck, and his head was nearly shaved. She couldn't help noticing that he wasn't really checking out any of the flooring samples and he hadn't even glanced at the blinds. Most people who came in the store wanted to touch. To feel the nap of carpets or the texture of tiles or vinyl flooring. They smoothed their fingers over planks of hardwood.

Tess grew more and more uneasy as he peered into the nook where tiles were displayed and then the room with wallpaper books. He disappeared briefly from sight and she heard a door opening and closing. Was he using the restroom?

No, because he came into sight again, sauntering toward her. He must have opened the door just to find out whether anyone was in there. He'd quit making any pretense of glancing around.

She moved a few steps closer to the front of the store and the big picture windows. No pedestrians were in sight.

The cop raked her with his gaze as he approached. She fought the instinct to back up even when he stepped a lot closer than she was comfortable with.

"Alone in here, are you, *Ms*. Granath?"

"Momentarily." She raised her eyebrows. "I take it you're not interested in new flooring."

He sneered. "Just wanted to see what a woman willing to lie to get a good cop in trouble looks like."

Fortified by anger, she slowly, insolently, crossed her arms. It gave her some pleasure that, despite this paramilitary creep's bulk, their eyes were level. He might have more muscle than her, but he wasn't any taller. She strove to sound confused. "I know some good cops, but I haven't gotten any of them in trouble."

He bared his teeth and leaned in. "You know who I'm talking about, bitch. What, were you spreading your legs for that *chico*?"

She rolled her eyes. Really? Was that the best he could come up with as a slur, calling Antonio a little boy? Or was he being considerate in deference to her feminine sensibilities? Yeah, probably not.

"Am I meant to be insulted? If so, it didn't work. Antonio seemed like a pleasant man. Obviously, Andrew Hayes's girlfriend agreed with me." She stuck out her chin, matching the creep's body language. "I'm hoping she didn't realize her boyfriend was so crazy, he'd kill a man just because he dared talk to her."

"Well, here's something to think about." He stepped back. "Watch yourself when you're out on county roads. You end up in a head-on collision? We're going to be *real* slow bringing the jaws of life to pull you out." He shook his head. "Got to give a little to get a little, *Ms*. Granath."

He turned and walked away. The bell attached to the top of the door rang and he was gone.

Her anger swirled and disappeared down the drain, taking all her starch with it. Tess discovered her knees were knocking and her legs felt like Jell-O. With a whimper, she sank onto a heap of carpet samples, where she did nothing but tremble for several minutes.

Not until her hand had quit shaking did she reach for her phone.

"WHAT DO YOU mean you didn't see a name?" Zach scowled at her over the dinner table. "It should have been right here." He tapped his T-shirt right where the nameplate would presumably have been pinned on a uniform shirt.

"I looked. He must have taken it off."

"Describe him again."

He was mad that she'd called Detective Easley instead of him. And, since Easley apparently didn't work on Mondays, all she'd done was leave a voice mail. As she had repeatedly pointed out to

Zach, the man today hadn't committed a crime. He hadn't even threatened to come after her. All he'd said was that she wouldn't get very good service from the sheriff's department. Knowing it would make him even more furious, she hadn't repeated the jaws-of-life reference, only saying that they wouldn't hurry to help if she were to be in an accident, and Zach himself had once said the same.

Now she patiently did her best to describe the deputy again. The lack of distinguishing features clearly annoyed Zach all over again.

"That could be anyone," he grumbled when she was done.

"The shaved head isn't that common, is it?"

"Half the younger guys go for that look."

"You won't, will you?" Tess wrinkled her nose. "It's kind of creepy."

He ran his hand through his hair as if for reassurance. "No."

She tried a tentative smile. "You wouldn't be able to pull it when you're frustrated."

His look said he was not amused. "Brown eyes. You're sure?"

"Or a brownish hazel."

He grunted. "Call me next time, okay?"

Tess refrained from rolling her eyes. "I will, but what could you have done?"

"Hung around until Greg got back."

She managed to coax him into telling her about

his day. He was expecting three bids on the job of replumbing his house, and had stripped and sanded the molding in two of the bedrooms. He'd pretty well ruled Sam Doyle out as his sister's killer, although he seemed embarrassed when he admitted that he had offered him the chance to bid on the job.

"He actually seemed like an okay guy," he finally admitted.

When she rose to start clearing the table, Zach took the dirty dishes from her hands. "You worked today, I didn't."

"But you cooked," she protested. Hamburgers, potato salad and green beans.

"You deserve to relax."

Tess laughed and kissed his stubbly cheek. "You're more worked up than I am."

His scowl returned. "Why weren't you scared?"

"I got mad," she said. "Only after he left did I realize I was scared, too. But… I don't know." She took a moment to analyze her reaction. "His voice wasn't familiar. Plus, this didn't feel like the other threats. I could be wrong, but my guess is this guy was just expressing his support for a fellow deputy. I don't think he was part of the earlier threats or slashing my tires. I mean, if he was, would he really show his face? And go with such a *weak* threat? 'If you get in an accident on a county road, you can't count on us.' That's kind of underwhelming."

"Also an offense that could get him fired if Stokes identifies him." Zach sounded a lot more grim than she felt. He went into the kitchen with the dirty dishes.

She trailed him as far as the doorway. "Will you report it?"

He swung to face her. "Hell, yes!"

She might have objected, except she couldn't forget the way the deputy had checked out every corner of the store to be sure she was alone. He'd used her vulnerability *because* she'd been alone as an implied threat.

She retreated from the doorway as Zach went back to the dining room to finish clearing the table, then decided to take him up on his offer. She'd done more than her share of meals and dishes this week.

Not in the mood to work, she took her book from her purse and went to the living room, turning on the lamp beside the sofa. Dusk purpled the sky. Comfortably ensconced, she thought about getting up and closing the blinds, but she'd been enjoying looking out at her garden earlier. The roses needed deadheading—

Out of the corner of her eye she caught movement outside. She turned her head sharply. A big, dark shape stood on her small front lawn.

Instinct brought her to her feet. "Zach?"

Oh, God—it was a man. She was sure it was—

only he didn't have a face. And he was swinging something. What—?

The window shattered and something shot past her, close enough she felt the wind. It smacked into a framed watercolor on the far wall, making glass explode again.

Screaming, she dropped to the floor and covered her head.

CHAPTER FIFTEEN

IT WAS DAMN near killing Zach to see the stress on Tess's face. Although if she tried to hide it, that might be worse.

Detective Easley had come to talk to them, as had Detectives MacLachlan and Clayton from the SIU.

They'd found a softball on her living room floor. A piece of paper bearing another threat had been wrapped around it with rubber bands. Zach still shuddered, knowing how close it had come to Tess's head. He had a feeling it had been intended to hit her.

God help him, when he'd heard the window break—

He inhaled a ragged breath. Tess could have been shot. He'd had a brief vision of a Molotov cocktail exploding at her feet.

Instead it had been one more effort to terrify her.

He'd taken a moment to be sure she was okay then torn out the front door, running full-out. Unfortunately he'd been close to a block behind the man by the time he made it out to the street.

The man had leaped into a dark SUV; tires had squealed as it accelerated. The light had been too dim for Zach to make out the license plate number.

The first responder had taken the softball and the note wrapped around it into custody. Within twenty-four hours Easley reported the lack of any useable fingerprints.

The surveillance cameras? Useless because he hadn't put one on the front of the house. He'd been so damn sure they wouldn't risk being seen by a neighbor.

He'd have felt worse, except Tess insisted the guy had worn a dark ski mask or had pulled a shirt up over his lower face and a hood down over his forehead. Something to disguise his face.

The couple days since then had sucked, in Zach's view. He didn't like leaving Tess potentially unprotected because he had to go to work every day. He did his job, but worried he might be distracted and screw up. The two of them had made love every night with a kind of ferocity, stunning in its intensity, but he didn't like knowing what was behind her desperation and the way she clung to him afterward.

Driving into her garage on Thursday evening, he wished like hell it was Saturday. It felt as though it should be.

He was reaching for the remote to close the garage door when he saw in the rearview mirror that another car had pulled in behind him on the driveway. He turned to look at the gold Toyota Camry. Not the newest model, but only a few years old.

Instead of closing the garage door, Zach got out of his pickup and went to meet the older man who had climbed out of the Camry. One good look and Zach thought, Oh, hell. The guy was tall, thin, mostly gray, with a mouth that drooped a little on one side. And he had Tess's eyes.

"Mr. Granath," Zach said resignedly.

"Deputy Carter." The faintest slur softened his consonants.

"Uh, yeah." He held out his hand, because what else could he do? "It's good to meet you."

Tess's father cocked one eyebrow, either because that's what he did or because the muscles on the other side of his face didn't work right. "Interesting to find you here," he said.

Zach winced. "I guess Tess hasn't told you." Thank God the front window had been replaced yesterday, he reflected, since he didn't know how much Tess *was* telling her father.

The front door opened and Tess appeared on the porch. Her gaze flew to Zach's. "Dad!" she said brightly. "I didn't expect you."

"Only way I can find out what's going on," he muttered.

Zach went in through the garage to give father and daughter a minute to themselves. Once inside, he endured an awkward introduction that neither man needed.

Finally, Tess threw up her hands. “Zach is staying here because of all the stuff that’s been happening, okay?”

And because he was sleeping with her. But, hey… He kept his mouth shut.

Dinner was already on and she made it stretch for three. While they ate, Mr. Granath extracted most of the story from Tess with strategic silences, that skeptical, raised eyebrow and some inspired guesses. Zach admired his interview skills, although he didn’t enjoy having them turned on him.

On the whole, however, he decided he liked her father, who accepted the appearance of a previously unannounced live-in boyfriend better than he might have.

Nevertheless, Zach was relieved when he left.

Tess stumbled all over herself apologizing, which annoyed him.

“It was bound to happen.”

“Yes, but I know you didn’t want—”

“Tess, it’s no big deal,” he said with a little more bite. “You told him I’m here to keep you safe. What father is going to object to that?”

“Yes, but I didn’t mean—”

“Drop it.” If he sounded testy, that’s because he was. He was glad to be able to turn on a Mariner game and pretend he gave a damn.

Friday night he suggested they go out for dinner and maybe see a movie. Getting away from the house would be good for her. He vetoed the thriller she suggested, on the grounds that it struck a little too close to home, so they went for a comedy that had them laughing enough to loosen him up.

Her, too, he decided as he held her close to his side through the exiting crowd. Her cheeks were pink and she tucked her hand into the back pocket of his jeans as they crossed the parking lot.

"Well, look who's here," said a man behind them.

Zach shot to instant readiness as he turned, nudging Tess to a position half behind him. Crap—it was Hayes with a woman and another couple. If he had to guess, the other man was the brother. There was some resemblance.

"Hayes."

The other deputy's expression was ugly. "Both witnesses, looking real cozy," he sneered. "Do those *special* investigators know how friendly you two are?"

"Being threatened has been a great bonding experience." Zach switched his gaze briefly to the woman, whose head was bent so she didn't have to meet his eyes. At least she was capable of some shame.

Hayes grinned. "Threatened? I don't know what you're talking about. What d'ye say, Tyler? You heard any threats?"

His brother guffawed. "Not me. Something got you scared, Carter?"

"Scared? No. Just a little irritated. But, you know—" He shrugged. "I don't have to worry about it, because the special investigators seem pretty competent to me. Detective Easley with CCPD, too." He let his gaze rest on Hayes. "They'll catch whoever is doing it."

Hayes pushed his girlfriend away and took a step toward Zach, his hands curling into fists. "You think you're hot shit, but you're nothin'. You hear me? You got Stokes mouthing crap he doesn't mean, but the rank and file, they're behind me. Sure as hell, nobody will ever call *you* for backup. I got a right to defend myself and my girl, too. Neither of you saw that stupid Mexican go for my gun."

Zach only shook his head. "Didn't know your girl was there and needed defending," he said mildly.

Tess tugged urgently at his pocket. And she was right. It was time to wind this up.

"Now, if you'll excuse us?" He nodded. "Enjoy your movie."

Hayes's mean eyes narrowed. "Run along. Your time will come."

Zach tensed. "Guess you know how to issue threats, after all."

Hayes took a step closer, his girlfriend obviously reluctant at being dragged along. "When I threaten you, you'll know, asshole."

Zach nodded politely then took a chance and turned his back, steering Tess to his pickup. He unlocked it with the remote before glancing back to see the four walking toward the theater. An angry voice carried across the lot. Easy to guess which of the two men was mad.

Neither he nor Tess said a word until they were locked in the cab of the pickup. Then she expelled a breath.

"Well. Stay in, go out—end result is pretty much the same."

"We can't get away from it, can we?" His hand was steady when he started the engine, but inside he was at a full, roiling boil. What had he been thinking, going unarmed tonight? What if Hayes and his brother had attacked him and Tess?

Last time I go anywhere without my backup piece, he vowed.

"Could have been worse," he said after a minute. "What if we'd known they were sitting two rows behind us throughout the movie?"

"I think I'd have suggested we change theaters. Some blood and gore on the screen might have seemed way more appealing."

Surprising himself, Zach laughed.

ZACH DOGGEDLY MADE time to keep digging into Sheila's murder despite everything else going on.

Maybe, if he was honest with himself, *because* of everything else.

He hated being excluded from the ongoing investigation into Alvarez's death. Being out of the loop so he didn't know what, if anything, the detectives had learned, grated at him.

And then there was Tess. If he hadn't already discovered the limitations of his ability to protect her, the softball whistling by within an inch of her head had been an eye opener. Now he had to add the confrontation in the parking lot, with him stupidly having gone unarmed.

Too much was happening that left him feeling helpless and he detested it.

At least, by God, he was making progress toward finding Sheila's killer. He already knew considerably more than the detectives at the time had.

Shelby Womack finally took one of his phone calls, but only to insist he leave their mother out of this. Then she'd hung up on him.

He and Bran were talking regularly. Bran shared what he'd learned from a couple of their father's other friends. He'd set out to determine whether they might be possible suspects, as well as to pick up more names of anyone who might have been around the Murphy household back then.

What Zach couldn't figure out was why Bran was helping when he hadn't tried very hard in all these years to find Sheila's killer. Zach wanted to feel a brotherly accord. Sometimes he actually did. But then a niggle of suspicion would surface. What if Bran had taken on Dad's friends as part of an effort to steer Zach *away* from Dad?

What if he hadn't investigated because the killer's identity wasn't a mystery to him?

Zach instinctively rejected that option. Bran might have a suspicion he didn't want to acknowledge. But if he'd *known* Dad was guilty, he wouldn't still be defending him. Zach didn't doubt Bran had loved Sheila too much to close his eyes to that.

Tess surprised him a little when she suggested they invite his brother and Paige to dinner on Sunday night. He'd had the impression she didn't much like Bran, although she hadn't said as much. She had obviously guessed that Zach hadn't been seeing his brother in his off hours because he didn't want to leave her alone.

Bran accepted for himself, but said Paige had plans with a girlfriend that weekend. While they were on the phone, he listened in silence to the latest about Zach's conversation with Shelby Womack and to the update that Zach had found the record of Sylvia Womack's remarriage and change of name. She and the new husband lived in Mount Vernon, midway between Everett and Bellingham, where her daughters lived.

Tess spent the day at the store Saturday. Zach picked her up after work, with the plan being that they'd eat out after he talked to the former Mrs. Womack—if he got lucky and caught her at home. He had decided he wanted to see her face when he asked his questions.

He'd had time to change quickly, so he wasn't in uniform when he rang the doorbell of a nice older home on the hill in Mount Vernon. He didn't like leaving Tess in the truck, but he was confident they hadn't been followed and she'd promised, cross her heart, to lean on the horn if she saw anything worrisome at all.

An attractive woman with short, stylish dark hair opened the door. Zach recognized her from her driver's license picture.

"Mrs. Needham? My name is Zach Carter."

Her expression didn't change, which either meant she was a hell of an actor or that neither daughter had told her about his calls.

"Your ex-husband handled my parents' insurance." He paused. "Their names were Michael and Gayle Murphy. I imagine you remember my sister's murder."

She looked startled. "Of course, I do! Oh, my. You're one of the Murphy boys? But didn't you say your last name is Carter?"

He explained and asked if she would speak to him about her ex-husband.

Finally wary, she said, "I don't understand."

"I'm a police officer, Mrs. Needham, as is my brother. I imagine we were both influenced in our choice of career by what happened. I recently moved back to the area, and he and I have joined forces to look into Sheila's death. Detective Nolte, who I believe spoke to you back then, mentioned your husband's name to me."

Her fingers tightened on the door. He could see her giving thought to closing it in his face.

"I'm hoping," he said quietly, "that you won't feel you owe him any loyalty."

Her mouth thinned. "I do not." Indecision held her for another minute before she sighed. "Is that your wife in the truck? She's welcome to come in instead of sitting out here."

"I thought you might be more comfortable answering my questions without any additional audience."

She studied him, probably trying to determine how trustworthy he was, then nodded. "Very well."

She led him to a living room with elegant, brocaded sofa and chairs, Persian rugs over gleaming hardwood floors and dainty side tables with Queen Anne feet. He had a feeling this room was for show, not daily use.

She sat in a wing-backed chair, her posture very straight, her hands folded on her lap. "I wasn't aware that Duane's name had ever come up during that investigation. Why on earth would it?"

Here's where it got awkward. If she didn't

know her husband had cheated on her with Zach's mother, did he have to tell her? She was already having to live with far more damaging knowledge of her ex.

"The investigators spoke to as many people as possible who'd had occasion to be out at the house," he said diplomatically. "I am retracing their steps and widening the investigation. In trying to track down Duane, I reached your daughter, Andrea."

Her expression changed.

"She told me that her father had molested both her and her younger sister. That…caught my attention, since Sheila was raped."

"Oh, no," she whispered. "I never knew that."

"My parents might have wanted to keep it from me, too, but I found her body."

"I'm so very sorry," she murmured. "And I do see why you're asking about Duane, but I can assure you it couldn't have been him."

"Detective Nolte told me you'd said he was home in bed with you every night."

She blinked at that. "I vaguely remember him saying something in passing about seeing Duane out late at night. I thought it was odd." Her cheeks turned pink and she wrung her hands. "If he'd asked me directly for…well…an alibi for Duane, I would have told him the truth. But it wasn't information I was volunteering to anyone."

He waited, certain she meant to tell him.

"We were having some marital difficulties, you see," she said with apparent difficulty. "I had begun to suspect there was another woman because—" Her blush deepened. "Well, we weren't having relations. At all. I even wondered if he was gay and couldn't tell me.

"Eventually he did admit to having cheated on me, although I never found out with whom. Of course, I had no idea then of his perverted tastes… If he preyed on other young girls, I'm not sure I want to know. I hate him enough already."

"I understand," Zach said gently.

"What I'm leading up to is that he agreed to attend a church retreat with me. The focus was on strengthening marriages. It was that weekend, at a small resort on Guemes Island. My sister kept the girls so we could go. You probably know how limited the ferry service is to Guemes. But even if that wasn't true…there is simply no way he could have left without my knowing."

Zach was dumbfounded enough to recognize that, in his eagerness, he'd reasoned ahead of the facts; something he knew better than to do.

It shouldn't be a surprise that Duane Womack wasn't the only pedophile who had had something to do with the Murphy family. Yet, despite knowing Duane's taste for girls entering puberty, Zach had still let himself believe he had found his man.

He made a last-ditch effort. "It's been a lot of years. You're certain it was the same weekend?"

"Yes. We were on the ferry when Duane turned on the car radio to the news and we heard about the murder. We were both so shocked. He told me your parents were among his clients and what a nice family you seemed to be."

"I see." He smiled crookedly. "Then I can only apologize for asking questions that must remind you of times you'd rather forget."

She rose when he did. "But you had to ask." At the door she squeezed his hand. "I hope you do find the man who did that. The very idea that he got away with it!" Her ferocity reminded him that she knew quite well who had hurt her daughters, and that she, too, lived with the knowledge she'd failed to protect them.

He thanked her and, feeling curiously numb, went to the truck, aware of Tess watching. She unlocked the door and he got in, sitting there for a minute and staring straight ahead.

Finally he made himself tell her. "It wasn't him."

"What did she say?"

Zach repeated the gist.

Tess listened, little lines creasing her forehead.

"Well," she said sturdily, "that's one more name you can cross off your list."

He nodded. "This is how investigations go. You find a promising lead and then it doesn't pan out. You back up and try another route."

When he still didn't move, Tess asked, "Are you okay?"

Honestly? He didn't know. Numb wasn't quite right for what he felt. A sense of failure? Maybe. He'd told Tess the truth—this *was* standard in an investigation. But this wasn't a standard investigation, not when the victim was his sister.

He made himself fire up the engine, even as his frustration built, filling him until there was no room left. Man, he hated dealing with so many emotions he hardly understood. It was like getting punched over and over, never knowing where the next blow was coming from. He was reeling from this latest one.

But sometime in the silent drive back downtown, Zach formed a resolve that hardened until it felt like a rough-sided chunk of cement in his chest.

It was past time Bran admitted what he knew instead of playing along for his own reasons. Time they found out what being brothers actually meant.

Wasn't it convenient, Zach thought, that he'd be seeing Bran tomorrow?

THE NEXT EVENING Tess insisted on cleaning up after dinner to give the two men time to talk. Conversation over the meal had been labored, probably in part thanks to her presence. Truthfully, she didn't yet feel comfortable with Bran and had been disappointed that Paige wouldn't be accompanying him. Without help from another woman, her every effort at being chatty had dwindled into an awkward silence.

Zach was being unnaturally quiet and, as far as she could tell, his brother was not a real outgoing guy. Or maybe some underlying tension between the brothers spilled over into everything that was said and unsaid. She didn't know, but once they'd finished their pie, she'd had enough.

She had just turned off the water with the intention of leaving the casserole dish to soak when she heard Zach's voice from the living room, raised in what sounded like anger.

"You expect me to believe that?"

Clutching the hand towel, Tess stood utterly still. Did she want to intervene? Or should she flee into the backyard?

But—what a shock—she was too nosy to do either. She sidled toward the living room, stopping just out of sight of the two men.

I'll listen only long enough to find out what's wrong, she told herself. Okay, justified to herself.

"Believe what you want." Bran's cool voice had chilled.

"So you completely lacked curiosity. You never once said, 'Hey, Dad, did *you* suspect anyone'?"

"You think he wouldn't have told the police? Get real."

"I think you're a police detective, which makes

it a real oddity that you never looked at her killing as a cold case. I mean, here you are, right in town. Just didn't occur to you, huh?"

A protracted silence ratcheted up Tess's worry. But there were no thuds or grunts, so they weren't going at it physically. What were they doing, glaring daggers at each other?

"I was…trying to honor what I thought Dad wanted," Bran said, his voice altered almost beyond recognition. It was slow and heavy. "I think he was afraid—" He stopped.

"Of what? That if the lid came off the can, the cops would be looking at him again?"

I shouldn't be listening, she thought, but her feet didn't move.

"That it was one of Mom's bed buddies!" Bran yelled. "That he'd be humiliated if it got out, that she'd be destroyed if she understood it was her fault Sheila died! Don't you get it? He loved her even after everything."

Heart pounding, Tess began backing away. But then she did hear a thud, as if one of the men had thrown something.

"Oh, screw this!" It was Bran again, sounding enraged. "You're on a vendetta against Dad, aren't you? Why have I been bothering to help? Believing in Dad would mean you have to admit how bad *you* screwed up. And you can't do that, can you?" He spat out an obscenity. Moments later the front door opened and slammed closed.

Tess scuttled back to the kitchen and turned on the faucet as if she was just finishing up. But when Zach didn't come to the kitchen, she couldn't stand it another minute.

"Zach?" she called.

There was no answer.

She went to the living room but found it empty. Bedroom? Bathroom? He wasn't anywhere.

Oh, heavens—had he followed Bran out?

Tess hurried to the front door and flung it open, expecting the worst, but Bran's Camaro was gone and she didn't see Zach, either. She called his name softly and was answered by silence.

Had he followed Bran and the two had agreed to go to a bar or something? He'd have told her, wouldn't he? And…the front door had been unlocked. *He* had left it unlocked after all his lectures to her.

Her disquiet grew until her stomach cramped.

The man she knew was passionate, yes, but also strong, determined, calm under stress. He'd been a rock for her. And now he was either crumbling or—

Looking out at the empty front yard and the dark street and sidewalk, she thought back to their past few days. Her terrified awareness of the faceless figure out front, followed by a missile exploding through the front window. Zach yelling, racing after Hayes or whoever it had been. Then the scene after the movie the very next night.

She had tried to joke about it. Now Tess's heart cramped at the memory of what he'd said, and of his oddly distant, resigned tone.

We can't get away from it, can we?

Maybe his mood didn't have anything to do with finding out his cold case investigation had to move on from Duane Womack. Maybe what was really getting to him was his forced realization that his role of protector wasn't going to be as short-lived as he'd imagined.

If being stuck with her had begun to chafe, it was no wonder his temper was short.

And, no, she would not let herself cry. She might be totally wrong about what was going on with him. And if she wasn't? Well…he'd done a lot for her, but he hadn't promised to grow old with her.

She could only pray he didn't suspect how she felt about him.

Suddenly aware of how frighteningly vulnerable she was standing there in plain sight of anyone, Tess hastily retreated inside, closed the door and turned the dead bolt.

She didn't exactly look forward to letting him back in.

CHAPTER SIXTEEN

"SO, WHAT DID you do today?" Tess asked as she spread the napkin on her lap. As conversational openers went, it wasn't brilliant, but she was scraping the bottom of the barrel here.

It was the next day and she had come home from work to find Zach's truck already in the garage. The moment she'd stepped in the house she'd smelled dinner cooking and saw that his hair was damp from a shower.

Zach glanced at her. "Doyle stopped by and I gave him a key. He says they can start Wednesday or Thursday."

"Are you having him go ahead and plumb the second bathroom upstairs while he's there?"

"Yeah. That'll be the most time-consuming part of the job." He shrugged. "I bought new windows. Today I replaced about half of them. Picked up paint samples, too."

"For the exterior?"

He nodded. "I can see a few clapboards that need replacing, but most are in good shape. I might be able to do that work and paint next weekend. How was your day?"

Apparently he was going to make an effort. They were on a roll.

"Truthfully, pretty boring," Tess said. "Greg and I have talked off and on about closing on Monday as well as Sunday. I think I'm going to push for us to do it. More often than not, we both end up working six days a week and I'm tired of it. Mondays are the slowest for us, and I have to believe people will come a different day instead of going to a competitor." She made a face. "Anyway. I filled my day browsing manufacturer's catalogs and chatting with a few people I know aren't ready to actually buy yet. If ever. They just like to dream."

And don't we all, she thought wryly.

"So you were alone a lot."

"More than sometimes," she admitted, waiting for him to grumble. When he didn't, she decided to tiptoe into what had become a delicate subject. "Did you think any today about where to go with your investigation?"

He took a bite, his expression not changing. "No."

O-ka-ay. Tess wasn't about to push it. She nodded and continued eating. Let *him* make a stab at conversation.

"Tess… About last night."

On any topic but this one.

"Forget about it." She pushed back from the table. "I'll put coffee on."

Zach hadn't moved when she eventually returned. It didn't look as if he'd even taken another bite. "I'm sorry," he said.

"You already apologized. That's enough."

Turbulent blue eyes met hers. "It was inexcusable."

"We all go off the rails once in a while. Now, can we not talk about it?"

He'd been gone an hour and a half last night. He had taken a long walk, he said, which she'd had no reason to doubt. And, yes, he'd had to ring the doorbell. When she'd let him in, he had been gasping for breath. "I suddenly realized—" puff, puff, puff "—that I didn't remember locking."

"*Or* mentioning that you were going out."

"God, Tess. I'm sorry."

"I'd have reason to complain if I were paying you for twenty-four-seven bodyguard services." Sounding composed had taken some serious effort. "Now, if you don't mind, I'm going to bed. Please lock up behind you."

When he had appeared in the bedroom a short while later she'd kept her back to him, hoping he couldn't tell her whole body was rigid.

He'd been smart enough not to reach for her.

This morning they had both gone about getting ready for the day without exchanging more than a few words. "Excuse me."

"Would you like scrambled eggs if I make some?"

"No, thank you."

That made her, and probably him, too, feel exceedingly awkward this evening.

She went back to the kitchen to pour the coffee then cleared the table as he watched, brooding.

Once the dishwasher was loaded, she retreated to the living room and turned on the TV instead of returning to the table where he still sat. There had to be something worthwhile on, she thought desperately. She found "Antiques Roadshow" and settled down to watch—or, at least, to pretend to watch. Thank goodness the show filled the silence.

Zach stalked into the living room and tapped the power button on the TV, which went dark. He glowered at her. "Damn it, Tess, we have to talk about this."

"No, we really don't. You were mad at Bran, you needed to cool off."

"And I left your house wide open."

Fine, she thought. He wanted honesty? She'd be honest.

"Yes, you did." She met his gaze square-on. "I dropped from your radar. But I think I mostly dropped from it several days ago. It's been pretty clear to me that you want out of this protector gig." When he started to open his mouth, she shook her head fiercely. "Your feeling that way is understandable. This crap is going to go on and on and on. Maybe till death do us part."

He winced. It felt like a stiletto into her heart.

"It's not that." His fingers raked his already disheveled hair. He took a couple of paces away from the television then back. "I've just been hit by a lot lately."

He had, and she knew it, but her temper flared, too. There was a great excuse for hurting other people. Not.

"Haven't we all."

He snorted. "Your little sister wasn't murdered. You're not hitting one dead end after another, trying to figure out who did it."

"My father had a stroke and it's only a matter of time until he has another one. *You* have a mother."

He looked stung. "Do I? After I asked which of her screw buddies might have raped and murdered Sheila?"

"You have a brother, too," she said quietly. "One you'll lose if you keep on like this."

"Lose? I haven't had him since he chose Dad over me."

Tess blinked, shocked out of her hurt feelings. "Zach, you were boys. He wasn't choosing your father over you. He chose him over your mother."

"Bullshit!" He was breathing hard. "We could have stayed together."

This wasn't going anywhere good and Tess knew it was her fault as much as his. She'd been foolish enough to hope he could free himself from his past. She should have known better. Was it even possible?

"Has it occurred to you that maybe it *has* been too many years since she died?" she asked softly. "That you might not find her killer?"

"No." He sounded implacable. "Failure's not an option."

"Zach, you might fail. You have to know that." Once upon a time he'd admitted as much.

Now he stared incredulously at her. "You think I should quit. Is that it?"

"I didn't say that. But *you* need to wonder whether this hasn't become some kind of obsession."

The taut lines of his face told her how angry he was. "I'm looking for justice. It's my job!"

"But it's not your job." Saying all this might not be the right thing, but if his swings in mood and surliness had to do with his investigation and not her, it couldn't be healthy for him. "It's a…quest."

"I'm a detective." He took the few steps needed to bring him to the coffee table, only feet from where she sat. He loomed over her, glaring down. "I've spent years developing the know-how and skills to get to the point where I could nail the creep who killed my sister. And now you're saying…what? Let it go?"

"I don't know." Tess hugged herself.

"Well, I do. Nothing will stop me, including this shit with Hayes." His stare could have blistered her skin. "Do you understand?"

She shivered. "Yes. *I* certainly can't stop you."

"What are you asking? For a big gesture here to prove you're everything to me?"

"I'm not stupid enough to do that."

"Good," he snapped with another angry look, "because it's not happening. You know what this is about." A slashing gesture took her in. Her house. Her worth to him.

Tess's usual confidence deserted her and she shriveled inside. "I do now," she whispered.

"You expected more."

She lifted one shoulder. "I suppose I...hoped."

"I don't do relationships. I never have. I thought I'd made it clear." He paced, the words coming faster and faster. "I want to nail Sheila's killer and get out of this town. There's just too much—"

He stopped, shook his head. He seemed to be talking more to himself than to her. "And now I can't go even if I wanted to, because of you."

Somehow that felt like the final blow.

"Zach, I absolve you of responsibility for me. I am an adult. I knew the risks when I accused a police officer of murder. I don't even understand why you think it's your job to protect me. I don't live or work in your jurisdiction, so it's *not* your job."

"You're a woman alone."

"By choice." She had to get through this. She could fall apart when she actually was alone. "Zach, you need to leave."

He stopped, shock transforming his face. "What are you talking about?"

"You heard me. I want you to pack and go." She'd managed to say all that without a tremor in her voice, which was reason to be proud. "You're off the hook."

"I'm not leaving you by yourself."

"Yes. You are." *Show no weakness.* "I was willing to accept your help when it felt as if we were in this together. When I thought—" Tess swallowed, unable to finish, after all.

"Thought?"

She shook her head. "It doesn't matter. Let me repeat. You need to go."

How could he look so stunned when he'd been such a jerk? No—that was understating his behavior. He'd been purposely hurtful. Hoping she'd react exactly as she had and set him free?

Maybe.

"Tess."

She said nothing and didn't let her gaze waver.

"God." He shook his head, bewildered. "Yeah. Okay. I guess I was asking for it."

You think?

His usual athletic grace missing, he stumbled out of the room. Rigid, Tess listened to him go down the hall. The wait seemed longer than it probably was.

He reappeared with his black duffel bag slung

over his shoulder and paused in the kitchen doorway. "If I left anything..."

She nodded. She couldn't even look at him now, but her peripheral vision told her he hadn't moved.

"I didn't mean the things I said." His voice was husky, strained. "I've been...panicking."

Obviously.

"Goddamn it, Tess!"

"Please go." How many times did she have to say this?

He went. The door into the garage opened. A moment later she heard the deep rumble of his pickup starting and her garage door rising.

When it went back down, she realized she should have asked for the remote back so he wouldn't have access to her house.

But really, did it matter? She didn't need it and *he* wouldn't use it. Why would he, when he'd gotten what he'd secretly wanted? Because, yes, he'd be plagued with guilt. She knew him that well. But beneath it would be relief. Tess had no doubt at all that within a day he'd have worked his way around to blaming her for tonight's blow-up. So, okay, maybe he should have been more tactful, but she was the unreasonable one.

On her head be it, he'd think, frustrated and mad.

And he was right. The decision had been hers. He'd have stayed if she'd allowed him to, because he was a man of conscience who took what he perceived as his responsibilities seriously. Look at his utter determination to find justice for his little sister.

The first tears blurred Tess's vision. She'd never in her life felt so alone.

ZACH PARKED IN his garage but didn't get far when he emerged into the chill night. He mumbled an obscenity. With shocking suddenness, he felt all his uncertainty, fear, passion and rage escaping, as if he'd pulled a cork from a bottle. The duffel thudded to the ground and he flattened both hands on the rough side wall of the garage, bent his head and kept swearing. And, shit, he was crying. Everything he'd felt, too much, poured out of him. His knees gave way. His hands slid down the wall, stinging, until he knelt on the grass, sobbing for the first time since he was a child.

What did I do?

Exactly what he had meant to do, on some primitive level he didn't even pretend to understand. He loved her, and that terrified him, so he'd made *her* push him away. Because then it wasn't his fault?

But it was. All of it.

He heard her soft, ragged voice. *I suppose I... hoped.*

He could say he was sorry. He could...what? Promise her forever? To stay on in this town that had him tangled into emotional knots? The place where his life had been severed in two? Where he'd found Sheila so horrifically dead? Where he'd lost his family, the brother he loved, all faith in the forever he couldn't promise Tess?

However much I love her?

Where he'd been turned into a pathetic, sobbing bundle of uncontrollable emotion?

The sobs kept ripping through his chest, shaking his whole body. He couldn't seem to stop. He was breaking down, with no idea what would be left when he was done.

It was a long time before, dazed, he found himself lying flat on the grass he'd mowed just today with Tess's lawn mower.

His fingers gripped the grass and earth beneath it as if they were all that held him from falling into an abyss.

He kept breathing and finally made a head-to-toe assessment. Face wet, eyes swollen and burning hot. Fingertips and the fleshy pads at the base of his thumbs stinging.

Slivers from the garage wall, he decided.

His stomach muscles felt as though he'd done a few hundred sit-ups. Legs…weak. Feet…okay. Zach was vaguely surprised to find any part of him was okay.

He lay there for what had to be another ten minutes before he managed to push himself to his hands and knees then stagger to his feet. Pure willpower kept him going, had him stooping to grab his bag. He made it up the porch steps, the pungent scent of lumber and fresh stain in his nostrils. No surprise his hand shook when he struggled to put the key in the lock, but he managed that, too.

Inside, he didn't stop until he reached the bedroom, where he dropped the bag on the floor and collapsed onto his bed.

He rolled over and stared up at the ceiling, what little he could see of it with only diffused light from neighbors' homes and the distant streetlamp.

This what you wanted?

No. God help him, no.

Tess's house was home now. No, *she* was home.

This town could be, he realized, as long as he had her.

Took care of that chance, didn't you?

Yes. He thought of himself as a decent man, one who felt compassion, who was capable of kindness. The need to protect dominated his personality, for obvious reasons. And yet he was a man who hadn't felt much that was really personal in so many years he'd forgotten what it was like. He'd come back to Clear Creek to find Sheila's killer. Everything he'd found instead was unexpected.

His brother and all the tangled emotions that had come with the reunion.

Tess. Yeah, she'd blindsided him. Because he'd sensed from the beginning he could feel too much for her, he would have avoided her if it weren't for that overdeveloped need to protect. And now, it was too late.

He thought about that for a few minutes, feeling something ease inside him. No, he wouldn't travel back in time so that he wouldn't meet Tess, even if he could. She *was* everything to him.

Blew that, didn't you?

Sheila.

He'd been so damned sure of himself, he thought. Mighty detective who could find answers where no one else had been able to. What he'd never let himself examine were his reasons for *needing* those answers. Tess had called it an obsession, and he guessed his plan to come back someday and hunt down a murderer had been that.

But what he let himself understand for the first time was that he'd been trying to accomplish something else. Had he thought he could undo everything that had gone wrong? Prove the flaws in his family hadn't been to blame?

Or was Bran right? That what Zach had really wanted was to prove Dad was responsible, and therefore he'd made the right choice himself despite what he'd learned about his mother? And, hey, that would have meant Bran had made the wrong choice, not Zach.

So I could blame him *for my pain?*

Nobility in action.

He reached the point where he could sit up, feet on the floor, although he groaned getting there. Man, what he'd give for a hot shower, or even to be able to immerse himself in a bath.

A thought floated into his mind. Jacuzzi? Might be worth the extra bucks.

He dragged his fingers through his hair, imagining what it would look like when he went into work tomorrow morning. What *he'd* look like.

I have to fix things with Tess, he thought. That was central. He had to believe she would understand and forgive him.

The rift with Bran had been his fault. He could fix it, too. He had to. Tess was right. A little wryly, it occurred to Zach he must be in training to be a husband. But she *was* right more than wrong.

He did have a brother and a mother. He could mend his relationship with both. And, please God, with Tess.

Whom he'd left alone and unprotected.

And… Jesus. How much time had passed?

The numbers on his digital clock jolted him. He'd left her house two hours ago.

Slammed by fear, he pictured her huddled on the sofa where he'd left her. Or had she gone to take a shower? With it running, she wouldn't hear a window shatter.

Again.

If anyone had been watching the house, they'd

have seen him leave. The light in the garage came on automatically when the door rose. He'd backed out without so much as looking around.

Without thinking, he was moving, searching for his phone and keys. He wouldn't try to make his peace tonight, but he could park out front and watch her house.

Keep her safe.

FEELING SORRY FOR herself wasn't very productive. Tess emerged from a prolonged bout of self-pity thinking more clearly.

It took her a while, but she eventually worked herself around to believing that maybe the real truth was in what Zach had said at the end.

I didn't mean the things I said. I've been...panicking.

Until the past couple days, when he'd changed, he hadn't acted like a man staying with her only because he'd felt responsible for her security. He might not be in love with her, but Tess believed he cared. Maybe enough to spook him. Given his childhood and the example his mother had set, it would be no surprise if he didn't believe in love that could last a lifetime.

Was he capable of changing? She had no way of knowing. And, after tonight's scene, she couldn't exactly go after him. It was up to him now. All she could do was wait and hope.

Too bad she felt a little short on hope right now.

Even though it wasn't especially late, she was so exhausted it was hard to heave herself up from the sofa. She did go to the kitchen and make sure the door into the garage was locked. It was. *He didn't forget.*

She bumped into walls a couple of times as she made her way to her bedroom, turning out lights as she went.

A hot shower would feel really good, but took more energy than she could muster. Plus…she wouldn't be able to hear anyone coming. Like the first hint of an injected drug, fear trickled into her veins, but she couldn't succumb to it. Wouldn't. What was she going to do, call Zach and beg him to come back?

I could go to Dad's.

But she swayed where she stood, too tired for that much effort. Besides, if someone was watching the house, she'd be followed anyway. Her father didn't want to admit how much the stroke had stolen from him, but she wouldn't put him in the position of trying to protect her from a muscular, brutal, furious man like Andrew Hayes.

She made herself brush her teeth, trying not to look too closely at herself in the mirror. Blotchy skin and red, swollen eyes were so attractive.

Bed.

Hazily she thought, Won't answer the phone if it rings. Screw 'em. They can leave a message.

If anything else happened…it only took a couple seconds to dial 911.

She dropped like a rock into sleep.

TESS LURCHED TO a sitting position in bed, blinking. She wasn't awake enough to know what had alarmed her. Had her phone rung? No. She kept listening, but heard nothing.

Maybe just a nightmare.

Her eyelids felt too heavy to keep open, but she didn't lie back down.

Nothing.

Finally too groggy to stay upright, she let herself sink back against the pillows and pulled the covers up over herself, preparing to surrender to sleep again.

A hard hand gripped her jaw, covering her face. Fueled by terror, she bucked and grabbed for the thick forearm and wrist, digging in her nails. Tess sucked in air through her nose and released it as a scream. The sound that emerged was no more than a prolonged whimper, smothered in that palm.

It smelled funny. Oh, God—he wore latex gloves.

"Bitch," the man whispered. "Wouldn't listen, would you?"

Her bedside lamp came on, momentarily blinding her.

When her eyes adjusted, she saw Andrew Hayes

leaning over her, his weight on the forearm that pressed cruelly hard on her chest. He *wanted* her to see him. Flooded by the implications, Tess let go of his wrist and went for his face and eyes.

Somehow he flipped her, trapping her arms beneath her body.

"Just wanted you to see what's going to happen," he growled.

Face turned to one side, she focused on her bedside stand. He was barely visible out of the corner of her eye. Then fear ran through her. A pillar candle sat in a small dish.

"Sorry, babe, you're gonna knock over this candle. Throw yourself off the bed to grab it, but on the way down, you hit your head on the corner here." Thick fingers encased in white latex caressed the edge of her bedside stand. "It's a shame you brought a couple days' newspapers with you to bed to catch up on."

"Nobody will believe—"

His laugh was ugly. He grabbed a handful of her hair and used it to drag her from the bed.

"Lights out," he said, and slammed her head down on the sharp corner.

ZACH RAN FOR the garage, impatient with the length of time it took the door to rise.

Tess's mower was still in the bed of his truck. He'd planned to unload it in the morning and not even noticed it when he'd left her house a few hours ago. It would give him an excuse to go back, he thought.

He barely slowed for stop signs, hoping not to see flashing lights in his rearview mirror. Having to pull over, even wait while a ticket was written, would be an unendurable delay.

Of course, when he reached her house, driving slowly by, it was dark except for the porch light. Back one was on, too, he could tell.

She did have the cameras, he reminded himself. Neighbors. Annoyingly enough, none of whom seemed to own a dog or else the dogs were brought inside at night. The times he'd come and gone on foot in the dark, he hadn't once heard any barking.

He circled the block, uneasily noting half a dozen vehicles parked at the curb rather than in driveways or garages. This wasn't a neighborhood with three-car garages. Teenagers would have to park on the street rather than in the driveway if their parents left first in the morning.

He especially noted a couple of SUVs—even paused to jot down license plates from two that were large and dark. But, face it, half the vehicles on the road these days were full-size or crossover SUVs.

Finally he chose a place to park, not quite in front of her house but with a decent view of it. He touched his Glock, lying on the passenger seat beside him. Despite the chill, he rolled down his window so he could hear anything untoward.

Then he struggled to stay awake.

CHAPTER SEVENTEEN

THE NIGHT AIR was cold enough to keep him awake, thank God. Zach turned off the dome light, in case he saw something and wanted to get out surreptitiously.

A light came on in Tess's house, barely visible toward the back. It wasn't bright. A bedside lamp, he thought. Her bedroom. She was probably getting up to use the bathroom.

He relaxed slightly, rolling his shoulders to release tension. A minute or two passed.

The light seemed to flicker. Bulb burning out? Or she'd turned it off and then back on quickly? At the thought that she couldn't sleep, guilt stabbed him.

But as he watched, the quality of the light seemed to change from a soft, pale glow to...orange. Jesus. Fire! Gaining strength with shocking speed.

Zach grabbed his handgun, shoved it into his waistband at the small of his back and jumped out of the pickup. Just as his feet hit the pavement, he heard what he thought was a door closing somewhere nearby.

He ran for the house, vaulting her picket fence and hardly feeling the shrubs scrape at him. Almost to her porch steps, he paused long enough to pull his phone from his pocket and dial 911.

"Fire," he said hoarsely, and gave the address. "Hurry."

A shape burst from the dark on the other side of the house. Somebody, dressed in black, running away. For a fraction of a second Zach was torn. He could catch that scum, tackle him, cuff him—but Tess would still be inside.

DESPITE AGONIZING PAIN in her head, Tess struggled to open her eyes.

Have to.

A different kind of pain licked at her arm. Burning.

Fire! The word exploded in her head and she opened her eyes a slit. She lay on the floor and saw flames leaping across it. Now her quilt caught. Oh, God. Oh, God. She hurt. Her stomach heaved. She clumsily lifted a hand to her head where she discovered her hair was…wet.

She pushed herself under her bed to what looked like sanctuary, then kept squirming even though starbursts in front of her eyes told her she was about to lose consciousness. But…she wasn't safe under here, even if it *felt* safe. Dark and protected, but… Fire! That was it. The bed would burn. Was burning.

Have to keep moving.

Her stomach heaved again and this time she gagged on whatever she'd brought up. Bile tasted sour in her mouth.

Keep going.

By the time she wriggled out from the other side of the bed, flames had started to crawl up the wall above it.

Could she get to the door if she went around the foot of the bed? But when she peeked, all she saw was fire. He must have crumpled newspapers all over the floor.

He.

Tiny frightened sounds broke from her throat. For comfort, she reminded herself that, if he hadn't come in the front, at least he'd be captured on camera. Zach would know what happened. Nobody would believe she'd knocked over a candle.

Except...the receiver was in here with her. Did the cameras store digital images or were they only in the receiver? She had no idea. Couldn't think.

But she was already crawling toward the bookcase where she'd set the receiver. She could break the window. Throw it out onto the grass, even if *she* didn't have the strength to stand and climb out.

ZACH TOOK THE couple steps in one leap, wishing she'd given him a key. He realized belatedly he still had the garage remote in his truck...but going back for it would take too long and he'd still have to pick the lock on the door into house. Or kick it in. Either way, too slow. Instead he slammed a booted foot through her front window, then did it again and again until he could climb through. Inside, he could smell the fire.

As he ran down the hall, glass shattered somewhere in the house. From the heat?

Please, God, no. Let me be in time.

Fire showed beneath her bedroom door and smoke seeped out. Placing himself to one side, he cautiously opened the door. Flames climbed her bedcovers and the wall above her bed, eating the wooden frame and the bedside stand. A dozen or more smaller fires burned on the floor, too, which struck him as unnatural. *Can't smell gas, though.* Smoke filled the room. The window was broken and the night air coming in was feeding the flames.

"Tess!" he roared then saw movement beyond the fiery bed, just beneath the window.

She was trying but failing to pull herself up, her hands gripping the windowsill.

There was too much fire and heat between them.

Zach bolted back across the hall and yanked the comforter from the guest bed. No time to wet it down. He took in a deep breath and held it before plunging into Tess's room. For a terror-filled second he couldn't see her at all, but a few feet in he saw that she had collapsed and lay completely still now. He flung the comforter open over the flames crawling across the floor and then ran across it even as he felt searing heat rising around his legs.

He reached her as he heard sirens in the distance.

He put his mouth up to the hole in the window and sucked in a desperate breath. Then, using his shoulder and forearm, he knocked out more glass. Jagged edges sliced through his sweatshirt, but the knowing meant nothing, not right now.

He bent and scooped her up. God. He didn't want to toss her out, but he might have to.

The sirens screamed right outside now. Zach had Tess half resting on the windowsill when a firefighter in full gear appeared right outside.

"I'll take her," he called above the roar and the sirens, reaching for her.

With help, Zach maneuvered her to fit through without coming into contact with the shards of glass still clinging to the window frame. When her weight left his arms, he took his turn. Another pair of gloved hands reached out to help.

The minute his feet touched the ground he fell to his knees, gagging and coughing.

ZACH SAT, SLUMPED, in the small waiting room. His own minor burns and cuts had been treated, although they still hurt. He wasn't about to take a painkiller that might knock him out. His eyes burned, too. A fireman had found him a T-shirt, which he wore in place of his bloody sweatshirt. It was his racking coughs that scared him most. He'd only been in there for a matter of minutes. Tess's exposure had been so much greater. What if her lungs were damaged?

When he heard footsteps in the hall, he raised his head.

Tess's father limped into the tiny room, his face transformed by fear. "Tess?"

Zach had called from the ambulance, figuring she'd want her dad there.

"All I know is that she has a concussion," he said hoarsely. He had to hack some more before he could go on. "They put a few stitches in, too. She was…" He stopped. Unconscious and bloody, she'd been a ghastly sight. Her father didn't need to know how bad she had looked. "She has some burns, too. I don't think they're that bad." He hesitated. "She inhaled smoke."

After a moment John Granath lowered himself heavily into a chair one seat away from Zach's. "Have the police made an arrest?"

"Not yet, but they should be able to. I know the bastard went out her back door. The camera should have caught his face if he wasn't wearing a ski mask." He coughed until he felt as though he was being turned inside out. When he could talk again, he said, "Tess broke the glass in her window so she could throw the receiver out into a shrub. She wanted to make sure—" His throat closed up. He doubted she had expected to escape herself, but, by God, she had been determined to ensure the arsonist was caught.

If he hadn't gone back to her house—

Something else he couldn't think about yet.

More steps in the hall had him stiffening. But instead of a doctor, Bran appeared. His alarmed expression eased when he saw Zach.

"Isaac called me. Damn. They're not keeping you?"

Zach shook his head. Isaac was the firefighter friend who had helped with the roofing. Zach hadn't noticed his presence tonight.

"I'm all right." After a bout of coughing, he lifted his head to see worry on his brother's face. "It's Tess—" His voice broke.

"But you got her out." Bran sat in the chair on the other side of Zach and rested a hand on his shoulder. "No reason she shouldn't be fine."

He couldn't say anything.

Bran looked past him. "Bran Murphy," he said. "I'm Zach's brother."

"John Granath. Tess's father." The slur in her father's voice was more apparent than it had been the first time Zach had met him.

"Have the doctors told you anything yet?"

"I only know what Zach told me."

Bran nodded. His hand stayed on his brother's shoulder. "I talked to Easley. It was Hayes. His face was hard to see when he went in, but when he let himself out the back door, the camera caught him dead-on. They found the license plates you'd jotted down, right where you said they were on your console. It so happens, one of those SUVs belongs to Hayes's brother. City and county cops are looking for both of them right now."

Zach heard a raw sound. It took him a minute to realize it came from him. He felt too much, but not what he'd have expected. Probably rage and satisfaction were there, but deeply buried beneath the fear for Tess that his heart pumped out with every beat.

"I'm sorry," he heard himself say. The time seemed right. "For what I said the other night. I was an idiot."

"Yeah," Bran said quietly, huskily. "But I was, too. We can work it out. I…missed you. All those years."

Zach nodded. Words were beyond him. He had to squeeze his eyes shut against the sting of tears.

They all sat in silence for a long time after that. He was finally able to straighten and wipe his eyes with the hem of the T-shirt. He caught Bran's quick glance, but his brother didn't say anything, and if Tess's father noticed, he didn't comment, either.

Eventually, Bran went to get Zach something to wet his throat. He brought back a cup of coffee for Tess's dad and a cold bottle of water for Zach.

A few swallows eased his sore throat, but not the hard grip of fear compressing his chest.

As bad as waiting was, though… He mulled over a strange awareness. Having Bran here made a difference. Their shoulders brushed each time either shifted in his seat. Zach flashed back to that long-ago, terrible morning, after his father had pulled him into the house and yelled, "Call 911, Gayle!"

Mom had done so, then pushed past her husband to look out the back door. Zach could still hear her screams.

It was Bran who had put an arm around Zach and taken him to the living room, where they'd huddled together, mostly invisible, as the police and medics and eventually a medical examiner came and went. Bran had never left Zach. Not once.

This felt…a little like that. As if he had a grip on sanity only because of the man at his side.

"You have a brother," Tess had reminded him.

Now he thought with faint amazement, *I guess I do.*

Footsteps came and went in the hall outside the small waiting room. There were other patients here, after all. He'd heard an ambulance not long ago, after which someone had been rushed by on a gurney. It had gotten so he had quit stiffening each time. But suddenly a doctor dressed in green scrubs filled the doorway. He introduced himself, though two seconds later Zach couldn't remember his name.

He was smiling. "She's awake. She has a heck of a headache, which the coughing isn't helping, but she's lucid and remembers what happened."

He kept talking but Zach had slumped forward, elbows braced on his knees, trying to deal with the flood of relief. *She's awake. She's lucid.*

"She keeps saying, 'Tell Zach the receiver is outside.'" The doctor shook his head. "Whatever that means."

"We found it," Bran said after a quick glance at Zach. He stood and held out his hand. "Detective Bran Murphy, HCSD. I'm Zach's brother. This is Tess's father."

"Ah." The doctor shook hands first with Bran then with John. "I can't let all of you back there, but I think your daughter would be glad to see you, Mr. Granath."

Her father shook his head. His smile was wry, maybe an after-effect of the stroke, but…maybe not. "I suspect it is Zach she needs to see most."

Zach shot to his feet. "You're sure?"

John nodded, his eyes wet now, too. "Yes."

"Then follow me," the doctor said.

TESS FELT AS if her head had been split open by an ax. Every time she coughed, she came close to blacking out from the pain. She *wanted* to black out.

Moaning, she remembered she was supposed to push a little button for pain relief. She did. Maybe her head didn't feel like a melon that was about to fall into two separate pieces afterward, which was a minor improvement.

"Tess."

Hearing the ragged, deep voice, she forced her eyes open. "Zach," she whispered. "It was you." Somebody—she didn't recall who—had told her he was the one who'd gotten her out. "You came back."

"I did." His expression was anguished. "I wish I hadn't left."

She reached out for him and their hands met, his clasp careful. "They'd have waited until I was alone," she said in a small, rough voice. "Would have happened—" a coughing bout wrung her out "—sooner or later."

"God," he said. He looked around and found a chair, letting her go long enough to pull it closer to her bed. Then he took her hand again. "I've never been so scared."

"Me, either."

"Your dad's here," he said.

She licked dry lips. "He…okay?"

"Scared, too."

She'd have nodded if she didn't know what that would do to her head. "It was Hayes," she managed to choke out. "He turned on the light so I could see him. Told me what he was going to do. 'Sorry, babe, you're gonna knock over this candle.'"

Zach did some serious swearing, which caused *him* to start coughing.

Tess focused enough to see the array of tiny cuts on his arms, colored by disinfectant, and the bandage that added bulk beneath the T-shirt on his shoulder. "You're hurt."

"Nothing major. It'll take a day or two for my lungs to clear. But you—" His voice broke.

"Head hurts," she said fretfully.

"I know. I know, sweetheart." He stroked her cheek and temple, the bridge of her nose, his fingertips gentle, comforting.

She let her eyes sink closed.

"I shouldn't ask," he said softly, as if he thought she might have nodded off, "but I will. Give me another chance, Tess. Please."

Tess opened her eyes. He was leaning over her, a different kind of anguish darkening his eyes and making his voice shake.

"I…got scared. I've never felt anything like this before. Please," he repeated. "Maybe I don't deserve it, but I need you to forgive me. I…figured out a lot of things after I left you."

"Because I could have died?"

"No. God. I was already plotting what to say to you."

"What were you going to say?" Tess whispered.

"I love you," he said hoarsely. "That's what I needed to tell you."

Relief and an astonishing feeling of joy filled her until she wondered if she was still touching the bed at all or had floated upward. Her head still hurt, but, for this minute, her awareness of pain became unimportant. "Oh."

Zach's laugh was shaky. "Oh? That's the best you can do?"

"I love you, too." Looking up into his very blue eyes, she remembered the first time she'd done so, when she'd felt an instant, powerful connection. If that had been the beginning, it had only gained strength.

"I kind of hoped so," he admitted. He leaned over and pressed the softest of kisses to her lips. "I don't want to let go of you," he murmured, "but I think your dad needs to see you, too."

She did want to see her father but… "You'll come back, won't you?" Begging made her feel a little pathetic.

"Yeah. I'm not leaving you tonight."

Tess fumbled for the button and pushed it again, sighing at the relief. "Wait," she said when Zach stood. He hadn't released her hand, but he was leaving. "Hayes. Has he been arrested?"

"Not last I heard, but he will be." His voice had hardened, reminding her that he was a cop.

"Good."

He smiled, bent, kissed her again and then said, "I'll be back."

BRAN CAME BY the hospital midmorning the next day to let Zach know that both Andrew and Tyler Hayes had been arrested and were still being questioned.

"Lieutenant MacLachlan joined Easley. They let me observe. Christine Campbell was there, too," he added.

Tess was sleeping, so Zach had taken a break to grab a bite in the cafeteria. Her doctor had decided to keep her for another twenty-four hours, to be sure the blow to the head didn't have further consequences, and until she was breathing better.

Zach had piled the food on his tray, while Bran had only taken a cup of coffee and a pastry.

"We've got him for attempted murder, when he might have dealt down the Alvarez killing to manslaughter," Bran said with obvious satisfaction. "Idiot."

Zach could think of a few stronger words but left them unsaid. "The manslaughter would have kept him from ever working as a cop again, though."

"Sheriff Brown stopped to ask me how you are." Bran's mouth quirked. "Wanted me to tell you that the entire department is behind you. Take as much time as you need, he said, but they'll be glad to have you back at work." Grinning at his brother's expression, he added, "He held a press conference. I recorded it for you. His sincerity is deeply moving."

Zach snorted.

"Delancy is keeping his head down and not saying a whole lot. I'm seeing some chagrin on a few other faces. Everyone else is genuinely concerned."

"Somebody put that threat in my mailbox."

"I'm with you. Somebody else is involved in this." He drained his coffee. "Easley and MacLachlan are leaning hard on both the Hayeses. One will crack."

Zach pondered that and agreed. Poor impulse control seemed to be a familial trait. "Hayes has a big mouth when he's mad."

Bran made an acknowledging noise. "The brother is backtracking frantically. Claims he had no idea his brother was going to assault Tess and set the fire. He thought Andy was just going to try to scare her again. 'Something harmless.' I quote," he said dryly.

"Hard to buy that when Andy had a bundle of newspapers under his arm and a candle and stand."

"Yep. Even harder to argue with camera footage. Plus, he still had a book of matches in his pocket when he was picked up."

Zach knew this grin was fierce. "The DA is

still going for second degree murder for Alvarez, isn't she?"

"Oh, yeah."

The two men looked at each other. Zach pushed his tray away.

"We won't give up on Sheila," Bran said after a minute. "We need to know now."

"We do," Zach agreed, "but Tess got me to thinking. I...really don't believe Dad would have done anything like that. I haven't said that, and I should have. I held on to too much anger, for a lot of reasons."

"I guess I did, too."

Zach lifted an eyebrow. "You going to relent where Mom is concerned?"

"You mean, agree to see her?" Bran grimaced. "Probably. I guess seeing her won't kill me. Just so you know, it'll be more for your sake than hers, though. Might make your wedding awkward otherwise."

Zach felt a squeeze of pleasure and, yeah, a jolt of panic, too. Marriage? Was he really going there?

Yeah.

"*You're* the one with an upcoming ceremony," he pointed out.

If Bran had any doubts, he didn't share them. "You're right. You'll have to get in line."

"Not like I've asked Tess to marry me."

"But you will, won't you?"

She was his everything. Of course he would be.

"Probably." Who was he kidding?

Bran nodded.

"I need to get upstairs." Zach pushed back his chair and grabbed the lunch tray.

He stopped when his brother said, "I've been thinking..." It sounded awkward enough to make Zach curious.

When Bran stalled, Zach prodded. "You've been thinking...?"

"Yeah. Uh, speaking of weddings... Would you consider being my best man?"

Floored, he said, "You have some good friends."

Bran smiled crookedly. "But only one brother."

"Yeah." Zach had to clear his throat. "It would be an honor."

"Good. Thanks."

They bussed their trays, everything important already said, and parted in front of the elevators.

THE DAMAGE TO Tess's house had been primarily confined to the one corner, but was still substantial. The fire had reached the hall and the bathroom and leaped up through the ceiling before firefighters had put it out. The stench permeated the entire house.

Her wardrobe was history, she discovered almost immediately. Without thinking, she had asked Zach to grab her some clothes to wear home. He'd said, "Yeah, about that..."

Tess called a woman friend, who'd gone shopping for the basics for her.

Zach and she opened windows to start airing her house out and discussed whether he would do the work on it. But she decided not as that would prevent him working on his own house. Her insurance would cover the cost of bringing in a contractor.

Plus…somewhere in that discussion, they'd decided she would move in with him once he had working plumbing, instead of the other way around. Neither had said, "This house will go on the market." They hadn't needed to.

On the positive side, she had plenty of furniture to fill his empty rooms, even with some having been destroyed by fire or damaged by the smoke.

In the meantime, they would be staying at her father's—in separate bedrooms.

Tess hated not being able to sleep with Zach, but knew it might be just as well. She had a headache that wouldn't quit. Sex wasn't happening. Neither, for her, did work. Greg had someone they'd used before to fill in for Tess at Fabulous Interiors.

Putting in long hours every evening, Zach wasn't at her father's much. Having his bathroom back together had become a high priority for him.

On the Sunday after the attack, Tess decided she felt well enough to make the trip to his place.

She admired the dishwasher he'd installed and

the work he had accomplished in the bathroom. She knew the bathtub surrounding could wait, but that he couldn't set the sink in place until the tile was finished on the countertop. She offered to start the tiling.

"I like this," she said, stroking the vanity. It was solid maple finished in a simple, Shaker style. "White walls, though? Really?"

"It's primer." He defended himself. Of course, she already knew that. "You can pick the color, within reason."

She was laying out tiles when a knock came on their front door. Zach went to answer it. While he was gone, she began marking tiles she'd cut to allow for the sink to be inset.

She could tell from the voices that their visitor was male. When Zach returned, he had his brother with him.

Bran nodded in greeting. "You're looking better."

She wrinkled her nose. "You mean less like a zombie?"

He laughed because…well, yes, the swelling and discoloration had made her face so ghoulish, she'd have frightened kids if she'd dared go out in public. "The yellow is an improvement over purple."

Even Zach smiled. So far, he hadn't displayed much of a sense of humor where her injuries were concerned. She'd had a little trouble laughing, too.

"Just wanted to tell you both that Tyler rolled on his brother's best bud. Stokes fired Doug Gundry today."

Tess didn't remember ever hearing the name before, but she could see that Zach knew it.

"I've barely met him. We're not on the same shift." He shook his head. "He didn't know me at all."

"He claims he didn't have anything to do with the dead rabbit, only put the flyer in your box because Andy asked him to. He denies being part of the threats or hammering your pickup, but Stokes says he's lying. Easley and the SIU guys will be talking to him. Losing his job may be the least of his troubles."

"So…it's over." Tess was having a little trouble believing that.

"Except for testifying in three or four trials," Bran said.

"Three or four…?" Why hadn't that occurred to her? "Oh, no."

"Oh, yes." Zach wrapped an arm around her shoulders. "You'll be a star."

At her look of horror, both men laughed.

"I'm here to work," Bran said. "What can I do?"

He might not have seen the pleasure Zach tried to hide, but Tess did.

"I thought I'd replace the rest of the windows today. You game?"

"I am." With another nod at Tess, Bran retreated from the bathroom.

Zach kissed her. Lightly. But it didn't stay that way. Desire flared and his arms came around her hard. He nipped her lip and she parted her lips for him. Suddenly they were straining together, Tess's arms locked around his neck, her breasts aching for his touch.

He eased his mouth from hers and groaned. "Damn, Tess."

She gave a tiny whimper of protest.

Zach rubbed his cheek against hers. "We can move in tomorrow night."

"We do have a bed here."

Zach groaned again. "We do. Want me to get rid of Bran?"

A giggle bubbled out. "Once you've gotten all the work out of him you can."

"You're right. I'm really looking forward to this place looking like a home."

Her small, secret fear gave a twinge. "Is that how you think of it?"

His eyes were as blue as the heart of a flame. "You're my home," he said gruffly. "But...yeah." He finally tore his gaze from hers to look around. "For now."

"For now?"

He shrugged. "We might want a bigger house someday. Once we have kids."

Just like that, he'd told her everything she

needed to know. Her heart settled. Humming with contentment, she teased, "Getting ahead of yourself there, guy."

He met her eyes again. "Am I?"

Seeing that he wasn't any surer about her than she'd been about him, she rose on tiptoe to press her lips to his. "No," she murmured. "We'll definitely have kids."

"Deal," he said, his shoulders relaxing. He kissed her again quickly then backed away. "Better get to work, if we want to move in anytime soon."

Tess smiled as she returned to marking tiles. She was really glad he'd chosen ones she liked so much. It was a good omen.

* * * * *

Book two of the miniseries
BROTHERS, KEEPERS,
Bran Murphy's story,
THE BABY HE WANTED,
is available May 2016 wherever
Harlequin Superromance books are sold.